ISBN 979-8-9907799-9-0 (Paperback)
ISBN 979-8-9907799-2-1 (e-book)
ISBN 979-8-9907799-5-2 (Laminate hardcover with Dust Jacket)
ISBN 979-8-9907799-8-3 (Laminate hardcover)
ISBN 979-8-9907799-1-5 (Paperback)
ISBN 979-8-9907799-7-6 (Audiobook)

Cover design by Jermaine Haggerty, GraphixMain, LLC
Published by Rooted Through Stories
2143 Springs Road, Ste 55, #199
Vallejo, CA 94591
Visit the author's website at www.TamaraMorganAuthor.com

❀ Formatted with Vellum

DONE IN THE DARK

A NOVEL

TAMARA MORGAN

For my mother, Beverly Ann.
My beautiful hummingbird,
who always did the best that she could,
loved me unconditionally,
and believed I could do anything.

CONTENTS

PART I

THE PRESENT - 2005

1

ALL GOODBYES AIN'T GONE

"Every shut eye ain't sleep, all goodbyes ain't gone, and what's done in the dark always comes to light!"

Satisfied she had conveyed her urgent message, the old woman relaxed her grip on her granddaughter's wrist, closed her eyes and sank back into a restless sleep.

In just six weeks Ella Maxwell had gone from diagnosis to hospice. Towards the end she had stopped eating, drinking and talking; she didn't seem to recognize anyone. So her granddaughter, Karina Bishop, was shocked when she had grabbed her with surprising strength and spoken so clearly. Within hours, her beloved Mama Ella was gone.

Ten days later, Karina smoothed the hand-sewn quilt and looked around the bedroom to confirm all was in order. Mama Ella's dog-eared Bible rested on the nightstand, as it had ever since she took up residence over sixty years before as a new bride in the modest home on the border of North Oakland and South Berkeley.

Karina looked at herself in the mirror. She didn't focus on the red double-knit suit with the skirt resting just at her knees, or the strand of creamy pearls given to her by Mama Ella for her

3

eighteenth birthday, or the miracle of her naturally curly hair having been woven into a perfectly smooth French roll. Instead, she gazed into her green eyes that changed colors depending on her mood. Today, they were more hazel than green and puffy from crying. Her hand shook as she uncapped the gold tube of lipstick and swiped it across her lips. Try as she might, Karina couldn't shake the sense of foreboding that lingered after hearing her grandmother's last words.

"Pull yourself together! Mama Ella has been planning this day for years and you will not ruin her celebration by feeling sorry for yourself! She wanted us to rejoice, not be sad!" She dabbed at her eyes with a tissue, squared her shoulders, and walked out of the room that had been witness to her joys, sorrows, and secrets for nearly forty years.

Fall was Ella's favorite time of year. It seemed only right that she was laid to rest on a beautiful September morning surrounded by all those she loved. At her expressed wishes, the word had spread to wear either red or yellow; black was for mourning, but Ella wanted everyone to be joyful for the blessings of life.

The small house was overflowing with friends and loved ones, all waiting for Karina and her small family to lead the procession. Outside, Reverend Carol Amos, the spiritual leader of All Souls Baptist Church, addressed the growing crowd. Her rich alto voice commanded the attention of those assembled.

"Welcome everyone to a glorious day. We are here to celebrate the life of one of our most loving and well-known church members, Mother Ella Maxwell. For nearly sixty years Mother Maxwell poured into All Souls. Join us as we walk for her, every step commemorating the indelible mark she made on our lives."

Seventeen-year-old Samaya Bishop, looking radiant in her daffodil summer dress and curly hair pulled back from her face with a red headband, reached for her parents' hands and took the first step. Behind the Bishops marched the All Souls choir jubilantly singing *Wade in the Water* as their white robes, adorned with yellow and red ribbons, billowed in the breeze. Behind the choir, nearly one hundred people of all ages joined the walk and the chorus. Surprised to see at least that many more waiting at the church to say goodbye to her grandmother, Karina turned to her husband in amazement. "How did so many people know?"

Zander Bishop towered over his petite wife. His bald head gleamed with shea butter. His dark brown eyes were set off by jet black eyebrows, and his full lips were framed by a neatly trimmed mustache and goatee. He cut a handsome figure in his custom-tailored suit with a yellow tie and pocket square and wore a Rolex on his wrist with a mother-of-pearl dial catching the sun.

Zander smiled and kissed Karina's forehead. "I know how important Homegoings were to Mama Ella. I lost track of how many times she traveled to say goodbye to elders at churches all over the country. So I made sure her obituary and the details of her Homegoing were published in every major newspaper from here to Texarkana." As Zander turned to acknowledge the greetings of the many visitors, he missed the fleeting look of worry that passed over his wife's face.

Ella's ornate casket stood at the front of the church. A simple woman in life, Ella had surprised the family by leaving explicit instructions that she wanted to be buried in a mahogany casket with gold-plated fixtures and the most comfortable lining and pillow they could find. "If these old stiff bones are going to be spending eternity in a box, it had better be the best box my insurance money can buy!" she'd said with a laugh. Even contemplating her own death could not thwart Ella's wicked sense of humor.

As they walked to their seats, Zander noticed an unfamiliar couple several rows back. The man was consoling a woman whose resemblance to his wife was uncanny. They had the same bone structure and bearing, but where Karina's skin was a warm bronze, hers was more like a sun-kissed ivory. At that moment, the woman turned her head and looked right at him. Taken off guard, he nodded politely and turned to accept more handshakes and condolences.

Karina mused over how strange it was to bury Mama Ella

almost eighteen years to the day of her parents' funeral. Her memories of that day were still hazy. She'd been in shock, barely able to put one foot in front of the other. But she remembered the matching caskets positioned where Mama Ella's was now. She shook her head, willing those memories to remain locked away.

Though she knew she should take comfort that Mama Ella was going to 'a better place,' despite her grandmother's efforts Karina's faith in a benevolent God was shaky at best. She hung her head, mind racing, as tears silently streamed down her face. An hour later the eulogy had been read, favorite songs sung, and prayers prayed.

Reverend Amos addressed the crowd, "Now, brothers and sisters, we will open up the floor for some of you to say a few words about Mother Maxwell. I know we've all been touched in some way by her kindness, but there's not enough time for everyone to speak. The family has allotted fifteen minutes for tributes. We'll then make one last procession to view Mother Maxwell in her beautiful red dress before heading to Rolling Hills Cemetery. Those of you who wish to speak, please line up to my right."

Karina tried to pay attention to the accolades being showered on her grandmother but her mind kept wandering. She thought of the many times she and Mama Ella had sat at the kitchen table drinking sweet tea and planning the future. The memories of tilting her head backwards over the kitchen sink so Mama Ella could massage shampoo into her scalp made her smile. She thought of the pride in her grandmother's eyes at her college graduation, and her smile of joy when Karina and Zander stood at the same altar where the casket now rested, vowing to build a life together. Suddenly a strangely familiar voice broke through Karina's meandering thoughts.

"It's been a long time since I've been here. I recognize some of you, but there are a lot of unfamiliar faces too. Y'all look so beautiful in your red and yellow. I wish I'd known there was a chosen color, but I'm just grateful to be here to say goodbye to Mama Ella."

Karina frowned as she looked up at the speaker. A rush of whispering and rustling built throughout the church as dozens of attendees shifted their attention to Karina, their stares and raised eyebrows questioning the identity of the newcomer.

It was the woman Zander had noticed. She wore a sleeveless navy-blue sheath that accentuated her figure while still being appropriate for the occasion. She had startling green eyes, eyebrows that arched naturally, and long honey-colored micro braids that trailed down her back. Standing next to her was an equally impressive-looking man in a perfectly cut suit. He was tall with golden skin, nearly black eyes, close-cropped hair, and a neatly trimmed goatee. He stood close to the woman and held her hand as she spoke.

Karina willed herself not to panic as recognition sank in. She watched the play of emotions cross the woman's face as she spoke of Mama Ella making her 'walk and talk like a proper lady' and teaching her how to bake from scratch. Karina marveled at what appeared to be genuine grief causing those eyes so like her own to well up and overflow with tears.

"I knew that if I didn't come here today, when I meet my maker Mama Ella would be right there and she'd say, 'Candace Janese Maxwell,' – cause you knew Mama was serious when she called you by your full government name - " nods of agreement and titters of laughter made her pause before continuing - "she'd say, I don't care how long you'd been gone you know you was supposed to be at my Homegoing!'" Laughter echoed throughout the church.

"All goodbyes ain't gone . . ." Mama Ella's last words echoed in Karina's head. Suddenly everything started to spin and she slipped out of consciousness.

Eugenia Jenkins saw Karina slump over and hurriedly directed the ushers to carry her to the ladies' lounge. She frowned and muttered to herself, "Now why that girl feel the need to make an appearance after all of these years? Giving folks something to gossip about instead of keeping the focus on Ella!" Eugenia had been Ella's next-door neighbor and best friend for over forty years. There was nothing that she didn't know about Ella's family.

A few minutes later Karina felt a rush of cool air on her face as she came to consciousness surrounded by concerned women waving fans and praying.

"Excuse me ladies, I think my wife could use a little fresh air." Zander made his way to the middle of the circle of fluttering church ladies and helped Karina to her feet.

"Thanks for rescuing me," Karina whispered.

Holding hands, they walked outside to the church garden and sat on a bench under a willow tree.

"Are you feeling better?" Zander asked.

Karina took a few deep breaths. "Yeah, I'm mostly embarrassed. I never understood why people pass out at funerals, and now look at me, in the spotlight." Her voice trembled as she unconsciously twirled a button on her jacket.

"There's no reason for you to be ashamed. Mama Ella meant the world to all of us, but no one was closer to her than you. Everything you're feeling is natural."

"It's not Mama Ella. I mean, of course it's Mama Ella, but I wasn't prepared for Candi to be here. The nerve of her to do this to me! Now, of all times! It's just too much!" Angry tears welled up in her eyes.

Zander pulled her close. "Try to relax, Rina. She was bound to come home eventually. When we met in high school all Mama Ella could talk about was that 'one day' the infamous Candi would come home. Maybe it's for the best. If you think about it, other than Samaya, Candi is your only close blood relative. Don't you think Mama Ella would be happy to know the two of you are together again?"

Karina pulled away from him, her face twisted into an ugly expression he'd never seen before. "Did you talk to her? Did she say something to you?"

Zander's confusion was obvious. "Calm down, baby! No, I haven't spoken to her. But even before she spoke, I could tell she was a blood relative; she looks so much like you I had to do a double take."

"She may be blood but she's not family. She hasn't been my

family for a long, long time. Candi is a selfish, cold-hearted bitch, and her being here can only bring more upheaval into our lives."

Gently taking his wife's hands in his, he whispered, "Baby, I know you're hurting, but you haven't seen her since you were seventeen years old. Maybe she's changed. Don't you think you should give her a chance?"

Karina let go of his hands and stood up. "No, Zander, we are way past second chances."

Zander started to speak, but Karina held up her hand to silence him. "She's never going to change, and I'm not going to let her get close enough to hurt me or my family ever again."

Karina hurried back into the church. As luck would have it, she ran right into the one person she was hoping to avoid.

"Excuse me," Candace murmured as she wiped her eyes with a tissue, not realizing who had bumped into her. Both women gasped when they looked at each other.

"You're going the wrong way. The bathroom back here is reserved for the pastor and officers of the church." Karina said in a haughty tone.

"Been a long time little sister," Candace said in a carefully neutral tone.

"Not long enough," Karina responded coolly.

"It's gonna be like that, Rina? At our grandmother's funeral?" Candace sighed.

"I don't know what you're talking about," Karina maintained her calm demeanor.

"I'm not into games, Karina. I know I'm the last person you wanted to see today. But Mama Ella was my grandmother too, and I have a right to be here." Candace's voice trembled slightly.

Karina glanced around and seeing no one nearby said, "I don't care what you think your 'rights' are. You lost any 'rights' when you abandoned this family seventeen years ago."

Candace jerked as if Karina had struck her. Before she could respond, Karina held up her hand and said with a withering look, "Save it, Candi. I don't have time for your tired excuses. I'm here to celebrate Mama Ella's life. I don't give a damn about what you have to say."

"Is this grief or did you grow up to be a cold ass bitch?" Candace snapped. She took a deep breath, and spoke more calmly, "I don't have any excuses, but there are two sides to every story, Rina. Before you judge me, you need to think back to how you treated me. I may have left the family, but you made damn sure that the door slammed and locked behind me."

"Oh come on Candi, you don't get to play the victim. I was here and you weren't. Period."

Just then Samaya came around the corner with a quizzical look on her face. "Ri-Ma?" she said, dark eyes darting from her mother to the stranger she now knew to be her aunt. "Is everything okay?"

Karina plastered a smile on her face and threw a warning look at her sister. "Everything's fine, sweetie. I was just coming to look for you."

Samaya walked to the women. "You missed the viewing; she looked so pretty." She struggled to hold back tears and said, "The cars are lined up and everyone's waiting for the family to get in the limo to head to the cemetery."

Karina attempted to steer her daughter back in the direction from which she'd come. Candace deftly stepped in between them. She glanced at Karina. "Ri-Ma?" Without waiting for an answer, she turned to Samaya and said with a smile, "I take it you're my niece?"

Karina jumped in. "This is my daughter, Samaya. As a toddler she'd try to mimic Mama Ella and call me Rina. That morphed into Rina-Mama and then Ri-Ma. It stuck."

Samaya smiled widely and held out her hand, "Hi."

Candace laughed and held out her arms. "Girl, you are not gon' shake your Auntie's hand! Give me a hug!"

Karina held her breath as Samaya and Candace hugged.

Candace held Samaya at arms' length, taking in her smooth complexion, sparkling bright eyes, and the Maxwell pointed chin. "Samaya's an unusual name. I like it."

"Thank you, Mama Ella named me. Sometimes people call me

Sammi." At the mention of her great grandmother, Samaya's eyes brimmed with tears. She grabbed Karina's hand. "Ri-Ma, I don't want to go to the cemetery . . . I just can't stand the thought of them throwing dirt on Mama Ella's casket!" Samaya's shoulders shook as she cried quietly.

"Shh baby, I understand." Karina said, holding her close. "But you know Mama Ella wants us there to bear witness. It's only her body in that casket. Her spirit is all around us."

A few minutes later, Samaya smiled weakly at her aunt. "Sorry, I guess I lost it for a bit, but I'm okay now."

"You have nothing to be sorry about, honey." Candace brushed a thumb across Samaya's cheek to wipe a tear away.

Karina pulled Samaya closer. "We'd better hurry before your dad comes looking for us." She guided her down the hallway.

Samaya stopped and looked back at Candace. "Auntie? Aren't you coming? There's plenty of room in the family car. It's just Ri-Ma, Zandy and me." She grinned, "Oh yeah, Zandy is my dad, Zander. It's cooler than Daddy."

Candace and Karina answered "no" at the same time. Samaya frowned.

Karina explained, "Candi has been afraid of cemeteries ever since she was a little girl. No matter what the grown-ups said, they couldn't convince her that they were peaceful places. Candi would start crying in the car, and when we got there she'd either pass out or start running to the gates to get out. Finally, our parents said that she shouldn't be forced to go anymore."

Candace added, "And I never went to another cemetery. I know Mama Ella will understand." She turned to Karina. "But you and I need to talk, little sister. The sooner, the better."

Karina's lips tightened, but she shrugged and said, "Sure, how long are you in town?"

"Actually, I moved back to the Bay Area a few months ago," Candace said.

Try as she might, Karina could not mask her dismay. "What? You live here? Where? Why?" She stuttered.

Candace smirked. "Thanks for the warm welcome. We're in

Concord, not too close for your comfort. Why? Lots of reasons, but mainly because this has always been home, and it was time for me to come back. We can talk more about that when we catch up."

"Alright, I'll meet you at Mama Ella's house tomorrow at 11 o'clock," Karina said.

"I'll let myself in," Candace replied.

"You still have the key?" Karina's astonishment was evident.

Candace's smile faded. "It was all I had of before," she whispered. "I keep it with me all the time. I just hope the locks haven't been changed."

The sisters locked eyes. Karina sighed and said, "No, Candi, the locks were never changed. You just never used the key."

As they walked to the limo, Samaya ran back to Candace and pressed a yellow rose into her hand. "I took this from the bouquet next to Mama Ella's casket. I was going to throw it in at the graveside, but I think you should keep it."

Fighting back tears, Candace said, "Thank you, sweetheart," and hurried out the side door.

Once they were settled in the back of the limo Samaya turned to her mother, "Ri-Ma, where has Auntie Candi been all these years? And why didn't you ever talk about her?"

Karina patted her hand absentmindedly. "I don't know, sweetie, out of sight, out of mind, I guess. This is Mama Ella's day, let's focus on her."

Samaya threw a questioning look at her father, but he shrugged. Samaya started to say more but noticed that her mother was studying the funeral program and quietly crying again.

Nick Myers found Candace sitting on the church garden bench, lost in thought. "I figured you'd be hiding out somewhere until everybody cleared out."

"That was the plan, but I ran smack into the person I was avoiding," she said, patting the spot beside her.

Nick unbuttoned his jacket and sat down, stretching his long legs out in front of him. "So how'd it go?"

"Let's just say she didn't welcome me with open arms." Candace leaned her head on his shoulder.

"Well, you've been preparing yourself for this, but she hasn't. You showing up out of the blue probably threw her for a loop." He put his arm around his wife. "But my concern is how you're doing? You're grieving and dealing with being back here. What's going on in your head, Sweetness?"

"It's a lot," she confessed. "Seeing Karina after all this time. She's so gorgeous and poised – bitchy and mean – but still amazing. My mini-me grew up into a woman, and a mother, and I missed it all! I have a teenage niece, babe!" She held up the rose. "She gave me this." Looking off into the distance, she whispered, "I should've come home sooner."

"You're here now. We're here now. C'mon, say it for me," he prodded.

Candace squeezed his hand as they recited the words that had guided their lives for the last several years: "God grant me the serenity to accept the things I cannot change, the courage to change the things I can, and the wisdom to know the difference." They sat quietly, holding hands.

Nick cleared his throat. "Let's indulge ourselves a little. C'mon Sweetness."

"What? Where are we going?"

"It's a surprise." He lightly smacked her backside as she stood up.

"Nick!" She slapped his hand. "We're in the church garden!"

"This is sanctified love, girl. God knows my heart." He grinned.

Candace laughed. "You're a mess! Come on, take me to my surprise."

Twenty minutes later, Candace clapped her hands in delight. "Babe! I cannot believe our favorite ice cream shop is still open!" They walked inside. "I think this is the same booth we sat in the first time we came here. Do you remember?"

"Do I remember? I don't know which one of us was more scared!" Nick laughed loudly.

"When that firetruck and ambulance pulled into the parking lot my heart was pounding so fast I thought I was having a heart attack," Candace said.

"The last thing I wanted was to run into your dad when we'd cut class to be here." Nick shook his head at the memory. "I think we were both about to pee ourselves!"

"But as always, you took care of me. Remember? You gave me the car keys and told me to slip out the side door while my dad was treating that sick customer."

"While you were sneaking out, I chatted it up with the busboy and then strolled out the front door right past your dad, the other paramedic, and the firefighters waiting outside. But I got spooked when I didn't see you in the car."

Candace chuckled, "I had curled myself into a ball and covered myself with your jacket. All the firefighters knew me and my sister; any one of them would have ratted me out for cutting school."

Her expression grew somber. "That was less than six months before Daddy and Mommy died. Only you'd understand that a sundae with all the toppings chases the clouds away."

Nick leaned across the table to kiss her nose.

"Not to take away from the moment, but based on how Karina acted earlier I'm sure tomorrow is gonna be interesting, to say the least." Candace said.

"Tomorrow?" Nick asked.

"We agreed to meet at Mama Ella's house to talk."

"Are you up for that so soon?" He frowned.

"It's soon, but then again it's been a long time coming. I'll just have to roll with the punches." She shook her head. "I don't understand why she's so angry. I know that I let her down by leaving – even before that, really. But I'm the one who ended up battling the demons, not her."

"You're the psychologist baby, not me, but maybe she needs forgiveness?"

Candace frowned. "Forgiveness from me won't mean anything if she hasn't forgiven herself."

"Block me so no one can see me, please!" Karina instructed her best friend, Sonya Morris.

"Girl, you're entitled to take a minute and rest your feet. You don't have to hide over here in the corner," Sonya fussed, but obligingly maneuvered herself so that she hovered over Karina's petite form.

"I just don't want anyone to ask me another doggone question. This has got to be the longest repast in the history of homegoings!" Karina slipped one foot out of a stylish pump and lifted her leg to rub the ball of her foot. "I think they're chewing slower so they can drag out the gossip about Candi."

Sonya laughed, making her dimples deepen. "Of course everybody's talking about Candi! Even you have to admit it was dramatic when she walked up to the podium and started speaking." She pushed her overlong bangs out of her eyes. "Candi always did have flair, didn't she? And she looks good! I don't know what I was expecting, but she seems to be doin' alright. And that man with her?" Sonya fanned herself with her hand. "He is fine!"

Karina frowned. "Girl. That was Nick Myers."

"Shut up! The boy she ran away with? I can't believe they're still together after all this time!"

"Right? And he has the nerve to look like an upstanding citizen."

Sonya studied her friend carefully. "So are you happy to have your sister back?"

Karina slid her shoe back on and stood up. "Hell no!" She slapped her hand over her mouth. "Dang, you got me cussing at the repast. Candi no longer has a place in this family. She paid her respects, and now she can go on back to wherever she's been all this time. I'll talk to her tomorrow and make sure she understands that."

"Rina, I've known you a long time so don't try to play me. I know how close you and Candi were and how much it hurt you when she left. Mama Ella always said she'd be back. Maybe this is God's plan – for Mama Ella's girls to be back together. See if you can find it in your heart to forgive her for leaving."

Karina didn't answer.

"Just sleep on it, Rina, okay? And you know you can always call me. Even if we just breathe on the phone together."

Karina nodded, and hurried to the ladies' room, wiping her eyes.

Zander watched them from across the room with concern. Excusing himself from the group of elders at the table, he headed towards Karina, but Elliott Jeffers, his de facto brother and best friend, blocked his path.

"Hey Zander, sorry to leave you hanging after the celebration. For trial to be starting on Monday, our wunderkind associate is not as prepared as he should be. I had to run to the office to get him focused."

Elliott, a few inches shorter than Zander with a muscular build and a head full of wavy black hair, was often mistaken for his brother. Elliott had moved in with the Bishops a week after his tenth birthday, when his father died of lung cancer. The boys had attended elementary, middle and high school, college and law school together. It was no shock to anyone that they ended up at the same prestigious law firm.

Zander chuckled. "Give the kid a break. His daddy may have hooked him up with this job, but even rich white boys can't fake being trial lawyers. Nobody better to teach him the ropes than us – if he's willing to learn."

"True, true. Anyway, did I miss any more drama?"

"No, thank God. Candace didn't come to the cemetery or the repast, and Karina is avoiding the subject."

"I hope she sticks around." Elliott rubbed his hands together. "That is a woman worth getting to know. I mean, damn! She even looked good while she was up there crying. She's like Karina with a little spice swirled in there." Elliott raised an eyebrow. "We might end up married to sisters after all."

"Have some respect man!" Zander fussed. "We're at Mama Ella's funeral and you're trying to push up on her granddaughter? Not to mention that dude with her might be her husband."

Elliott smirked. "Settle down! If so, she's safe. I've sworn off married chicks – for real this time." Elliott waved away Zander's disbelief. "But anyway, what's the story? All these years you never mentioned Karina having a sister."

"I don't know the whole story, Eli. From what I gather, the girls grew apart when their parents died. Candace couldn't handle it, I guess. She missed most of their senior year of high school and ran away a few months before graduation. Mama Ella would mention her from time to time, hoping she'd come home, but I think Rina had given her up for dead. There's some bad blood between them, I know that much." Zander leaned back against the wall. "Today was a big shock."

Elliott looked around the banquet hall. "Rina is always on point but she looks exhausted." Zander followed Elliott's gaze to see Karina coming out of the ladies' room.

"Good looking out. Lemme get her home. She's put in enough face time," Zander said.

"Much love, brother," Elliott said as they exchanged hugs.

Ten minutes later Karina looked at her husband in awe. "How did you do that?" she said.

"Do what?" Zander asked, buckling his seat belt.

"Get us out of that repast so fast? It would've taken me an hour to say my goodbyes!"

"Are you complaining? Want me to turn around?"

"Hell no!" Karina laughed. "I've been ready to go for hours! Don't get me wrong. I love my folks, and I appreciate them coming out to honor Mama Ella, but why is it that every repast becomes a high school and family reunion?"

"It's good to hear you laugh." Zander reached for Karina's hand.

"I don't know what I would've done without you these past weeks. Thank you, baby." Karina said.

"There's nothing I wouldn't do for you, my love. And Mama Ella was my grandmother too." Zander took advantage of the red light to kiss Karina. "Speaking of which, do you want me to get Eli to cover for me tomorrow so I can come with you to meet with your sister?"

"No!" She said quickly. "This is something I need to do alone. Candi and I have to get some things off our chests, and then she can be gone again. This time for good."

2

LEAVE THE PAST IN THE PAST

"I give up!" Karina threw off the comforter and sat up. She had tossed and turned all night. Karina realized that what she needed more than anything was to feel her grandmother's spirit. She dressed quickly in a tracksuit and went downstairs. She pulled her hair into a messy ponytail and grabbed her purse and keys. In the garage, she started to open the door of her coveted Jaguar, Zander's gift to her for winning Teacher of the Year twice in a row. "I'd better take the Camry. All I need is for Candi to think I'm showing off," she murmured to herself.

As she headed down the hill toward the MacArthur Freeway, Karina's mind jumped from one thought to another. *Where has Candi been all this time? Will Mama Ella rest easy if I make Candi leave? What if Zander starts asking questions?*

Karina was so engrossed in her thoughts that she almost missed the exit. By the time she parked in the driveway, her burst of energy had evaporated, and all she could think of was how good it would feel to lie on Mama Ella's bed and pull the quilt over her head.

Entering the foyer, she dropped her keys into the basket atop the polished entry table. Mama Ella's brightly colored sweater hung on the coat rack next to the door. Karina smiled at the memory of her grandmother putting on that sweater nearly every day. "I don't have to worry about matching! My sweater has all the colors of the rainbow!" Mama Ella would laugh.

Steeling herself for the memories that would surely overwhelm her, Karina tried to suppress the sadness and focus only on the comfort the house had always brought her. She walked slowly down the long hallway, peering at the family photos that told the history of the Maxwell and Lanier families. It was lined with faded black and white portraits of Texas and Louisiana ancestors interspersed with bright color images of Candace and Karina as children, and their parents. The Maxwells and Laniers had sharecropped neighboring plots of land in the Jim Crow South. Langston and Jewel's grandparents had announced their betrothal when they were still in diapers, envisioning a future of Maxwell/Lanier land as far as the eye could see. Their dream was for their families to own all of the land that their ancestors had been forced to cultivate for generations.

Karina ran her fingertips over the wedding pictures – Ella and Horace Maxwell dressed simply and clasping hands; Doris and Chester Lanier, a bit more glamorous, smiling widely; Jewel and Langston, beaming as they realized their grandparents' dreams; Karina and Zander with flower girl Samaya clinging to Zander's leg.

Karina nearly jumped out of her skin when she noticed Candace sitting at the dining room table, quietly flipping through a photo album.

"What are you doing here? Did you spend the night?"

Candace looked up. "No, Karina, I didn't spend the night. I could barely sleep so I came here hoping to find some peace. But what if I had?"

Standing up and pushing past Karina, Candace walked into the living room and opened her arms. "Are you still trying to keep all of this from me?" she asked, indicating the furniture and knickknacks that were so familiar to both women. "Isn't it enough that you had it, and her, to yourself for all these years?"

"Stop being so dramatic!" Karina snapped and walked past her to stand in front of the bay window.

"Dramatic?" Candace moved closer to Karina. "You really are a piece of work! You got to have a fairy tale life while I got the nightmare. You had Mama Ella all to yourself, the career of your dreams, a beautiful daughter, and you married up – yeah, I Googled your husband – his folks are rich and he's a lawyer at a fancy firm. You have a big house on the hill and I'm sure cars to match." She paused, "You have so much, but you've never had to be accountable, have you?"

Karina spun around. "You're delusional. My life is far from a fairy tale. And accountable for what? I took care of Mama Ella when she got sick." Karina's voice grew shrill. "I worked hard and reached for my dreams while you were running the streets. I deserve my husband, my daughter, my career, and everything else I have! You don't know anything about me, and you need to keep your nose out of my business!"

"You're telling me how responsible you've been," Candace said. "But I asked you about accountability. See, I blew up my life, but I own the outcome. All this bitterness you're throwing at me doesn't make sense. Running away was wrong; I know that. But why does it erase our first seventeen years?" Candace tilted her head to the side, a quizzical look on her face.

"Rina, we were as close as two sisters could be. I've spent so many hours trying to understand what I did to make you so angry at me and why your self-esteem took a nosedive when *you* were the one who could do no wrong. I dealt with my issues in therapy and took accountability for my mistakes. But what about you? We both know that if it wasn't for you our parents wouldn't have died that night."

"How dare you try to put that on me, Candi? I was the good girl. You were the one who snuck out. Everybody knows that. *They were looking for you!*"

Candace grabbed Karina's arm. "They were looking for me because you sent them there! You sent them to a place they didn't know shit about - not because you were worried about me. Unh-uh, you sent our parents to their death out of pettiness and insecurity. Those are the facts, little sister."

"Shut up! It wasn't my fault, and you know it!" Karina snatched her arm away, angry tears streaming down her face. "After everything you've done, why would you come back? Are you here just to ruin my life?"

She ran down the hall and out the front door, slamming it behind her. She stood on the porch, hands on her hips, breathing deeply to calm herself.

"Karina! What's wrong with you, slamming the door like that? Come over here!" Eugenia was sitting on her porch next door and motioned for Karina to join her. Karina walked over and sat down beside her.

"What did Candi say to get you so upset?" Eugenia asked. "I saw her car pull up hours ago. She just sashayed into Ella's house like she been here the whole time!" Eugenia clucked her teeth. Before Karina could respond, she continued, "Whatever she said, you need to just ignore it. That girl ain't earned the right to cause tears or trouble."

"She was talking about our parents, Miss Genie. About the accident. Saying that it was my fault!" Karina's voice shook.

Eugenia sat back and sighed heavily. "Y'all was just kids. Trying to divvy up blame don't help nobody. Candi did some things that made you do some things. What do they say? Chicken and egg? When it comes down to it, only God can judge." Eugenia reached out to pat Karina's hand but she pulled away.

"Sounds like you think it was my fault too."

"Oh Rina, it was an accident. That's what you need to hold on to."

Eugenia leaned close and spoke in a hushed tone, "And as for the rest, whatever you do – leave the past in the past. If you're thinking about clearing your conscience, Karina – don't. Y'all did what Ella thought was right."

Karina nodded. "Yes ma'am. Mama Ella always made sure I understood the need for keeping our secret. She had such a strong faith in God that it was hard to question her decision." She took a deep breath. "Now I'm just not sure about anything."

"Try not to worry. When it gets to be too much Karina, just take it to the Lord. I'm gonna be praying every day as well. Mark my words, Candi ain't gonna let no grass grow under her feet. She been gone too long to stay around here long."

Karina stood up. "Thanks for letting me sit with you, Miss Genie. I needed to pull myself together. Lemme get on back to the house and deal with Candi. Love you." Karina hugged the elderly woman and left.

She'd been gone for less than fifteen minutes, but the smell of bacon was unmistakable. Memories of her grandmother sprang to mind. Whenever there was a big day ahead – first day of school, spelling bees, field trips – Mama Ella made the girls a hearty breakfast. Bacon, sausage, grits, ham, eggs, French toast or omelets – the menu varied but the comfort was consistent. Glancing in Mama Ella's room to see her Bible in its usual resting place, Karina felt her grandmother's spirit surrounding her, bolstering her courage, and giving her the strength to face whatever the future held. As she stood there, working out in her mind what to say to her sister, she detected the distinct smell of burning bacon.

Karina rushed into the kitchen to find Candace sitting at the breakfast nook looking off into space, tears streaming down her face. Karina turned off the stove and took the skillet off the fire. She then slid into the seat across from her sister. Candace blinked in surprise and wiped the tears from her face.

"I made enough for both of us," she said in a hoarse voice, looking down at her hands.

"I didn't know I was hungry until I smelled the bacon," Karina said with a slight smile.

For the next few minutes, they played out a familiar routine in silence. Candace gathered the eggs, butter, and cheese from the refrigerator. She turned the dial to "2" before slipping two slices of bread into the toaster for Karina. When it was time to make her own toast, she moved the dial to "8" preferring the crunchy toast that Mama Ella always made for her. Karina set out the plates and prepared the eggs – sunny side up for Candace and scrambled for herself. Without breaking the silence, they moved to the table and sat in their childhood seats – Karina on the right facing the window and Candace facing out into the kitchen.

After they'd been eating for a few minutes, Candace cleared her throat. "I didn't come here to fight with you. Can we maybe start over?"

Karina wiped away a tear and gave her a lopsided smile. "Breakfast was a good idea. Mama Ella must've been guiding you."

Candace sopped up the egg yolk with her toast and took a bite. She smiled at Karina. "It seems that you've done pretty well for yourself," she said.

Karina searched her sister's eyes but could discern no negativity. "There were some rocky times, but overall I'd say I've been blessed," she said with a shrug.

Candace said, "And you look good. No more knobby knees, I see!"

Karina had to laugh. "Remember when you made that collage of pictures of models to prove to me that skinny legs were in?"

"Yes!" Candace slapped the table as she laughed. "I was trying to get you to wear skirts or shorts to school. It would be eighty-five degrees outside and you still wouldn't let those legs out!" She grew serious. "Really though, you look great, Rina. Tell me about yourself."

Karina hesitated, nervously playing with the tendrils that had escaped her ponytail. She looked around the kitchen, noting the cheeriness of the lemon-yellow walls and bright white molding. Glancing at the crisp white cotton curtains with intricate, hand-stitched trim brought to mind Mama Ella sitting at the sewing table tucked into the far corner late into the night. The thought of her grandmother steadied her nerves and she met Candace's quizzical gaze as the words came tumbling out, "There's not really a lot to tell. I live up by Merritt College. I'm an elementary school teacher but I'm on a leave of absence right now because of Mama Ella."

"You always were just like Mommy," Candace said.

Karina grinned. "Nope, I don't have her patience. My little

hooligans drive me crazy. Anyway let's see, me and Zander dated senior year and then during college and got married right after graduation," Karina rattled off.

"Rina! Slow down! What about your daughter? Do you guys have other kids? How did y'all meet? What kind of law does Zander practice? C'mon gimme something!" Candace cajoled.

"Alright, alright! I met him at a Berkeley High basketball game that Sonya dragged me to while you were in Texarkana. He was the point guard for St. Mary's during our senior year. He got a scholarship to play for Howard University. He was hoping to go pro, but he messed up his knee sophomore year. After graduation he went to law school at Boalt Hall on the U.C. Berkeley campus. Now he's a trial lawyer. He made partner a few years ago."

Karina continued, "Let's see, what else? Samaya is an only child. I had a few miscarriages and an ectopic pregnancy. Then a couple years ago we lost our little boy – he was stillborn. A few hours later I had an emergency hysterectomy."

She grew quiet for a moment and then resumed, "Samaya is a senior at Berkeley High. She's a dancer – just like you were. Ms. Bennett is her teacher too. She's good enough to get a college scholarship." Karina pursed her lips in annoyance. "That is assuming she graduates. Miss Samaya is going through a troublesome phase right now."

Karina looked at Candace. "Enough about me. You look good, too. What have you been up to all these years?"

Candace shifted in her seat so that she could look out the window into the garden. "Some things are better left unsaid, so we'll leave those first few years to your imagination. Let's just say it wasn't how I thought it would be."

Candace was momentarily lost in thought as she remembered parts of her past that she had no intention of sharing with her sister. "Nick needed to get out of town fast and I wanted to be anywhere but here. We made our way to Reno and stayed there all this time." She paused. "A lot of bad things happened," she finally said.

As Karina watched the emotions play across her sister's face, she felt an unexpected ache in her heart. Without thinking, she took

Candace by the hand. "I know I wasn't there for you then but I'm ready to listen now, if you'll let me."

Candace's expression was inscrutable. "I've finally learned not to dwell on things that can't be undone. I don't feel like talking about that part of my journey just yet," she said.

"I understand." Karina let go of Candace's hand. Biting her bottom lip, she picked at the woodgrain of the oak table. "It feels like the past is full of landmines anyway. Plus, I'm not much of a talker either."

Candace's laugh broke the tension in the room. "Karina Joelle Maxwell! You have been a talker since you were nine months old! That's all you ever did was talk! Remember Daddy said you were destined to be a lawyer or a politician because you were born with the gift of gab?"

Karina blushed and joined in the laughter, her alto combining with Candace's soprano in the familiar tune that had filled the small house during their childhood years.

"Okay, so that wasn't exactly accurate. Let's just say that I've learned to be more judicious with my words. Do you remember Sonya Morris?"

"Of course, I remember Sonya, our third amiga! Y'all are still friends? That's so cool."

Karina nodded. "Yeah, other than Sonya I don't have a lot of girlfriends or people I confide in, so I know what it's like to be a private person."

Candace leaned forward, elbows on the table. "I do know what you mean, Rina. Over all these years I've probably only made one real friend. And even with her I never completely let myself go. I guess Nick is my closest friend."

After a few moments Karina asked, "Did you ever get married?"

"Yeah, twice actually. Both times to Nick!" Candace chuckled. "The first time was soon after we got to Reno – you know it was all part of the romantic us-against-the-world thing we had going on. But life got crazy and that wasn't any kind of marriage . . ." Her eyes grew distant. "Five years ago when we'd slayed our dragons and life was really good, we renewed our vows."

They sat in silence, each lost in thought. "I can't believe how good it feels to be home again." Candace took a deep breath. "If only I'd known it would feel like this." She turned to her sister. "Rina, every once in a while a memory will hit me and it almost takes my breath away, it seems so real!"

"Like, remember when Mommy used to drive that red Bronco and we'd head out to Sacramento to visit Nana Lanier?" Candace asked.

"And we'd roll the back windows all the way down and stick our heads out while she was flying down the Freeway—" Karina chimed in.

Candace finished the thought, "And we'd almost suffocate our silly selves?"

"Mommy would just shake her head and keep on driving. But when Daddy was in the car, she'd act all stern-'Girls, you sit down and put on your seatbelts, you know that's not safe'-then she'd shake her head and tell Daddy, 'Those are your crazy daughters.'" Karina mimicked their mother's voice.

"Yep, but I'd catch her eye in the rearview mirror and she'd wink." Candace felt like she was eight years old all over again, reveling in the love that shone from her mother's hazel eyes.

After breakfast the sisters cleaned up, each automatically assuming the responsibilities they always had. Candace washed, Karina rinsed. Candace wiped down the countertop and table, Karina put the dishes away. Once done, they walked to the living room and sat watching the kids play in the school playground across the street.

"This is the first time I've been in this room since Mama Ella passed," Karina shared. "I just couldn't bring myself to sit in here without her. For weeks, we had a hospital bed in the corner."

Candace sniffed back her tears. Turning to face Karina, she spoke softly, "I didn't know Mama Ella was sick when Nick and I moved back a couple of months ago. I intended to come sooner, but I procrastinated. Trying to get my nerve up—" Candace's voice broke.

"I'm shocked that you're still with Nick!" Karina changed the subject. "Just goes to show that you can't predict the future. We figured Nick was either gonna end up in the penitentiary or dead before he turned twenty-one. Mama Ella prayed every night for a year that you would see him for who he really was and come on home."

Candace shook her head. "Nick was never as 'street' as you guys thought. Hell, as I thought. He was the little brother of a dope dealer trying to impress the girls with his big talk, borrowed gold chain, riding in his brother's flashy car. And yeah," Candace laughed ruefully, "I fell for it hook, line, and sinker! But after I got to know him I realized he was different. He was smart but he liked the attention that being 'Slick Nick' got him." Candace closed her eyes. "Now I know how desperate he was to fit in - a boy with no mother or father, just an older brother who had raised him since he was five years old - back then we all bought into the façade."

"Was it really just a façade?" Karina's tone and expression betrayed her skepticism. "I mean, I was there for at least part of it. I remember seeing the money that you were holding for him one time, and then you started using drugs, too."

Candace's first inclination was to snap at Karina, but after a few moments she said, "You're right, he was no angel. I'm just saying that wasn't the real Nick. He got in over his head. And all I was 'using' when I was at home was some weed."

Karina hadn't realized she was holding her breath. She exhaled. "So, what changed?"

"Once we got to Reno and we were on our own, it was different. Real different. Johnny was dead. There wasn't anybody to tell Nick what to do or how to be successful, so he tried to figure it out on his own. He thought he could do what Johnny had done to build a mini empire out of nothing. He had some cocaine that he'd brought with us and thought he could just show up in a strange town and be the big man." Candace's brow furrowed.

"We trusted the wrong person and everything went bad. We ended up using coke and to numb the pain." She met her sister's gaze. "But we had unconditional love for each other. That, and help from some guardian angels, got us through."

"For years I told myself I hated you. I blamed it all on you – Mommy and Daddy dying, being on the streets – hell, me being hooked!" Candace spoke softly, her eyes averted.

Karina frowned. She waited for the familiar rush of intense anger – the only emotion she'd allowed herself to feel over the past seventeen years whenever Candace had come to mind. But now, getting to know the woman the child had grown into was more important than indulging in her anger.

Candace continued, "But I learned in recovery that I would always lose if I kept playing the blame game. I was the one who got myself all turned around. Nobody forced me to run away. I was the big sister and I should've set a better example. I finally learned that I had to be accountable for my actions in order to heal. And that I had to give myself permission to heal."

Candace forced herself to meet Karina's gaze and reached out to touch her hand. "Rina, I know it hurt you when I went to Texarkana and then ran away. It's not that I was trying to desert you, I just couldn't bear to see all that hatred in your eyes. So much of it was my fault and at the end of the day I was too much of a coward to face the music. It took sobriety, prayer, and a lot of therapy to get to this point." Tears ran unchecked down her face. "I'm hoping that we can forgive each other. I've missed my family."

Somehow all the hateful speeches Karina had memorized and practiced seemed to evaporate. Gone was the monster that had haunted her dreams for years. Instead, the sister she had adored and clung to for the first sixteen years of her life was sitting right in front of her. Realizing that neither of them wanted to talk about the day Candace ran away, and without thinking about the complications or consequences, Karina pulled her sister close.

"Candi, I missed you too and I'm sorry I haven't done the work to forgive you. Therapy probably would've been a good idea," she admitted. "I'm not sure how to make everything right between us. It may not even be possible. I've been so angry with you for so long and I still don't understand how you could've done it, or why you did it. But I do know that Mama Ella would want us to try to get along. Can we try to move forward without revisiting the past?"

"My therapist brain tells me that's not healthy, but my sister brain says to do whatever I can to get my family back," Candace said.

"Maybe we should just listen to our sister brains, at least for now," Karina said.

The slamming of the screen door made them jump.

"Ri-Ma?" Samaya poked her head through the doorway. "Oh, good! I wasn't sure you'd still be here." Karina reached up to hug her daughter.

"Hey Auntie, how are you today?" Samaya asked.

Candace embraced her and leaned back to look at her face. "I'm good, Sweetie. I can't get over it. You're like a perfect mixture of me and your mom at the same age. Every feature that one of us wanted from the other one, you got. You see it, Rina?"

Karina looked from Candace to Samaya. "There's definitely the Maxwell woman resemblance. Samaya, what's up?"

Samaya looked around the room. "I wasn't sure I could come back here," she sighed, "but it doesn't feel like I thought it would. I can feel Mama Ella's presence. It's like she has her arms wrapped around me. It's not sad, it feels safe. Does that sound crazy?"

Before Karina could respond, Candace walked over to Samaya and took her hands in her own. "No, Sweetie, not crazy at all. I feel it too and it's been so many years since Mama Ella held me you'd think I wouldn't remember, but I do. She's here. In the fabric of this couch, how her bedroom smells like lavender, in the way those pictures are arranged on the walls, in that Bible that she wore the print off of; Mama Ella is right here." By the time Candace finished speaking, they were all crying.

Karina squared her shoulders. "And because she's here with us, I can hear her telling us to stop all this crying and get on with the business of life!"

"On that note," Samaya said in a pleading tone, "Ri-Ma, can I talk to you about something really important?"

"I'm going to go out and explore Mama Ella's yard and give you two some time to talk. Maybe I'll do some watering." Candace said.

Karina and Samaya sat in the chairs in front of the living room window, facing each other. "What's wrong, sweetheart?" Karina said.

"Nothing's wrong. Zandy just said I should talk to you. I didn't want to bother you because I know you're upset, but there is a time issue." Samaya averted her eyes.

"Talk to me about what?"

"Well," Samaya took a dramatic deep breath. "Ms. Bennett says that I am one of the best dancers in the class."

Karina's shoulders slumped. "Yes, Samaya, we all know that you are a talented dancer. What's your point?"

"Why do you have to get that tone with me, like I'm doing something wrong or bothering you?" Samaya grimaced and stood up. "My point, Mother," she mimicked Karina, "is that because I'm so good I have a chance to perform with a dance troupe that one of the Alvin Ailey dancers is putting together."

Dropping the attitude, Samaya knelt in front of her mother. "Ri-Ma, this would be so cool! I'd have to work hard to catch up with the other dancers cause they've been practicing together all summer but Ms. Bennett thinks I can do it. We would perform all over the country from Halloween until Christmas."

Karina put her hand on top of Samaya's. "Halloween 'til Christmas? It's September! I know you don't think you're going to take off from school for the rest of the semester! This is your senior year, Samaya!"

Samaya stood up and started to pace. "See, I knew it! I told Zandy you wouldn't even listen to what I had to say before getting all negative. I wouldn't be *taking off*, Mother! It's an academic program. We'd have tutors and mandatory study hall and I'd get credit for the semester. It would help my chances at getting into college, not hurt them."

Samaya plopped down on the couch. "Why won't you ever let me do what I want? This is *my* life! I would've thought you'd want me to leave since you're always so worried about me hanging out with my friends."

Karina leaned back against the chair and closed her eyes, forcing herself to count to ten before responding.

"Samaya, the world doesn't revolve around you. I just buried my grandmother – the woman who raised me from the time I was your age; the woman who helped raise you." She sat up to look at her daughter, who was sniffling and wiping away her tears.

"Did you even think that I might be drained? That I might not feel like arguing with you or being pressured to make a big decision? Did you think about the fact that you've been grounded for a month because you keep sneaking out of the house, drinking, smoking and partying with your friends? And that your irresponsibility might make us think you can't handle being away from home?"

"That's not fair, I—"

"Let me finish," Karina said, silencing her. "Did you consider that I might be a little preoccupied since my sister has appeared out of nowhere after nearly twenty years? Let me answer that for you. *No.* It didn't occur to you because you're selfish, Samaya. You're a selfish little girl who wants to be treated like a responsible young woman but won't act like one."

"Ri-Ma, you never talk about your sister! How am I supposed to know it matters to you that she's back? And what does any of this have to do with the dance troupe?" Samaya grabbed her jacket. "Just forget it. I told Zandy you wouldn't listen."

"I'll bet Zander didn't tell you to come track me down at Mama Ella's house while I'm talking to my long-lost sister to ask me about this dance troupe, did he?"

Deflated, Samaya looked down at her feet. "Well, no. He said I should ask you in a day or two after you'd gotten some rest."

"That's what I thought. But you couldn't bring yourself to wait, could you?"

"No. I mean yes, I guess I could have. Look, I'm sorry, okay? I was gonna wait but then I ran into Ms. Bennett at the yogurt shop and she asked me about the funeral and how everybody was doing and then she asked if Mama Ella's passing was gonna affect me joining the troupe and she wanted to set up a meeting with you guys to talk about the details and she said that it was okay if I didn't want to leave right now and that she could talk to Regina Walters about taking my spot."

Samaya stopped just long enough to take a breath. "But Ri-Ma I just can't lose my spot to Regina! *I hate Regina.* And you know I'm a better dancer than her. And then I ran into Darnell and he said that even though he'd miss me he'd be really proud of me if I was in a professional dance troupe and that he wouldn't be with anybody else while I was gone. When I dropped him off at home I saw your car here so I came in to ask you."

Karina studied her daughter's face as if she were a stranger. "It's really amazing to me how you can suddenly 'hate' Regina after being best friends with her for more than half your life. I have to wonder if Brandy is suddenly your best friend because she's Darnell's cousin. And didn't your Dad tell you to stop driving that boy around town?"

When Samaya started to speak, she held up her hand to stop her. "You know what? That's not the conversation for today. Sammi, today is tough for me, okay? I'm sure Ms. Bennett will understand that your Dad and I will need some time to decide. Why don't you get all the information together for us to look at? We need to know all the details, like who is in charge of the program, where the troupe will stay, who will chaperone, how the academics will be handled, dates, cost, everything."

Samaya ran to her mother and gave her a hug. "Thank you, thank you, thank you! I'll get everything together right away. I have Ms. Bennett's home phone number!"

"Samaya, I didn't say yes! You always do this. You don't listen and then you get your feelings hurt when things don't go your way." Samaya's eyes grew stormy and she crossed her arms across her torso.

Karina groaned. "Listen to what I'm saying. Give us the information and we'll look at it. And do not call your grandparents for support. Dad and I will decide if it's okay. But I am not inclined to let you do something that requires maturity away from home if you continue to demonstrate immaturity at home. Do you understand?"

"Yes, Ma'am, I understand. Can I go now?" Samaya frowned.

"Can you go now?" Karina mimicked. "Yes, please go. Like I

don't have enough on my mind without having to drop everything to deal with your make-believe crisis." Karina stormed out of the living room and sought refuge in Mama Ella's room.

Outside, Candace moved away from the open window. She sat on the porch steps, transported in time. *Samaya could be me and Rina could be Mommy! Was I really that selfish? She shook her head. What a difference a lifetime makes.*

The screen door slammed behind Samaya. She plopped down on the steps and stared unabashedly at her aunt.

"It's crazy how much you and Ri-Ma look alike! But she dresses like an old lady and you've got style, Auntie!"

Laughing, Candace studied her niece's face just as closely. "People used to think we were twins. Probably because our mother insisted on dressing us alike until we were ten years old!" Candace took note of Samaya's designer jeans and purse. "I don't think your mom dresses like an old lady, but if she does, maybe it's because you get all the money in the clothing budget."

"I'll have you know I am a good sales shopper." Samaya pouted, then she laughed. "But seriously Auntie, you have to help Ri-Ma get up with the times. She'd look so cute in that outfit you're wearing." Samaya glanced with appreciation at Candace's snug-fitting jeans, cashmere sweater and high-heeled boots.

Candace found herself giving in to the teenager. "Okay, if Rina and I go shopping, I'll make a few suggestions."

Samaya grinned. "You're cool Auntie. I hope you'll stay for a while. Maybe my mom won't be on my case so much if she has somebody to talk to. She hates that I'm growing up. You showing up might be just what she needs." Samaya jogged to her car parked in the driveway and waved to Candace. "Later Auntie!" Her radio blasted an Alicia Keys song as she drove away.

Seeing seventeen-year-old Samaya took Candace back in time to when she and her sister were that age. *I thought I knew everything back then. And Rina did too. We were both so wrong. Isn't that funny? Miss know-it-all and her boyfriend had a baby before they got married — she didn't mention that part. Lord knows she would've held that over my head.*

"Stop it, Candace!" She admonished herself. "Live in the now.

Digging up the past won't do you a bit of good." Candace hoped the forgiveness that she had granted Karina in therapy would hold up in real life.

Meanwhile Karina sat on Mama Ella's bed lost in thought. She almost dared to hope that Candace was back for good. She wondered if it was really possible to forgive and be forgiven.

PART II

THE PAST - 1986/1987

LOOSE LIPS

Langston Maxwell's voice seemed to bounce off the walls. "Karina, why are you in my chair? I want to watch the CBS News Special about the crack cocaine epidemic. It's 1986, I would've thought things would be getting better for Black folks, not worse."

Without looking up from her book, Karina moved to the couch, and continued reading. At sixteen, reading was her favorite pastime. Looking up from her sewing machine, Jewel Maxwell added, "I've been wanting to watch that news special too – that is, if you think you can tone down your commentary so I can hear it!"

"Woman I keep telling you comedy is not your strong suit!" Langston replied.

"If only I was joking!" Jewel snickered. "Seriously though, I need to watch this one and the ones the other networks are airing so I can be prepared for our community action meeting this weekend. We need solutions. The money they're spending on admiring the problem would be better spent bringing genuine opportunities back to so-called urban America. Most of these boys out there on the corners are trying to survive or help their families survive. But they don't want to show that, do they?"

"Here we go." Langston grumbled. "Jewel, some of those

precious kids you taught once upon a time are too far gone. These knuckleheads are slinging dope, joining gangs, terrorizing their own neighborhoods, and shooting each other. Do you know that most of the 911 calls we're getting are for overdoses or shootings? And they're coming from the flatlands. Poor folks turning on each other. The white folks in the hills are living their lives as usual." Langston said.

"I know, Lang, but it's still a small minority of our kids. The world loses sight of the Black and brown kids who are on track for college and meeting their goals. They're future teachers and firefighters like us. As for the knuckleheads, why let them sit in jail exposing them to more violence! Get them educated! Teach 'em a trade! And don't be misled – those folks in the hills are consumers. And their kids get busted at school with contraband more often than our kids do!" She gave her husband a stern look. "Why are you getting me all riled up, Langston?"

Langston chuckled, "Ya gotta admit, it's pretty easy, Baby. And yes, I know where the money that's being funneled into the community is coming from. But our kids have got to be smarter and stop turning on one another. That TV special is not gonna show the world that they're victims, you can count on that!"

Rolling her eyes at her husband, Jewel said, "Karina, go check on your sister."

Karina groaned, "Mommy, I'm at the best part of the book!"

"That's the thing about books, you put them down and come back and the characters are right where you left them."

Karina sat up. "Mommy, there's nothing wrong with Candi."

Jewel frowned and glanced at Karina. "What do you mean nothing's wrong with her? She's been having terrible stomach cramps for hours now. That cyst may have come back. Find out if the hot water bottle is helping. Matter-of-fact, it probably needs to be refilled, so turn the tea kettle on before you go upstairs." Jewel turned back to her sewing.

Several minutes passed. Langston said, "Why are you still sitting there? Your mother told you to go see about your sister."

"Daddy," Karina kept her eyes on the floor, "there's no point in me going upstairs."

Before Langston could respond, Jewel stood and walked over to the couch. "Karina, these days I expect your sister to give me attitude, but not you. What do you mean 'no point'?"

Karina hesitated. Only ten months apart and in the same grade in school, Karina had always been Candace's shadow. When Candace learned her ABCs, Karina learned hers. Karina had learned to spell Candace's name before her own. When it was time for Candace to go to school, Karina threw such a fit that the principal let them start kindergarten together. They read, played, bathed, sang, danced, and cried together. They looked so much alike that people routinely took them for twins, the only noticeable difference was Candace's skin tone was like tea with a heavy pour of cream and Karina's was a warm bronze. Images of all the good times she and Candace used to have together flashed through Karina's mind.

But that was the old Candace, before she started hanging out with Tiffany Peterson. The new Candace couldn't be bothered with who she now referred to as her "little sister" and avoided at all costs. The new Candace rolled up the waistband of her skirts to make them shorter. The new Candace called herself "C.C." and cut school more than she went. She got away with it by forging their mother's signature on notes to the attendance office. The new Candace was sneaky and mean, and made Karina feel plain and lonely.

Karina took a deep breath. "There's no point in checking on Candi 'cause she's not there."

"What the hell do you mean she's not there?" Langston's voice boomed. "Candace! Get down here right now!"

Jewel hurried up the stairs calling Candace's name, while Karina wished she could suck the words back in.

Jewel ran back downstairs, "She's right, the blanket is pulled up but she's not there." Worry etched her typically smooth brow. "Karina, what's going on? Where's your sister?" Jewel demanded.

Karina bristled, "Why are you yelling at me? I didn't do anything. I'm right here."

Langston stood towering over her. "We don't have time for this, Karina. You knew your sister had snuck out and now you're trying to act all innocent?"

Karina stood up and backed away from her father. "How does this get to be my fault? I'm the good girl! I'm the one who gets good grades, follows the rules, and dresses like I have some sense. I'm not the one cutting school, smoking, doing drugs and screwing drug dealers!" As the last words crossed her lips, Karina slapped her hand to her mouth wishing she could stuff them back inside.

"What!" Her parents exclaimed.

"Karina Maxwell sit your narrow behind down and watch your mouth." Jewel's measured tone had the desired effect. "Tell us what you know right now!"

Cowed, Karina told them, "You know she hangs with Tiffany and her crew now – but you haven't seen how they dress – always in tight clothes and makeup so they'll look older. She never hangs out with me and Sonya anymore. She stopped going to our SAT prep sessions."

The hurt and anger that she'd been bottling up for months poured out. Karina told them everything she knew or even suspected. "They go behind the swimming pool building before and after school to smoke. And not just cigarettes – she used your oregano to practice rolling joints last night when she was supposed to be studying for her Spanish test. There was no point in her studying Spanish, anyway. She hardly ever goes to eighth period."

"Rina, are you making this up?" Langston asked. "I know you and Candi didn't spend a lot of time together this past summer and you've been feeling left out. But it's natural for you girls to branch out and make separate friends."

"Daddy, I'm telling the truth!" Karina yelled. "Even though she's been treating me like crap, Candi has always been my best friend. I wouldn't be telling on her if I wasn't scared."

Jewel frowned, "Scared? Scared about what? Is there something else?"

Karina twisted the hem of her shirt. She'd gone this far. "It's her boyfriend and his crowd."

Langston frowned. "Michael? Michael's a pretty good kid. You're telling me he's mixed up in this mess?"

"No Daddy, Michael's not her boyfriend anymore. They broke up before school let out for the summer. Her new boyfriend is this guy named Nick."

Langston's voice boomed. "Who the hell is Nick and why am I just now hearing about him? Where did she meet him?"

"I really don't know. She doesn't tell me anything anymore. All I know is that Nick is a drug dealer and that he picks her up from school sometimes in a flashy car. Usually, Tiffany's boyfriend is with him. I'm pretty sure Candi sometimes holds his money or maybe his drugs for him so if the police hassle him, they won't find anything."

Langston seemed to be having trouble breathing. Jewel cut Karina off, "Rina, get your father some water. I think we've had enough true confessions for now."

Karina walked to the kitchen, glancing back over her shoulder to check on her father.

After Langston had steadied his breathing he turned to Rina and asked quietly, "So where is she now, Li'l Bit?"

"I'm not sure." Karina averted her eyes and studied the patterned wallpaper as if she'd never seen it before. "She's not with Nick though. He's still in Juvie."

Langston frowned. "He's in 'Juvie'? Y'all are so comfortable with criminals that you have nicknames for jail? If she's not with this Nick character, then who is she with?"

Karina hesitated. Langston started pacing around the room. "Rina now is not the time to try to protect her. You've been doing that for too long as it is! Do you know where she is?"

"Karina, it's almost midnight. Who is your sister with? When is she coming home and how will she get in?" Jewel asked.

Karina swallowed, "She was going to meet Tiffany and some other people. I don't know where. She usually only goes out when Daddy is at the Fire Station, so I was surprised she went out tonight. She always comes back before it gets too late because she knows I can't stay awake late. She climbs the plum tree and then I open the window and help her inside. We had this big argument because I told her I didn't want to have to wait up for her because I have a history test in first period tomorrow. She said she'd come back soon, but I figured she was lying."

Jewel closed her eyes at the realization that Candace had been sneaking out frequently enough to have established a routine. "Why do you think she was lying?"

"Because I think she went to the sideshow and I know those don't even get started til late."

"The sideshow?" Langston was beside himself. "Are you talking about over by the skating rink in East Oakland where kids cruise and drag race? Didn't someone get shot there last month!" Langston was livid. "My baby girl is out there with that trash?"

Karina nodded, "I think so, Daddy."

Langston headed for his bedroom. Jewel hurriedly followed behind him, tossing over her shoulder, "Karina, go get ready for bed. When Candace comes home, open the window for her and get back into bed. Keep your mouth shut."

Karina rushed to her bedroom and lay on the floor with her ear next to the central heating grate. Years before, she and Candace had discovered they could hear whatever went on in their parents' room by listening at the grate. As they'd gotten older and understood what the sounds coming from the room meant, they'd decided it was better not to listen.

"Langston, what are you doing? Put that gun away! Who are you going to shoot? You don't know where she is or who she's with."

"I'll find her and I'll find somebody to shoot!" Langston's voice bounced off the walls. "What do you want me to do Jewel, just sit here knowing that our daughter is in the streets with drug dealers? You don't know how bad it's gotten out there. I'm starting not to recognize some of these neighborhoods. The dealers don't even try to hide what they're doing. They're taking over apartment buildings and entire blocks as though they're corporations. And the users are walking around like zombies."

Langston sat down abruptly on the edge of the bed. "Baby, I

was at a call a few weeks ago trying to revive a guy who was probably my age. We got him in the ambulance and a woman kept pulling on my sleeve. I thought she was his daughter maybe and wanted to ride with him." He looked at his wife. "Do you know what she said to me, Jewel?"

Frowning, Jewel said, "What Lang?"

"She said 'before you take him, lemme suck you off. Just ten dollars.' It hurt me to my heart, baby. She wasn't much older than our girls. That's why I have to go now. I can't let Candi be out there in those streets."

Karina heard drawers opening and closing. "Where did you put my bullets woman? You are not supposed to hide a man's bullets!"

Jewel's voice was steady, "Langston. I didn't hide the bullets. You're in a frenzy and don't know what you're doing or where to look. Would you just sit back down for a minute and talk to me? Candi is not a crackhead. I know we missed some signs but I don't believe she's on drugs. Okay, she might smoke some weed but that's not the end of the world." Her voice softened, "C'mon Lang. Calm down. We're going to fix this. We are not going to lose our baby to these streets. We've worked our entire lives to keep them away from all of this."

Karina couldn't make out the rest of the conversation. She got up off the floor and flung herself across her bed. *This is bad. Real bad. Daddy could go to jail and it'll be my fault.* She shook her head angrily. *No! It'll be Candi's fault! She's so stupid! I told her about the shooting at that sideshow last month and that she shouldn't go. Now look what she's done! Daddy's about to have a heart attack and Mommy's all worried and stressed out.*

Karina looked at the clock on the night table between the two beds. *12:45! What the hell is she doing? She hardly ever stays out this late on a school night, especially when Daddy isn't on shift!* Karina punched the pillow. *She's so selfish. She knows I have a big test in the morning.*

"Rina." Jewel gently shook Karina awake.

Karina rubbed the sleep from her eyes. "What time is it?"

Glancing at the clock, she sat up. "2:30! Mommy, what's going on?" Looking over at her sister's empty bed, she frowned, "Where's Candi?"

Jewel whispered, "She's not back yet, baby. Daddy and I are going to look for her. We'll be back soon."

Karina grabbed her mother's arm. "Mommy, no, just wait for her to come home! You don't even know where to look!"

Her father answered from the bedroom doorway, "You thought she was going to the sideshow, so we're gonna head over to that skating rink parking lot where the last sideshow was. Maybe she's there. If not, we'll find out if there was one somewhere else tonight. Do you know anywhere else where she hangs out, Rina?" Noticing her hesitation, Langston said, "Now is not the time to keep secrets, Karina. Your sister could be in trouble."

Karina's eyes filled with tears, "I don't know, Daddy. Sometimes when they cut school they hang out at Tilden Park, up by Lake Anza or at the Berkeley Marina, but I don't know where they go at night."

She got out of bed and ran to her father, throwing her arms around his waist. "Daddy please, please don't go. I bet she didn't even go to the sideshow. Candi's all talk, she's not really like those other girls. She was probably just trying to impress me. Daddy, I have a bad feeling about this. You and Mommy don't need to be out there with those drug dealers!" Karina could feel the imprint of her father's gun in his waistband. Her body was shaking as he pried her arms from around his waist.

"Girl, stop being so silly. Only thing bad that's gonna happen is your sister is gonna get embarrassed in front of her so-called friends and she won't leave this house again until she's eighteen years old." Langston managed a distracted smile. "Jewel, why don't you stay here with Li'l Bit while I go look for Scoot."

"There's no way I'm letting you confront these kids by yourself, Langston. I have no desire to visit you in the hospital, penitentiary, or morgue!" Jewel said sharply. "Karina, stop crying and get back in bed. You need to be ready for that history test. If your sister comes home before we get back, call us on your dad's mobile phone."

"Daddy has a mobile phone?" Karina frowned.

"I have the on-call phone from the Station – the number's on the refrigerator," Langston said.

Jewel and Langston each kissed Karina before hurrying out.

"Love you guys," Karina whispered, leaning against the door.

Nearly two hours later Karina heard tapping on the window. She could just make out her sister's smiling face in the early dawn light. Karina pushed aside the curtains and yanked open the window, steadying Candace as she climbed in. As soon as Candace's feet were safely inside, Karina sat back on her bed to resume her vigil. She had been looking up from her book every few minutes to check the clock ever since her parents left.

Candace whispered as she tiptoed around the room. "Rina, I had the most amazing night!" She quickly changed from the skintight leggings, too small spaghetti strap tank top, and off-the-shoulder cropped sweatshirt that stopped above her belly button, into a pair of sweatpants and an oversized t-shirt.

Her voice dropped. "Well, it started off bad, really, really bad," she paused, lost in thought, even her heavy makeup couldn't mask her vulnerability, "but it ended up being the best night of my life."

Candace stashed the taboo outfit under a stack of sweaters in the corner of her closet. Turning back to the dresser, she slid the gaudy hoop earrings and long ropes of fake pearls into her jewelry box, and reached into the top drawer for the makeup removal wipes she kept to erase the traces of her nocturnal field trips. Karina sat motionless, watching her.

While removing the layers of foundation, blush, mascara, and false eyelashes that made her look two shades darker and two years older, Candace whispered conspiratorially, "Rina, I met this guy named Rell. He's so fine and nice and such a good kisser!"

Karina frowned. "Hold on. You met a guy and kissed him? What about Nick?"

Looking at Karina through the mirror, Candace blushed. "I

know how it sounds but it's all so confusing, Rina. I love Nicky, but sometimes he makes me nervous. Plus, he's still in Juvie and I don't know when he's getting out." Hardly able to contain her excitement, Candace buried the soiled wipes in the trash. Throwing herself dramatically across Karina's bed, pulled her close, and whispered in her ear, "Rina, we did it!"

Karina pulled away and her eyes narrowed. "Did what?"

Candace giggled. "You know what I mean. We did it!"

Karina's jaw dropped. "You had sex? With a stranger?"

"I know, I know. It sounds crazy but Rell's not really a stranger. I've seen him playing ball at the Rec center over the summer even though he never saw me. He always seemed nice. Anyway, first he helped me get away from these guys that were bothering me and then we walked and talked, and he was telling me stuff about myself. Rina, it was like he could see inside my soul or something."

She leaned back against the wall and hugged her knees close to her chest. "He told me I was special, not like the other girls at the sideshow – you know, like Tiff and them." She paused when she saw the look on her sister's face. "Don't look at me like that, Rina! You're always telling me the same thing."

"Look at you like what, Candi? Like you are the most gullible person in the world?" Karina sneered.

Candace ignored her. "He helped me get out of East Oakland. I couldn't find Tiffany and them. We went up to Cal. He's the schoolboy type, Rina! And we just wandered around for a long time. We followed Strawberry Creek and went over the bridge – you know where you and I used to study after our summer classes? It was always so, I don't know, private I guess, that it felt like the perfect place to sit with him. Then he put down his jacket for us and we just laid there, talking; then we started kissing and it just happened." Candace couldn't suppress her happiness.

Karina got up and walked around the room in circles. "You mean to tell me you just happened to meet your soulmate, he told you you're special, and then he fucked you in the dirt at Cal over by the bridge where the homeless sleep? Yeah, that's real romantic Candi."

"You can be so mean sometimes, Rina! I don't get it. We used to be so close but now it's like you get off on hurting me." Candace moved to her own bed. "Why do you have to make it sound so dirty? It was special."

"How is it that you're the older sister? You're so naïve. Or just plain stupid." Contempt oozed from Karina.

"I guess you can't understand it because you're still a little girl. Another woman would understand, but you just sit here with your books and your daydreams hiding from the rest of the world because you're scared." Happy to have finally gotten the upper hand in the conversation, Candace turned away and started to get in bed.

Karina grabbed Candace's arm and spun her around.

"Scared? Yeah, Candi, I'm *scared* to run around town like a whore, piling makeup on my face, hiking up my skirt to show my ass, and tying my shirts so my belly is out. I'm *scared* to pretend that I haven't been an honor student all my life, just like you, and dumb myself down to be accepted by Tiffany and her stupid friends."

She loosened her grip and stepped back. "But not you. You're brave enough to pretend that you don't want to be a psychologist because that's not cool. You're brave enough to cut school every day so you can sit in Nick's car or hang out in somebody's basement drinking and smoking weed, or God knows what else."

Stunned, Candace's eyes brimmed over with tears. "Is that what you really think of me? *You know me, Rina.* I'm not one of those fast girls. Most of the time I don't even get high, I just hang out with them while they do it." She plopped down on her bed.

"Yeah, I like to look cute, but what's wrong with that? I still want to be a psychologist. I do my homework, or enough of it to get by. It was just a fun summer, you know? And now I'm having a hard time getting back into the swing of school but it's not like I'm about to drop out or anything." Tears ran down her cheeks. "And what do you have against Nicky? You don't even know him. All that drug stuff you're talking about? That's really his brother, Johnny. Nick is just dabbling in it, trying to fit in and raise some money. You'd actually like Nicky if you knew him. Did I ever tell you he can draw, like artist level drawings? He could be a professional!"

Candace's voice lowered to a barely discernible whisper. "But that's not the point. I don't understand why you hate me so much, Rina. What does any of this have to do with you? I told you about Rell because I thought you'd be happy that I found somebody who sees me for who I really am but all you can do is tear me down. What kind of sister are you?"

Karina snorted, "You are too much! Now I'm not a good little sister because I don't idolize you anymore? Because I'm not still trying to follow behind you and imitate everything you do? You love being the center of attention! You and Nick deserve each other; I'll bet he's just as misunderstood as you are." Her tone grew urgent. "Candi, you know he's slinging crack! I don't care if his brother is the big man. Nick is trying to make a name for himself and you're right there by his side. You've seen the news. You see what crack is doing to people. How can you be part of that?"

Karina's words were like a physical attack. Candace scooted away from her and clutched a pillow to her chest, willing herself not to cry.

"Candi, you wanna be so grown, at least be woman enough to look at yourself in the mirror. You put our whole family in danger by being with Nick. What if somebody thinks you hold his stash? Huh? Who's stopping them from coming here? You know Daddy has a gun that he's not afraid to use. What will happen if he has to shoot one of these drug dealers? He'll go to jail! You're so selfish!"

When Karina yanked open the bedroom door, Candace jumped up and grabbed her arm. "Where are you going?" she whispered. "It's 5 o'clock in the morning! You're gonna wake up Mommy and Daddy."

Karina pulled her arm away. "They're not here Candace!" she shouted as she headed downstairs.

Scurrying behind her, Candace said, "Not here? What do you mean? Where are they?" As the girls reached the landing, she said, "Oh no, did something happen to one of the grands?"

Karina continued down the stairs. Glancing back, she threw her words like poison darts. "Like you care! No, they're out looking for you."

"What do you mean looking for me?" Candace asked in shock.

Karina looked up from the foyer. "Just what I said. They've been out looking for you for the last couple of hours."

"What? Why? Where would they go?"

Karina sighed. "Probably to East Oakland to see if you were at the sideshow or down alleys or something wherever the other potheads hang out." Then she walked down the hall to the kitchen, with Candace trailing after her.

"Potheads? They don't know I smoke. Wait, Rina, you didn't?" She pushed Karina against the wall. "What did you do?" She was crying so hard she struggled to get out the words.

"What I should've done a long time ago. You need help. Somebody has to stop you from ruining your life." Karina pushed past her sister, ignoring the tentacles of doubt pulling at her conscience. "So yeah, I told Daddy and Mommy you snuck out and they went to get their precious baby."

Candace sat down at the kitchen table suddenly looking much older than seventeen. "You are so stupid! I don't care what you think about me, but why would you send Daddy out there to get into it with the D-boys? Johnny and his crew are serious trouble, Rina. They're trying to make a place for themselves in the drug world now that Felix Mitchell is dead. They're not gonna let some girl's daddy get in the way."

Karina looked at her sister in horror. "Felix Mitchell? The drug kingpin whose funeral was in the papers the other day? Candi, tell me you are not in that deep!"

"No, I'm not, we're not. But that's what Nick's brother does, and I've seen a little of what goes on. Trust me, Daddy does not need to be in that mix. You know how crazy he can get, Rina. And what about his blood pressure?" Her voice broke. "Do you hate me so much you'd take a chance on Daddy getting hurt just to hurt me?"

Karina sighed and sat opposite Candace. "I don't hate you. I just hate what you're doing, and I hate that you hate me."

Candace started to respond, but Karina cut her off, "I don't think Daddy would go to the Village to look for you. I told him you guys were probably going to the sideshow and he mentioned the skating rink. Anyway, all that stuff about sideshows is a lot of hype, isn't it?" There was a plaintive note to her voice.

Candace frowned. "First off, I don't hate you. You sound stupid. The sideshows used to just be young guys hanging out in their cars and having fun, but now the D-boys have been coming to show off their fancy rides and listen to rap music. I've only been a few times. Tonight, Tiffany took me to one near the Village. Everybody was all hyped up, passing around bottles and weed. Then these boys from Richmond showed up and started talking mess. Some fights broke out and things got wild fast."

Her eyes started to tear. "I got separated from Tiff and these guys started messing with me, touching on me and stuff. That's how I ended up leaving with Rell; he got me out of there. If it wasn't for him, I don't know what they would've done to me."

Karina banged her fist on the table, causing the salt and pepper shakers to jump. "There you go again! You keep making this be about you and all I care about is where Mommy and Daddy are!"

Candace shrugged, a worried expression on her face. "I don't know." Glancing at the clock, she gasped when she saw it was nearly 6 o'clock. "Maybe we should go look for them, Rina. There was a lot going on at the sideshow tonight. It was definitely not someplace Mommy and Daddy would have fit in or been welcomed. I wish we could get in touch with them."

"I'm such an idiot!" Karina got up and ran to the phone. "Daddy has the Fire Station mobile phone with him! Read me the number!" she demanded.

Candace scanned the many notes and post-its on the refrigerator. "Where is it? Where is it?" she repeated. "Got it!" She called out the numbers to her sister.

Karina dialed and the girls anxiously waited for their father to pick up, but after several rings, a recording came on offering options of which button to push for help. Karina tried again, only to get the same results. The girls looked at each other in fear. "You know he'd answer if he could." Karina's bravado disintegrated and she cried in earnest.

Candace hugged her sister. "Don't worry, it's gonna be okay," she murmured unconvincingly. "Let's go find them."

Taking their mother's car, the sisters checked the spots closest to home first, putting off venturing to the site of the sideshow. There was no sign of Langston's distinctive sports car anywhere. Last year, in a fit of what Jewel called his "middle age crisis," Langston had traded in his dependable minivan for a classic 1967 Corvette. He and his friends were working on restoring 'his baby' on their days off. Langston loved the way the car drew attention.

"Foolishness!" Jewel often said. "You just watch. That bad back of his is gonna seize up one day and we'll have to call the fire department to get him out!" Despite her criticism, Jewel secretly enjoyed riding in the sporty car with Langston. It made her feel young and carefree.

Candace pulled Jewel's practical Volvo to a stop a half mile away from the housing project run by Felix Mitchell, a notorious drug lord and leader of a criminal organization dubbed the '69th Village Mob.' Mitchell had devised an ingenious drug supply and delivery system using the housing project as a base of operations. Apartments were commandeered for the cooking, packaging, and storage of heroin and crack and the counting and bundling of money. Children as young as six years old were recruited into the organization as lookouts and to pass drugs to customers. Workers patrolled the entrances and exits of the housing development with automatic weapons. Law abiding tenants lived in fear, knowing that the police were unwilling or unable to protect them. The arrest and conviction of Mitchell had not resolved the many issues of the community.

"Nicky told me it got worse on the streets when Felix got a life sentence. He said more gangs started challenging the 69 Village Mob, trying to take over territory and stuff. And since Felix got murdered in prison, there's been all kinds of rumors and talk about retribution," Candace said.

"All the people showing up for his funeral the other day was unbelievable," Karina said. "And the fact that they showed it on TV is wild! Sonya's cousin actually went and he said it was fancy like something you would expect for somebody like Dr. Martin Luther King, Jr."

"I almost went, but at the last-minute Tiffany's sister chickened out."

Karina rolled her eyes. "That would've been dumb!"

"Whatever! I didn't go. But I saw the horse-drawn carriage."

"Not just that! Four Rolls Royces and ten limousines. The papers said at least 10,000 people were there." Karina said.

"People at the sideshow were all worked up about Felix's murder and talking mess about who was really behind it. It's like they were feeding off each other's energy." Candace shuddered.

"This is as close as we can get," Candace said. "The actual sideshow was up ahead but there were a lot of people, so the crowd stretched all the way to here. I didn't go any closer, but this was bad enough. There were some dudes right over there rocking a car."

"Rocking a car? What do you mean?"

"There was an older man, maybe Hispanic, driving a beat up Volkswagen bug. He was trying to get through the crowd, but they wouldn't let him pass. Then these dudes surrounded the car and started rocking it back and forth like it was a toy. I don't know what happened next cause that's when those guys started grabbing on me."

"Grabbing on you? What are you talking about?"

"I tried to tell you before, but you wouldn't listen. I got separated from Tiffany in the crowd. These guys started messing with me, talking nasty and touching me. I started running and Rell kinda just appeared out of nowhere and helped me get away."

"Sounds romantic," Karina said with a smirk. Noticing Candace's hurt expression, she quickly added, "Just kidding. Actually, it sounds really scary. I'm glad your newfound soulmate came to the rescue! All he needed was a white horse!"

They both laughed, breaking the tension. Karina said, "Candi, I don't think Daddy and Mommy would've come here, though. I thought the sideshow was at the skating rink, so that's where I sent them."

Candace shook her head. "Nobody was going back there after the shooting last month. But there's usually more than one sideshow going on at a time. Hopefully you're right and they went somewhere else. Let's get out of here."

Suddenly Candace stuck her head out of the window. "Rina, look!" She pointed to the ground between the railroad tracks. At first Karina didn't see anything unusual. There was broken glass mixed in with fast food wrappers, empty beer bottles, crack vials and soda cans. Suddenly, she saw what Candace was pointing to. Karina opened her car door and jumped out, ignoring Candace's admonition that it wasn't safe. As soon as she got out of the car, several young men who had been lounging on a bus bench not far away stood up and sauntered in the girls' direction. Karina was oblivious to their approach. She squatted down to peer closely at the striped, red, black, and green ball. Candace rolled down her window and hissed angrily, "Karina, get your ass in the car now!"

Frowning, Karina turned and saw the men approaching. She snatched the ball off the ground and ran back to the car. Candace pulled away from the curb before Karina's door had fully closed, leaving the smell of burning rubber in their wake. Something hit the side of the car with a thud and liquid splashed all over the back window. Neither girl said anything, but Karina reached for Candace's hand.

A few minutes later Karina broke the silence. "Candi, this is Daddy's," she said, opening her clutched fist to reveal the antenna ball that Langston's Jamaican coworker had given to him. Langston loved the tricolored ball imprinted with the words 'Black Power'. Candace's mouth and lips were dry. She wouldn't or couldn't look at her sister. "We don't know that's his, Rina. We're in the middle of East Oakland where just about everybody is Black. You think Daddy is the only person with a Black Power antenna ball? Be serious."

Karina clutched the ball tightly in her hand. "Well, I've never seen another one, have you?" Taking her sister's silence as agreement, she continued, "What if it is Daddy's? What does that mean?"

Candace remained silent, tears welling in her eyes as she recalled the frenzied crowd tipping the Volkswagen back and forth. As if reading her sister's mind, Karina exclaimed, "Oh my God!" and fell silent. The girls didn't speak again during the drive home.

When they turned onto their block, a police car was parked in front of their house. A uniformed female officer stood on the front porch, ringing the doorbell. Candace pulled into the driveway and turned off the engine. The girls sat in the car holding hands until the police officer knocked on Candace's window and escorted them inside the house.

Fifteen minutes later, Ella Maxwell ran inside the house and gathered the girls close. "I'm here, Mama Ella's here," she murmured over and over. Candace wept unceasingly. Karina sat quietly, barely registering their grandmother's presence.

"Mrs. Maxwell, I'm Sargent Namasaki." The officer handed her a business card. "We spoke on the phone. I'm truly sorry for your loss."

Ella stumbled over her words, "Uh, yes, thank you Sargent. I still don't, I mean, I'm having a hard time getting my mind around this. Can you tell me more?"

Sargent Namasaki nodded. "Would you like to step over here with me?" She gestured to the dining room, out of earshot of the girls.

"I'll just be right over there," Ella told the girls.

"Ma'am, I just have the preliminary investigation. Our detectives will be in touch when they have a full report, but it's pretty straightforward." She flipped through her notebook and then looked up at Ella. "I know this is very painful. Let me know if you want me to stop at any time, okay?" Ella nodded.

"Mr. and Mrs. Maxwell were driving a 1967 red Corvette. At approximately 3:30 a.m. they arrived at the railroad intersection at 66th Avenue and East 12th Street in East Oakland. This had been the site of an unauthorized sideshow a few hours before. Patrol Units had already shut down the sideshow and most of the attendees were gone by the time the Maxwells showed up. Apparently, Mr. Maxwell and some youth exchanged words and the youth began to rock the Corvette."

Ella interrupted, "Oh my God!"

"But the youth had not anticipated that Mr. Maxwell would be carrying a gun."

Ella's hand flew to her throat. "A gun! Lord have mercy, what was he thinking? And with Jewel right there in the car?"

"It's not something we would advise, that's for sure. The gun was registered, ma'am, and Mr. Maxwell did have a permit to carry it outside the home. When Mr. Maxwell brandished the weapon, the youth started to disperse. According to witnesses, no one had been paying attention to the warning siren of the oncoming freight train until the light shone on the intersection and the Corvette."

"Oh, sweet Jesus." Ella looked like she was going to faint.

"Ma'am, would you rather wait for someone to come sit with you?"

"No, no. I need to be able to talk to my granddaughters." Ella took a deep breath. "Keep going."

"Several witnesses corroborated that Mr. Maxwell tried to start the car, but it stalled. Mrs. Maxwell's door handle broke off when Mr. Maxwell tried to get her out, so Mr. Maxwell reached in from the driver's side to pull her out. Somehow she was stuck. Maybe her foot or her leg. Witnesses heard Mrs. Maxwell begging Mr. Maxwell to let her go and get out of the way, but he ignored her. Just as he pulled her free, the train made contact." Sargent Namasaki closed the notebook. "The only solace I can offer you is that they died instantly."

Ella blinked, keeping the tears at bay. She knew she had to be strong. She walked outside onto the patio that overlooked the vegetable garden that had made Jewel so proud. "Lord give me strength to get me and these girls through this," she prayed.

4

WHAT'S DONE IS DONE

All Souls was overflowing with family, friends, firefighters, and community members. The tragic circumstances of the deaths of a beloved teacher and dedicated firefighter also drew media attention. Candace was inconsolable, while Karina remained dry-eyed and frighteningly removed. Ella's brow furrowed at the widening chasm between the sisters. They'd barely spoken to each other in the last week.

When the ushers handed out orange decals to all those planning to join the procession to the cemetery, Candace's face paled. Ella took one look at her and turned to Eugenia. "Genie, would you mind staying with Candi until we get back for the repast?" Candace smiled gratefully at her grandmother.

Eugenia squeezed her hand, "Whatever you need, girl." Eugenia took Candace's hand and led her away, "Candi, let's make sure the tables are set up for the repast."

Karina groaned, "Will it ever end?"

"What are you talking about?" Ella asked.

"The Candi Show! You should've made her come to the cemetery, Mama Ella. Why should she be spared?"

Ella inhaled sharply. "Candace hasn't been to a cemetery since she was eight years old. Why would I force her to come now? That would be cruel, Karina."

On the drive to the cemetery Karina stared unseeing out of the window of the limousine. She was unable to put her thoughts into words. *What about what I need? How am I supposed to do this without Candi? Our parents are being put in the ground and she won't even be there to hold my hand.*

A month after their parents' service, Ella called the girls into the living room to talk about their college plans. Patting the couch beside her she gestured for them to sit down. Candace, eyes swollen, plopped on the floor. Karina, stone-faced, sat in one of the wing chairs. Frowning, Ella looked closely at them."What's the matter? Did something happen?"

Karina studied the grain in the oak floor as though she'd never seen it before. Candace sniffed, glanced at her sister, and then said morosely, "it's nothing Mama Ella."

"Obviously it's something. Your face is all red and puffy and Rina, you look like a statue." She looked at Karina, then at Candace. "This has to stop. This is a time for sisters to pull together as a team. You need to be able to lean on each other."

"There's no team anymore, Mama Ella. Mommy and Daddy were our team leaders and now they're gone." Karina cut her eyes in her sister's direction. "Thanks to Candi."

Ella gasped and Candace's eyes spilled over. "Karina Maxwell, shut your mouth! Who are you to cast blame? You apologize right now!" Ella demanded.

Karina's expression didn't change. She said softly, "I'm sorry for upsetting you, Mama Ella, but I can't apologize for what I said. It's true. I know it and Candi knows it. If it wasn't for her, Mommy and Daddy never would have been there in the first place."

She stood up over her sobbing sister, fists clenched, arms held tightly to her sides. "It's your fault, Candi! Because of you, Mommy and Daddy will never get to see us graduate. Daddy will never walk us down the aisle." Her voice broke, but she forced herself to continue, "Mommy will never rock our babies to sleep." She paused, narrowing her darkened green eyes, and lowering her voice to a menacing whisper, "I will never forgive you. I wish it had been you instead of them."

Ella flew from the couch and slapped Karina across the face. Karina's head jerked from the force of it. "Shut your mouth right now! How could you wish death on your sister? Blaming her won't bring your parents back. Nothing will." Ella's voice shook with fury.

Candace was sprawled on the floor sobbing, unable to speak in the wake of Karina's words and her grandmother's fury. Tears filled Karina's eyes, but she maintained her stoic expression. Ella continued, chest heaving, words flying out of her mouth. "I can't believe you'd be so hateful. Candace will have to live with her part in this mess for the rest of her life. It's not for you to decide how much she should suffer or what her punishment should be. That's not your place or mine. All we can do is accept it and move on; do you hear me?"

Karina answered in a raspy whisper, "Mama Ella, no matter what you say, we all know the truth. We all know it was Candi's fault, whether or not I say it." Seeing her grandmother's eyes narrow, Karina stepped back. "Fine," she mumbled. "I won't say it again, but it's still true." Karina headed for the front door.

"And just where do you think you're going?" Ella snapped.

"I have to get out of here," Karina's quavering voice belied her calm exterior. Hand resting on the doorknob and shoulders shaking with restrained emotion, Karina kept her back to the room. "Please Mama Ella."

Candace spoke for the first time, her voice fragile and reedy, "Let her go, Mama Ella. Please just let her go."

A flurry of emotions passed over Ella's face. After a few moments she said, "Fine, but be back in one hour. I—"

Before she could finish, Karina yanked open the door and stepped onto the porch, closing the door quietly behind her. Ella sat on the floor next to Candace and pulled her head onto her lap. Stroking her hair, Ella looked deeply into the eyes that were so like

Langston's that she had to look away for a moment to compose herself.

"It's gonna take her time, Scoot, but Karina will work all of this out and you two will be close again. This is just her pain coming out in the only way it can. You've been able to cry but she hasn't, so her feelings are all bottled up and her grief is manifesting itself as anger." Ella laid her head back onto the couch cushion, eyes closed, while she continued to smooth Candace's hair. "She'll get past it. She has to." Her voice lowered to a whisper. "We all have to."

"But Mama Ella, she's right. If I hadn't snuck out that night, Daddy and Mommy wouldn't have come looking for me. That's just the truth. Rina's right, it's my fault." Her voice caught in her throat.

"Candace Janese Maxwell, you listen to what I'm saying. Yes, you did sneak out and yes, your parents did go looking for you. That's true. You can't change that. But Langston knew better than to jump out of his car getting into a scuffle with those boys. He knew not to carry a loaded gun going to look for teenagers. He and Jewel both knew that car was held together with glue. They were parents who were determined to find their daughter, but you know what? There was nothing that you or they or those kids or even that train conductor did to bring about their deaths. God put them there at that time and place. God is the one who allowed that train to come through right then, and you know why?"

Candace shook her head.

"Because it was their time. Plain and simple. Because God needed them more than we did. It's beyond our comprehension why God makes the choices He does, but we have to have faith and learn not to question His will."

Candace knew there was no point in arguing with her grandmother, but she also knew that her sister was right. She had put the ball in motion and she was sure that God would punish her.

When Karina returned, Ella redirected the conversation. "I know it's really hard making plans for the future right now, but that's what you have to do. You're both graduating this Spring and college applications are due in less than two weeks. Have you been working on your personal statements?"

Candace said quietly, "Mama Ella, I can barely concentrate on my homework. I'm tired all the time; I fall asleep in class. I think I want to take a year off."

Karina snorted, "I hope you're not trying to blame your shortcomings on Mommy and Daddy's deaths. You started screwing up as soon as the semester started."

"Did I ask you for your opinion, Karina?" Candace snapped. "You know what, Miss High and Mighty? I've had just about enough of you always on my case and having something to say about everything I do or say!" She crossed the room to stand in front of Karina. "I don't even know you anymore. You're mean and spiteful. Mommy would be ashamed of you!" she said.

Ella knew she needed to let this play out between the girls, so she sat in her chair, her eyes jumping back and forth from one granddaughter to the other.

"Don't you dare try to tell me how Mommy would feel about anything! Because of you, there is no Mommy!" Karina hurled the words at Candace.

Chest heaving and face flushed, Candace pointed her finger in Karina's face, "Yes, Mommy and Daddy were looking for me and they got killed. But let's not forget it was you who sent them there," she spat.

Shock rendered Karina speechless. Candace went on, "You were so jealous of me and of the fact that I was out there making friends, having fun, and doing stuff you wanted to do but were too scared to try that you wanted to hurt me. So you tattled like a three-year-old."

Candace leaned closer and whispered, "They wouldn't have ever gone there if it wasn't for you. If you wanted to get me in trouble all you had to do was tell them I had snuck out and when I got home I would've been busted. But you wanted more than that. You wanted to humiliate me by having Daddy come act a fool in front of all of my friends." She poked her finger into Karina's shoulder. "But it backfired. You were a petty little bitch, and now Mommy and Daddy are dead. So yeah, Rina, some of it's my fault, but them dying? That's your fault."

Karina clenched her fists and stood toe-to-toe with Candace. "You're pathetic, you're gonna try and put this off on me when you—"

"Enough!" Mama Ella's voice reverberated throughout the small house. She pushed her way in between the teenagers, causing Karina to fall back onto the couch and Candace to stumble in the opposite direction.

"I've had enough of both of you! Your parents are turning over in their graves right now. Calling each other names, placing blame, casting judgment when you know that's only for God to do! You're gonna have to find a way to forgive each other because truth be told, you both played a role in this situation."

Noting how each girl flinched, Ella said, "You heard me right! One thing you've always been able to count on from me is honesty, isn't that right?" When they nodded, she went on, "Then you better listen to me and accept what I'm telling you."

"Candace, you were immature. You did silly and unsafe things." She turned to Karina. "And you manipulated the truth out of jealousy." The girls studied their feet.

"What's equally true is that neither one of you is responsible for your parents' deaths, neither one of you. But you should've behaved better. You know it, you regret it, but there's not a damn thing you can do about it, is there?"

Shaking her head, Ella answered her own question. "No, there's not. What's done is done. Your parents are gone. Death is a part of life. That sounds cruel, doesn't it? But that's the way it is. I lost my mother and my father and both my sisters when I wasn't much older than y'all. I grew up and made another family and God took my twin babies, then my husband and now my son and daughter-in-law."

She sighed, "All that loss, yet and still I have an abiding faith in God. It was God's decision to take Langston and Jewel, not yours. That decision was made years ago when they were born. It just wasn't revealed to us then." Taking a deep breath, Ella said, "You mark my words. Each of you will regret the words you said today."

She turned to Karina. "You've been mean-spirited and vicious for weeks. I've been trying to let you grieve in your own way, but it stops right now. Hurting your sister is not going to bring your parents back. And Candace, I've watched you flinch every time Karina starts in on you, and you finally struck back, but you're just as wrong as she's been. Yes, you made some poor decisions. All you can do is to make better ones in the future. Do you hear me?" She waited. The only sound was the ticking of the grandfather clock. "Do you?" Ella demanded.

"Yes ma'am." The girls mumbled.

"From now on, I don't want to hear another word about blame or fault. We are a family and we're going to pull together and act like one."

Ella noticed a glint of sunlight reflecting off one of the many gold and silver picture frames adorning the mantelpiece. She walked over and picked up the wedding photo of Langston and Jewel. She ran her fingertips over the faces of her son and beloved daughter-in-law before carefully repositioning the frame. Shoulders sagging and suddenly looking every one of her sixty-seven years, she said, "I think I need to lie down for a little while."

The girls rushed to her side. Wordlessly, they escorted her to her bedroom, took off her shoes and helped her onto the bed. Ella didn't have the strength to talk. It was as though the weight of her loss had suddenly hit her. She closed her eyes as soon as her head hit the pillow. The girls tip-toed out of the room, closing the door behind them. Once in the hallway they looked at one another; neither said a word. Candace made her way to their bedroom. Karina grabbed a book from the living room and settled down on the couch to lose herself in the imaginary world of a book.

The next morning there was no trace of the sad old woman who had retreated to her bed. Ella flitted around the kitchen making breakfast while watching the morning news on the small black and white television that sat on the counter.

The girls hadn't spoken to one another since the blow up the day before and neither knew how to cross the chasm they'd created.

"We didn't finish talking about college applications last night," Ella said. "Deadlines are coming up. Where are you both in the process?"

"Mama Ella, my personal statement is done. Mommy and I worked on it right before school started. And my counselor already helped me fill out the application forms. I just need checks for the application fees," Karina said softly.

"Okay, just write down who each check should go to and how much and I'll give them to you tomorrow. What about you, young lady?"

Candace summoned the courage to speak up, "Mama Ella I was serious last night. I really don't think I'm ready for college right now. I'll be lucky if I pass this semester of high school. Daddy and I had talked, a bit, about me going to community college or even cosmetology school instead of a four year and I think that's what I want to do."

Karina huffed, "If talking 'a bit' means you said you wanted to do it and Daddy said you must have lost your cotton-pickin' mind, then I guess you're finally telling the truth for a change!"

Candace snapped, "Karina, who asked for your two cents? And for your information, both Daddy and Mommy talked with me about what I want to do next year. They knew I wasn't a brainiac like you and that was okay with them as long as I had a solid plan for my future."

"Actually, Jewel mentioned to me you were trying to convince them to bypass college and learn a trade instead. But she also said that she thought you might get serious about dance." Ella said. "What happened to that? You're an excellent dancer, Candace. Your dance teacher would surely help you get a scholarship." She slid the scrambled eggs onto the plates that had been laid out on the kitchen table.

"I don't know if I want to dance anymore, I'm out of shape and

I haven't been to practice in weeks. And anyway, Ms. Bennett doesn't play. She's not gonna let me waltz back in after all this time. Plus, I don't know the routines and they're all getting ready for the Winter Dance Recital."

"Why not talk to her about it? And apply to a university just in case. If you get in and decide you don't want to go, what have we lost? A fifty dollar application fee? In the scheme of things that's not much."

Ella noted Candace's dejected expression. Her heart ached for the child. "I understand that it's hard to make big decisions when your emotions are so raw. Let's keep your options open, okay?" As was her habit, Ella cleaned off the countertop before sitting down to eat.

"Girls, sit down and eat this breakfast. What are you two waiting for?"

Karina jumped off the counter and slid onto the breakfast nook bench. Candace clung to the door jamb, her face a peculiar shade of gray. Ella frowned. "Candace, are you alright?"

"My stomach hurts." She ran out, barely making it to the bathroom. She kneeled in front of the toilet, dry heaving since her stomach was empty.

Ella followed her and applied a cool cloth to her forehead. "That's what I mean. You all have to stop this nonsense. Stress will tear at the insides of your stomach until you can't even walk straight." She sucked her teeth in annoyance. "Look at you! Thin as a rail. How much weight have you lost over the last two months?"

"I don't know. I just don't have much of an appetite and when I do eat, the food tastes like cardboard."

"That's what grief will do to you, sweetheart, but you still have to force yourself to eat. Come on in here and drink some bicarbonate of soda--that'll settle your stomach and nibble on a piece of this toast."

Karina hadn't moved from the kitchen. She didn't look at Candace or show any interest in her. Candace sat down but pushed the plate of eggs away.

Ella handed Candace a piece of toast and said, "Now about this school situation. I'll tell you what. You apply to at least one California State University and keep your high school grades up and I'll seriously consider letting you start at a cosmetology school in the fall, if that's what you really want."

Karina shook her head. *There she goes, playing her manipulation games with Mama Ella. Candi isn't gonna graduate, and she knows it. And since when did she want to be a hairstylist? She's full of shit.*

"Well, I'm gonna live up to the potential that Mommy and Daddy always knew I had." Karina said, digging into her breakfast with relish, ignoring her grandmother's disapproving frown.

"Genie, I'm worried about Candace," Ella confided in her best friend.

Stirring her tea, Eugenia nodded thoughtfully, "I don't blame you. She looks terrible. The grief is just tearing her up. Has she been back to school yet?"

"I sent her back a couple of weeks ago, but she's just not herself. And she's lost so much weight. The poor girl was only about 115 pounds soaking wet from the beginning and I'd be surprised if she's 100 pounds now."

"That's too much weight to lose for such a tiny girl," Eugenia agreed.

"It's not just that. She's listless and not interested in anything. Jewel always complained about her watching too much TV, but now she just listens to her music or sleeps. She doesn't go out with her friends. She doesn't seem to have an interest in anything. Not even boys and you know how boy crazy that girl is!"

Eugenia laughed softly. "Grief hits everybody different. And although nothing good can come from placing blame, it is a fact that Langston and Jewel were looking for her and that she wasn't where she was supposed to be." She studied Ella's expression for a sign that she might have crossed a line but was fairly sure she was on solid ground after twenty-five years of friendship.

It didn't occur to Ella that Eugenia should bite her tongue. "I know," she said with a sigh. "Girl, you got to pray for me. I'm trying to make peace with this. But some days I get to thinking that if Candace hadn't been so headstrong, maybe the Lord wouldn't have seen fit to take Lang and Jewel."

"Now Ella, you know that's not how God works. If it was meant for Langston and Jewel to go and to go together, then that's what was gonna happen. May not have been that particular train, might have been a car accident or heart attacks or what have you, but if their time was up, it was up."

"I know, but it's hard to accept it. It's wrong to blame Candace but girl, sometimes when I hear Karina laying into her, I understand how she feels. Then that feeling passes and I look at that girl-child trying so hard to be a woman before her time and my heart aches at the thought of her carrying this burden for the rest of her life. She's hurting so bad, Genie, and I don't know how to help her." The usually composed Ella allowed a few tears to slip out of the corner of her eyes.

"You're helping her every day, just by being there for her." Eugenia tried to console her.

The women sat silently for a while, watching the bees hover over the rose bushes.

"Don't beat yourself up too much, Ella. Lang was your only son and I swear it seemed like you birthed Jewel. Even the most devout among us have doubts and get mad at God for taking our babies away from us. I know firsthand what you're going through."

Ella nodded, remembering when Eugenia got word that her husband had been killed in Vietnam and more recently, when her grandson was shot and killed by a stray bullet. She'd certainly had her share of loss and grief.

"Even though you feel like blaming Candace sometimes, you and I both know that she didn't have the power to bring about Lang and Jewel's death – only God has that power. And it ain't like Karina didn't play a part." She patted her friend's hand.

"You're right, Genie. I know you are. I just have to keep praying for forgiveness and for strength. Lord knows I love these girls with all my heart." Ella pulled her multicolored sweater closer to her body as a gust of November wind blew through the backyard. A mischievous glint came into Ella's eyes. "But I'll tell you one thing."

Eugenia leaned closer. "What?"

"As much as I don't want Candace to be making herself sick about all of this, I have to admit I'm glad she seems to have put her defiant and whorish ways aside for a while. I don't think I could take having to worry about her running the streets."

Candace was stunned. She sat in the kitchen breakfast nook near the slightly open window, a forgotten piece of dry toast and a lukewarm cup of tea on the table in front of her. *Mama Ella blames me for Mommy and Daddy dying?* Candace felt the bile creeping up into her mouth and rushed to the bathroom. She straddled the toilet, dry heaves mixing with her sobs. When she was done, she remained on the floor, resting her head on the toilet seat.

Ella was still outside, talking to Eugenia. Laughter filtered through the bathroom window. *She called me whorish! Rina can just make up lies about me and Mama Ella believes her? That means Mommy and Daddy probably believed her too. They died thinking I was whorish, but I wasn't! I wonder if guilt can kill you. I can't eat, can't sleep, my stomach hurts. Maybe this is my punishment.*

Candace sat back, pulling her knees close to her chest. An hour passed. No one came looking for her. She stood up and studied her face in the mirror, noticing how sallow her skin had become. She'd lost so much weight that her naturally thin face looked skeletal. "Good. I look the way I feel. I don't deserve to be happy or pretty. I don't even deserve to be alive."

Every day since the accident Candace had thought about suicide. Sometimes she lay in bed imagining how she would kill herself. Shooting was out of the question; she had neither the guts nor the gun. Cleaning solutions were aplenty but were they poisonous? She gagged from the smell of most of them, so she figured she would just throw them up. And Mama Ella's medicine cabinet offered only baby aspirin, Vaseline, Vitamin C, Epsom Salts, and cod liver oil. *Maybe I could drown myself in the bathtub!* Candace turned on the taps in the tub.

While the water was running, she returned to her room. *Should I leave a note? What is there to say?* The ticking of the grandfather clock echoed in the house while she chewed on the top of the pen. Finally she jotted down, "I'm sorry. I'm sorry about everything. I love y'all."

She looked around the room. Although she and Karina had only been living there for two months, it felt like home. Years ago, Ella had turned Langston's old room into the girls' room. The twin beds were covered with white chenille bedspreads. At the end of each bed was a neatly folded afghan that Mama Ella made for them in their chosen colors, blue for Candace and yellow for Karina. She wistfully ran her finger over the framed photo of her parents taken at their tenth wedding anniversary celebration.

She then gently placed the note on her sister's bed. Karina might not be able to say it, but Candace knew that she was suffering. She knew Karina as well as she knew herself. It was Karina's forgiveness she craved.

Candace heard Mama Ella singing softly to herself in the kitchen. The closer she got to the closed bathroom door, the faster her heart beat. She picked up her pace, realizing that the tub would be close to overflowing because she'd taken so long.

"God would've sent me a sign if I wasn't supposed to do this," she whispered. Closing her eyes, she pushed the shower curtain aside and gingerly lowered her foot over the side of the tub. Expecting to meet water, she stumbled when her foot came into contact with only air. Opening her eyes, she looked down. The water was gushing from the faucet and running down the drain. "How could I have forgotten to put the stopper in?"

The sound of pounding on the door startled her so much that she almost fell. She grabbed the shower curtain and the rod came tumbling down onto her shoulders.

"Candace, what in the world are you doing in there?" Mama Ella sounded annoyed. "Why are you letting that water run for so long? The tub has to be ready to overflow! Don't make a mess in there."

Candace turned off the water and slid down to sit inside the empty tub. Fifteen minutes later she climbed out. After replacing the shower curtain and rod, she double-checked to make sure she left the bathroom as she'd found it.

Walking down the hallway, Candace spied a small brown envelope on the table in the foyer. A letter from Nick! She hurried to retrieve it and ran to her room to read it in private. For the first time in days, she smiled.

Hey Baby,

I know it's been awhile since I put pen to paper, but I had a lot on my mind. It's been real hard being locked up in here when I know you're out there by yourself, hurting. I keep saying it every time I write to you but I just want you to know that I'm so sorry about your Moms and Pops. That was such a fucked up thing that happened to them. But I don't want you to be blaming yourself. Couldn't nobody have predicted that shit, Candi, for real. I just wish I could be there to hold you close and kiss your tears away. Man, you got a brotha trippin' in here. I mean, I know I'm supposed to be all cool and shit and be the playa, but on the real, you're everything I want in this world. I don't know how to explain it Candi but I know, deep down in my heart, that we're supposed to be together forever. Do you know how bad I want to make love to you? How excited I am to know that I'm the only man you'll ever be with like that? That makes me feel like a big man in here, baby. You know I ain't usually one to be talking about my feelings and stuff but you been heavy on my mind and I

don't want to lose you. I know you ain't had a way
to come visit me. I ain't mad about that. Tell you
the truth I don't really want you to see me in
here, locked up and shit. My release date is April
25th. I can't believe they got me doing 10 months
for some bogus shit but you know my brother is
taking care of me in here and I'm earning the
respect of the OGs so it's all good. Anyway, baby it's
about to be lights out so I'm gonna have to let you
go . . . for now. Write me back and send me some
pictures, okay. Your man loves you.
    Slick-Sorry-Nicky

Candace closed her eyes and clasped the letter to her chest. "Oh Nicky, why did I even take a chance on losing you? Nothing about that night is special anymore. It ended up being the worst night of my life. Now I'm an orphan and the little bit of family I have left hates me. But Nicky, you're my other half. When you get out, you'll take care of me." Candace murmured to herself as she smiled and lay back on the bed, imagining the reunion with Nick. She didn't notice her sister entering the room.

"Nice to see somebody is happy around here," Karina said sarcastically. "You don't have to go to school anymore? You get to lay around reading letters from your jailbird boyfriend?" She tossed her backpack on the floor and plopped down on the bed.

"Fuck you, Karina. Leave me the hell alone!" Candace sat up. "I don't feel good, and I don't want to deal with your bullshit today. So just save it." She stood up quickly, then felt dizzy and grabbed the chair to steady herself.

Karina said softly. "What's this?" She held out the note that Candace had left on her bed.

Candace blushed, "It's nothing. I just don't wanna fight with you anymore. If an apology will do the trick, then hey, I'm apologizing."

"So you're not really sorry for anything. You're just saying it to get along?"

"I'm not saying that. I'm really sorry about everything. Sorrier than you could know, but I don't know how to make it right. I can't make it right and I'm tired of everybody trying to make me feel even worse than I already feel."

Karina lay back on her bed and stared at the ceiling. "I believe that you're sorry."

Candace's breath of relief was premature. Karina turned to look at her. "But I don't know how to forgive you. Every time I see you I think about Mommy. You look so much like her. Then I think about her being gone and you still being here and it just doesn't seem fair." Karina raised up on one elbow and studied her sister's face. "I'm not trying to make you feel bad and I know it's wrong for me to say that but that's how I feel right now, Candi. I hope it will pass but I don't know if it will."

Candace felt as though she'd been stabbed. There was something about Karina's matter-of-fact tone that made her words even more cutting. Candace realized she'd lost her sister when she lost her parents. Without a word she left the room. Walking into the dining room, she chose a jigsaw puzzle from the closet. Hours later she hovered over the table, dinner untouched, desperate to create a beautiful picture out of random jagged pieces.

A few days later Ella perched on the edge of the kitchen chair; the corkscrew cord of the yellow rotary phone pulled taut to reach the table. Candace sat in her usual spot in the nook working on a word search puzzle.

"Charlene, I just don't see how I can do it. I can't leave the girls and I'm Interim Director of the NICU right now. We're getting more and more premature babies, some of them drug exposed, with longer hospital stays. Can't we hire Deacon Washington's daughter to stay with Aunt Izora? She's grown by now, isn't she? I'm forgetting her name."

Ella smiled, "That's right, Maybelle. Brown-skinned girl with the long legs. I remember a few summers ago, she just about gave her daddy a heart attack when she pierced her nose." Ella chuckled. "Deacon told me that the stroke affected the strength on Aunt Izora's right side, but is she dealing with any other deficits?" Ella listened intently, scribbling on a note pad. Candace craned her neck and tried to read the notes upside down.

"Charlene you don't have to feel guilty for needing to go take care of your daughter! Don't be silly! I can't believe you waited this long! Poor Kelly just had premature twins and has a three-year-old up under her feet and Harold has to leave the country for a month to nail down a promotion? Of course, you need to be with her!" She paused for a few moments, listening to Charlene speaking on the other end.

"Chile, it's no wonder Aunt Izora has been bragging on her goddaughter for so many years – you are a force of nature! It's because of you we could bring her home instead of sending her to a convalescent hospital and it's because of your commitment to her physical therapy that she's able to function so well." Ella's voice was firm. "You make your travel arrangements and I'll work with the Washingtons on a plan."

Candace waved her hand in front of Ella's face.

"Mama Ella," she whispered. "Mama Ella, let me do it." Ella ignored her. "Mama Ella!" Candace's voice grew louder. "Let me do it!"

"Hold on a minute please Charlene. This chile is acting like the sky is falling! What is it Candace?" Ella snapped.

"Let me do it, Mama Ella! I can take care of Aunt Izora."

"L'il girl git outta here. What do you know about taking care of a disabled old woman? And you'd go crazy in slow ole Texarkana!"

Ella turned her attention back to her phone conversation. "I'm sorry Charlene, now tell me about Maybelle. Are you sure she's capable of taking care of Aunt Izora? "

"Mama Ella!" Candace banged the table with her fist. "Will you please listen to me?"

Ella frowned. "Charlene? Let me call you back in just a few minutes. I do believe my grandchild has completely lost her mind."

Before Ella could chastise her, Candace began to lay out her plan. "Mama Ella, this is perfect! I need to get away! I can't think about anything but Mommy and Daddy. I don't have any friends anymore. I can't stand to be around Tiffany and her girls knowing that Daddy and Mommy hated for me to hang out with them. My old friends are all on Rina's side and Rina hates me and —"

Ella's brow furrowed and she tried to interject, but Candace said, "I know I deserve it, but it still hurts, Mama Ella. It hurts a lot. I can't concentrate on my schoolwork. I can't shake this flu. And Aunt Izora needs help. It doesn't make any sense for you and Charlene to pay somebody to take care of her when I can do it for free." She stopped to take a breath, giving Ella a chance to jump in.

"You're still in school, Candace." Ella reminded her.

"I'm failing anyway, Mama Ella. That's just the truth. Maybe this way you can convince the principal and my teachers to let me catch up on my own so I can graduate on time. They call it "independent studies." I could mail my homework and assignments back here and Karina could turn them in for me. This could actually save my senior year Mama Ella!"

"I heard my name. What am I being volunteered to do?" Karina came into the kitchen and began rummaging through the refrigerator.

Mama Ella responded, "Nothing for you to concern yourself with at the moment, Rina. And it's mighty funny you're willing to admit you're failing your classes now, Candi, but when I asked you yesterday, you told me everything was fine!"

"No, I told you everything will be fine. And it will! Especially if you let me do this."

"No Candace, I don't think so," Ella's wavering voice belied the rejection. "Taking care of Aunt Izora is an important job. It requires a level of dedication and responsibility that you haven't exhibited in a very long time."

"That's fair, I've been a brat for months. But I can be responsible, Mama Ella. You know it's true. Remember when I helped you take care of Daddy Horace before he died? You told everybody what an excellent nurse I was. And for my first three years of high school I volunteered at the Senior Center and the Hospital. Your own nursing colleagues told you how helpful I was and elderly people love me, Mama Ella! You know I'm telling the truth."

"That's different, Candace. That's going in and out whenever you feel like it but Aunt Izora requires a different level of care. You'd be her primary caregiver. No, I don't think it's a good idea." Shaking her head Ella reached for the telephone.

"Please Mama Ella, you haven't thought it all the way through."

Ella pulled her hand back and sighed, "What haven't we covered, Candace?"

"I heard you and Mrs. Jenkins talking about Aunt Izora last week. You said that Aunt Izora isn't sick and that her mind is clear, but she just can't walk or do a lot of things for herself, right?"

"You always have had a bad habit of eavesdropping on grown folks conversations, Scoot!" Ella frowned slightly and Candace ducked her head. Ella continued, "It's true that Aunt Izora is competent, but she's still very challenged by the physical issues. She has to wear a diaper at night and has to be cleaned if she has an accident. She has to have each meal cooked and sometimes she may need help with eating. She has to have her clothes washed and her hair combed and help to brush her teeth. That's too much work for a teenager."

"You were gonna pay Maybelle! She's only a couple of years older than me and you don't even know if she has any experience with the elderly or sickly people. But you know I do, Mama Ella. You can even have Maybelle check on me every day. I know how to cook and comb hair. I don't have a weak stomach or anything like that when it comes to cleaning or bathing her. I helped with that kind of stuff when I was volunteering. I could sit with her while I'm doing my homework. Or I can read to her and watch TV with her. I can make sure her skin doesn't get too dry, and that she doesn't stay in the same position too long so she won't get sores. Can't we just try it out for a while, Mama Ella, please?"

"I need to think about it some more, Candace. Aunt Izora is my mother's only remaining sister and my favorite aunt. I loved spending summers with her and Uncle Franklin in Texarkana. The thought of her needing care and me not being able to go to her just tears me up." Ella's voice broke.

Karina interrupted, "Mama Ella, please don't feel bad. I'm sure Aunt Izora understands that you can't leave the hospital right now. She always brags about the work you do with the babies in the NICU."

Ella smiled. "Thank you Rina. That's true. She's always been supportive of my career."

Candace clapped her hands. "Yes! And having me there will be like having a piece of you there with her! You've taught me everything I know and she knows that. We were all just down there together last year – well year before that – we made a connection, just me and her. Please let me go take care of her. For your sake too," she pleaded.

Karina said, "Now I don't know about all that. If the poor old lady is already sick, why would we let Candi go make her worse? That just seems cruel."

"Shut up, Karina," Candace snapped.

Ella bit the inside of her cheek. "I need to pray on it."

"Okay, I'm gonna pray on it too. Pray you say yes!" Candace bounced over to Ella and kissed her on the cheek. "Thank you, Mama Ella. This will mean so much to me."

Karina rolled her eyes and went back to the living room to read her book.

It took many prayers and several telephone calls with Charlene and Deacon and Mrs. Washington, but Ella finally agreed to step out on faith and let Candace go to Texarkana to care for her beloved aunt.

The day after Thanksgiving, Ella pulled into a parking place at the Oakland Airport. "Check your purse again to make sure you have everything," she said.

Candace sighed, "Mama Ella, I have everything! I have my ticket, I have my wallet with my I.D., I have my address book with names, addresses, and phone numbers of every relative and friend of the family within 100 miles of Aunt Izora. I have Deacon Washington's and his wife, Jackie's, phone numbers. I have Charlene's mobile phone number and the phone number to her daughter's house. I know that Deacon Washington and Maybelle are going to pick me up from the airport and take me to Aunt Izora's house. I have change for the pay phone and money hidden in my bra and my sock and the secret compartment of my purse. I have everything!" Candace failed to mask her exasperation.

"Don't get mouthy with me, Candace! Remember, I don't have to let you go!" Ella warned.

Worried that her grandmother might indeed change her mind, Candace contritely responded, "I'm sorry, Mama Ella. I didn't mean to be snappy. I'm just excited to be going somewhere. The last few months have been so miserable."

"As usual, you're making a dumb decision that everybody else will have to scramble to make up for. Poor Aunt Izora will probably starve to death." Karina said from the backseat.

Candace turned to face her, "Damn, Karina! Why do you have to be so negative all the time?"

"Not negative, just real. Mama Ella's spending all her overtime money sending you to Texarkana cause you can't handle having to deal with the problems you created."

Mama Ella banged her fist on the steering wheel. "I am sick and tired of all this arguing. Karina, if you can't be positive then be silent, for goodness' sake. And Candace, don't you ever curse in my presence, do you hear me?"

When the girls murmured their assent, Ella twisted in her seat to glare at Karina. "You need to give your sister some space and some credit. Candace can take care of Aunt Izora. She did a great job helping me with your grandfather when she was only fifteen. And I am so tired of hearing you play the blame game. God took your parents and we all have to learn to live without them. Blaming Candace is just your way of avoiding dealing with your own feelings."

She turned back to look at Candace, her voice softening, "You've been okay these last few days, but you need to let Jackie know right away if you run a fever or your flu symptoms come back. We can't let Auntie get sick."

"Okay Mama Ella, I will, but I don't feel sick anymore."

"What a coincidence," Karina mumbled under her breath.

Ella glanced at her watch. "We have a few minutes to go over the plan one last time."

When the girls groaned, Ella laughed. "Too bad! Now, Charlene sent us Aunt Izora's daily schedule and a list of her medicines . . .."

5

RELIEF FROM GRIEF

Candace felt as though she had been holding her breath for months. She watched through the tiny window as the plane taxied down the tarmac and clapped her hands in delight when the wheels lost touch with the ground. The mere thought of not having to look into Karina's accusatory eyes or listen to Mama Ella be nice, knowing that she also blamed her for their parents death, was like a hundred-pound weight being lifted from her shoulders. She was proud of herself for handling the connection between flights without having to ask for help.

But as she got closer to her destination, anxiety started to creep in. Candace had been so intent on convincing Mama Ella that she could handle the task that she hadn't really given much thought to the details. *What if Aunt Izora gets sick? What if she dies? Oh God! That's all I need is for the entire family to blame me for something else!* For the rest of the flight Candace alternated between elation and despair as she contemplated her immediate future.

"Ladies and gentlemen, we're beginning our final descent into Texarkana. Please bring your seats to their full upright position and return your tray tables to the locked position."

Candace kept her purse close and tried to be aware of her

surroundings. Mama Ella had impressed upon her that a young woman traveling alone was an easy target. She was relieved that she recognized Deacon Washington as soon as she saw him. The last time she'd been to Texarkana was three years ago. Deacon Washington had picked her and Karina up from the airport and taken them to Aunt Izora's house. That was when the then seventy-seven-year-old was spry and full of life and happy to have the teenagers visit her for a week while their parents were on an anniversary trip. At the time, Maybelle had been an eighteen-year-old high school graduate who couldn't be bothered with the younger girls. Now, the age difference didn't seem as vast. Candace noted her lavender Sassoon pants, t-shirt knotted above the belly button, and Farrah Fawcett feathered bangs. *Miss Maybelle would fit in just fine in the Bay Area, but she'd have to lose that country name!*

The drive to Aunt Izora's house didn't take long. Deacon Washington filled Candace in on the progress of the church renovation fundraising efforts. Clearly bored with the conversation, Maybelle twisted around in her seat to talk to Candace. "So what did you do to piss your parents off so much that they sent you to backwater Texarkana as punishment?"

Tears unexpectedly welled in Candace's eyes at the thought of what she had indeed done to warrant punishment. Before she could answer, Deacon Washington nudged his daughter with a frown.

"Maybelle turn around and leave that girl alone. Maybe if you'd listen when your momma and me talk, you'd know when to keep your mouth shut!"

Catching Candace's eye in the rearview mirror, the Deacon's eyes were warm and compassionate. "Candace I heard about your parents and I sure am sorry. What a terrible accident! I know you and your sister and Ella Mae are just beside yourselves in grief. We been praying every Sunday that the Lord gives you the strength to get through it."

"Thank you," Candace murmured, looking away. She didn't want his pity and she didn't deserve his compassion.

Maybelle turned to face her again. "I'm sorry. I didn't know. That was stupid of me. I was just trying to make conversation."

"It's okay. Anyway, to answer your question, I asked if I could come. I needed to get away from everybody and everything."

"Whenever you think you want to talk or want some company just call me, okay? Or just come over. You'll see, our house is only about a block away from Miss Izora's house."

"Thanks."

Fifteen minutes later they entered a different part of town. Gone were the paved sidewalks and neon signs. They passed Inspiration Baptist Church, where Aunt Izora had worshiped for the past fifty years. Deacon Washington pointed out the site of the new church that had been in the planning stages for at least five years. Finally, they turned off onto Homestead Road. Maybelle pointed to a neatly painted well-kept single-family house set back from the road. "That's where we live." She winked at Candace. "Well, that's where Daddy and Momma live. I'm just staying there until I get my money straight and move into my own place."

"Don't pay her no never mind, Candace. She been singing that song ever since she graduated from high school. That girl don't wanna go nowhere, she cares too much about her designer clothes." Deacon Washington chuckled and Maybelle sucked her teeth.

"Whatever Daddy! I been saving my money and if I get that job at the mall next week I'll have enough money to move by next Spring."

"Well I'll surely pray on it cause me and your momma are ready for you to take your loud music and late-night telephone talking somewhere else."

The loving banter between father and daughter brought a lump to Candace's throat. After they passed the Washington's house there were no other homes in sight. She hadn't remembered Aunt Izora's house being so isolated. "Deacon Washington, where are the rest of the houses? I remember there were a couple of them and a little store on this street."

"You got a good memory. They were actually trailer homes that people had fixed up and put on cinder blocks so they looked like real houses. They'd added little gardens and flower patches too. The store was a little shack that Brother Jamison ran as a side business.

But the owner of the land decided to sell and the new owner evicted everybody. Said he was gon' build some brand-new single-family homes or some kind of fancy subdivision but so far all we've seen is a lot of looky-loos. Been about a year now."

"Why didn't Aunt Izora have to move?"

"Your Aunt Izora owns all the land on this side of the highway from where the church sits all the way down to the river. She's a smart woman, 'specially when it comes to finances. I wouldn't be surprised if she finds a way to get some of that land on the other side of the highway."

Candace took in the expanse of land that Deacon Washington was talking about. They'd passed the church a mile back and she still couldn't see Aunt Izora's house. Candace decided to one day be the kind of woman who inspired the respect and admiration she heard in Deacon Washington's voice.

Finally they pulled into the gravel driveway of a well-maintained house. Candace climbed the three stairs to a wide planked porch and smiled to see the cushion covers she and Karina helped Mama Ella make for the porch swing three summers ago. Chrysanthemums spilled from large pots on each side of the double oak door.

Suddenly the door was flung open. Izora's goddaughter, Charlene, scooped Candace up in her arms. "Oh baby, it's so good to see you. I'm so sorry about your mama and your daddy. I know it feels like the world has come to an end, but I promise you, Candi, it'll get better. Just take it one day at a time." Charlene squeezed Candace's hand. "How was your flight? Are you hungry? I know you must be tired. Were you scared to fly by yourself? Truth be told, I'm a little scared to fly by myself. But I only have to go to N'awlins, so it shouldn't be too bad."

Candace was spared from having to respond because Charlene never stopped talking as she quickly herded her into the family room. "Mama Zora, look who's here! It's Candi. Ain't she done grown up to be a beautiful young lady?"

Candace smiled widely when she saw Aunt Izora. She was sitting in a comfortable chair with a walker next to it. She looked exactly the way Candace remembered her. Her thick white hair was pulled back into a long braid and her deep blue eyes contrasted beautifully with her cinnamon tinted skin.

"Hi Auntie. It's so good to see you. You look gorgeous!" When Candace bent over to kiss her, Izora pulled her closer, using her left arm to hug her. Candace inhaled the familiar smell of vanilla that she had always associated with her aunt, tears suddenly pricking her eyes.

Izora whispered, "I'm here, sweet girl, I'm here. Don't let this dead arm fool you. Auntie's mind is clear as a bell. You can take all that stuff you been holding and hand it right on over to me. We'll talk after everybody else is gone, okay?"

Candace nodded, scared that if she spoke, the tears would spill over.

After saying goodbye to Deacon Washington and Maybelle and getting her things put away in the guest bedroom, Candace joined Charlene and Izora in the den.

"Perfect timing. I need to go over this list of medicine with you and to show you where everything is. Then it'll be time for her dinner and to help her get ready for bed."

"When are you leaving for New Orleans?" Candace asked.

"First thing in the morning. I wanted to help you get settled first."

For the next several hours Candace got a crash course in how to care for a partially disabled but still feisty elderly woman. Charlene revealed a pantry and deep freezer full of enough food to keep a family of ten satisfied for months. "Why in the world does Aunt Izora have all this food?" Candace asked.

Charlene laughed, "I know, it's crazy, isn't it? It's her one eccentricity – she always wanted to be ready to entertain. But I have to admit that I added a few things when I found out you were coming. Ella Mae said that you're a good driver and I'm gonna leave my car here with you but Mama Zora shouldn't be left alone for long periods of time. Either Deacon Washington or his wife, Jackie, will come over every Saturday afternoon for a few hours to sit with her so you can go out. You can do whatever shopping you need to do, see a movie, go to the mall, you know – feel like a teenager for a while. How's that sound?"

"That's fine, Charlene. Don't worry about me. I haven't felt like a normal teenager in a long time. I don't think I'm gonna be wanting to go anywhere."

"A month is a long time, so we'll keep the arrangement just in case, okay? If you need to go somewhere during the week or if something happens, just give the Washingtons a call. Jackie is across town every day taking care of her parents – that's why she couldn't take care of Mama Zora – but they can be left alone in an emergency. And the Deacon may be running errands but he's never too far."

"We'll be fine, Charlene. I promise."

She patted Candace's shoulder, noting how the bones jutted out. "I know you will baby. I'm not worried. But I want you to eat some of this food. You're nothing but skin and bones!"

"I haven't had much of an appetite since my parents died. I had the flu for a while, and I just don't have much interest in food." Noticing Charlene's frown, Candace quickly added, "But don't worry, I'm not sick anymore, and I'll eat enough to keep my strength up."

Under Charlene's direction Candace prepared Aunt Izora's dinner, dispensed her medicine, helped her to the bathroom, and helped her get ready for bed.

Charlene handed her a small bronze bell. "Even though Mama Zora is doing really good and her voice is strong, the doctors warned us she's in danger of having another stroke. I've been keeping this bell close in case of emergencies."

Izora snorted, "You're just a worrywart, Charlene! My arm may not work and my legs are a bit weak, but otherwise I'm fine. Y'all need to stop treating me like an invalid!"

Candace giggled, and Charlene rolled her eyes. "Yeah, yeah, heard it all before. Nobody said you were an invalid, Mama Zora, you just need help with things. That's all I'm saying. We want to keep you safe and with us for a long, long time."

Charlene made sure Candace knew how to lock up behind her, and finally the day was over.

An hour later, Candace lay in bed wide awake. *I didn't cry all day! I knew this was the right thing to do.* She went back over everything she'd learned about caring for Aunt Izora, determined to prove that she could be useful to the family she had left.

After a few days Candace had gotten into the swing of things. The routine was comfortingly predictable. Up by 6 o'clock, Izora called for Candace to help her get out of the embarrassing diaper. Candace got her to the bathroom – Izora detested the bedside commode – and then assisted her in the shower or with a sponge bath, depending on Izora's mood. After gently moisturizing her still supple skin, Candace helped Izora get dressed for the day. Next was the part Candace loved, combing her aunt's luxurious hair. The thick, slightly wavy, pure white hair cascaded down to the small of Izora's back. Candace first applied a light oil dressing to the edges and on the scalp and then brushed it gently. Finally, she wove the hair expertly into a long French braid and captured the end with an elastic band so it wouldn't unravel.

"I'm gonna make us French toast this morning, okay Auntie?"

Izora smiled and studied Candace. "You're too skinny, girl. If you want me to eat, you're gonna have to eat with me."

"I'll try, Auntie. I had the flu for weeks and it took my appetite. I'm better now, but my appetite hasn't come back yet."

"We'll just have to entice it back. After we eat, I want you to go over to that cabinet in the dining room and pull out those cookbooks. Your Uncle Franklin and I used to have such a good time playing what we called 'around the world' with them. We would randomly open them up and cook whatever we landed on. That's what we're gonna do while you're here. We'll fatten you up in no time!" Izora laughed heartily and for a few precious minutes Candace forgot to be sad.

By her second week in Texarkana Candace's inner clock was

synchronized with her aunt's. To Izora's surprise, Candace was up and dressed by the time she was ready to get up. After breakfast, Izora typically watched television or read while Candace sat at the kitchen counter doing her homework. Sometimes Izora would tell her to read her assignments out loud and would ask her questions about the material. Candace found that talking to Izora about her studies helped her to focus.

For lunch Candace usually made them soup and sandwiches or a chef's salad. The one thing that hadn't resolved itself was Candace's appetite. She found she couldn't eat too early without feeling sick and that nausea would pop up from time to time throughout the day, causing her to grab onto a chair or the counter to steady herself. Candace made sure to conceal her discomfort so her aunt wouldn't worry.

The 'around the world' game made dinner a fun adventure. The cookbooks represented every country and culture that Candace could think of – Italian, French, Japanese, Soul Food, and more. They worked out a routine – Izora chose the cookbook of the day and Candace poured through it to pick a dish she thought she could cook. There were some wonderful successes: chicken parmesan, teriyaki beef and rice, smothered steak. But there were a few losers too. When that happened, they trashed the experiment and settled for grilled cheese sandwiches and soup while watching Jeopardy. Aunt Izora went to bed by 8 o'clock, leaving Candace time to read, think about her future, and write letters to Nick.

Dear Nicky,

I'm sorry I haven't written in a while, but I think about you all the time. I have so much to tell you! I'm not at home— I'm in Texas! Crazy, huh? I came the day after Thanksgiving to take care of my Great Aunt Izora. She's hella cool . . . especially to be so old. She's 80! A few months ago, she had a stroke and now she can't get around too good and needs help with personal stuff and cooking. But her mind is sharp and she's a lot of fun to be around. Rina couldn't understand why I wanted to take care of an old lady, but I needed to get away.

Baby, I think I'm the loneliest girl in the whole world. At least getting away from the Bay Area helps a little. At home, every time I turn around I see a reminder of my mom or dad. Plus, Rina is being such a bitch to me. I mean I know she's hurting just like I am but she blames me for everything—even though she's the one who sent our parents out that night! She hates me now, and she used to be my best friend (other than you Baby). I really miss my sister. Sometimes I pray that God had taken me instead but then I wake up and nothing has changed.

Anyway, sorry to be such a downer. How are you? I can't even imagine how hard it must be for you to be locked up for something you didn't even do. I hope Johnny really appreciates you. Take it from me, Baby, if your sibling turns on you it hurts really bad. I'm gonna ask if I can stay here until after Christmas. The last thing I want to do is wake up Christmas morning without smelling my mom's turkey or hearing my dad's laugh and then have to sit across from Karina and Mama Ella looking at me like I'm a criminal. (You know what I mean. . . no offense, Baby. I mean, you're not a criminal cause you didn't even do it.)

Write back to me at this address, okay?

Love, Candi

P.S. I LOVED your letter! You are so romantic. I'm saving myself for you cause you're my soulmate. Xoxoxoxoxoxox

"That's it, I'm done with all my make-up work!" Candace closed the history book with a sigh. "I'm going to pack all of this up and mail it off this afternoon so Karina can turn it in for me before the teachers leave for winter break. I know she'll be shocked that I got it all done."

"Won't your sister be happy that you're all caught up?" Aunt Izora asked.

Candace grimaced, "I doubt it. She'll probably assume I got the answers wrong, anyway."

"Why do you say that, Candace? You've both always been on the honor roll. I've tried not to stick my nose in it, but there's something off between you and Karina. What's going on?"

Candace's eyes filled with tears as she resolutely focused on organizing her schoolwork. "Nothing Auntie. Everything's fine." She mumbled.

Izora pushed herself up onto the walker and made her way over to the dining room table where Candace sat. "Look at me, Candace."

Candace turned to face her aunt and the tears spilled over.

"It's time you and I had a talk. You need to get it all out, baby."

"Oh Auntie, I can't say it out loud. You'll just be one more person who hates me!" Candace broke into tears that wouldn't stop.

Izora sat next to her and pulled her close, allowing her to cry as long as she needed. "Darling, there is nothing you could do to make me or any of us hate you."

Candace interrupted her, "That's not true. I heard Mama Ella say right after the funeral that she couldn't stand to look at me sometimes because it was all my fault."

"You know, grief can make us say and do all kinds of things that we regret. I'll bet you've said things to your sister that you didn't mean or wish you hadn't said, right?" Candace nodded. "Did you ever talk with Ella about what you heard?"

"No ma'am."

"Has she told you that what happened wasn't your fault?"

"Yes, lots of times."

"Ella loves you more than life itself. That was just grief talking. But one day soon you should tell her what you overheard." She paused for a second. "Now let's talk about what's going on with you and Karina and why you don't want to be home."

"It's a long story, Auntie."

"I got nothing but time, Baby."

Candace grabbed a throw pillow and hugged it tightly. "Last summer, I started hanging out with this new girl, Tiffany. We — Karina and all of our friends — used to think she was slutty, but we didn't even know her. She and I ended up working together at the Rec center and I realized she was cool so I started hanging out with her. It turned out she was part of a faster crowd and I guess, well now I know, I started acting different. Me and Karina grew apart and started fighting a lot. Then I got this new boyfriend, Nicky."

She stopped to look at Izora, starry-eyed. "Oh Auntie, he's so fine. And he treats me so sweet." Her eyes dropped to her clasped hands. "But Nicky's parents aren't around and his older brother, Johnny, is into street stuff. I knew my parents wouldn't approve of me being with Nicky so I started sneaking around. Rina knew I was sneaking around with Nicky. I knew she didn't like it, but I never thought she'd rat me out to Mommy and Daddy. I didn't realize she was so jealous of me. The night of the accident Rina told them I had snuck out and that I was at a side show where drug dealers and gang bangers were."

Izora frowned, "Why do you assume Rina was jealous of you? Don't you think she might have been worried about you? You two have always been so close. And what you're describing does sound pretty dangerous."

"I know, but Auntie, she sent Mommy and Daddy there to make a point. She wanted to embarrass me in front of my new friends. To show how square I really was. That's how mad she was at me for making new friends! It all came out when I got home that night and we had this horrible fight." Her voice grew quieter. "But they never would've been on those railroad tracks if it wasn't for me. So, Karina's right, it's my fault they're dead." Her shoulders shook as the tears returned.

Izora gave her time to pull herself together. "I understand why you feel that way and I know Ella has already explained to you that God doesn't work that way."

Candace took the tissue Izora handed her and blew her nose.

"Yes ma'am. That's what I'd like to believe, but Rina won't let me. She's made it very clear that she can't stop hating me because it's all my fault. So, it's just easier for me to be away from home."

"Sweetheart, I knew you were grieving, of course, but I had no idea you were carrying all of this. No wonder you haven't been able to move on. I need to think on this some but we'll bring you and your sister back together again, mark my words."

Candace gave a weak smile. "I hope you're right, Auntie. In the meantime can I ask you for an early Christmas present?"

"Of course," Izora said.

"I really want to spend Christmas here with you. I'm not ready to face a Christmas at home without Mommy and Daddy and with Rina hating me." She pleaded.

"Let me think it over and discuss it with Ella." Izora said.

"Knock, knock! How y'all doing today?" Jackie Washington said, slamming the screen door behind her.

"Hey Miss Jackie, how you doing?" Candace liked the petite, fast talking, always busy woman with the tightly curled gray afro. She reminded her of Mama Ella.

"Cain't complain, baby, cain't complain." Jackie set her purse down on the counter and stepped into Izora's view. "Hey there Miss Izora. I'll say! You sure look good today. I like you in that purple caftan, purple suits you." Looking a little closer, she continued, "And I daresay you may have put on a pound or two. That's good. You know, the doctor said your appetite needed to pick up."

Candace laughed as Izora nodded and said, "We've been experimenting with recipes. Let's just say we ain't missing no meals!"

"So, Miss Candace is a cook? Well, it looks like you are filling out a little too, Missy! I think you and your Auntie are good for each other!"

She turned to Izora. "Lemme check you out, Miss Izora." Jackie had been a registered nurse for thirty years before going into semi-retirement to care for her parents.

Candace could barely sit still. She thought that she'd taken good care of Auntie, but what if the change in diet had been bad for her?

"I'll say, Miss Izora, this chile must be the medicine that the doctor should've ordered for you a long time ago! Your blood pressure is perfect, your blood sugar is just fine, and I do believe that grip of yours is stronger."

Turning to Candace she admonished, "Now young lady even though she's doing fine you still have to be really careful about what she eats and don't forget to check her blood sugar at least twice a day, three times if it's elevated."

Candace jumped up and grabbed a clipboard from the counter. "I check it every day and keep a record right here, just in case the doctor ever wants to see it."

"My, my! What a wonderful job you've done!" Miss Jackie said, looking at the chart. "You've been keeping a record of everything that Miss Izora eats and drinks, as well as her urine output, medications, and blood sugar! Who told you to do this?" she asked.

"Nobody, it just made sense. I know everybody is worried that I won't be able to take care of her, so I didn't want there to be any questions. Plus, it's not hard. I just write it down as I do it."

"Excuse me, you do know I'm sitting right here!" Izora huffed. Everyone laughed. "Jackie, will you please put Charlene's mind at ease? I want her to stay with her grandbabies a little longer, but she worries about me so much," Izora asked. "Ella and I have already discussed it and Candace will be staying until after the new year."

"What?" Candace squealed. "Auntie you didn't tell me! Thank you, thank you, thank you!"

Two hours later, after speaking with Charlene and sampling the best fettuccine Alfredo she'd ever eaten, Jackie gathered her things together to leave. "I'm glad you're staying until the new year Candace, but if you change your mind and want to go home all you have to do is call me, alright? The first holidays are always hard to handle after you lose people you're close to."

"I'm not gonna change my mind, Miss Jackie. I can't handle Christmas at home this year. I'd rather it was just another day."

"Well now we cain't have you treating Christmas like just another day! I tell you what, I'll have the Deacon come get y'all on Christmas day, about 1 o'clock and you can have dinner with us. That okay with you Miss Izora?"

"But I was thinking I could cook something special for me and Auntie . . ." Candace quickly chimed in.

Izora overruled her, "Yes, that sounds fine, Jackie. It'll do Candace good to get out a bit."

"That settles it." Jackie said. "In the meantime, I'm gonna send Maybelle over here on Saturday morning to give you a little break."

"I don't need a break, Miss Jackie. I'm fine." Candace frowned, annoyed at having been ignored by both women.

"Everybody needs a break every now and then. I've been nursing folks for a long time. I know what I'm talking about. Go take in a movie or do some Christmas shopping for your sister and your grandmother. I can mail your packages off for you."

Candace sighed. She hadn't given any thought to Christmas presents. She supposed they'd expect to get something from her since she wouldn't there in person. "Okay, thank you." She finally agreed.

<hr>

Karina made a small "x" under the date on the calendar that hung in Ella's kitchen.

She murmured, "Today makes twenty-one days since she left, only nine days to go."

As irritating as it had been to be around Candace in the weeks after their parents' death, Karina had been secretly terrified for her to leave. She'd never been away from Candace for more than two days. Even when Candace had started to break away from Karina at school, the sisters' long-established routines – helping prepare dinner, grousing about homework, sniping at each other for real or imagined slights, folding laundry – reassured Karina that they were still connected.

But everything had changed in the blink of an eye. To Karina, the sale of their childhood home was like losing another family member. The rambling Victorian house had always been aswirl with activity – cookouts with firefighters and their families in the backyard, impromptu talent shows put on by Karina, Candace, and their friends, Jewel's many strategic planning sessions with other like-minded community activists, Langston and his buddies painstakingly restoring the Corvette. And there was always music playing – R&B competing with jazz, classical, and hip-hop.

Spending time at Mama Ella's was part of their childhood – it was just as familiar as home and brought with it the special connection between grandmother and grandchildren – but it wasn't a neighborhood gathering place. Sharing a room with Candace, even when they weren't speaking to one another, was a little slice of normalcy in Karina's shattered world. Keeping track of the days until her sister would be back home helped her believe she wouldn't be lonely forever.

"Rina, I talked to Candace and Charlene today." Ella said.

Karina turned from the calendar, slipping the pencil in her pocket, and sat at the table where her homework was spread out. Feigning nonchalance, she shrugged. "Oh really?"

Ella frowned, "That's it, 'oh really'? Don't you want to know how she's doing?"

Karina pretended to read a passage in her textbook, randomly highlighting words to make it look like she was focused. "Not really, Mama Ella. I try not to think about her."

"You and I both know that's not true! Li'l Bit, you need to let this anger go. You and your sister should cling to each other right now, not push each other away."

"Mama Ella, Candi is the one who left, not me. What's the point of sitting around thinking about someone who decided to leave? And just because I don't want to talk to her on the phone doesn't mean I'm pushing her away. She'll be home in a week, anyway."

"That's what I was going to tell you. Candace asked if she could stay with Auntie until New Years. I told her she could."

Karina blurted, "She's not coming home for Christmas?"

"No. She feels like Christmas at home without Jewel and Langston will be too hard. I wasn't sure how you'd feel about it, but I was thinking that you – or even the two of us – could go to Texarkana and spend Christmas with Candi and Auntie. What do you think?"

"No! Please Mama Ella, don't make me go!" Karina pleaded. "Christmas is going to be bad enough without Mommy and Daddy. I've never had Christmas anywhere else. Can't we serve dinner at All Souls like we always do?"

Ella searched her granddaughter's face. "Do you want to call Candace and talk to her about it? She asked to speak to you earlier today."

"No, that's okay. It's not a big deal. The decision's already been made. She'll be home in a few weeks and we can talk then." Deftly changing the subject, she said. "When winter break starts, I'm going to pick up more shifts at the coffee shop, okay?"

Ella frowned. "All you do is go to school and work and hang out here with an old lady. You gotta keep living, baby."

Karina refused to give in to the tears. She stood up and hugged her grandmother. "You worry too much. And anyway, Candi is the one hanging out with an old lady. You're a young whippersnapper!"

Ella laughed at Karina's use of Daddy Horace's favorite expression. "Stop trying to change the subject."

Karina sighed, "Okay, Mama Ella. If it'll make you feel better, I'll go to the basketball game with Sonya tomorrow. She's been trying to get me to go out."

"Yes, that will make me *and* you happy, Rina."

"It's gonna be weird going without Daddy, though." Langston had been an avid basketball fan. Karina shared his love for the game and had been his plus one to high school, college, and even NBA games since she was ten years old.

"There will be a lot of firsts that are hard to face, and some things may never feel exactly the same, but you have to allow yourself to have fun and invite joy back into your heart."

Despite her misgivings, Karina was looking forward to the basketball game. Her school was playing the local rival and it promised to be a nail biter. She'd even relented to Sonya's constant nagging and agreed to make an effort to look cute. Apparently Karina's "uniform" of plain blue jeans and different color t-shirts every day was wearing on the fashionable Sonya's sensibilities.

"You're the prettiest girl I know and you refuse to let it show!" Sonya complained as she rummaged through the closet. "I can't believe Candi left all of her best outfits!"

Sonya squealed when she found what she'd been looking for. "Girl this is it! Everybody will wear red and white or red and gold to show their school spirit, but you are going to stand out in the crowd." She laid out a pair of snow-white brushed denim Jordache jeans and a forest green sweater. "This sweater is perfect! It'll draw attention to your amazing eyes. Hurry up and change so I can do your hair."

"My hair?" Karina looked up in alarm. "Sonya, I never said you could do my hair! This is too much. It's a basketball game, not a party. My ponytail is just fine."

"Rina, you have to give that tired ponytail a rest. You have all this beautiful hair and you don't do it justice. Now just sit down and let me work my magic!"

Twenty minutes later Sonya and Karina stared at her reflection in the mirror. Sonya had unleashed Karina's naturally curly hair and let the moisturized curls flow down her back, framing her face on one side and clipped behind her ear on the other, a la' Janet Jackson.

"You look beautiful," Sonya whispered. "Maybe I found my calling."

Feeling uncharacteristically confident, Karina peered into the mirror and joked, "don't get ahead of yourself, girl. I think it's the model!"

"Whatever!" Sonya rolled her eyes and then secured her own jet black hair with a wide gold stretchy band into a high ponytail and let the long loose curls swing between her shoulder blades.

"Are you seriously going with a ponytail after talking about *my* ponytail?" Karina fussed.

"Now Rina, all ponytails are not equal. I am five feet eight inches tall and this magnificent ponytail adds another four inches. Even if I wasn't spectacular already - which, of course, I am - I will be pulling more attention than most of the players on the court. And that, my dear, is the plan!" Sonya did her best to keep a straight face but burst into laughter. Karina joined her as they primped in front of the mirror.

"Okay, I see your point." Karina conceded. "My ponytails never make that kind of statement!"

Mama Ella paused while washing dishes, happy to once again hear laughter in the house.

Karina and Sonya did indeed turn heads when they walked into the gym. Karina was relaxed and having fun for the first time in months. She couldn't help but notice the rival team's point guard. He was confident, but not cocky. She had to restrain herself from cheering for him when he blew by her team's defense to score the winning basket. She wondered if she'd imagined him stealing glances at her a few times. When he walked over to her after the game she knew it hadn't been her imagination.

"Hey, I was hoping I'd catch you!" He was even better looking up close.

Karina was flustered, despite her interest. "Me? Do I know you?"

He smiled widely. "Not yet, but I'm about to fix that. I'm A, um, Zander." He reached for her hand.

Karina smiled back, trying hard not to blush. "Nice to meet you, A, um, Zander. That's an interesting name."

"I was gonna say A.J. 'cause that's what people call me, but I prefer Zander."

Karina noticed he was still holding her hand. She smiled. "I like Zander. You're a good player. You made my team look bad!"

"It's a team sport. We work well together." Zander shrugged. "So what's your name?"

"Karina." She noticed Sonya trying to catch her eye. "Well Zander, it was nice to meet you but my ride is leaving." She finally slid her hand out of his and began to walk away.

Zander frowned, "But we didn't get a chance to finish our conversation."

"Didn't we?" she asked.

"Can I call you?" he shouted, hoping he didn't sound as anxious as he felt.

"You don't have my number!" Karina called out over her shoulder, picking up her pace when Sonya warned that her mother would come look for them if they weren't at the pickup spot on time.

Zander ran to catch up with her. "Can I come to see you tomorrow and get your number?"

Karina laughed, "Come see me where?"

"At the Brick Wall on your campus – tomorrow at 12 o'clock."

"You're coming to see me at one of the most well known hangout spots at your rival school?" Karina's smile gave her answer. She grabbed Sonya's hand and ran the last few yards to Mrs. Morris's car. She smiled the entire ride home. Life was suddenly looking much better.

The next few weeks seemed to fly by as Karina and Zander got to know one another. Zander helped distract Karina when Candace didn't come home for Christmas by taking her ice skating. And to her delight, he invited her to his family's annual New Year's Eve party.

At the party, Karina snuck into the guest bathroom to call Sonya. Sonya answered sleepily, "Happy New Year, but aren't you supposed to be at Zander's family party?"

"Girl, wake up! I gotta tell you something. I'm still here – I'm in the bathroom – and guess what?"

"I dunno, they got fancy towels or something?"

"Zander just asked me to be his girlfriend!" Karina almost screamed.

"What!" Sonya said, sitting up in bed.

"Yes! I think I'm in love."

Karina stopped marking days on the calendar.

"Hey Scoot, how are things going?" Ella said. Candace was happy to hear her grandmother's voice. Christmas hadn't been all bad being away from home, but the memories had been hard to suppress.

"Hey Mama Ella! We're good here. How are you guys?"

"We're doing alright. We miss you, though. As old as I am, seems like I can't remember a Christmas without you and your sister tearing through gifts like crazy people." She chuckled.

Candace smiled as memories rushed at her. "I know, it was weird being away from you guys. Where's Rina? Can I talk to her?"

"She's gone to some basketball game. I'll tell her to call you when she gets home."

"That's okay. You know she's not gonna call. She never does." Candace couldn't hide the sadness in her voice.

"Well, I'm calling, and I want to know everything that's going on. How's Auntie doing and how bored are you?"

Candace laughed, shaking off her sadness. "We're both good. I'm not bored, honestly. We're having fun. We even play checkers every night."

"Checkers! I don't think I've ever seen Auntie play checkers."

"And we have a puzzle that we're working on. It's a picture of Times Square in New York. It's got 1500 pieces, so I think it's gonna take awhile. I taped some pencils together to make her a long stick that she can use to move the pieces on the left side around without having to reach."

"That was pretty smart of you, Missy!"

"Thank you! I didn't want her to have to watch TV all the time. You know they say it rots your brain!" They shared a laugh. "And let's see, what else? We've been having dinner from around the world. We pick new recipes to try almost every day. Have you ever made chicken catch-a-story?"

"Cacciatore!"

"Close enough, Mama Ella! Have you?"

"No, but I've eaten it."

"Well Auntie says mine is the best she's ever eaten, and she had the real thing when she went to Italy with Uncle Franklin."

"That's pretty impressive. I'm surprised that you're going the extra mile to learn all of these new recipes and spend quality time with Auntie. And I hear from Jackie that Auntie is doing quite well from a health standpoint."

"It's not as hard as I thought it would be. We have our routine and we have fun together. It makes me feel good to prove I can be responsible."

"I'm glad Auntie has had this time with you, Baby. But don't you think it's time you came on home? Don't you miss your friends and your sister?"

Candace twirled the phone cord between her thumb and index finger. "Sure, some days I miss my friends, but then I remember that my old friends have been gone for a while and my so-called new friends disappeared when times got hard."

"What about Karina?"

"What's the point in missing Karina? She doesn't miss me. And I can guarantee you she doesn't want to spend any time with me . . ."

"So, you're gonna hide in Texarkana? For how long, Candace? Life goes on baby, no matter how hard it is, no matter how much we don't want it to."

"I know, but can't I just get through the school year?"

"The school year! This is your senior year, Candace! You're missing once in a lifetime events!"

"Mama Ella, I don't want to go to prom or grad night or any of that stuff. I just don't want to. And I can get my diploma without being there to walk the stage."

"I'm putting my foot down about that, Candace. It's one thing for you to skip the prom. Lord knows you've been to enough parties and to every formal dance that you heard about since you were fourteen, but graduation is non negotiable. I'll be there to watch you and your sister walk across that stage if it's the last thing I do!" The conviction in Ella's voice was unmistakable. Candace knew not to push the issue.

"Okay, okay. Home in time for graduation. Can we agree to that?"

"I just don't know Candace. That's five months from now. That's too long for you to be away from us."

"Mama Ella, please just think about it. I've been getting good grades since I've been here and my teachers have been supportive. And I'm doing a good thing here with Auntie. We talked about it and she's happy to have me here. It gives Charlene a chance to spend time with her grandbabies. They need the help. Please don't make me come home. Can that be my birthday present? It's so hard for me to be home when I know Mommy and Daddy will never walk through that door again." Candace could barely hold in the tears.

"Calm down, calm down. I never thought you'd be begging to stay in the boondocks away from all your friends. I'll think about it and call you in a couple of days. I—"

"Thank you, thank you, thank you!"

"Candace, I didn't say yes. I said I'd think about it!"

"I know. Yes ma'am. Okay. Please think about it and call me back, okay?"

"Okay. Now tell Auntie I love her and we're keeping her in our prayers."

"I will."

"And I'll tell your sister you said hi."

Candace sighed, "Okay." It was easier to go along with her grandmother's dreams of a joyful reunion between her and Karina than to convince her that their bond had been severed forever. "Love you. Talk to you soon."

Candace sat at the counter for a few minutes after hanging up the phone. *God, please make her say yes. I'm not ready to face Rina again. It hurts too bad.* She wiped her eyes and put on a cheerful smile.

"Auntie, Mama Ella said to tell you she loves you and that she's keeping you in her prayers."

Izora nodded. "Did you ask her if you can stay?"

"Yes, she said she'll think about it. She's worried about me missing out on the rest of senior year. I tried to explain to her I don't want to do any of that. It makes me sad to even think about being around all of those people. It's like I'll be putting on a mask and pretending to be the old Candace, but I'll never be her again, Auntie."

"I understand that your whole life has been upended by the tragedy of losing your parents and this rift with your sister. You'll never be exactly the same girl as you were before, but we all grow and change, darlin'. That's part of life. Time will go on and you'll heal; so will Karina. And the two of you will come back together – that's God's love. But you need to do some healing on your own right now and sounds like Karina does too. You shouldn't feel guilty about that. Women, Black women, especially, have to learn to take care of themselves cause most of the time ain't nobody else gonna do it. That's just the way of the world. Auntie here is gonna help you take care of you. I may need your help to get my body stronger, but I'm gonna help you get your spirit stronger. Deal?"

Candace threw her arms around her aunt's neck. "Deal! I love you so much, Auntie."

"I love you too, Scoot."

"Are you ready for dinner? I am starving! I feel like I haven't eaten all day!" Candace said, standing up.

"Nowadays you're always hungry. You got a tapeworm?" Izora teased.

"Very funny Auntie! I only had two meals today and a couple of snacks. I guess my flu finally passed."

"Go ahead and get started with dinner. This one has lots of

steps. We've never tried Japanese before. And it shouldn't make us too fat! While you do that, I'm gonna go to my room and call Ella Mae. I think we can work out the logistics of you staying here a while."

Candace held her crossed fingers up in the air and then pulled out the cookbook and began gathering the ingredients.

6

OUR SECRET

Candace and Maybelle sat on the back porch enjoying the rare January sunshine. Maybelle stretched one long leg in front of her and bent the other at the knee, polishing her toenails bright red. In a jean skirt, white t-shirt and red flip-flops she could easily have been one of Candace's high school classmates but Maybelle was quick to point out that in just one month, on her twenty-first birthday, she'd be a grown woman.

"In every sense of the word," she said with a wink.

Maybelle had taken to stopping by in the evenings a few times a week. She told Candace about her boyfriend, Lamont, who was a UPS driver. She loved to talk about her sex life, regaling Candace with stories that might or might not have been true. Candace never had much to add to these conversations, choosing to allow Maybelle to think she was still a virgin.

"I gotta get home to take me some medicine." Maybelle said, standing up.

"What's wrong? You look fine."

"I feel my period coming on. If I don't start taking something right away, I'll get cramps and I won't be able to sleep tonight."

"I know what you mean! I don't know why I always get such bad cramps. My sister can just throw on a pad and keep on with her day. But me? I'll be all in the bed curled up and crying for two days every month."

"I feel for you! When you feel it coming let me know and I'll help you with Miss Izora for a couple of days. I know how it is to wanna stay curled up. When are you due?"

Candace paused for a moment. "Umm, next week, I think." She grabbed the garden shears and began to cut flowers. "I'm gonna take these inside to put in a vase for Auntie." She reached for the door. "You coming?"

"Naw. I'll cut through the yard. You know I'm too lazy to waste any steps!" She laughed. "And I need my Midol! I'll see you tomorrow or the next day." She closed the gate behind her and headed toward home.

Candace let go of the door handle and sat down on the top step frowning. She actually couldn't remember when she'd last had a period. Just then Aunt Izora called for her. "Coming Auntie!" Candace jumped up and ran inside.

Over the next few hours, Candace fell into the usual routine: she made dinner and dessert, cleaned up, played a game of checkers, watched the news and helped her aunt get ready for bed. She hadn't had time to think about her period but the question was always there in the back of her mind. "Goodnight, Auntie. I think I'll go to bed now too."

Izora asked, "Are you feeling sick?"

"No, just tired. A lot on my mind." Candace kissed her aunt's forehead. Izora grabbed her wrist as she turned to go. She had a surprisingly strong grip. "What's wrong, Auntie?"

"You'll be okay, Scoot. Just trust in God."

Candace patted her aunt's hand in reassurance. "Auntie you're so dramatic. I'm fine. Just ate too much of that rich food we've been eating!" Her giggle sounded forced even to her own ears. She quickly turned and left the room.

She paced around her bedroom, trying to focus. The last several months had gone by in a blur. She didn't remember the last time she'd had her period. She hadn't had one since she'd come to

Texarkana. The box of tampons that Ella had packed for her sat unopened.

She lay on the bed and tried to remember. "Let's see. I came here the day after Thanksgiving. That's about six weeks ago. I must have had one right before I left," she murmured. She thought back to the weeks preceding her departure. She remembered the constant fights with Karina. She remembered that she'd flunked her AP Lit test the first week of November. She remembered Thanksgiving. *She did not remember having a period.*

Candace sat up suddenly. *My cramps are always so bad. When was the last time I used the hot water bottle? Think Candace, think!* Then a memory crystalized. Her shoulders sagged; her face crumpled. It was the night her parents died. *I was faking like I had cramps but I had just finished my period a couple of weeks before. That's how I got to go to bed early and was able to sneak out the window.*

Candace ran to the kitchen and grabbed the calendar off the wall. Back in her room she studied the calendar. "Hmm . . . my period started on August sixth and my cycle usually comes every thirty days like clockwork, so I should have had another one on September sixth." Candace willed herself to remember. "The funeral was September ninth – I'll never forget that. I definitely wasn't on my period at the funeral."

The weeks following her parents' death had gone by in a haze. She had eaten, showered, combed her hair and brushed her teeth but she couldn't remember any of it. All she remembered was crying all the time and wishing that it had been her instead of them. She threw the calendar on the floor in frustration.

"Okay, Candace, breathe. It's just stress. So I missed a couple of periods. Big deal. It's not like we didn't use protection." *But what if the condom broke?* Candace thought about all those months of vomiting and bouts of nausea. She thought about all the weight she'd lost in the fall but that she'd suddenly gained at least ten pounds in the past couple of weeks. *I can't be pregnant. I just can't be pregnant!* She looked at herself in the mirror, turning left, then right. Her fingers splayed across her belly. *If I was pregnant I would be big as a house by now. There's no way I'd still have an almost flat belly. No way.*

Candace turned off the light and lay on her side, cradling her body. She finally fell asleep, the words *I am not pregnant, I am not pregnant* running through her mind over and over again.

The next day she called Maybelle and asked her to come over while Aunt Izora napped. The girls sat on the back porch so she could hear the bell if it rang.

"What's up?" Maybelle asked. "Why you look so sad?"

"Can I trust you to keep a secret? A huge secret?" Tears threatened to spill from Candace's eyes.

Maybelle grew serious. "Candi, we're like cousins. You can tell me anything and I won't tell a soul. What's the matter?"

Candace studied the ants milling around in the dirt and then said in a small voice. "I'm not a virgin."

Maybelle giggled, "Is that your big secret? Girl, you don't have to be ashamed or nothing. I know how it is to be in love and not be able to wait."

Candace smiled wanly, "That's not the secret. It's much worse than that."

Maybelle's expression turned serious. "Is everything okay?"

Candace shushed Maybelle and quietly opened the screen door so she could check on her aunt. Then she said, "Okay, Auntie is still knocked out. You absolutely promise that you won't tell anybody, no matter what the secret is?

"I'm about to be a grown ass woman. What would I look like running around telling secrets? What is going on with you?"

Candace inhaled deeply and took a leap of faith. "I haven't had a period in a long time."

"How long?" Maybelle frowned.

Candace looked at her feet and whispered, "August, I think."

"August!" Maybelle shouted and clapped her hand over her mouth. "Lord have mercy!

Candace started crying. "I know! I just, I just didn't even think about it with everything that's happened. Mommy and Daddy. School. Karina. I had the flu. It wasn't until you started talking about your cramps and Midol that it hit me."

Maybelle pulled Candace into an embrace. "Shush. You're just gonna make yourself sick." The girls sat in silence for a while and then Maybelle said, "Well damn girl. You done swore me to secrecy about something that ain't gon' be a secret much longer!"

Candace threw her a panicked look. "But it has to! Nobody can know!"

"If you're as far along as you say, it ain't much we can do to keep this a secret, Candi."

"Stop it! You're assuming I'm pregnant," Candace whispered, "but that doesn't have to be what's wrong. We used protection! I probably have a tumor or something."

"A tumor, okay." Maybelle smirked.

Candace swatted at Maybelle's arm. "Don't tease! I'm serious. I've been sick for months and losing weight. I probably have cancer or something. This is gonna be so hard for Mama Ella."

Maybelle tried to keep a straight face. "Candi, if you thought you had cancer you wouldn't have told me about not being a virgin and swearing me to secrecy. But let's just get you to the clinic and find out for sure."

"How are we gonna do that without anybody knowing?"

"You haven't had a day off since you've been here. We'll ask my mama to watch Miss Izora tomorrow so we can explore the city and I'll take you to the clinic."

"You think you can find one that will see me?" Candace asked.

Maybelle's expression was unreadable. "Chile, this ain't my first rodeo."

———

The Women's Health Clinic was tucked into the bend of a strip mall that offered everything a teenager could possibly want or need. There was K-Mart, Payless Shoe Source, a donut shop, a bar-b-que joint, four fast food restaurants and a video store. Maybelle parked the Deacon's car in front of the K-Mart just in case it was spotted by someone from the congregation. Walking quickly with their heads down, Candace wondered why a place that promised confidentiality would be smack dab in the middle of the busiest strip mall in town.

When they reached the entrance, Candace took a deep breath and hesitated before opening the door. She had the uneasy feeling that once she crossed that threshold life would never be the same. The receptionist barely looked at her when she handed her a form to fill out.

Maybelle nudged her. "The sooner you turn in the form, the quicker they'll see you."

Date of last menstrual period? Candace's hand trembled as she wrote August 6th. She looked up at the calendar on the wall next to the receptionist window - Today is January 30th - and swallowed. She quickly completed the questionnaire, deposited the clipboard in the slot and sat down

The pelvic exam was the most embarrassing and invasive experience of her life. After a few minutes the doctor said, "Okay Candace, you can sit up. You're pregnant, but you already knew that didn't you?"

The air was suddenly sucked out of the room. Candace struggled to breathe. A look of terror flashed across her face. "No! Please check again, please check again!" She laid back and put her feet into the stirrups.

"Candace, stop." The doctor put a hand on her arm. "Sit up, honey. There's no need to check again. The urine test is positive, your uterus is enlarged and you haven't had a period in five months. What did you expect to hear?"

Tears rolled down Candace's face. "I, I don't know," she stammered. "I've been going through a lot. My parents died. My sister isn't speaking to me. I don't have any friends. I didn't even think about my period until earlier this month. Can't it be stress? Maybe it's a tumor! Did you check for a tumor?"

"It's not a tumor. We'll set you up with one of our psychologists to talk about the things going on in your life. We need to get you healthy mentally as well as physically. We'll also need to check you for STDs that you can contract when you have unprotected sex. If you do have a STD, you'll have to contact each of your sexual partners."

"I only had sex once and we used protection. I don't know how this happened." She closed her eyes. *If Mommy and Daddy weren't already dead this would kill them.*

The doctor sighed, "I get so many girls in here who got pregnant their first or second time. You can't leave it up to the guy to supply the condom or assume he's putting it on right. One mistake and you get pregnant."

"No kidding." Candace smiled wryly. Gathering her resolve she asked, "How soon can I get an abortion?"

The doctor frowned and opened her mouth to answer.

Candace anticipated her response. "I know, I know, abortion is a big step and you want me to think about it. Trust me, Dr. Moore, all I've done for the past week is think about it. That's my only option. My family can't ever find out."

"Candace, it's far too late for an abortion. You're going to have this baby. You do still have options, though. If you're not able to care for the baby or you feel it would be in his or her best interests to be placed into a more stable home, we can help you with the adoption process. One of our social workers will talk with you about that. You've got plenty of time to decide, the baby won't be here for four more months. In the meantime, you're going to need to take better care of yourself. You'll need to meet with the nutritionist so you can learn what to eat to get to a healthier weight."

Candace was speechless.

"I'll leave you to get dressed. We can talk more at your next appointment. We'll schedule more time and give you an ultrasound so you can see the baby and hear the heartbeat.

Back in the lobby, Candace motioned for Maybelle to leave.

Once outside, Maybelle peppered her with questions. "Well, did they confirm it? What's next?"

Candace's face was blank. "It's not a tumor. Can you take me home, please?" They walked to the car in silence. After driving a few miles Maybelle pulled off to the shoulder of the road.

"Candi, I know you're scared but you can't just ignore this. A baby is not going to go away. You're gonna start showing soon."

Candace started to hyperventilate. Maybelle made her lean over and take deep breaths. "I didn't mean to upset you, girl. You know I'm on your side, right?"

Candace nodded, still trying to settle herself. "It's not you. I appreciate you so much. I'm just so scared! I can't have a baby! And this will break my grandmother's heart!"

"I hear ya, I really do. But you are gonna have a baby."

"Just keep your promise," Candace implored. "You swore you wouldn't tell anyone!"

"I told you I wouldn't tell and I won't, but girl you're gonna have to tell it yourself pretty soon."

"I know. I just need some time to think."

"Okay. You know you can call me anytime." Maybelle squeezed Candace's hand and pulled the car back onto the road. Ten minutes later she dropped Candace off at Izora's house.

Letting herself in the house, Candace did her best to look and act normal. "Hey, Miss Jackie. Hi, Auntie." Coming around to kiss Aunt Izora's cheek Candace managed to avoid meeting her eyes.

"Where are your bags? I thought you were going shopping. And where is Maybelle?" Jackie said.

"Just window shopping. I walked all through the store but didn't find anything I had to have. Maybelle headed on home." Candace struggled to hold back tears and turned her head away slightly.

"Girl, you might be the first teenager I ever met who didn't find something that she just had to have!" Jackie teased.

Candace forced a laugh and changed the subject. "Did you guys have a good afternoon?"

"Oh, yeah, we just sat here watching a movie and eating," said Izora.

"Did you have lunch? There's some tuna salad in the refrigerator." Jackie said.

"Yeah, I ate." Candace lied. Food was the last thing on her mind.

Jackie started to gather her things. "Well, Miss Izora I'm gonna get on outta here. The Deacon is leading Bible study this evening and I promised I'd make something sweet for him to offer the folks afterwards." She turned to Candace. "Let me know when you want to get out again, okay? I know Maybelle is itching to take you out to a party, but you gotta be careful about going anywhere with that fast thang. Now that she's knocking on twenty-one's door she thinks she should be able to do whatever she wants with whoever she wants." She clucked her tongue.

"I keep telling her daddy that she's spending too much time with that driver boy. Before you know it, she's gon' turn up pregnant. You mark my words. But you know daddies, they cain't never see the fault in their little girls. I birthed her and I still know that she's wild."

Izora patted Jackie's hand in reassurance. "Think of it this way, she made it through high school and she's nearly twenty-one. She's a preacher's kid but maybe not as wild as you paint her in your head."

"You've always had a soft spot for her, Miss Izora. Let's hope you're right. I'm gonna put it in the Lord's hands. That's all I can do. I'll see y'all in a few days."

"Thanks again, Miss Jackie." Candace closed the door behind her, grateful to be done with the references to pregnancy. Candace flipped through the small pile of mail on the counter and found an envelope addressed to her. *Nicky!* She grabbed the letter then ran to her room to read it but her hands were shaking so much she dropped it and the pages scattered. *Just like our relationship is going to be in pieces.* Candace felt her eyes begin to well with tears as she kneeled to pick up the pages. Passages caught her attention and the ink got blotchy as her tears fell.

That's right baby! I'm out!

Johnny came through for a nigga!

Johnny done come up, Boo!

I'mma be his right-hand man.

It's time for you to come on back home, baby.

I know you don't wanna be back with your grandmother and your sister. So lets get a place together. You'll be 18 next month so caint nobody stop you from doing what you wanna do. Think about it, okay? I'll have my money straight by April 1st.

I'm dreaming about you every night and you know what I'm dreaming about!
Love your only man, Nick.

Candace jammed her fist in her mouth to muffle her sobs. *My life is over. Nicky loves me. but there's no way he'd understand about Rell and he would never raise another guy's baby. If Nicky finds out about this baby it will be over for us, forever.*

"Happy birthday!" Izora screamed as soon as Candace entered her bedroom in the morning. For the first time in weeks Candace flashed a genuine smile. "Auntie, how'd you know it was my birthday?"

"Ella told me and Jackie that February fifteenth was a very special day."

"Really?" Candace's eyes started to fill with tears.

"We're having a party today." Izora sang.

Candace's smile disappeared. "No, Auntie, I don't want a party. It's no big deal, really."

"Too late! And eighteen is very much a big deal." Izora insisted.

Candace dreaded having anyone come over to celebrate her birthday. She still hadn't figured out what to do about the pregnancy and lived in fear of discovery. She knew from her clinic visit that the baby was due around the May twenty-fifth, putting her at a little over five months pregnant on her birthday. Thankfully she wasn't showing, she just looked like she'd put on a few pounds.

The day's mail was full of surprises. There were birthday cards from Mama Ella and Nana and Papa Lanier. For as long as Candace could remember, the Lanier grandparents had sent her and Karina birthday cards intended for little kids – the ones with elephants or silly clowns or puppies and kittens that said something silly like "who's the big girl of the day?" or "somebody deserves a treat" and inside would be the crispest, cleanest twenty dollar bill they'd ever seen. They used to joke that Nana and Papa must wash and iron the money before they put it in the card. On the outside of this year's card was a little girl jump-roping while her pet poodle looked on.

"I guess this is a special birthday! Two twenty dollar bills!" Candace smiled, touched that her elderly grandparents had thought of her.

Next in the pile was a fancy card from Karina. She recognized her sister's handwriting immediately. She tore open the envelope. A Black ballerina was depicted on the front and on the inside was an inspirational verse followed by a short note from Karina: "Happy 18th to you from me." *That's it, no 'I love you,' nothing about missing me or wanting me to come home.* Candace sighed and stood the card on the mantle next to the others. Finally, there was a letter from Nick. Candace held it close to her heart and closed her eyes. *Finding out about this baby is gonna hurt him so much.*

Later that day Maybelle, Lamont, Deacon Washington, Miss Jackie and Aunt Izora presented Candace with a homemade 7-up cake, a K-Mart gift card, a cassette tape of Janet Jackson's *Control* album and a wrapped present from her grandmother. Candace ripped open the wrapping to reveal a small gift box. Inside was a strand of pearls.

Candace gasped and her hand flew to her mouth. "These were Mommy's!" The enclosed note from Ella made tears spring to her eyes. 'Candace, darling, your mother always planned to give you these on your 18th birthday. She told me that her mother had given them to her on her 18th birthday and that she planned for you to give them to your daughter when she turns 18. You hold on to them and cherish them. We love you and miss you, Mama Ella.'

Candace couldn't control her sobs. The loss of her parents, the kindness of these strangers, the baby growing in her belly – was all too much. Izora realized that these weren't typical happy birthday tears and took Candace in her arms like a baby. She waved the others off and rocked her, crooning in her ear, until Candace finally fell asleep. Deacon Washington carried her into the bedroom and eased the door shut before returning to the living room.

"Poor chile, she's been through too much over the last six months. It's taken a toll on her." Jackie said.

Maybelle replied carefully, "We talk sometimes. I think she's depressed."

Jackie nodded, "I think you're right. I'd been so glad to see her putting on a few pounds. She was starting to look healthy, but now it looks like she's dropping weight again. Miss Izora, is she taking care of you alright?"

Izora nodded. "Grief hits everyone differently. She'll be okay. It just takes time."

The Deacon rubbed his beard. "Well, if she keeps on like this, we either gon' have to take her to the doctor or get her back to her grandmother."

Candace was finding it hard to stay awake all day and hard to sleep at night. Her body felt different, heavy. Her appetite was fickle. Sometimes she was famished an hour after eating a full meal and at other times the first swallow of food gave her terrible heartburn. But worse than the physical effects of pregnancy was knowing that soon her secret would come out.

"Sorry I overslept, Auntie. I hope you weren't calling me for too long." Candace shuffled into her aunt's bedroom, still rubbing her eyes. She'd woken with a start and jumped out of bed without donning the oversized terry-cloth robe she'd taken to wearing around the house in the mornings. The small mound of her belly was clearly visible through her cotton nightgown. At six months pregnant, she was unusually small. She could still get her jeans on but she couldn't zip or button them. With the right top, her belly wasn't noticeable at all.

Izora looked closely at Candace as she opened the curtains and moved around the room, gathering the toiletry items. She'd suspected Candace's secret for some time and the unencumbered view of her belly confirmed her suspicions. Later that day, Candace lay on the couch wearing a loose sun dress watching the soap operas with Izora.

"Come sit over here next to me, Candace." Izora said.

Candace frowned as she hurried over to her aunt. "Is everything okay, Auntie? Are you feeling sick?"

Izora took Candace's hand. "When are you due?"

Candace gasped. She couldn't meet her aunt's eyes. She pulled her hand away and sat down heavily on the floor at her aunt's feet. "How did you know?"

"I am eighty years old, girl!" Izora pursed her lips.

Candace managed a small smile. "Yeah, I guess you've seen your share of pregnancies, huh? Auntie I'm so ashamed!" Her face crumpled. She lay her head on Izora's lap and the story poured out. Izora let her tell it in her own way without interruption.

"Sit up, Candace. Blow your nose and look at me. I want you to know that I'm not ashamed of you. You made a poor decision and decisions have consequences. You already know that. Sometimes girls get pregnant on their first time, even when they use protection and sometimes they don't. The dice didn't roll your way. The God I believe in is a forgiving God, who knows your heart. It's up to us to be practical and deal with the here and now. When is this baby coming?" Izora's eyes were soft but her tone was matter-of-fact.

Candace was so relieved to have someone take control. She tried to match her aunt's demeanor. "Around May twenty fifth I think." Her voice cracked. "Auntie, this is gonna break Mama Ella's heart! I tried to convince the doctor at the clinic to give me an abortion but she said it was too late. I can't be someone's mother! And this baby won't even have a father! Rell seemed like a nice guy, but I couldn't find him if I tried!"

Izora patted her shoulder. "Hush, child, you're getting yourself all worked up again. I'll tell you what. You get started on dinner and let me think for a spell, okay?"

Candace stood up, "Okay. I appreciate you not being angry with me, Auntie. I know I've disappointed you."

Izora frowned. "Candace, I've never put you girls on a pedestal. You and your sister are smart, funny, beautiful and perfectly imperfect human beings. You'll each make your fair share of missteps. It's how you recover that matters most. Is this a big one?" Izora shrugged and waved her good hand in the air. "At this point in your life, for sure. Is it the worst thing that will ever happen to you? I hope so but I doubt it. If I'm disappointed about anything, it's that you didn't know you could confide in me. I'll always be here for you, Scoot, no matter what. And I know that Ella Mae feels the same way."

Candace frowned and Izora said, "Now don't get all bristly with me. I said I won't tell her, so I won't. Now get on in the kitchen and let me think!" Izora smiled.

An hour later, Candace and Izora were eating dinner.

"This is delicious, Candace. You really ought to consider culinary school." Izora said, as she finished her meal. "Alright, I've given the situation a lot of thought and I think we can pull this off."

Candace frowned, "Pull what off?"

"I'm going to insist that you stay here until the last minute before graduation. I'll tell Ella I'll send you home on June 8th for your June 17^{h} graduation. That gives us two weeks of wiggle room from your due date. It's tight, but God willing we'll make it. And if not, we'll come up with a reason to buy a few more days. We'll get Jackie to help us find a family to adopt the baby. Believe me, that won't be hard. There are lots of couples praying for babies."

"Oh my God! Auntie, really? You'd do that for me?" A cloud passed over Candace's face. "Auntie, is it wrong for me to give her up? Before I got here Karina kept saying that I was selfish. Is this being selfish? I don't want to be a bad person, but I'm just not ready to be a mother!"

"You have no reason to be ashamed. The best mothers put their children first. My sister Sophia made the same decision many, many years ago and it was the right decision for the baby even though it broke her heart."

"Auntie Sophie! I never knew that!" Candace said.

"And you still don't! That's a secret that I promised to keep." Izora said. "I'm only telling you now to help you understand that it's up to you, not Karina or anyone else, to define what's best for you and this baby."

Candace felt the despair lift from her shoulders. That night, she slept soundly for the first time in months.

Several weeks passed. Candace's belly was still a barely noticeable bump, but her hips were filling out and her face was fuller. Izora hadn't spoken with Jackie about Candace's situation because Jackie's hands were full caring for her parents. Her mother had broken her hip and her father was adrift without his wife of sixty-five years scheduling his days. Izora reassured Candace that when the time was right, they would tell Jackie and she would help them find a home for the baby.

Candace laughed in delight whenever she felt the baby moving. She placed Izora's hand on her belly and they both smiled at the faint flutters. "Auntie, she doesn't move very much. Do you think she's okay?" Candace bit her lip.

"Every baby is different. You're healthy, so she's healthy." Izora had lived long enough to know that each baby grew and developed in his or her own way in his or her own time. Although she didn't have any living children, she'd had a son who died of pneumonia when he was three years old. She was confident that Candace's baby would begin to grow quickly now that the stress of discovery was removed.

"I hope so, Auntie." Candace wasn't convinced. Every pregnant person this far along she'd ever seen was humongous. Not that she wanted to be fat, but she thought it was strange that her belly was still so small.

Maybelle didn't visit as often because she was helping her

mother take care of her grandparents but they talked regularly. "I guess you've been rubbing off on me." She told Candace over the phone. "I've been paying attention to how you take such good care of Miss Izora. I might even take some nursing classes. But don't tell my mama that! We'll just see how this goes first!" They laughed.

"How's everything going with you?" Maybelle asked. "Time sure is passing fast."

"It's all good. Aunt Izora knows. We're going to tell your mother and ask her for help finding a good home for the baby but please don't let the cat out of the bag! I think it's best for Aunt Izora to talk with Miss Jackie. And no need for anybody to know that you knew all about it."

"Amen to that!" Maybelle laughed. "As grown as I am, I think Mama would whoop me! Candi, I know it's not really my business but I think you're making a good decision. My mama does a lot of ministry work with Black couples who want to adopt but they run into so many roadblocks. A few times, she's introduced pregnant women to families that have been praying for a baby. They've been so happy."

"That's what Aunt Izora said. I feel good about my baby growing up around here with a family that can take care of her."

"Her?" Maybelle asked.

"I feel in my heart that it's a girl. I can't explain it." Candace replied. "Okay, I'd better let you go. Time to fix Auntie's dinner. Thanks girl. It helps to have somebody to talk to."

"No problem. Talk to you soon."

Before she knew it, it was the middle of March. With a little over two months to go, Candace was growing fearful. She wanted to confide in her sister, but each time she thought about calling her or writing her a letter, she imagined Karina's expression. At best, she'd be disappointed, at worst, disgusted. Candace couldn't bear to take that chance. She and Izora had agreed the time had come to confide in Jackie and to start making plans for the birth.

At 6 o'clock Candace stretched and yawned. It was getting harder and harder to get up so early. She listened to the silence of the small house. Satisfied that Aunt Izora was still asleep, she allowed herself to doze for another fifteen minutes before getting up.

Candace shifted in bed, awakened by the heat of the sun on her face. She smiled at the unfamiliar sensation. Usually, the sun wasn't so bright when she awoke. *The sun!* She squinted to see the time. *9 o'clock? Oh no! Aunt Izora must be mad at me!*

"Auntie, are you awake? I'm sorry I overslept. I don't know how that happened." She said as she walked the short distance to her aunt's bedroom. Once inside, she hurried to open the curtains to let in the sunshine. When she turned to help her aunt out of the bed, she gasped in shock. Izora's eyes were open but unseeing, and her right hand was hanging from the side of the bed.

"Auntie! Auntie! Oh my God!" There was no doubt about it. She was dead. Candace collapsed in despair. "Auntie please don't leave me. You're all I have. How can I get through this without you?" Candace sobbed and draped her body across her aunt's, her fingers absently playing with the beautiful mane of hair spread across her pillow.

***

It was April first and Candace knew she had to make some decisions. She'd gotten through Aunt Izora's wake and the funeral without anyone detecting the pregnancy. Candace had told the Washingtons that Mama Ella was under the weather and wouldn't be able to make the funeral. In reality, she hadn't told her grandmother about Izora's death because she knew Mama Ella would have been on the first plane to Texarkana. Candace wasn't prepared to face her grandmother. She still had a lot to figure out.

Candace sat on the back porch with Maybelle. "I miss Auntie so much. And after all these months of being so convinced everything was gonna work out, now it's all a mess all over again!" She rubbed her temples to relieve the headache that was a daily reminder of her dire circumstances.

"Charlene will be here tomorrow. She hasn't seen me since November. It was terrible for her that she had to miss the funeral because her grandbabies were in the hospital with pneumonia, but as bad as it sounds it was lucky for me. I know she's gonna notice that I'm pregnant as soon as she sees me."

"You want me to ask my mother to come over now? We can talk with her in private about the baby," Maybelle said.

"No, with Auntie gone I don't feel as comfortable with the plan. Your mother might feel obligated to call my grandmother."

"True, it is a big secret to keep. I think Miss Izora could have convinced her to keep it but I can't swear Mama would listen to you and me."

Candace shrugged, "Even if your mother would help me, I'm not gonna be able to hide this baby from Charlene. She's definitely gonna be on the phone with Mama Ella as soon as she sees me."

"So what are you gonna do?"

"I can't let Mama Ella be embarrassed by somebody else telling her. That's just piling wrong on top of wrong. I have to be the one to tell her."

"You're gonna call her yourself? I can be here with you when you call," Maybelle offered.

Candace bit her lower lip. "No, I have to tell her in person." She took a deep breath. "I'm going home."

Candace searched on the kitchen counter for her plane ticket. She picked up the telephone. Putting on her most adult voice, she said. "Yes, I'd like to change my reservation. I'm supposed to be flying to Oakland from Texarkana on June eighth but an emergency has come up and I need to leave right away."

7

HOME NOT SO SWEET

The flight home was tortuous. Candace's feet were swollen and she couldn't find a comfortable position. Sleep was elusive because her mind was racing. When she had decided on adoption, Candace hadn't fully considered that she'd be giving up a piece of herself forever. Within the past year she'd lost three beloved family members to death and been estranged from two others. Rubbing her belly, she wondered for the first time if she could stand to lose someone else.

But what was the alternative? The answers were no clearer when the plane touched down in Oakland. She hadn't called ahead for Mama Ella to pick her up from the airport – she wanted to spare her the shock of a public revelation. She took a shuttle to the nearby Coliseum BART station and paid the fare for the short BART train ride to Berkeley.

It felt strange to be in the Bay Area after so many months. She had grown used to the slow pace of the country. Candace didn't feel like the same girl. She didn't care about the latest fashions or who the popular kids were anymore. She saw a guy standing on the opposite platform, bopping his head to rap music blaring from his portable radio. He reminded her of Nick. *Will I ever get to be with my Nicky again?*

Once on the train Candace chose a window seat and watched the Bay Area cityscape pass by. From the window she could just make out the intersection where her parents had died. She wondered if the makeshift shrine of flowers, candles, notes and stuffed animals that friends and strangers constructed in the weeks after her parents' accident was still there. "Proof," a local morning news reporter had said, "that even in the midst of the crack epidemic, Oaklanders have not lost their souls."

Candace had been too ashamed to attend the midnight vigil at the crash site. Karina didn't go either, saying that the organizers were using their parents' death as a political ploy. Ella kept her opinion to herself and went to church that night instead. Candace closed her eyes, willing the barrage of memories to stop.

Half an hour later she exited the BART station and began the one-mile walk home. By the time Candace reached the house, she was exhausted. Despite the smallness of her belly the pregnancy was definitely taking a toll on her body. Her legs and feet were throbbing and there was a constant ache in her lower back that she hadn't noticed before leaving Texarkana. She was glad to see that Mama Ella's car wasn't in the driveway.

Candace reached into the side pocket of the backpack for the brass key. She remembered her tenth birthday when Daddy Horace had ceremoniously presented her with the key on a retractable ring that he pinned into her backpack. "Scoot, I trust you to take care of this key. This key isn't just about opening this door. It means more than that. It means that there will always be a place you can come to, no matter what. Your sister will get her own key when her time comes, but your key will always be yours." From that day forward Candace treated the key as if it were made of gold instead of brass.

She stood in the entryway, taking in the familiar sounds and smells. She hadn't realized how much she missed home. Candace smiled with relief when she entered the bedroom that she shared with Karina. Everything was just as she had left it. Her bed was made up neatly with her blue afghan lying reassuringly at the foot. She laid down on her bed and let the tears flow freely. She cried for everything she'd lost: her parents, her sister, her friends. She cried because the next few weeks were going to be even harder than the last few months had been.

It was nearly 3 o'clock. Candace assumed Karina and Mama Ella would be getting home soon. Looking at herself in the mirror she realized the thin sundress would give her secret away. When they moved to Mama Ella's house the girls had grabbed a few things to remember their parents by. Karina had chosen Jewel's silver bracelet and Langston's favorite book, *Invisible Man,* by Ralph Ellison. Candace had wanted something more personal, so she had chosen her dad's pajama pants and the extra-large t-shirt that Jewel had worn when she was pregnant with her. She was happy to put them on now; they worked well to camouflage Candace's extra weight and gave her comfort for the coming confrontation.

She decided to wait before unpacking her backpack. "For all I know, Mama Ella might tell me to get my pregnant ass out!" Candace said only half-jokingly to herself. She sucked in her bottom lip. *Mama Ella won't really put me out will she?* Candace was afraid to let her mind wander too far in that direction. Instead, she grabbed her afghan off the bed and went to the living room to wait. She wrapped herself in the afghan and curled up on the couch, waiting for the storm to hit. Just then she heard the jingle of keys at the door.

Ella was in a hurry as she entered. She tossed her keys into the basket on the table and set her purse down beside it. Glancing at her watch she mentally reviewed her to-do list again. A flash of blue in the living room caught her eye.

"Candace? Oh, my Lord, you almost gave me a heart attack!" Ella hurried over to her granddaughter.

Candace pulled the afghan closer and smiled. "Hi Mama Ella, I wanted to surprise you, not scare you!"

As Ella came forward to hug her, Candace raised a hand. "I think I'm coming down with a cold." Ella stopped in her tracks. Ella had worked in the Neonatal Intensive Care Unit for over twenty years. The newborn babies she cared for were so susceptible to infection that it was second nature for her family members to be extremely careful not to pass on what could be deadly germs to Ella. Candace blew her grandmother a kiss. Ella pretended to catch it in the air and threw one back at her.

Ella sat on the arm of the couch. "Candace, what are you doing here? How did you get here? Why didn't you call?" The questions tumbled out of her mouth. "Why would Deacon Washington put you on a plane without letting me know?" Ella's brow furrowed. "I'm gonna give him a piece of my mind!"

Candace finally got a word in edgewise. "Calm down Mama Ella. I told you, I wanted to surprise you! Don't be mad at Deacon Washington. I know I should've called, but I needed to see you; to talk to you in person."

The sound of a car horn blaring interrupted her. Ella opened the door and gave an acknowledging wave. Closing it again, she turned to Candace. "Darn it! That Freida is always right on time! And I haven't even gotten my things together."

"You're going somewhere?"

"Yes, I promised Freida that I'd go on a turnaround trip to Reno with her."

"Reno!"

"I don't know if you remember that Freida's husband passed away just about a month after Langston and Jewel's accident." Candace winced at the mention of her parents. "Freida's been having a real hard time moving on. She never had any children. She's been begging me to go with her on one of these trips and I finally said yes. I just got off work and came home to change and put a small bag together."

The horn blared again. "Okay, hold your horses!" Ella shouted, even though Freida couldn't possibly hear her. She clucked her tongue. "So country! She knows I do not like people sitting in my driveway honking their horns." She checked her watch again. "Look at the time. The bus is leaving in thirty minutes. No wonder she's having a fit."

Candace hadn't known her grandmother liked to gamble. As if reading her mind, Ella snorted and said, "I don't even gamble. I'll throw a few coins in the slot machine and maybe play a little bingo but I'm not a hard-core gambler."

"So why go?"

"Oh, I'm sure it'll be fun and Freida really needs to have some fun. We're going with a bunch of 'active seniors' as they like to call us, so we'll be in good company." Ella frowned. "Candace I'm so sorry that this is coming up on the very first day you get back home. I missed you so much and I want to hear all about Aunt Izora, and what you think about Texarkana."

The horn blared a third time. Ella opened the front door again, stuck her head outside and hollered, "Just a minute Freida!"

"I have a lot to tell you, Mama Ella, a lot to talk to you about. Not just about Texarkana, but it's okay. It can wait until tomorrow."

"I hate to leave you, sweetie, but Freida has so been looking forward to this. If I cancel now, it will just crush her." Ella hurried across the hall to her bedroom and began gathering the items she needed for her trip. She continued talking, raising her voice so Candace could hear. "Your sister is going to be so surprised to see you! She asked me just this morning when you were coming home. There's plenty of food in the fridge. Karina has a study group this afternoon but she promised to stay home this evening since I'll be out of town. She knows I worry if she's out late." Ella emerged wearing a stylish velour sweat suit and matching brown and tan running shoes.

"Don't you look cute!" Candace exclaimed.

Ella smiled. "Karina bought it for me for Christmas. Talking about I needed to get with the times. You don't think it makes me look too young?"

"Mama Ella, stop being silly! It looks really cute on you. You'd better hurry up; I think Freida might explode."

"You're probably right. She's not the most patient person and now we're in real danger of missing that bus. Still, I don't feel right about leaving you alone on your first day home, especially when you're not feeling well."

"Mama Ella, please go. I'll be fine." They exchanged air kisses and Ella left.

Candace couldn't decide whether she was more annoyed or relieved. The thought of working up the courage to tell her grandmother about the pregnancy all over again was overwhelming. On the other hand, Mama Ella was going to be upset that she'd kept Aunt Izora's death from her. Mama Ella adored her aunt and would have wanted to be at her funeral, or her homegoing, as Ella called them. She said it was an honor and an obligation to send someone off to their final resting place. Candace realized that she had made a very serious error in judgment. *To add to all my other bad decisions, I guess.*

Dejected and lonely, Candace wrapped her afghan around her shoulders and headed to the kitchen to find a snack. She felt achy and uncomfortable, and her back was throbbing. While she was rummaging in the refrigerator, Karina walked into the house. She'd seen Ella's car in the driveway and saw the door of the open refrigerator from the hallway.

"Hey Mama Ella, what you doing in there? Stealing a snack without me?" She teased. Candace poked her head around the corner.

"Oh my God! Candi!" Karina hurried down the hallway, arms open wide. "Mama Ella didn't tell me you were coming home today!"

As Karina came closer, Candace panicked, realizing that her sister intended to hug her. *I can't let her feel my belly!* Pulling her afghan closer, Candace smiled feebly and backed away, letting the refrigerator door close. "Hey Sis! Better not get too close. I'm coming down with something."

Karina dropped her hands to her sides and disguised her hurt with a shrug.

"Whatever." Karina turned away from her sister and opened a kitchen cabinet, surreptitiously wiping at her eyes. Putting on a bored voice, she said, "So what brings you home? Ran through all the country boys?"

"Sis, I just spent the last six months with an eighty-year-old lady in the country. The only teenaged boys I've seen were on TV!" Hoping to draw Karina into conversation, she added,

"Mama Ella already left for Reno. I didn't know she likes to gamble, did you?"

Karina started making herself a peanut butter and jelly sandwich. "I don't know. She goes to bingo sometimes. I think she was mainly going to be nice to Freida. Anyway, Mama Ella needs a real vacation. She works too much."

"I wish she'd just retire," Candace said.

"They're gonna have to kick her out. I don't know what she'll do when she doesn't have those babies to watch after."

The mention of babies reminded her that this was the perfect opportunity to break the news to her sister. Before she could form the words, Karina said, "So, um, are you planning to be home tonight?"

"Yeah, I just got home. Where else would I go?" Candace asked.

"How the hell do I know where you go or what you do? I didn't even know you were coming home today." Karina snapped. She turned and put the tops back on the jelly and peanut butter jars and muttered, "Just my luck."

"I've been gone for months and you have to give me that funky attitude on the very first night. Hell, the very first hour? What difference does it make to you what I'm planning to do?" Candace bristled.

"I don't really care what you do, Candace." Karina sighed, "I was planning something. My boyfriend is coming over and I thought we were gonna have the house to ourselves, that's all."

"Boyfriend? I really have been gone too long! You have a boyfriend you're bringing into Mama Ella's house while she's away?" Candace teased. "Little sister must be growing up!"

Karina didn't laugh. "You know what, Candace? I don't have time for this. Just forget it. I'll make other plans."

Candace grew serious. "I'm sorry I ruined your plans, Rina. I really am. I didn't know I was coming home today until last night. But it's kinda good that Mama Ella is gone tonight because I need to talk to you. It's import—"

Karina slid the sandwich into a plastic bag and carried it with her into the bedroom. Candace hurried after her, careful to wrap the afghan around herself.

"Where are you going?" She asked, watching as Karina changed into a pair of jeans and a yellow lace shirt that revealed a matching yellow tube top. She completed the look with big gold earrings. Candace was surprised to see her wearing the latest fashion. She'd always been the one to experiment with new styles and would have to beg Karina to try them.

"Not that it's any of your business, but I'm going to meet my boyfriend and tell him that we have to find somewhere else to go tonight."

"You can bring him back here. I'll stay in the room."

"Never mind, it won't be the same. Anyway, I'm outta here." Karina dropped the sandwich into her purse and grabbed the keys from the table.

"Wait, Rina. When will you be back? I really need to talk to you."

"Nothing's changed, has it? Why is everything always about you? You need to talk to me tonight? You've been gone almost six months, Candi. You didn't need to talk to me about leaving me behind before you decided to go to Texarkana. You didn't need to talk to me while you were gone. You didn't need to spend the first Christmas and New Years without Mommy and Daddy with me."

"Rina it wasn't like that. I had to go. Everything was falling apart. And it's even worse now. If you just listen to me, you'll understand. My life is a mess. I have to tell you —"

"I have a life too, Candi. I have school. I have a future to think about and I have a date with Zander. You will have to wait, just like you left me waiting for six months." She yanked the front door open then slammed it behind her.

Candace didn't have any more tears left. *It's like I never left. She still hates me. Mama Ella doesn't have time for me. And when I tell them about the baby, it's gonna even be worse.* Candace wandered back into the kitchen and sat at the breakfast nook, lost in thought. The baby was unusually active, twisting and turning and pushing against her ribs.

The constant movement plus the now steady throbbing in her lower back made her shift positions every few minutes.

Until recently the baby hadn't been real to Candace. Other than the "flu" that had lingered for months and some ankle swelling over the past several weeks, the pregnancy had been remarkably easy. The baby had only started moving a few weeks before, well into her seventh month. But the activity today was dramatic and unsettling. The smell of Karina's sandwich still lingered in the air, reminding Candace that she hadn't eaten since she'd left Texarkana. She made herself a sandwich and slowly chewed, while rhythmically rubbing her belly.

Her back was hurting more and she felt nauseous. *Maybe that sandwich wasn't a good idea after all. A warm bath might help.*

Candace drew a bath. She pondered her future as she soaked in the claw-foot bathtub. As afraid as she was to face Ella's wrath when she found out about the pregnancy, she was comforted by the thought of being with her grandmother when it was time to give birth. Ella had been a Labor & Delivery nurse for years before she transferred to the NICU. She would know how to get Candace through the ordeal.

She got out of the bathtub, realizing that the soaking hadn't helped her aching back. She looked at herself in the mirror. Her belly was so small compared to other pregnant women she'd seen. It was hanging low and it was tight like a drum. She put the t-shirt back on and went to lay down on her bed.

If she were honest with herself Candace would admit that she wanted to keep the baby. But she didn't want to lose Nick. "God, is there any way to keep this baby and keep Nicky in my life? I miss him so much." She wondered if God even listened to her anymore.

She thought about the last time she'd heard Nick's voice; it was the day after her parents' funeral. It was a good thing that Candace had answered the phone because no one else would have accepted a collect call from the California Youth Authority. She resisted the almost overwhelming urge to pick up the phone and call him right then. She was so lonely and scared, but she still hadn't figured out how to explain the pregnancy to him.

She had wanted Nick to be her first but she was never quite ready to go all the way. Yet somehow that night with Rell, she'd been more than ready. Candace pushed the memory away. "It seemed so special then but now it's like it happened to some other girl."

She used her hands to push her belly up a bit. The baby was hanging so low in her pelvis it felt like she was going to fall out. "You were created in that one perfect moment. I'll never be ashamed of you." Tears started to leak from the corners of her eyes. "I can't give you up to strangers! I have to find a way to keep you. But I don't want to give up Nicky either! Those moments with Rell weren't real. Nicky is my true soulmate! I can't imagine never seeing him again. I want to make that same kind of magic with him and one day we'll have a brother for you." Candace rubbed her belly gently and after a few minutes she finally drifted off to sleep.

Hours later moonlight seeped into the darkened room. Candace woke, startled and disoriented. The sound of Anita Baker crooning drifted into the room. *Rina must have brought her boyfriend back, after all.* Karina had never had a serious boyfriend. The idea of her and a boy in Mama Ella's living room listening to love songs - Candace squinted at the clock - after 3 o'clock in the morning was almost unimaginable.

The baby shifted, putting intense pressure on Candace's back. Then a wave of pain washed over her, taking her breath away. Scared, Candace called out for Karina in a weak voice. *Oh my God, something must be wrong. It's too soon for her to come. She's almost two months early!* Candace needed help. She needed Karina. She waited for another cramp to pass. This one was much worse than the others. Her legs were shaky. She used one hand to hold up her belly and the other to balance herself against the wall as she made her way down the hallway. There was a fire in the fireplace, but no other lights were on. Candace hesitated while another pain gripped her, nearly causing her to fall.

Candace was stunned to see Karina lying naked on the floor in front of the fireplace. A tall boy, also naked, was kneeling on the floor between her legs with his back to the doorway. Karina's eyes were heavy and she was breathing in short gasps. At that moment, Candace was hit with a strong contraction and she grunted. Karina's eyes focused on her sister standing in the shadowed doorway. Distracted by Zander's lovemaking, she moaned and closed her eyes. When she opened them again, Candace was gone.

Taking deep breaths, Candace slowly made her way back to the bedroom where she collapsed onto the bed. She waited for Karina. The pain grew more intense. She called out for Karina but she didn't come. She was dehydrated, weak and oblivious to time. She dozed off and on, sure that death had to be near.

At 6 o'clock Karina slipped into the room. Seeing Candace curled up under the covers and facing the wall, she breathed a sigh of relief. Embarrassed by what Candace had seen, Karina took care to be extra quiet as she grabbed a pair of jeans and a shirt and eased out of the room. Through the fog of her pain Candace thought she heard the front door creak. She raised her head a few inches off the pillow and opened her eyes.

"Rina?" Silence.

Her head fell back heavily. She tried to breathe slowly and deeply. *I need to call 911. Something is wrong with my baby.* But she was too weak to get up. Within thirty minutes she had begun to pant; pulling and twisting the sheets in agony.

"Somebody help me!" she screamed. She felt hot all over. At 7 o'clock she struggled to get up from the bed. She had to get help. She walked slowly into the hallway, stopping when the pains hit. She willed herself to get to the phone in the kitchen, but seemed so far away. When she made it as far as the bathroom, she knew she had to stop. The urge to get to the toilet was overwhelming but she didn't make it. She held on to the side of the bathtub when she felt something pop between her legs and bloody water gushed out. She sank to the floor with her back propped by the bathtub and pulled a towel from the nearby rack to slide under herself. Another contraction hit, this one harder and longer than all the rest.

Instinctively Candace began to push, grunting with the exertion. One push was all it took. The baby slipped out onto the towel with a gush of blood and fluid. Her skin had a bluish-green tinge. Candace had no idea what to do next.

"I need help!" she screamed. She nudged the baby and then put her ear next to its tiny mouth to listen. "She's not breathing! She's not breathing!" Candace screamed. She opened the baby's mouth and slid her finger in to make sure nothing was blocking her throat. Then she pushed on her chest gently, afraid to hurt her. The little arms and legs began to thrash.

"Oh, thank God!" Candace cried, "You're alive!" Suddenly she was gripped with another strong contraction. She braced herself and pushed to expel the placenta. It lay between her legs, still connected to the baby by the umbilical cord. Catching her breath, Candace closed her eyes and absently smoothed the downy hair on the baby's head. Suddenly she realized the baby had stopped moving.

"No! Please don't die!" The words tumbled out of Candace's mouth. She carefully pushed against the baby's chest with two fingers and tried breathing into its mouth but got no response. Candace held the baby to her chest and sobbed. Heartbroken, exhausted and emotionally spent, she gently laid the baby down on the towel again. *My baby is dead. I killed her too.* The agony she had endured for so many hours was nothing compared to the pain she now felt.

In a daze she pulled herself to her feet. She bent down and placed a small hand towel over the baby, unable to look at her. She wet a washcloth and cleaned herself up but avoided looking in the mirror. She grabbed an armful of towels from the cabinet and tried to clean up the bathroom, leaving streaks of blood and mucus along the tub and sink, then stuffed the towels in the clothes hamper. She turned and walked on shaky legs into the bedroom.

Suddenly she was hot, burning hot. Sweat beaded her brow and her upper lip. *I can't breathe. I can't breathe! I have to get out of here!* She snatched the soiled t-shirt over her head and replaced it with the sundress she'd worn the day before. She balanced herself by leaning on the bed and stepped into a pair of panties. Realizing that blood was still trickling down her leg, she wiped it with the t-shirt and rushed to the hall linen closet to get the box of sanitary pads that Ella kept there for them. She ripped the paper off two pads and jammed them into her panties end-to-end so that she was covered from front to back.

"I have to go, I have to go, I have to go," she repeated. Her underarms were sticky with sweat and she felt nauseous. She pushed her feet into her sandals, grabbed her backpack and headed for the front door. She glanced into the bathroom as she passed. Her eyes took in the blood smears and the tiny lump in the middle of the floor. She turned around. *I can't leave her there like that.*

She ran into her bedroom, looking around wildly for something to put the baby in. Her eyes landed on the shoebox on the top shelf of the shared closet. Candace used the shoebox that had once held her father's treasured Air Jordans to hold her own treasures: concert ticket stubs, friendship bracelets, photo strips from theme parks, notes passed during class, and the like. She dumped everything onto her bed and ran back to the bathroom.

Trying not to look directly at her little girl, she lined the shoebox with a towel and picked up the baby and the placenta all at once, keeping the towel that covered her intact. Less than ten minutes after giving birth, she gently placed the baby in the shoebox and closed it. Her hands shook so violently that she almost dropped the shoebox. Propping it against her hip, she slung her bag over her shoulder and opened the front door.

Closing the door softly behind her, Candace hesitated. She had no idea what to do next. She looked down at the shoebox she was carrying. *I can't just carry her around with me.* She noticed the garbage cans set out on the curb in front of each house. Candace hurried to the garbage can in front of Mama Ella's house and removed the lid. Several neatly tied green bags of trash were inside. She held the shoebox in both hands and placed it on top of the bags but couldn't bring herself to close the lid. Impulsively, she took the shoebox back out and placed it gently on the grass next to the garbage can. She then backed away from it and hurried to the nearest bus stop, willing herself not to look back.

The bus stop was only a block away but Candace felt like she was walking ten miles in lead boots. She hurt all over – her back throbbed, her head pounded and her privates were on fire. She tried to block out what had just happened but every time she closed her eyes she saw the baby, so still, so much smaller than she had expected. Her mind was fixated on the eyes that never opened. *What color were they?* And on those tiny arms and legs that were so strong, like they were swimming in the air before going so still. Candace felt the anxiety begin to build again. Her body was hot, so hot that she wanted to strip her clothes off right there on the sidewalk. The bus stop seemed so far away. Her chest felt tight. She started gasping for breath.

Candace stopped walking. She stood bent over with her hands on her knees, taking deep breaths. No one pulled their car over to check on her. No one came out of their house to ask if she was alright. Finally, the band tightening across her chest slowly released and she was able to stand upright. Wiping her eyes with the back of her hand, she trudged towards the bus stop.

The bus stop was directly in front of All Souls Church and gave her a direct view of Mama Ella's house. Candace could see the silver garbage can resting near the curb and if she squinted she could see the black shoebox resting next to the garbage can. She sat on the bus bench, eyes locked on the shoebox. *How can I just leave her there? She's not trash; she's my baby!* Suddenly, she knew what she had to do. *I'm going to bury her. I'm going to get her a pretty dress and say a prayer from Mama Ella's Bible and then bury her. That's the Christian thing to do. Nobody has to know; nobody but me and God.*

When Candace stood up from the bench a sharp pain shot across her abdomen that was so intense it made her cry out and nearly lose consciousness. She grabbed for the back of the bench and gingerly sat back down. Her body was covered in sweat and her heart was racing. She waited to catch her breath and tried again, determined to do right by her baby. Squaring her shoulders, she stood up and started to walk back home. Her determined expression gave way to shock and horror when she saw the city garbage truck in front of Mama Ella's house. Blue-uniform-clad men made their way from house to house heaving heavy silver cans onto their shoulders, walking to the back of the truck to dump the contents and then returning the cans to the curb.

"No!" Candace screamed and hurried towards her grandmother's house. Without looking, she darted into the street oblivious to the red light and the minivan turning directly in her path. The loud horn and curses shouted by the driver caused her to freeze in her tracks. The minivan came so close to her that she stumbled backwards and dropped her backpack. By the time she picked it up and made it safely to the sidewalk, the garbage truck had pulled away. The shoebox was no longer in sight.

Candace collapsed into a heap in the middle of the sidewalk. *I'm so stupid. I threw her away like garbage.* The self-recriminations reverberated through Candace's mind so loudly that she covered her ears. "Zora, her name is Zora." Candace whispered.

Looking toward the house again, she saw Karina's car in the driveway. *She can't see me like this!* Candace used the hem of her dress to wipe her face and slowly got to her feet. The nausea was almost overwhelming but the cramping had slowed down a bit. She swung her backpack over her shoulder and began to walk. She made her way to the next bus stop, a block away from the church. She sat on the edge of the bench and waited, willing the voices in her head to quiet down, until the bus came a few minutes later

---

Karina strummed her fingers on the steering wheel, waiting for the garbage truck to move past Mama Ella's driveway. When the truck finally moved, she turned into the driveway. She had reported for her six thirty shift at the coffee shop on time but was so tired she asked someone to finish out her shift. Nearly an hour later Karina sat in the driveway bracing herself for her sister's judgment. She stalled while she thought about the last twenty-four hours.

Candace's unexpected return had thrown her for a loop. *She should've never left! And now she shows up as if nothing has changed? I'm glad I had Mama Ella, but what would I have done without Zander?*

The mere thought of Zander made her smile. Karina had never

been in love before. Yes, there had been boys who she'd liked but this was different. Zander made her heart race and her stomach twist up in knots. He made her feel pretty and desirable. Karina loved knowing that she affected him, too. Zander was usually confident in everything he did, but Karina had learned how to look at him in a way that made him lose track of his thoughts and stumble over his words. It was exhilarating.

But there was always a little voice in Karina's head telling her that she wasn't quite as pretty, funny, sexy or interesting as other girls. She had always mimicked Candace. Now she wondered if that was because she'd realized from an early age that being herself wasn't good enough. The competition for her popular boyfriend – girls blatantly trying to get his attention, fawning over him after games and slipping him their numbers – ratcheted up her anxiety. Karina was careful not to complain too much; she didn't want Zander to realize she was so insecure.

They had talked about making love for weeks, but Zander knew she was a virgin and wanted to be sure that she was ready. She knew he had been with other girls but tried not to think about it and it wasn't something they talked about. When Mama Ella mentioned she was going on an overnight trip, Karina decided that the time had come. She and Zander would finally become one. She was so glad that she had waited for the perfect person. Not like Candace, who'd given up her virginity to a perfect stranger!

When she found Candace at home that afternoon Karina's first reaction had been pure joy; she had missed her so much. But when Candace put her hand up to stop Karina from hugging her, the past came rushing back to slap her into reality. It was a double whammy when she realized that Candace was going to ruin her and Zander's special night.

Zander had been so sweet when she rushed to pick him up and tell him the bad news.

"Why the tears, baby?" Zander kissed the corners of her mouth in concern.

"My sister showed up out of the blue today. It's like her main goal in life is to ruin mine!"

Zander laughed, "You always talk about how much you hate this mysterious sister of yours, but you obviously love her. Maybe it's good she's back – now I can finally meet her."

"No! You don't need to meet her." Karina said quickly.

"Why not? Think she'll take me away from you?" he teased.

Karina's face flushed and she angrily pulled her hand away. She would never admit to Zander how close to the mark he was. Candace always got all the attention. Candace was the more outgoing, confident, sexy sister. She had laid in bed so many nights, missing Candace yet thanking God that she hadn't been around to meet Zander first.

"Who said anything about you meeting her?" she snapped. "Why would I be worried about her more than any of the other girls always swarming around you, Alexander? Either you love me or you don't."

"Baby, relax! You know I don't care about your sister or any other girl." His soothing voice calmed her. He pulled her close and whispered, "You're all I think about, Rina. I love you, girl! I've never felt like this before. I can't wait to make love to you."

Karina felt the warmth spread over her lower body. "But that's the problem," she whined, "this was gonna be our night. We could spend the whole night together for our first time and now she's spoiled it!"

"We have all the time in the world. Let's take your car home so I can chauffeur you around. We'll go to dinner and the movies and see what the night brings, okay? In the meantime, you gonna share that PB&J sandwich?" He nudged her playfully.

Karina blushed as she remembered what the night had indeed brought. Her exhilaration had been momentarily interrupted by Candace's appearance and the look of shock on her face. Luckily, she had disappeared as quickly as she had appeared and Zander's passion consumed all of Karina's attention. After the lovemaking was over they had slept in each other's arms for a while before Zander gathered his things and slipped out the door. Karina had overslept and barely had time to wash up and throw on some clothes and make it to work on time.

Taking a deep breath and bracing herself for a fight, Karina got out of the car. She skipped across the dew drenched grass but when she reached the steps she remembered the garbage can. *I'd better move the garbage can back to the driveway now, or I'll forget and Mama Ella will end up doing it when she gets home. Shoot, Candace should move it. How many Wednesday mornings has she missed?*

Grumbling to herself, Karina turned and walked to the curb. Next to the garbage can was a black Air Jordan shoebox. Frowning, she picked it up. Just then she heard a faint mewling sound coming from the shoebox. Hands shaking she pushed off the shoebox top. At first all she saw was a lavender and white hand towel. The sound grew louder so she moved the towel to the side.

"Oh my God!" Karina whispered, shocked by the sight of a tiny baby, still covered in bloody fluid, waving its arms and legs and opening and closing its mouth. Instinctively Karina gathered the shoebox to her chest as she hurried into the house.

"Candi! Candi! Oh my God, you're not gonna believe this!" Karina was frantic. She ran to the kitchen and gently placed the shoebox on the table. "Candi! Help me!" She ran into the hallway, keeping an eye on the shoebox, and threw open the bedroom door. Candace wasn't there. Next, she checked the bathroom. No Candace. She rushed back to the kitchen and looked at the baby again.

Suddenly, she recognized the towel. Karina ran back to the bedroom and saw the things on Candace's bed – the pile of momentos that she kept in their father's Air Jordan shoebox, the same shoebox she'd found outside by the trash. Karina jammed her fist in her mouth to hold back the scream. "Candi, no, no, no!" Tears streamed down her face as she walked slowly back into the kitchen. The baby was still moving its arms and legs, furiously trying to get attention. Karina stroked its cheek, murmuring to it while she tried to get her mind around the situation. She was afraid to pick her up. Just then, there was a sound at the front door.

She called out, "Candi! Thank God! What have you done? We need to get help . . ."

But it was Ella who responded. "Karina? What's wrong? What do you need help for? Are you hurt?"

Ella hurried down the hallway and into the kitchen but stopped short when she heard the mewling and saw Karina standing over the shoebox. Stepping closer, she put her hand to her heart and closed her eyes briefly. "Oh Lord Jesus, please help us." She instinctively went into action. "Go to the hall closet and get that bag of baby things that Sister Prescott gave me to take to the hospital. I think there's a receiving blanket in there that we can use."

She quickly turned on the fire under the teakettle and switched on the oven, opening the door so the warmth would fill the small kitchen. She then carefully unwrapped the tiny bundle and examined it.

"Lord have mercy, this baby cain't be but an hour or two old! Puny little thing; probably premature. From this blue-green color it looks like she had some gen issues but she's pinking up nicely. And those lungs sure are working good now! Rina, grab my work bag too."

Quickly Mama Ella listened to the baby's lungs, severed her umbilical cord and cleaned her up. She showed Karina how to introduce a small amount of watered-down evaporated milk on the tip of her finger and then transition to little sips from a bottle. The baby drifted off to sleep, sucking on the pacifier that had been discovered in Sister Prescott's charity donation. Neither Karina nor Mama Ella allowed themselves to voice their thoughts until the baby was settled down. Finally their eyes met. "Where's your sister, Karina?"

Karina's eyes overflowed. "I don't know Mama. We argued yesterday and then I went out. She was asleep when I came home – or at least she was in the bed. She was still there when I left early this morning. I didn't hear anything. Mama Ella, you don't think, I mean, Candi couldn't, could she?" Karina's sobs filled the tiny kitchen as the enormity of what her sister had done hit her. Ella rubbed her back and let her get it out, her own eyes brimming with tears.

"Listen to me, Karina. This is important," Ella said. "We don't know what happened. All we know is that your sister was here, and she left and you found a baby outside."

Karina swiped her tears away defiantly, "No, Mama Ella, we know that the baby and Candi are connected because the baby was wrapped in your towels and put inside Candi's shoebox and there's blood on the bathroom floor."

Ella sighed, "Yes, Rina, we know those things too and yes, looking at this baby, you and I both know that she belongs to your sister. The resemblance is remarkable even at just a few hours old. But we don't know the why of it, Rina. What we do know is that Candace is out there somewhere and she's hurting, scared, and confused. She is not the kind of person to leave a baby on the curb."

Ella began to wring her hands and her voice had a slight tremor. "She has to be in a state of shock to do something like this. Oh Lord, why didn't she come to me? Did she think I wouldn't support her, Jesus?" Ella couldn't stop the tears streaming down her cheeks.

Karina thought her heart would break witnessing the anguish on her beloved grandmother's face. Karina wanted to throw something she was so angry. "Mama Ella, you can't blame yourself. There's no way we could know that Candace had turned into the kind of monster that would throw her baby in the trash to die."

Ella angrily dashed the tears away and frowned at Karina. "You watch your mouth! Don't accuse her of more than you know. I refuse to believe that Candace knew that baby was alive. I don't believe she meant to do her any harm. She must've thought she was stillborn."

This time it was Karina who frowned. "Mama Ella, come on! The baby was crying up a storm and waving her arms and legs. How could Candi have thought she was stillborn? And even if she did, why would she put her in a shoebox for the garbage man to pick up? I'm glad Mommy and Daddy aren't here to have to deal with the shame of what Candace has done. It's bad enough people are gonna be talking about this family once it all comes out."

"It's not coming out." Ella said matter-of-factly.

"What?" Karina squealed.

"I said, it's not 'coming out.' This is a family matter, and it will remain a family matter. No one needs to know about the circumstances of this baby's birth. It's no one's business. We'll just take care of this angel until your sister comes back and learns how to be a mother." Ella's tone was firm.

"Mama Ella, Candace is not coming back. She's gone. Probably forever. People don't put babies out on the curb for garbage pickup and then just wander back home." Karina looked at her grandmother in confusion.

"I'm the head of this family Karina, and I'll tell you what we're going to do. First of all, as I said, we are gonna take care of the baby. She's tiny but she seems healthy and between the two of us we can manage."

Karina opened her mouth to respond but closed it again when Ella held up a hand. "I'm not finished. Second, we are going to try to find your sister. She may be having complications and she's definitely going to be in shock and not thinking clearly. I need you to start contacting people she knows but you have to be discreet. I don't want to bring the police into it because they'll start asking a lot of questions. Find a picture of her because we may have to make flyers. Finally, we need to make sure we're telling the same story. I don't want to tell anyone that this is Candace's baby yet, just in case we can't get her home soon. So we're going to say that Cousin Jolene from Texarkana brought the baby to me to take care of because her husband is really sick and she needs to tend to him. That's only if we're forced to explain the baby to anybody, you hear?"

"Yes ma'am, I hear you. But if Candi doesn't come home soon what are we gonna do with the baby?"

"What do you mean what are we gonna do with her? We're going to raise her of course. What else would we do with your sister's child?"

8

A NEW START?

Candace was exhausted when she finally tucked herself into a seat at the back of the bus. She stared out of the window but barely noticed the cars and people as they passed. Her baby's tiny pale face kept creeping into her thoughts. Tears slid down her cheeks.

She got off the bus with a large group and walked aimlessly through downtown Oakland. The cramping had started again and she needed to get to a bathroom. She hurried inside a Long's drugstore and gathered extra strength Tylenol and maxi pads. At the checkout counter she mumbled to the cashier that she needed a bathroom.

The older African American woman searched Candace's face. "Are you alright darlin'?" The obvious concern in her voice almost caused Candace to break down but she held herself together. Avoiding the woman's eyes, she said, "Yes, ma'am, thank you. It's just bad cramps. I really need a bathroom."

The woman studied her for a moment and then nodded her head. Slipping a key ring in Candace's hand she whispered, "It's supposed to be for employees only but if you won't tell, I won't." Squeezing Candace's hand, she continued, "It's the unmarked door on the left. Leave the key on the counter when you finish." The woman reached into the cooler next to the checkout counter and retrieved a bottle of water and put it into Candace's bag. "Make sure you drink plenty of water when you take those pills – it'll help them work faster."

Candace lowered her eyes, unable to meet the sympathetic gaze. "I will. Thank you." Once inside the bathroom she cleaned herself up, frightened by the clots of blood that passed from her body. Candace used paper towels and soap to wipe away all traces of her daughter's birth and retrieved a clean pair of panties from her bag. She then threw the bloody towels and soiled panties in the trash.

She made her way through the throng of people rushing to get to their desks in the high-rise office buildings and found herself at Lake Merritt. The body of water known as the jewel of urban Oakland was a historical landmark and a magnet for residents and tourists of all ages. Joggers and walkers paced themselves as they made their way along the three-mile perimeter, ducks floated atop the surface and children's laughter floated across the lush green treetops from Fairyland.

Too much walking made the cramping worse, so Candace sat on the grass and leaned back against a gnarled tree trunk. She berated herself for not confiding in her grandmother before it was too late. Ella would have taken her to the doctor right away. *Maybe they could've saved the baby. Rina already blames me for Mommy and Daddy. If she finds out about my baby she'll never speak to me again.*

Candace sat there for hours, crying then dozing off and on. No one paid her any attention – she certainly wasn't the only one hanging out at the Lake with nowhere else to go. She wanted to go home, but knew it was out of the question.

She watched the sun go down while her body stiffened, and the cramping turned to aching. Her thoughts turned to Nick. *Nicky loves me! He's the one person left in this world who I can still turn to – as long as he never finds out about the baby. He can't know about any of it!*

Stiffly she got to her feet and began to walk up Grand Avenue away from the Lake. Half an hour later she slipped inside a supermarket customer bathroom. She changed her pad and downed four more Tylenol, grateful for the bottle of water the drugstore cashier had given her. She felt like she was 100 years old when she crossed the street to a phone booth and fished Nick's last letter out of her purse. She picked up the phone to dial his beeper number, praying that he would call the unfamiliar number back.

Candace struggled to stand up when the phone rang a few minutes later. "Nicky?"

"Candi? Baby is it really you?" She could hear the smile in Nick's voice. "Damn girl, I ain't heard your voice in so long!"

Tears streamed down Candace's face as she stood in the phone booth with her back to the street. Her voice cracked with emotion and exhaustion, "I'm sorry I didn't call before. Everything's been so crazy and now I just don't know what to do or where to go . . ."

"What the hell you talking about? Where you at?"

Candace told him where she was, then crumpled back to the ground with the phone receiver still in hand while she waited on her first and only love to rescue her from the nightmare her life had become. *At least Nicky still loves me.*

The Nick who pulled up to the curb fifteen minutes later was a different boy from the one Candace had last seen nearly a year before. His Kangol bucket hat, Adidas tracksuit and shoes, and oversized gold chains made him look like a member of Run DMC. There was a newfound hardness in his eyes, a small scar on his neck and a wariness in his movements as he jumped out of a renovated 1969 Mustang and scanned the area. His expression turned to shock when he saw Candace sitting on the ground in the phone booth. He ran to her, pulling at her clothes and searching for injuries. "Candi! What happened?"

"Nicky, oh Nicky, I missed you so much!" Sobs wracked her body as disjointed snippets of a story emerged. "Aunt Izora died! She died, Nicky! I came home, but everything is just a mess now and I can't be here anymore. My body hurts so bad."

He carried her to the car and carefully placed her in the front seat. Frowning as he tried to make some sense of the jumbled story, he interrupted, "Baby, why does your body hurt? What happened?"

Candace tensed up, realizing that she had said more than she intended. "Um, it's just so much all at the same time. I had a cyst. I thought it was just a bad period but it was a cyst like I used to get, remember? It busted and it made me sick and then I didn't get to the doctor in time cause of Aunt Izora and I probably have an infection and then me and Mama Ella had this big ole fight and I just left. And Karina is like a whole 'nother person. I just can't handle it all."

With each word, Candace's voice rose closer to the point of near hysteria. Nick didn't understand much of what she was saying, but what he did understand was that she had come to him. He caressed the side of her face, using the bottom of her shirt to wipe her tears.

"Damn, I don't even have a tissue but that's okay. I got you." He tipped her face, so they were eye-to-eye. "Candi, I got you. Always. I didn't get all of what you just said but it don't matter to me. Don't nothing matter to me but you. You don't need nobody else. You're eighteen now so we don't need nobody's permission to be together. You and me, baby. It's all about us." He kissed her gently on the forehead.

An insistent buzzing caused Nick to unclip a pager from his waistband. Frowning at the coded message, he said, "We need to head to the spot."

Candace lay back against the seat with her eyes closed. She said, "Nicky, where is the spot? Do you have your own place? I can't believe we're finally gonna be living together." Her voice began to drift off as sleepiness overtook her.

Nick answered distractedly, pulling into traffic on the MacArthur Freeway. "I been staying with Johnny, but yeah, we can get our own spot, Baby. Money ain't no problem. I'mma set us up real nice. We can go shopping and get whatever you want. But first I gotta take care of some business."

A few minutes later Nick parked the car in front of a rundown apartment building in North Oakland and hopped out to talk with two muscular men, clad in black, standing guard at the foot of the stairs leading to the upstairs apartments. After a whispered exchange the taller man nodded. Nick returned to the car to retrieve Candace and her backpack. As they walked past the sentries the shorter man whispered to Nick, "Johnny ain't in the best of moods, man. Might not be the time."

Nick scowled, but his shaky voice betrayed his uncertainty. "What the fuck makes you think I need yo assessment of my brother's mood?"

He kept walking, beckoning Candace to speed up. He whispered, "Follow my lead and don't ask no questions. We won't be here but a little while."

Candace frowned and wondered what she'd gotten herself into but it was too late to back out. Then they crossed the threshold into a world she'd never imagined.

Johnny, an older, toughened version of Nick, sat in the dimly lit apartment on a fake leather couch with a gun balanced on his knee. At five foot nine inches tall, he worked out daily so his muscles made him appear solid and bigger than he really was. He wore a tight white t-shirt and baggy jeans. His chiseled features were marred by a thick scar running down his left cheek – the remnant of a knife fight in juvenile detention at the age of twelve with an older boy who didn't live to tell the tale.

He finished snorting a line of white powder, wiped his nose with the back of his hand and barked at Nick, "Boy what you doing bringing this bitch in unannounced and shit?"

Candace, despite feeling woozy from blood loss and pain, reacted instinctively. "Who you calling a bitch?" She shot back. But her words had no bite, as she had to lean on Nick to keep herself upright.

Johnny ignored her outburst. "What the fuck is wrong wit her? She on the pipe? I don't want no crackhead bitches up in here, Nicky. Get her out!" He turned back to his lines.

"Naw, it ain't like that, Johnny. Hold on a minute, lemme get her settled." Nick took Candace down the hallway to a dark bedroom. There were boxes of sneakers piled haphazardly everywhere and piles of clothes with tags still on them. Bags and cartons of takeout food covered the floor and dresser. He pushed everything to the side and found a blanket and pillow. "I'm sorry it's such a mess in here, Baby. Ain't nothing but dudes around all the time but I'll get it cleaned up for you. Naw, scratch that. I'll get us our own spot tomorrow. But for now just rest. I'mma go holla at Johnny for a minute."

Candace was too weak to respond. The bed seemed to swallow her up. She heard the hum of the brothers' voices and prayed they were working out their differences. She had nowhere else to go. While she slept, Nick cooked up most of the brick of cocaine that Johnny wanted out on the streets in the form of crack before sunup. When Candace woke up she felt a little better. The bleeding was still heavy but the pain wasn't as bad. She found the bathroom and went looking for Nick.

"What's up, Li'l Mama?" Johnny said, having dropped his surliness of the night before. "Baby bro says you gon' hang with us for a while. Says you his Li'l Wifey." Johnny laughed and patted Nick on the back. "So, if you his wifey, that means you gon' be the lady of the house, I guess. We don't have no other hoes up in here. This is where we do bizness, ya know what I mean?"

Candace nodded, as if all of this made sense to her. In reality, she felt like she was in a bad movie. She understood that being called Nick's "wifey" and the "lady of the house" was supposed to cancel out being called a "ho." Candace talked a big game, but she was clueless about the drug scene. The weed that Karina found in their room was the closest she'd ever been to drugs. Rumors were always flying about Johnny and his crew but she hadn't paid much attention.

Johnny broke into her reverie. "Hey, can you fix us some eggs or something?"

"Yeah, sure. I can do that." She said confidently.

Candace started gathering ingredients to make breakfast. *Guess it's a good thing that I've been cooking for Aunt Izora all these months.* The thought of her beloved Auntie brought tears to her eyes. Images of the past few days began to crowd her head, causing her hands to shake.

Nick noticed the change in Candace's demeanor and said, "What's up Baby, still not feeling too good?" She shook her head, afraid that if she opened her mouth to respond, the whole story would come tumbling out.

Johnny said, "Well, we got some medicine for you! Just what the doctor ordered. Come on over here and take a little toot." He motioned her to the table where the mirror with lines of white powder lay.

Candace looked from Johnny to Nick and then to the mirror. *Why not? Maybe it will help me forget.* She walked over to Johnny but looked to Nick for guidance. He picked up a hundred-dollar bill, rolled it into a tight tube and showed her how to slowly sniff the line of powder. Candace followed suit. The shock to her brain caused her to abruptly sit back on the couch. The guys laughed. Within a few minutes she felt clearer and less melancholy. Candace giggled, "Alrighty then, how y'all like your eggs?"

"Hey Baby?" Nick shook Candace awake. "You wanna call home?"

Candace rubbed the sleep from her eyes. She groaned and grabbed her stomach as the pains that had become her constant companion shot through her again. The past twenty-four hours were a blur of pain, snorting cocaine to dull the pain, learning to cook and cut up crack and dreaming up plans for the future with Nick. She had finally crashed to sleep what seemed like only minutes ago. "Is it morning again?"

"No, you just took a nap." Nick laughed.

"Call home?" She murmured. "They don't want to hear from me. Why you ask me that?"

"Cuz my patna told me he saw some people putting up signs about you."

"Signs?"

"Yeah, missing signs. You know, 'have you seen this girl' type of signs." Nick looked over his shoulder. "Baby when Johnny finds out there're signs out there he gon' get paranoid. He ain't gon' want nothing to draw attention to our spot, you know?"

Candace sat up. "Let me think." But her head was so fuzzy.

"You got some stuff so I can wake all the way up?" She asked. Nick brought her the mirror and she snorted a few lines of cocaine.

"Nicky, I can't go back there. Mama Ella and Karina hate me. They may be looking for me, but if I go back, I'll be miserable. I wanna stay with you, Baby." She reached out to caress his thigh. "Can't I stay here with you?"

Nick used his thumb to hold one nostril closed while he snorted a line. "You know that's all I ever wanted, Candi. Lemme think this through. Johnny be trying to keep his foot on my neck but I got my own ideas and plans, you know." He kissed the side of Candace's neck.

"He keeps trying to restrict my access to the game. Sayin' he didn't work this hard for me to get caught up. He even had one of the boys get me an application from the Community College in downtown Oakland. Do I look like some sucka that's gon' walk around carrying a backpack and books?" Nick sucked his teeth.

"I know you wanna be like Johnny, babe, but I think it's sweet that he's looking out for you. He's just trying to make sure you survive all of this." She made a sweeping gesture.

"You don't get it. I'm ready to launch my own thing – get my own spot. Johnny is doing good, don't get me wrong, but I know I can take the game to the next level if he'd just trust me."

"I know you can do anything you set your mind to, Nicky. But what if you could be a professional artist or an architect? What if Johnny made that a reality for you?"

Nick's pager started to vibrate. "Oh shit! That's the emergency code!" He ran to the phone and dialed a number, his hand shaking. Candace could only hear snippets of the conversation but the panic in his voice was clear.

Nick ran back into the bedroom, gun in hand. "Candi, get up! We gotta go now!" Reaching into the closet, he pushed the top off one of the sneaker boxes, pulled out the wrapped brick of cocaine and stuffed it into a duffle bag. Candace's eyes grew big.

"What's going on?" Candace saw the fear in Nick's eyes.

"No time to talk. They hit Johnny and the boys. They're on their way here. We gotta go! Grab the money from the mattress and put it in your backpack. Here, catch this!" He tossed a gun to her.

Candace yelped, having never touched a gun before. "The money? What money?"

"Look under the mattress!" He yelled as he ran back to the kitchen and scooped up the loose powder cocaine and the crack they had been in the process of cutting up and packaging. Wrapping it all in a towel, he stuffed it inside the duffle bag. They heard the squeal of brakes in the distance.

"Oh shit, that's them! Hurry up!" Candace pushed the mattress to the side and saw a few stacks of money bound in rubber bands. She stuffed them in her backpack.

Nick pulled her into Johnny's bedroom to get to the balcony. "Okay, you're gonna have to jump onto the top of that car." Nick said. "I'm coming right after you."

Candace opened her mouth to say something and the next thing she knew Nick had pushed her out of the window. Landing on her butt sent pains shooting through Candace's lower belly. Just as she started to slip off the top of the car, Nick landed and grabbed her leg to steady her. They carefully made their way to the BART station, ducking into people's backyards, hiding behind cars, easing into liquor stores posing as customers, even mixing in with mourners at a funeral at a West Oakland church. It was the longest walk of Candace's life.

"Stop crying!" Nick growled. "You need to act normal." His eyes darted back and forth, surveying the empty platform, willing the next BART train to arrive.

"Well, excuse the hell out of me!" Candace said. Hurrying away, she said over her shoulder, "This is not my normal! I wanna go home."

"Girl, home is not an option anymore!" Nick easily caught up with her and grabbed her arm. "Everybody knows you're my woman. They shot Johnny. They're looking for me, the dope and the money. Who else you think they gon' come looking for? My woman! Don't be stupid. The safest place for you to be is with me!"

Candace tried to absorb all of this information. Her brain was fuzzy from cocaine and lack of sleep. She didn't ask herself who "everybody" was that would connect her to Nick after she hadn't been seen with him in nearly a year. *If I go home and 'they' come looking for us there, won't that just put Mama Ella and Karina in danger?* She sank onto a bench. *I can't count on God to take care of me or them. Look what He let happen to my baby. I can't be responsible for any more Maxwells dying.* Sighing heavily and stood up. *As if I really have a choice.* Adjusting the heavy backpack on her shoulder, Candace tried to ignore the shooting pains in her abdomen as she walked toward Nick. "So, what's the plan?"

He smiled and pulled her into a hug. Thinking fast he said, "The BART train that's coming will take us to the AMTRAK station. We'll hop on a train and go wherever it takes us. A new start, Baby. We got money, yayo and each other! That's all we need."

Candace winced as another pain sliced through her midsection. "Okay Nicky, I trust you," she said.

Twenty minutes later, when they reached the Amtrak platform, a train was pulling in flashing the destination "Reno." Nick laughed and swung Candace in a circle, kissing her on the lips.

"Reno, Baby! It's a sign!"

"A sign of what?" Candace asked.

"We are getting married!" he screamed. "Today!"

His laugh was so infectious that she joined in.

By the time they made it to Reno they were too tired to do anything but check into a motel. Luckily there was a taco truck right across the parking lot, so Nick got them some food. Candace tossed and turned in the motel bed. Something had to be wrong. The bleeding hadn't stopped. The pain was always there, like a monster inside of her. Cramping, throbbing and then stabbing or slicing through her abdomen so viciously she would cry out. Candace kept snorting cocaine and drinking vodka to keep the pain somewhat under control.

Nick was in a different kind of pain. His pager had been

bouncing all over the nightstand for hours. Every call that he returned brought worse news. Around 4 o'clock in the morning Candace awoke to the sound of heart wrenching grief. Nick had gone into the bathroom and turned on the shower but nothing could drown out his sobs. Candace pushed her way into the tiny space.

"He's gone. Johnny's gone. I thought he was gonna make it but he's gone." Nick was bereft. "All we had was each other. Ever since I was five years old, Johnny been taking care of me."

"What? Where were your parents?"

"Neither one of us had a daddy that we knew of. And when I was five and Johnny was seventeen, my moms overdosed on some bad shit – heroin I think. I barely remember her."

Nick started punching the bathroom wall until his fist was bloody and a hole formed in the plaster. "Fuck!" Tears streamed down his face.

Candace cried with him. Her own grief about her parents was still fresh and combined with the loss of her baby, her despair was overwhelming. The two of them sat on the bathroom floor, huddled together, and cried until there were no more tears.

Nick kissed her, hungrily. "It's just us, Sweetness. You're my forever family."

Candace stroked his face. "And you're mine, Nicky. You're mine."

Later that morning they went shopping for new clothes and wedding rings. By noon they had exchanged vows.

Slowly awakening, groggy and with her eyes still closed, Candace reached across the bed for Nick. Not finding his head on the pillow, she scooted closer until she felt the warmth of his body closer to the edge. *He must still be cutting the crack and putting it into vials.*

"Nicky," she whined, "when are you gonna be done working? I thought we were gonna watch movies?" She pulled at his arm, causing the cocaine that he was measuring to spill to the floor.

"Nigga! Don't you know betta than to let crackheads be around the yayo when you workin?"

Candace's heart raced at the unfamiliar voice. Her eyes flew open, searching the room as she scrambled to cover herself. The voice belonged to a man she didn't recognize leaning against the bedroom wall. He had skin like peanut brittle with grayish brown eyes and a wine colored scar that ran from his right temple to his chin. He wore a black and white Adidas tracksuit with matching shoes, a heavy gold chain around his neck and rings with what looked like diamonds on both pinky fingers.

Nick frowned. "Stan, this is my wife, Candace." Nick never took his eyes off Stan. He turned slightly towards Candace and said in a reassuring tone, "Candi baby, this is Stan, the dude Johnny always spoke of with such respect. The man I been trying to hook up with. He's about to sample the yayo."

Candace eyed Stan warily and sat with her back against the headboard, a thin bedspread pulled up over her shoulders. "What's up?" she murmured.

Stan raised his chin in acknowledgement. "No disrespect intended," he said, but something about the way he looked at Candace made her feel even more uncomfortable.

Stan smirked and leaned down to snort the two lines that Nick had prepared for him. Clearing his throat and wiping his nose with the back of his hand, he said, "it's cool. No concerns about quality." He stepped back to lean against the wall again and studied Nick silently for a few minutes.

"Here's the problem, youngsta. You don't have enough to make it worth my while to fuck with you. You say you got a few kilos – okay, mad respect for coming through with weight. But you ain't got no connect to bring more once that's gone. What's the point of me working with you?"

Nick nodded. "I anticipated that question. I could run these keys on my own but I'm offering to bring them to you and run 'em with you as a sign of good faith. I'm looking at the big picture. I don't wanna be in competition with you. When you get to know me you gon' learn I'm strategic, reliable and a hustler. I'm not just a dude you should have working for you. I'm the man you should be grooming to be your number two when the time comes. No disrespect to anybody you got working with you now, you know what I'm saying, but I was born and bred for this shit."

Stan nodded slowly. "I hear what you sayin' youngblood. You got heart, I'll give you that. I'm gon' marinate on this. You'll hear from me." He pushed the curtain aside a few inches and tapped on the window twice with the ring on his pinky finger and reached for the doorknob.

"Hope you enjoy that movie with the missus." They could hear his laugh even after he closed the door. A few minutes later, the bass from Stan's car shook the windows of the motel.

Candace relaxed her grip on the bedspread. "So was that a good meeting, you think?"

Nick bit his bottom lip, "I cain't call it. You know as cool as it would be to have Stan – you know, somebody as high up in the game as Johnny was – help me establish myself in Reno, I know how to sell dope! I think I need to start recruiting some unaffiliated dudes to work for me just in case Stan ain't interested. I don't wanna have to be out here standing on corners and shit."

Candace laid her head on his shoulder. "Are you worried?"

Nick pulled her close. "Hell naw! I told you, now that I have you by my side there's nothing that I can't do." He kissed her neck then pulled back. Placing the back of his hand on her forehead, he said. "Baby, you're burning up. How do you feel?"

Candace avoided his gaze. "I told you I'm still recuperating from the cyst, so I don't feel great, but I'll be okay. You don't need to worry about me." She started to wiggle away, but he stopped her.

"I'm your husband Candi. I'm supposed to worry. And it's been almost a week since you said you talked to the doctor about the cyst. Shouldn't it be better by now? Do you wanna call your grandmother?"

Candace stiffened. "Call my grandmother? For what?"

Nick rubbed her arm, "I know you don't want her to know where we are but I'm worried about you. You're not getting better, Baby. She'll know what to do."

"I can't rely on Mama Ella to solve my problems anymore. I'm grown now. I'm getting better, I promise. I just need a little something for the pain." Candace circled her arms around Nick's neck and kissed him deeply. "I'm sorry we haven't been able to make love yet, Mr. Myers." She clenched her jaw almost imperceptibly. "But how about we make that happen tonight? Just use a condom in case there's still a little bit of bleeding."

Nick closed his eyes and groaned. "You know how bad I want you, Candi. I've been dreaming about it for so long. But not like this. You're still sick. I don't want you sacrificing for me. When we finally make love, it's gonna be perfect. I don't want nothing coming between us – no rubber, no pain, no holding back."

Candace pushed him back onto the bed, trailing kisses down his torso. "I love you so much, Nicky. Just so you know, you're not the only one who's been dreaming about us making love. Candace smiled and kissed his lips. She grimaced as she shifted positions. "Babe, would it be okay to snort another line or two? My stomach hurts."

Nick jumped up. "Coming right up! Maybe we should get you some . I think it works better for pain."

"Don't we need a prescription for those?" Candace asked.

Nick laughed. "Yeah Baby, a street prescription. I'll get it filled in a few minutes." He looked over at her while he lined up the cocaine, a faint frown creasing his brow. "I gotta keep you real close. Sometimes I forget you don't know nothing 'bout these streets."

The next day Candace went to the taco truck next to the motel to wait for Nick to come back from what he called a "recruitment trip." She joined the trio of girls she had met the day before. Lucia, a petite 19-year-old Latina with smooth sienna skin, high cheekbones, and long curly hair, began searching in the pockets of her tight jeans and slid her hand under the breasts that were barely covered by a skimpy halter top. Then she checked the leather jacket on the bench next to her. Finding nothing, she asked Candace, "you got anything on you?"

"What do you mean?" Candace said.

Pam, a slender 20-year-old Black girl with reddish brown skin, long braids and fancy acrylic fingernails said, "She's asking if you're carrying some dope. Whenever any of us has some we share."

Candace said, "Oh! No, I don't have anything, but I'll ask my husband for some yayo when he gets back."

Michelle snapped, "Don't ever do that! Don't ever tell nobody that you can just get dope whenever you want. You gon' get yo ass fucked up out here in these streets!"

She seemed to be the leader of the trio. She was a white girl who wore her red hair in an asymmetrical bob and her green eyes were so startling that Candace wondered if they were real or contacts. Her silver dress was so short you could see her black thong under a white fake fur coat.

Candace bristled. "Thanks for the advice, but I'm not out here in these streets. I'm with my husband and he takes care of me."

Pam shook her head. "Girl, we was all with somebody before we was out here on our own. You'd be smart to listen to Michelle."

Lucia joined in, "Yeah, it's hard to know who to trust, but you need to have people who got yo back. Who'll tell you which dudes are cool, which ones just want you to suck their dicks and which ones gon' take forever to cum."

Pam added, "And which ones are undercover police you need to avoid."

"Every once in a while, you get some crazy ass muthafucka – that's when you have to have somebody strong to stand up for you; somebody that everyone respects." Michelle said.

Candace listened in fascination. *They think I'm gonna be a prostitute, like them? What would make them think that?* A car slowed a few yards away.

"Duty calls ladies. Newbie, more lessons to share next time." Michelle winked and then sauntered over to the car on four-inch stilettos.

The girls finished eating and Candace asked, "Do y'all stay around here?"

Pam answered, "We been sharing Room 6 for the past week or so. But we don't do no work out of the room, you know? That's like, home. Sometimes a motel manager will be cool but sometimes they won't believe you're not working there and they make you leave."

Lucia chimed in, "That's what happened at the last place. Manager swore she saw clients coming in and out but that bitch was lying."

"The social worker lady that comes around all the time in that bright ass yellow t-shirt helped us get this room. She talked to the manager, so hopefully we won't get kicked out," Pam said.

Candace had so many questions – *Do they have a pimp? How much of the money did they have to give him? Are they afraid of him?* – but she didn't know how to ask without being rude. She hoped that as time went on they would trust her enough to share these kinds of details.

"Well, since we're neighbors maybe I'll see you tomorrow." She said as she turned to walk back to her room.

9

OUT OF THE FRYING PAN

Candace was happy to see Nick walking up to their motel door. She was outside at the taco truck with Pam and Lucia. Just as she was about to call out, a car pulled into the parking lot, tires screeching, and came to an abrupt stop. The doors swung open and men with ski masks covering their faces jumped out and ran towards Nick. Candace screamed and started to run to the motel but Pam and Lucia dragged her behind the taco truck. Candace struggled to pull herself free.

"Let me go! What are you doing?" She panted.

Pam whispered, "Shut the fuck up! Do you want to get us all killed?"

Candace struggled, "I need to help Nicky! They're gonna hurt him!"

Lucia yanked Candace back. "What the fuck are you going to do to help him? They're wearing ski masks, Candi! They ain't leaving no witnesses. Now hopefully he's just getting shaken down for his dope and he'll be okay."

They crouched behind the truck in silence. Ten minutes later, the car was gone.

"I'm going to check on Nicky now." Candace said standing up. She looked at the girls beseechingly. "Will you come with me?"

Pam nodded but Lucia shook her head. "Sorry girl, but I got money to make and it's hard enough to do this shit with a fake ass smile. I don't need to see nothing that's gonna put me in a bad mental space. I'll check in with you later." She walked over to a group of women smoking cigarettes a few yards away.

Pam gave a half smile, "Sounds messed up, I know, but it's true. You gotta make yourself into a whole other person, while you're doing this. If you can figure out a way to make it easier, that's what you do. Snort a line, pop a pill, smoke, stay high, you know?" She looked at Candace's confused expression. "Naw, you don't know yet. Anyway, let's go check on your dude."

Candace ran as fast as she could across the parking lot with Pam right behind her. She found Nick sitting in the room on the floor, propped against the dresser. He had been beaten badly. A cut on the side of his forehead was oozing blood and his lip was split.

"Oh no, your face! Look at your beautiful face!" Candace started to cry. "Nicky, who were those guys?"

"Apparently, I tried to recruit the wrong muthafuckas," Nick said.

"But why did they beat you up?" Candace asked.

"That was just the cherry on top," Nick said. "They came to rob us. They took it all, baby. Everything."

"What do you mean 'everything'?" Candace asked, looking around the room.

"Just that baby. All the yayo and the money. Now that I think about it, it had to be Stan. Nobody else knew what I had." He shook his head, looking more disappointed than angry. "Damn, I really thought he was a standup dude."

Pam had been standing in the doorway, taking it all in. "Y'all got more trouble coming. I see 5-0 down the block. They coming in stealth, but they coming deep." She drifted away from the door.

Nick frowned. "Fuck! Candi, listen to me." He pulled her close to whisper in her ear. "You still have the locker key, right?" She nodded.

"Okay, good. I need you to walk away, no, run away, right now, Baby. Right now."

Candace started to cry again. "I can't leave you here like this!"

Nick struggled to stand. "Candace, we ain't got time for this shit. You're my wife. They'll take your ass to jail, too. You have to go now. Those muthafuckas cleaned us out, Candi. What's in that locker is all we have in this world. Guard that key with your life. I'll be out in a few days. Hang with baby girl out there. It'll be alright. You a survivor. You hear me?" He dug in his pocket and pulled out a few bills and coins. "This is all I got left. Take it and go. I love you, Candi. I'll see you soon."

"Hey, Miss Lady, you still out there?" He said in a stage whisper.

Pam appeared in the doorway, pulling her coat closed. "Yeah, but I gotta jet to my room."

"Take my wife with you, please. I'll make it worth your while when all this is over," Nick said.

Pam grabbed Candace's arm and pulled her away while Candace called out her last loving goodbyes over her shoulder. The girls fast-walked to the end of the building and entered Pam's room.

Just as their door closed, sirens started to blare and several police cars swarmed into the motel parking lot. Cops jumped out and the girls could hear them banging on a door and then the loud sound of the door being forced open.

"I don't think they saw us," Pam whispered as she peeked out of the window. Muffled sounds of furniture being upended and the cacophony of police officers' radio static kept Candace frozen in fear.

When she finally mustered the courage to peek through the curtains, she saw Nick being pushed out of the room by a police officer. His right eye was swollen nearly shut and he was limping. She turned to Pam in shock.

"What did they do to him? He didn't look like that when we were in the room! I'm not going to let them get away with this!" She headed to the door.

Pam grabbed her and slammed her down on one of the beds. "Sit the fuck down, girl, before you get yourself killed. Where did you come from? You ain't never seen what the police do to Black men slinging dope?"

Candace was crying. "What difference does it make where I'm from? They beat up my man and they should pay for that with their jobs! I don't care if he's selling dope or not. Arrest him. But it's not legal for them to beat him like that."

"No, it's not legal, but it's real life, Candi. And you about to deal with more real life. I'll do what I can to help you while your man is down but we all have to do whatever is necessary to take care of ourselves, you hear me?"

Candace watched as the police car drove away. Another officer stretched yellow crime scene tape across her motel room door. She turned to Pam. "Thank you for your help. Don't worry, I'll only be here for a few days. I'll find a way to pull my own weight. Can I use your bathroom?"

Once in the bathroom, Candace counted the money Nick had given her. Combined with what she had in her purse, she had a total of one hundred and forty two dollars. She hid the bus locker key under the insole of her shoe.

Two days later, Michelle shook Candace awake. "We need to talk." Without her makeup and 'work clothes,' Candace was beginning to think Michelle might be closer to thirty-five than twenty-five. The faint etchings of crow's feet were visible in the corners of her eyes, her lips were thin and tight without lipstick, and there was a hardness to her face that Candace hadn't noticed until spending two days in close quarters with her.

Candace groaned, finding it hard to uncurl from the fetal position. The pain in her abdomen had grown increasingly worse over the past forty-eight hours. "My stomach hurts so bad, Michelle. Do we have to talk right now?"

"You been laying up in here two days already and all you gave me was fifty dollars. Pam said she told you that everybody got to pull their weight. You gonna need to start working."

Candace managed to sit up in bed. "You know I only had one hundred and forty two dollars. I gave y'all fifty dollars and spent thirty seven dollars on food for everybody so far. I only have fifty-five dollars to my name, Michelle! What am I supposed to do? I thought Nicky would be out by now." She started to cry. "How am I supposed to find a job?"

"I got this dude, one of my regulars, that wants to spice it up. You and me can work together, help you ease in. That'll put some money in both of our pockets." Michelle said.

Candace's eyes widened. "You want me to have sex with some stranger?"

Michelle snorted. "Are you serious right now?"

Candace bit her lip. "Michelle, I can't do that. I told you that my stomach was hurting; I had a cyst that burst like almost two weeks ago and I'm still bleeding and in a lot of pain. I think I have an infection."

Michelle pursed her lips. "You can take some Tylenol. He'll wear condoms. Believe it or not, some dudes like that shit."

"That's just nasty!" Candace blurted out without thinking. "I mean to each his own, but Michelle I'm not doing it, okay? I'm just not going to do that."

Michelle huffed in exasperation, "You don't get it, Candi." She leaned closer and spoke softly. "I'm the one saying the words to you but I'm just the messenger. Antonio is tired of you just laying up in the room he pays for."

"Antonio? Is he your pimp?" Candace said.

Michelle sighed. "You're so square. Antonio is my man. We go way back; we built this up together. I help choose the girls and make sure they stay in check. Sometimes I work with them, sometimes I stay with Antonio. He watches out for us, makes connections for us and things you don't need to know just yet. All you need to know right now is that he's taken an interest in you. He's doing your dude a favor by making sure you're taken care of while he's locked down. So he set up this date for you and me."

Candace's head was reeling. "Um okay. You and this Antonio person and the other girls have an understanding. I'm not judging you. I'm really not. And Antonio is doing Nick a favor by setting this up so that I'll be taken care of while he's in jail? Wow, that's uh, very generous of him, but no thank you, I'll be okay." She got up from the bed and began to gather her things.

Lucia and Pam came in with burgers and fries. "Candi Cane! It's about time you woke yo lazy ass up!" Lucia teased.

Pam fussed, "Stop calling her lazy. I told you she was sick."

Lucia retorted, "Antonio ain't buying that sick shit no more, right Michelle?"

Michelle said, "I was just telling Candi about the date Antonio set up for us. He's gonna ease her in on a three way."

"Aw, that's cool," Lucia said.

Candace frowned. "I really, really appreciate you helping me out these last couple of days." She finished zipping up her bag and put on her jacket as the three young women watched. "I'm gonna see if Nicky is getting out today. If not, maybe the motel manager will let me get a room with my last little bit of money."

"They release prisoners from the city jail in the mornings, so if he was getting out he would have been here by 11 o'clock at the latest and it's 2 o'clock," Pam said.

"You're sure they only release them in the mornings?" Candace's shoulders slumped. She rummaged through her backpack. Her face turned red, and she looked at each of them with a scowl. "Who took my money?"

"Bitch, you owed us!" Michelle said.

Candace hurled herself at Michelle, fingers curled like talons as she went for her eyes. With a guttural roar, she kicked Michelle in her knee cap, knocking her off balance. It was over almost before it started. Before Michelle could recover enough to retaliate, Candace was spent; the pain in her abdomen was so intense that she nearly passed out. She lay on the floor, moaning and writhing in pain.

Michelle stood next to her, heaving and rubbing her eyes. "Bitch caught me off guard. What the fuck is wrong with her ass? I didn't even get a chance to touch her!"

"Told you she was sick," Pam said. "Lucia, can you score her some ?" She examined Michelle's eyes and patted her on the back. "You're alright. You slippin' though," she laughed.

"We'll see who's slippin'," Michelle grumbled. "Just make sure she gets her shit together by the time I get back tomorrow. Antonio will be coming through. It's about time she meets him face-to-face."

Later that night, Candace slid her tennis shoes on, checking under the insoles as she did every time for the bus locker key and the key to Mama Ella's house. She stuffed her backpack in the crack of the motel door so she could get back inside and slipped outside the room. Looking carefully around the parking lot, she hurried to the telephone booth. She picked up the telephone and dialed "0". "Operator, I'd like to make a collect call; tell them it's Candi." She kept one eye on the motel parking lot while waiting. Finally, she heard the voice she'd been longing to hear.

Karina stammered, "Yes, yes I'll accept the charges!" Relief flooded her body. "Candi? Is it really you?"

"Karina," Candace whispered, "I'm so glad to hear your voice! Oh, Rina, it's so bad!" She glanced at the motel door. "I only have a few minutes. Can you guys come get me?" Her voice broke. "I'm not like them, Rina. I can't do this."

Karina twisted the yellow telephone cord while she listened to her sister cry. Instead of offering an explanation or apology, Candace wanted a ride?

"It's been almost two weeks, Candace. You didn't think to call and let Mama Ella know you're okay? You broke her heart when you did what you did and disappeared." She thought about the soft cries coming from the shoebox on the curb. "Do you even wonder if she's still alive? Of course not. Same ole selfish Candi!"

Karina was so angry that she slammed the phone into the cradle. *How could Candi be so selfish and thoughtless? She never even mentioned the baby she threw away like garbage.* Karina closed her eyes and took some deep breaths until the pounding in her head quieted down. *She sounded scared.* Karina reached for the phone to call her back, then remembered she didn't have a number for Candace. She looked over at the pile of Missing posters on the kitchen table, waiting to be distributed by church volunteers. "What did I just do?" she whispered.

Two days later, Pam handed Candace a bottle of water and two contins. "Sit on the edge of the bed and I'll help you get undressed." Candace took the pills and followed Pam's instructions. She sat motionless while the girl removed the caked-on foundation and blush and scrubbed at her scarlet red lipstick. Pam used another wipe to gently moisten her eyelids and then pull off the strips of false eyelashes. She then unsnapped the black bustier and went to unzip the denim skirt when she noticed streaks of blood running down Candace's thighs. Pam turned Candace's face to meet hers. "Are you okay? The guys you been with are usually cool."

"The blood is always there," Candace answered woodenly.

"Well, let's get you into the tub. Does Antonio know about the bleeding? I wonder why he has you dealing with customers when you're bleeding," Pam said.

Michelle walked in while they were talking. "Miss I wonder this, I wonder that, do you want to talk to Antonio about all the things you wonder about?"

Pam jumped when she heard Michelle's voice. "Oh! You startled me! No," she mumbled, "but something's wrong, Michelle."

Pam pointed to Candace who lay motionless on the bed. "She's bleeding and she's burning up. I think she needs to go to the hospital."

Michelle threw her an exasperated look. "Don't be so dramatic, Pam!" She turned to Candace and said, "Make sure you clean yourself up before Antonio comes by."

She slammed the door behind her. Candace didn't flinch.

"Don't worry Candi Cane, I'm gonna take care of you." Pam said, wiping Candace's forehead with a cool cloth.

Two days passed. No matter how hard Candace tried, she couldn't stay awake more than a few minutes at a time. She raised her arm or tried to, but it felt like it weighed a hundred pounds. She tried to speak, but all that came out was a low guttural moan. Even in her sleep she heard faint beeping sounds.

"No identification. Roxie Stapleton brought her to the ER. Fetid vaginal discharge mixed with heavy uterine bleeding; postpartum approximately 10 to 12 days, fever of 103.5, BP 70 over 59, tachy, tox screen positive for cocaine, methamphetamines, and cannabis, ETOH 2.3, white blood count off the charts. Started her on broad spectrum IV antibiotics. Dr. Patel went in laparoscopically to clean up the uterus. Picked out pieces of placenta. Saved her from a hysterectomy, but God only knows how much scar tissue she'll end up with. She's young; maybe she'll bounce back. Lucky she's alive."

Candace willed herself to remain still, so the nurse wouldn't realize she had finally awakened. *Who is she talking to? The police? I gotta get outta here.* But she knew that was a pipe dream. She wasn't in pain, exactly, but her body felt foreign and heavy, so heavy. She drifted off to sleep again.

"Hey there, I can tell you're awake." Candace was startled by the sound of the woman's voice so close to her ear. "Don't be scared. You've probably seen me before. I'm usually out by the motels or the alleys, giving the girls food or clothes or helping them out when times get hard. I always have on a bright yellow shirt with our slogan, The Sun Will Rise."

Candace had seen her a few times around the motel. She was tall with tattoos covering both arms and shoulder-length dreadlocks. Even though her skin was very fair and sprinkled with freckles, Candace could tell she was African American. The broadness of her nose and fullness of her lips reminded her of Nana Lanier. She had a take-no-shit attitude about her that caused the pimps and hustlers to steer clear, and everybody on the streets treated her with respect. Candace had seen her handing out condoms, talking quietly to women, and meddling in business that wasn't hers. Pam told her she helped them get the motel room the girls were staying in when Candace first met them.

"Yeah, I've seen you," Candace groaned. "Why are you here? And where is here, anyway?"

Roxie gave her a cup of water. "Here is Washoe Medical Center. Why I'm here is less important than why you're here." She gave a quiet, rueful laugh. "Or maybe it's more accurate to say let's be grateful that you're still here." Her expression turned somber. "You almost died, little girl. I just happened to be at the taco truck when Pam started hollering for somebody to help. By the time I got to your room you were passed out in a pool of blood, barely breathing. It's been touch and go for a couple of days."

"Nicky? Is he here?" Candace whispered.

"I'm assuming Nicky is that pretty boy you came to town with. You don't remember he got picked up? You've been staying with Antonio's Angels, so to speak. I guess you ran out of whatever money or dope you had pretty quick, and the girls showed you how to survive."

Candace's eyes filled with tears as visions of the horrors of the past few days flashed through her mind. "From the look on your face, I think you're starting to remember what exactly that's meant for you. We can come back to all that. I'm Roxie Stapleton and you are?"

Candace sniffed, trying desperately to hold it together. "I'm, um, Mrs. Candace Myers."

Roxie laughed out loud. "Mrs. Myers, is it?"

The heart monitor started to beep faster and Candace snapped, "Don't laugh, I really am married! Nick is my husband."

Roxie patted Candace's arm. "Calm down, no disrespect intended. You just look like you're about 13 years old right now. My bad. Okay if I just call you Candace?"

"Yeah, I guess."

"Candace, can I get in touch with your family? I'm sure they're worried about you."

Tears silently streamed down Candace's face, and she shook her head from side to side. "I don't know. I just want to sleep." She turned her back to Roxie.

"I tell you what, you get a little more rest, and I'll come back tomorrow. My guess is that calling home sounds really scary right now, even though it may be the thing you want most in the world. I promise we'll figure it out together. And I'll help you do it when the time is right, okay?" When Candace didn't answer she said, "They're not gonna let you stay in here forever. I can help you find a place to stay so you don't have to worry about going back to that motel, alright?"

"Look at me, Candace." When Candace's eyes finally found hers, Roxie continued. "Nothing you've done in the past determines your future. I promise you that. Now, I'm putting my card here on the nightstand. Call me anytime, day or night."

Candace closed her eyes. She didn't trust herself to respond.

The next afternoon, Roxie greeted the nurse on duty. "Hey, Miss Bridget, how is little Mrs. Myers doing today?"

The gray-haired woman patted Roxie's arm comfortingly, "Oh honey, you try so hard but you can't save 'em all."

"What do you mean? What happened?" Roxie's voice trembled.

"Chile, early this morning her so-called 'husband' showed up. Came straight from the jailhouse; still wearing the city issued flip flops. He came in here acting the fool! Whooping and hollering, talking about where's his wife? What happened to his wife? And when he finally saw her, he broke down crying! He wanted to know what was wrong, and she kept trying to shush him. She told him she just had an infection. He was demanding to talk to the doctor, but she did not want that to happen. She got all wide-eyed and kept shaking her head at me when he wasn't looking. So, I just played along with it and told him that she was doing much better, she was out of the woods, yada yada yada. I left them alone. Ten minutes later, that girl was up and dressed and signing herself out against medical advice!"

Roxie exhaled. "Damn. I was really hoping I could get her home to her folks. This isn't the life for her." She squeezed Bridget's hand. "Well, I'm sure this won't be the last time either one of us sees her."

Bridget nodded and fingered the gold cross hanging on a chain around her neck. "I'll keep her in my prayers."

Three weeks later Karina was hanging out with Sonya at Mama Ella's house playing matchmaker.

"What if I promise to give you free hot chocolate at the coffee shop every morning for a month?" Karina pleaded.

Sonya pursed her lips. "You need to fess up, Rina. What's wrong with Elliott? I've seen him on the basketball court. He's a good player and he's hella fine but he doesn't have a date for prom?"

"You're beautiful, smart and talented, and you don't have a date for prom." Karina pointed out.

"That's different. That's because a bunch of us decided the beginning of senior year on a girls-only Senior Ball, remember? You're the one who fell in love and dropped out. Believe me, I could have a date if I wanted one!" Sonya punched her in the arm.

"I know, I know." Karina giggled. "But Sonya," she whined. "Think how perfect it would be for us to double date. Best friends with best friends."

"You know he's not my type, Rina."

"Yeah, you're all about the nerdy, dorky boys, and he's a popular pretty boy." Karina laughed.

"Hold on a minute, you know I love a good-looking brotha! I just like the boys that are into their books and have a future planned out, cause that's what I'm all about. Shoot, that's what we've always been about!" Sonya raised an eyebrow at Karina.

"Zander is on the honor roll and was accepted to seven top-tier colleges, thank you very much! Just because he's NBA bound doesn't make him a dumb jock!" Karina shot back.

"Calm down, I'm not trying to insult the love of your life." Sonya laughed. "I'm just saying that his boy doesn't come across as focused."

"You refuse to get to know Eli! He's really sweet, he's got a good head on his shoulders and his grades are even better than Zander's! They got into the same colleges, Sonya. Zander just gets more of the shine cause he's the point guard." Karina said.

"And he's cocky as hell! But fine, Rina. I'll go to prom with y'all, but make sure he knows it's not a date – we're just going as a group!"

"Deal! But I have a feeling you'll like him." Karina grinned.

"I wish Candi was going with us." Sonya said.

"Me too." Karina said. She thought about mentioning Candace's phone call then decided against it. *Candi will come home when she's good and ready. Everybody's gonna be so mad at me when she tells them I hung up on her. No need in telling on myself!*

"Has there been any response to the posters?" Sonya asked.

Karina shook her head. "No, but the church volunteers put up new ones every week." Karina said. She picked up a magazine featuring prom dresses and started flipping through it. "Hey, look at these dresses. I like the off the shoulder ones. What about you?"

Sonya grabbed another magazine from the pile and flipped to one of the dogeared pages. "I really like this one with the puff sleeves and the sweetheart neckline, but it's so expensive."

The girls spent the next several hours daydreaming about prom dresses and accessories.

Pam checked her watch. "Candi, we need to hurry up. Antonio said to be back at the spot before six with new outfits and we still need shoes!" They had spent the last two hours shopping at the mall and were running out of time when Candace saw a bookstore and pulled Pam inside.

Candace ran her finger along the spines of the paperback novels. "I miss reading. I just wanna pick out a book real quick."

"Are you sure you have extra money for a book?" Pam asked, biting her lip. "I'm not trying to get on Antonio's bad side tonight cause you wanted to play schoolgirl."

Candace frowned. "Yes, I have five dollars to buy a damn book!" She grabbed a novel off the shelf and stomped toward the register, grumbling to herself.

"I can't believe Nicky got arrested just two weeks after I got out of the hospital! I wonder if Stan set him up again. How else would they have known about the yayo in the bus station locker? With everything that was stashed there, Nicky's probably gonna get real time." Candace swiped away a tear as she left the bookstore. "Now I gotta keep answering to Antonio if I wanna survive. This is so fucked up."

Pam hurried to catch up with Candace. "Candi, you need to be careful what you say and who you say it around. Lucia is gonna meet us at the shoe place and you know she got loose lips. Last time you bad-mouthed Antonio around her, he ended up slapping the shit outta you and making you work so much you ended up in the hospital."

"Like I need you to remind me!" Candace snapped. A few minutes passed. "I'm sorry Pam. You always look out for me and I'm being a bitch to you for no good reason. It's just I can't believe this is my life. It's like I blinked and everything got turned upside down." Tears started rolling down her cheeks.

"Aw Candi Cane, don't cry!" Pam used the bottom of Candace's t-shirt to dry her eyes. They sat down on a bench.

Candace sniffed. "I'm being silly. It's just that my Senior Prom is next weekend. If I was home I would be picking out shoes for that. And Graduation is next month! How did I let this happen to me?" The tears came harder.

Pam let her cry for a few minutes and then said, "I'm taking a big risk here but I got enough money to buy you a train ticket if you wanna go home. But you gotta go now, Candi, before we hook up with Lucia and Michelle."

Candace's eyes glittered with gratitude, and she grabbed Pam's hand. "Pammy, you're the best friend I've had in such a long time. But you know what Antonio would do to you if he found out?"

Pam squeezed Candace's hand. "I'm a survivor, girl. I'll figure out a story to tell him. If you wanna go home, I'll help you get there."

Candace looked down at her lap. "Have you ever done something so horrible that you can never come back from it? Something that will haunt you for the rest of your life?"

Pam frowned. "Fuck, Candi, I'm not trying to send you back if the police gon' be trying to lock yo ass up!"

Candace laughed. "No, not like that. More like a stain on your soul, you know? My grandmother is the best person I know. And my sister is like my other half. If they knew my secret they'd hate me. Really hate me."

"Then don't tell them."

"I feel like, if they see me, they'll just know, somehow. And the things I've done here – I just feel dirty. I'm not the Candace they knew and loved. I never will be again." Candace shook her head thinking about Karina hanging up on her. "It's too late. I missed my chance to go back."

"Look, Candi Cane, I don't know your whole story just like you don't know mine. And you never have to tell me your secret. But I promise I won't ever judge you. No matter how we got here, this is where we are today. And we gotta do the best we can with what we got right now. I'm trying to stay alive and figure shit out one day at a time. Fresno is in my rearview mirror, and it has to stay there. That Senior Prom shit and Graduation is from another life that you ain't living no more. So, if you ain't going back, you gotta stop thinking about it. Put Berkeley in your rearview is the best advice I can give you. Whenever I start thinking about my old life. I block it out."

Pam hunched her shoulders. "And when I can't block it out by myself, I pop some and smoke some weed. You need to figure out how to block it out."

Candace nodded slowly. "Do you have some ?"

Pam reached into her pocket and pulled out a few pills. "You owe me, though."

"I'll pay you back." Candace said and swallowed the pills dry.

Candace pulled Pam to her feet and hugged her close. Then they walked to the shoe store to meet Lucia and Michelle.

<hr>

Two weeks later, a guard escorted Nick from his cell to a chair facing a plexiglass window, with a telephone receiver hanging at his right. "Fifteen minutes, Myers."

Nick stared at Candace for a moment before picking up the phone. "I hate for you to visit me in here. I told you not to come." Nick's eyes mirrored the hardness of the other prisoners.

Candace frowned and snapped, "Why you have me sitting here holding the phone like an idiot? And you know I hate being out here without you, so you should know I'm coming whenever I can."

They sat in silence for a full minute, staring at each other. Candace smiled, "Hey Baby, let's start over. We don't have much time. So, how you doing? I'm so lonely out here without you. I miss you; do you miss me?" She said in a sing-song voice and placed the palm of her hand on the plexiglass.

"Why are you wearing so much makeup? What's wrong with your face?" Nick peered more closely at Candace through the plexiglass.

Candace covered her cheek with her hair. "Nothing. Why you have to be so critical all the time?" she pouted.

"Candi, don't try to play me!" Nick's grip on the phone receiver grew tighter. "What the fuck is wrong with your face?"

Candace closed her eyes briefly. "Nicky, it was taken care of, okay? This guy got out of pocket, but Pam's dude took care of it."

Nick's eyes narrowed. "Hold up. Something's not adding up here. Where were you at that some guy got out of pocket? And what does that mean? He put hands on you?" He stood up and his voice grew louder. "Pam's dude? You talking about that punk ass pimp Antonio? Why would he be anywhere around you? You work at a fucking bookstore! Why you even rubbing shoulders with hos and pimps while I'm locked down?"

"Myers, settle down or I'll terminate this visit!" The guard yelled from the doorway. Nick grabbed the chair and sat down.

Candace's legs were bouncing under the counter where Nick couldn't see them. She licked her lips. "Calm down, baby. You know me, Pam, Lucia and Michelle made friends back when we first got to town. If it wasn't for Pam I woulda died! So yeah, I see them from time to time when I don't have a shift at the bookstore," she lied. "It's no big deal. We went to grab some fish the other night and these dudes there got outta pocket with us. Antonio came through and straightened them out." Candace was chewing gum and talking fast, her eyes darting around the room.

"Is that right?" Nick said slowly.

Candace nodded and began to pull at the threads of her shirt.

"Baby, let me ask you something," Nick said softly. He stared at Candace for a few minutes without saying a word. She looked away and started picking at her cuticles. An announcement over the loudspeaker stated visitation would end in five minutes.

"Candi, are you using?" Nick asked.

Candace's mouth tightened. "What? Why would you ask me that? Using what?" Her voice grew shrill. "And where would I even get anything from? You trippin'!" She stood up and picked up her purse. "I'll see you next week. I'll try to get some extra hours at the bookstore so I can put some money on your books. Love you!" She hung up the receiver. Without meeting his gaze she blew him a kiss and hurried away.

Nick watched her walk away, then hung up the receiver. "Love you too, Sweetness."

———

Several weeks later, Candace stood in the shadows of the motel parking lot watching Pam, Lucia and Michelle get arrested for possession with intent to sell heroin, crack cocaine and . Nick was still in jail. She was all alone. She would need to fend for herself and keep herself supplied with the and crack that she had come to rely on.

She slowly learned which casinos she could hang out in to find johns and which ones would immediately kick her out. She figured out the hard way who was selling real crack and who was selling pieces of soap. Sometimes she begrudgingly accepted a warm meal from Roxie Stapleton but she would shy away from too much personal talk.

Candace grew more and more anxious. She didn't have a good sense of which johns were safe to get into a car with and giving blow jobs in alleys wasn't very lucrative. It was hard without somebody like Antonio to keep the johns in line but she refused to go slinking back to him. She finally decided that Ryder was worth the risk. She had met him at one of the casinos downtown. He was a pimp but he assured her that he wasn't trying to be *her* pimp. He just admired her hustle and worried it wasn't safe for her to be standing out on corners. He said he didn't mind setting up dates for her as a favor. And to top it off, he was very generous with and crack that he cooked himself. Candace was relieved to have found someone she could trust.

The first few dates went really well. Candace got high, the clients were well behaved and she got to keep the motel rooms all night. She made enough money to buy herself some clothes and toiletries and to get her hair braided. One day Ryder offered her a chance to service a private party at one of his clients' homes. Candace jumped at the chance when he paid her one hundred dollars in advance with the promise of nine hundred dollars more at the end of the party.

That evening Ryder dropped her off in an unfamiliar residential neighborhood and promised to pick her up later. A well-dressed woman with curly strawberry blonde hair ushered Candace into an opulent home. The starkness of plush white carpet and black leather furniture was offset by colorful abstract art on the walls. Jazz played quietly in the background. Candace saw nearly a dozen white men lounging in small groups, some drinking and smoking cigars. A few scantily clad brown girls were scattered around the room. They were working girls, like her. There were white women dressed in black pants and crisp white shirts carrying trays of champagne and hors d'oeuvres. Bowls full of colorful pills and mirrors covered with lines of white powder with straws next to them were placed strategically throughout the room. Huge bouquets of fresh flowers sat on glass tables. Candace felt the knot in her stomach release when she saw that it was a sophisticated party.

A man with startling blue eyes wearing an expensive suit beckoned for her to join him. One of the women hurried over with a tray of champagne flutes. Candace didn't notice when the woman slipped powder into her glass and swished it around. She took the glass and sat on the man's lap while he slid his hand up and down her leg.

"You're so sexy," he whispered in Candace's ear. "Come with

me," he said, after Candace downed her second glass of champagne. He grabbed a champagne bottle and led her down a long hallway. Candace started to feel woozy and put a hand on the wall to steady herself. He slipped an arm around her waist for support as they entered a bedroom. The man took a swig of champagne and put the bottle on the nightstand. He took off his jacket and threw it on the bed. He pushed Candace onto the bed. The empty glass slipped from her hand and bounced to the carpeted floor. Candace felt her eyes get heavy, then everything went black.

Candace struggled to wake up. Her head felt like it was filled with cotton, her tongue was as dry as sandpaper, she couldn't breathe, she couldn't swallow, she couldn't move at all as though she were paralyzed or weighed down by something . . . *what kind of dream is this? What's happening?* She forced her eyes open. Icy blue orbs bore into her eyes without blinking. The man's hands were clamped around her neck. His naked body was sweaty and lay heavily on top of hers. She tried to scream but no sound came out. His grip grew tighter. Candace had no idea how much time had passed. She flailed and bucked. Her hands clawed at his. Her eyes bulged. She was starting to weaken until she saw the champagne bottle.

Hope gave her a burst of energy as she grabbed the bottle and smashed it on his head. When he let go of her she wiggled from under him and hit him again, as hard as she could, on the side of his head. He fell backwards off the bed and lay on the floor not moving. Candace jumped off the bed. Her dress had been ripped open from neckline to hem and her panties were missing. She grabbed the man's jacket to cover herself, pushed open the window, eased her legs over the sill and jumped down to the grass below.

She was in a garden. On the other side of the hedges was the driveway of the house next door. She could see the top of a boat and an RV over the hedges. When she heard the man groaning she slipped through the hedges and crouched in the darkened driveway. She used the sleeve of the jacket to wipe the tears from her eyes. *I was never supposed to make it out of there alive. They drugged me. What did he do to me while I was knocked out?* Candace could still see his eyes staring down at her as he squeezed tighter and tighter. She concentrated on taking shallow breaths and willed the tears not to fall.

Suddenly she heard footsteps coming towards her. She tugged at the tarp that covered the boat, but it was too taut for her to loosen. He was getting closer. Her heart racing, she tried the door of the RV and was shocked to find it unlocked. She slipped inside, locked the door behind her, then climbed up into the crawl space over the seats. She reached into the jacket pocket, hoping to find something to use as a weapon. *A mobile phone!* She heard him stop in front of the door. He tried the handle but she'd locked it. He circled the RV looking for a way in but after a few moments she heard his footsteps receding. She waited a few more minutes to be sure he wouldn't hear her voice. She opened the phone. The battery was almost dead.

Karina stood in the foyer of Mama Ella's house and checked herself out in the mirror for the hundredth time.

"Girl, would you get outta that mirror? You look fine. It ain't like you haven't seen the boy just about every day since January!" Ella grumbled. She was tired, having worked a twelve-hour shift at the hospital and just picked up a fussy teething Samaya from Eugenia, who often watched Samaya when Ella was at work and Karina at school.

Karina ran her tongue over her lips to enhance their shine and smiled at herself. "Mama Ella, tonight's special."

"And why is that?" Ella grudgingly smiled at her granddaughter, grateful to Zander for putting a smile on Karina's face.

"Because he's leaving for D.C. tomorrow and it's the last time I'm gonna see him for months!" Karina's smile lost its luster as the reality of the impending separation hit her. She walked into the living room where Ella was and slumped into a chair. "Mama Ella! What am I gonna do without him?" she whined miserably. "He's the only person I have to talk to."

"What am I, chopped liver?" Ella teased.

"You know what I mean! After Mommy and Daddy died and then Candi went to Texarkana I felt . . . lost. Then Candi ran away and now you're either working or taking care of the baby. Zander became my new best friend. I tell him everything."

"Everything?" Ella's brow furrowed. "Karina, you can't tell that boy about your sister or Samaya!" Her voice lowered to a whisper and she leaned forward, capturing Karina's gaze. "No one can know the truth."

"No Mama, I didn't tell him." Karina sighed. "I guess I don't tell him everything. And anyway, why would I tell anybody what a horrible thing Candi did? How do you think that makes our family look? You don't have to worry. That's a secret that will never come out." Karina stood and walked over to the portable crib, marveling at the fact that Samaya had survived the first harrowing days of her life. "Poor little baby. How are you gonna feel when you find out what your Mommy did to you?"

"Miss Samaya will be just fine. She's going to grow up strong and smart, just like you. There's no reason for her ever to know what Candace did. When Candace comes back, the baby won't even really understand she was gone for a while."

Karina snapped, "Mama Ella, it's been months! What makes you think Candi is coming back? She tried to kill the baby and threw her away, Mama Ella. She's never coming back. Don't you get that?"

Ella scooped the half asleep baby up and rocked her rhythmically. "I don't know where you bought your crystal ball but I don't have one. What I do know is that your sister is a good girl, deep down inside, and that she can't survive without her family. We're all she's got, Rina, just you and me and this baby. Candace will find her way back to us." Ella's voice grew sharp, "And stop saying she tried to kill her. We don't know that. She might've thought the baby was dead already. You can't know what she was thinking or feeling. She had to be in shock."

"Believe what you want, Mama Ella, but there's no way Candi's coming back. And how could she have thought the baby was dead? She was crying! I heard her!"

"Yes, she was crying when you found her but that doesn't mean she was crying or even breathing when Candace put her in that shoebox. Live a little longer, Karina, and you'll learn that you can't know everything. Only God does."

"What I do know is that you're gonna run yourself ragged trying to take care of a soon-to-be toddler and work full time. What are you gonna do when I start college next month? Much as I love you both, I don't plan on coming here every day to babysit."

"Watch your mouth talking to me like that! Samaya is your only niece in the world, so yes, I do expect you to help out when you can. As for the rest of it? God will take care of the details. We just have to pray that Candace is okay and keep her business to ourselves until she comes home. Now I need to run next door to Genie's for a minute – watch the baby."

Karina hurried to get a cloth diaper to throw over her shoulder. "Please don't mess up my outfit, Samaya! I know you're teething and unhappy Sweetie but I wanna look good for Zander tonight, okay?" She kissed the top of the baby's head and rocked her to sleep. Just as she put her down, the phone rang. Karina ran to the kitchen to grab it.

"Hello?" she whispered, craning her neck to make sure Samaya hadn't stirred.

"Oh, thank God! I was so scared nobody would be home, Rina!" Candace could barely talk through her tears. "Listen, I don't know how long this phone's battery is gonna last, so we have to talk fast, okay?"

Karina was stunned to hear her sister's voice. "Candi?" She said.

"Yes Rina, it's me!" Candace whispered. "Rina, I'm in trouble, bad trouble. I need help. They must have drugged me. He was chok—"

As soon as Karina heard 'I'm in trouble,' Candace's voice began to fade. Karina was transported back to the morning Candace climbed through their window jabbering about the Sideshow and how much trouble she'd been in right before her 'soulmate' rescued her. *Here we go again.* She interrupted Candace's babbling, "Candi, is there ever a time that the world doesn't revolve around you? *I need, I'm in trouble, please help me* . . . Do you ever think about anyone else?"

"Rina, stop! You can hate me, okay? Whatever. This is life and death."

"You have the nerve to talk to me about life and death?" Karina scoffed.

The mobile phone battery beeped. *One percent! Oh no!* "Rina, listen to me!" Candi's voice grew more urgent. "I need you to send money for me to get home. I have to get out of here before they find me. Please, Rina! Send money to Western Union in my name, use Mommy's name as the password, okay? This phone is gonna die Rina, tell me you're gonna send the money, please. I'm your sister and I'm begging you!"

"You're gonna pull the sister card now? I was almost happy to hear from you but this reminds me how glad I am that you left. You only think about yourself. I don't have a sister anymore, Candace!"

"Rina, you don't mean that! Please send it! I'm in—"

The doorbell rang. *Zander!*

Without another word, Karina hung up the phone. She stopped in the foyer to check her lipstick before opening the door.

10

A PACKAGE DEAL

Ernest Bishop sat in the leather club chair that gave him an unobstructed view of the Bay Bridge, San Francisco, the Golden Gate Bridge and Alcatraz Island. Purchasing the three-story home in the coveted Hiller Highlands of Oakland, strategically adjacent to the cities of Piedmont, Berkeley, and Montclair and just minutes away from the exclusive Claremont Hotel and Spa, had served notice to his white counterparts that his infiltration was permanent and cemented his position in the ranks of the elite Black social circles that were so important to his wife.

Not that Ernest didn't appreciate the finer things in life. His bespoke suits, Italian shoes, Cuban cigars, and top shelf aged Bourbon were carefully curated. His prowess as a mergers and acquisitions attorney for a prominent San Francisco law firm had led to the establishment of his own respected law firm. Ernest had the right connections – fraternal, social, corporate and political – to get things done. But he never forgot that he came from a Georgia working-class family and was not destined for prestige. He had created his own destiny.

Ernest nursed his cognac and sighed heavily as Bettina breezed in and planted a kiss on his cheek. "Uh oh, cognac alone on a

Sunday evening, not a good sign." She sat down in the twin club chair and slipped off her pumps. Ernest looked up and winked at her, "You look like one of the models in the Ebony Fashion Fair, not an organizer!" He took in her snug fitting couture dress. "The rubies really kick it off, Betty," he said, referring to the earrings and necklace he'd recently gifted her for her birthday.

Unlike her husband, Bettina Bishop, nee' Sinclair, was born into the Black elite. Her father was a Morehouse man who went on to Meharry to become a doctor. Her mother, a Spelman woman, traced her lineage back to the original founders of her sorority and served as a dean at one of the nation's Historically Black Colleges and Universities. Bettina taught English to college freshmen and was an active member of social organizations that were committed to the cultural, social, educational and economic survival of African Americans.

Bettina preened under her husband's praise for a moment, then frowned. "Hey, don't try to distract me! What's going on with you?"

Ernest pursed his lips. "Your son. He and Elliott are up to their shenanigans again. They had Freshman year to get settled. Now it's time for them to grow the hell up."

Bettina sat up, "Oh no! I thought Alexander had straightened up his act. I was surprised, though, when Janesa Ward told me this evening that he and her daughter, Sofia, have been dating. I thought he was serious about Karina. I hope that boy hasn't been leading Sofia on; she's such an innocent young lady."

Ernest laughed, "They're not all innocent – trust me on that!" He paused, a slight frown on his face. "This may or may not be about Sofia. Hell, it may or may not be about Alexander - could be Elliott. You know I don't make any distinctions between the two of them – they're both are a mess. But at least Elliott handles his academics. Alexander tends to think he can get by on his good looks."

"He looks just like you!" Bettina teased.

Ernest rolled his eyes. "Lucky for him! He called earlier today sounding downtrodden. Talking about they're flying in tonight and need to talk to me in person. It can't be good if they have to fly all the way from D.C. to talk about it." Ernest downed the rest of his drink.

Bettina frowned and stood up. "I'll go get changed and then I'll put some food together. Sounds like this may be a long night."

"No, this is a father-sons conversation that's way past due. Not trying to be old-fashioned, but I gotta ask you to stay out of this one, at least for the time being."

Bettina conceded. "I understand. But be prepared to spill it when you come to bed!"

An hour later, Zander and Elliott entered the house. The young men were so similar in looks, bearing and style that most people on campus believed them to be brothers. In fact, their fathers had been best friends and the boys had been raised together. Elliott was such a jokester that he was frequently underestimated by his competition, whether in the classroom or on the basketball court, to the detriment of the opponent. Zander, on the other hand, came across as more serious and focused, when in actuality he could be flaky and indecisive until push came to shove. Both of them were highly sought after by the young ladies on campus.

The three men greeted one another with obligatory hand clasps, hugs, and pats on the backs, genuinely happy to be together for the first time since the holidays. After seeking out Bettina to say hello and reassure her that they had all their body parts, the guys came back downstairs to raid the kitchen and talk with Ernest.

"So tell me what's going on." Ernest said. He looked first to Zander and then to Elliott. "It must be big or you wouldn't have flown all the way home."

Zander cleared his throat. "Yeah Dad, I needed to talk with you in person." He straightened and bent his legs repeatedly, then flexed his fingers, eyes roaming around the room..

Elliott interrupted. "I do too, Unc." His voice cracked..

Ernest frowned. "How can you both have fucked up at the same time?" He walked over to the bar and poured another cognac. "Something tells me I'm gonna need another drink." As he was pouring, the guys walked over to the couch and sat down.

Elliott looked to Zander and then to Ernest, "um, maybe I should go first." Zander nodded.

"So, Uncle, I messed up – again. I don't want to have to keep asking you for money—"

Ernest began to speak, but Elliott said, "Please Uncle, just let me get this out? You always tell me I'm like a son to you and you've treated me like a son ever since Pops died. But his insurance can't possibly have covered everything since I was ten years old. Forget about basic stuff, but the AAU camps and tutors and all of that? And now college? Even with the basketball scholarship, it's a lot. And now we're getting ready for law school and that's gonna cost a grip."

This time Ernest did interrupt, "Elliott, I hear you and I appreciate what you're saying, but I made my decision a long time ago, so basically, you're trying to be all up in my financial business right now, which I do not appreciate. And stop beating around the bush, boy. What happened?" His tone was brusque.

Elliott hung his head. "I made a bad investment. And now I don't have enough money to cover my expenses for the rest of the semester."

"A bad investment? What the hell are you talking about?" Ernest's frown deepened.

"I know this dude who gets computers and sells them to students on campus at a discount. So, I invested some money with him and we were gonna split the profits 50/50. It was a sure thing, Unc! But, um, he's not available right now to get me my money."

Ernest stood up and paced the living room. "So what you're telling me is that you gave your, excuse me my, hard-earned money to some clown who was stealing computers and reselling them and he got popped?"

"I don't think he was actually stealing them, Unc. I think the deal was that he had a connect at the company who was using his employee discount to get them cheap and then something didn't go quite right and um . . . "

"Boy, shut the hell up!" Ernest shouted. "You cannot make this shit sound any better or smarter. And your stupid ass wants to go to law school!" He looked at Zander. "Did you 'invest' in this scheme, too?"

"No sir," Zander mumbled.

"Well, what's your problem? I may as well know everything I'm working with." Ernest shook his head and sat back down.

"Mine is worse, Dad." Zander took a deep breath. "I promised you last year that I'd do better with my studies and my time management and I've really been trying. My grades are great and Coach made me a starter . . ."

Ernest interrupted, "Are you trying to sell me some Girl Scout cookies or something? Get to the point, man! Yeah, you were fucking up last year, sniffing after every girl that smiled at you or opened her legs and you needed to settle the hell down or deal with the consequences. So what happened Alexander?"

"Um, this one girl – a freshman – has been hanging around a lot. You know, we go out sometimes or she comes over and stuff. And well, she's cool and all but now we have a problem."

Ernest hung his head. "Please tell me you're not talking about Sofia Ward?"

Zander stammered, "How, how do you know Sofia?"

"Because less than three months into her freshman year she's so sprung that even her mother knows how much she likes you, ya dumb ass!" Ernest growled.

Zander's eyes widened. "What? I mean, we've been kicking it, but it ain't serious."

The room was silent as Ernest locked eyes with his son. "So, what's up, Alexander?"

Zander squared his shoulders. "Okay, straight up. Sofia is pregnant. She says it's mine and I believe her because she's pretty square and she's only been hanging around me since she came to campus a few months ago. We agreed that she's gonna get an abortion but she's terrified her mother will find out if she uses her insurance. She can't tip off her parents by using her credit card. I don't have the money either. I would've borrowed it from Eli but he invested his money in computers." Zander kicked Elliott.

"So, the reason both of you are here is that, for once, you can't bail each other out of the dumb shit you got yourselves into." Ernest fumed. Looking at Zander, he scooted to the edge of his chair. "I have the perfect solution for you."

Zander closed his eyes and took a deep breath. "I knew you would, Dad! What should I do?"

"Marry her."

"What?" Zander and Elliott said in unison.

"Marry her." Ernest repeated. "She's beautiful, smart, comes from a great family, has her own money . . . I mean, what else are you looking for?"

Zander frowned. "Marry her? Dad, I don't want to marry Sofia! I mean, she's cool but I don't like her like that. I could never marry her."

Ernest laughed sharply. "You weren't thinking about all that when you put your dick in her with no protection, were you? How many times have I told you to wrap that shit up? You don't want to marry her? You're gonna marry somebody sooner or later – you might as well marry her. It'll make your mother happy."

"Dad, there is no way I'm going to marry Sofia. This is not 1950. When I get married, it's going to be to Karina – just not yet. If I have to be the one to tell Mom, I'll bite the bullet and tell her, but I'm not marrying Sofia. And I'm not having this baby either. There's gotta be a way for me to help Sofia get the money." He abruptly stood up and started to walk toward the front door.

"Sit your ass down!" Ernest bellowed. Zander froze. "Have you finished telling me what you will and won't do? In my house?"

Elliott stared at Zander hoping he was conveying encouragement to sit back down on the couch. Zander sat. "Dad, I meant no disrespect. I apologize."

Ernest closed his eyes and composed himself. He downed the rest of the cognac in his glass. "Had you not gone off half-cocked, you would have realized that I was being facetious. It's clearly not a good idea for you to get married to Sofia. You're not mature enough to be a husband and certainly not to take on the responsibility of being a father. I'm not even going to speak on how ridiculous you sound talking about Karina as your future wife in the same conversation as telling me you got this other little girl pregnant. Not to mention that Karina is a package deal – she comes with a toddler."

"I'm going to help you handle this situation and we're going to do everything in our power to ensure that your mother and Janesa Ward never find out about this. Do you understand me? But hear this loud and clear. This is the one and only time I will give you money to keep some girl out of trouble. Do you understand me? Wrap it up, zip it up, get your shit together or I'll cut you off. Do I make myself clear?"

"Yes, sir." Zander's relief was palpable. "But Dad, Karina *is* going to be my wife one day and I *will be* Samaya's dad. I know how that sounds but it's true." Zander's expression was resolute.

Ernest rolled his eyes and turned his attention to Elliott. "And as for you, Elliott, you're gonna have to take the hit for this one. I'll cover your debt but Betty has to be told something about why y'all flew all the way from D.C. looking for a handout. You'll be forever known as the failed computer bandit." Ernest chuckled.

Sonya and Karina were lounging in Sonya's apartment overlooking Lake Merritt. "Okay, let's get it over with." Sonya said.

"Get what over with?" Karina looked confused.

"The Zander issue."

"What Zander issue? What are you talking about?"

"Rina, ever since he went away to school every time we hang out, there's a 'Zander issue' we need to work through." Sonya laughed.

"You make it sound like I'm creating issues but I'm not. I just don't think he's being faithful."

"There are never any pictures of him with other girls on MySpace. You guys talk at least once a week and write letters, and when he comes home to visit y'all are inseparable. Seems like you're looking for a problem."

"I'm not looking for a problem. I just can't help but notice things. Like why did Zander and Eli come to town last weekend for only twenty-four hours? Who does that? All he told me is they needed to talk with his dad. Why the secrecy? The only thing he'd keep secret is another girl."

"You see what you just did, right? You took established facts and then inserted an imaginary girl into the mix. And you made it Zander's imaginary girl instead of Eli's – Casanova Eli! I'm not going to entertain this today. Instead, we're going to examine your life."

Karina rolled her eyes.

"Nothing against Zander, girl, but these are your best years. Your poor pussy probably has cobwebs and you are missing out on prime dick! This is why I've avoided monogamy in order to conduct research."

At Karina's raised eyebrows, Sonya said, "Yes, research. Dudes get to sow their wild oats, so why shouldn't I?"

Karina snorted. "Oats? Girl you been making oatmeal, cookies, and trail mix."

"Very funny. You know I'm discreet. But I owe it to myself to get to know me before I commit to making someone else happy. There are specific issues I have to resolve. For instance, what's my favorite position? Do I like giving blow jobs or is receiving more my thing? Does foreskin matter? Is there really a correlation between shoe size and dick size? These are critical pieces of information."

Karina couldn't hold her laughter any longer, "You should be on stage. I'll just stick with my Cream of Wheat, thank you very much."

"Come on, let me give your phone number to my boo's cousin. He's fine and manages the Sprint store in Emeryville."

Karina shrugged. "I'm not interested in anybody else."

Sonya continued, "Well, you're hardheaded, and loyal. But if you should change your mind, I'm telling you, he has very large feet. Not that I have anything against Zander. But you know my saying . . ."

They said in unison, "What's good for the goose, ain't got nothing to do with the gander!"

"You are a mess! Just keep on telling me your juicy stories. That's all the raciness I need until I see Zander."

The beginning of her Junior year of college was challenging, to say the least. Karina eyed the desk and floor littered with thick books, highlighters and index cards filled with scribbles that she had to transform into a coherent research paper to conclude the semester. A goal that seemed impossible to reach since Mama Ella broke her hip.

By the grace of God, Ella had exited the Cypress Freeway just minutes before the Loma Prieta earthquake hit. The devastating six point nine earthquake was felt as far as San Diego and Nevada and took the lives of sixty-three people. When Ella saw the Freeway collapse, she parked her car and went to help, knowing that her nursing expertise would be needed. Despite the efforts of dozens of people working to extricate drivers from the rubble, forty-two people died in the collapse. An hour later, Ella too needed help when a strong aftershock caused her to stumble and fall, breaking her hip.

Because of Ella's fall, Karina had given up her campus apartment and adjusted her work schedule and study sessions to help Ella get to her doctors' and rehab appointments and relieve Eugenia from caring for Samaya. Finding time to study and work on her research paper had been challenging, to say the least.

Even though it had been over two years since Candace left, Karina couldn't bring herself to get rid of her sister's things. Every so often she would freshen up the blue afghan, plump the pillows and rearrange the baby doll, as if Candace might suddenly show up and life would go on as before. Karina thought back to their last conversation. *Why did I have to be such a bitch? She said she needed my help. I could have at least sent money through Western Union like she asked. And why didn't she ever call back?*

Suddenly, the door flew open. "Ri-Ma, Ri-Ma, whatchudoin?" Samaya was like a small tornado, blowing through the house, wreaking havoc wherever she touched down. Karina scooped her up. "Thinking about you, Scoot. That's what I'm doing. Thinking it's time for you to go to school."

"Go to school like Ri-Ma! Go to school like Ri-Ma!" Samaya wiggled out of Karina's grasp and flew through the house. "Mama, Mama, I go to school like Ri-Ma!"

Karina had to laugh. *Sammi's too smart to watch soap operas all day long at Mrs. Jenkins' house. But sending her to preschool means answering questions.*

Months ago, Karina had discovered Samaya's birth certificate tucked away in Ella's bible. Ella had been annoyed about her snooping and downplayed Karina's concern that it listed her as the birth mother. "It's just to cover our bases," Ella said, reassuring Karina that she would get the birth certificate corrected as soon as Candace came home. *But Candi isn't coming home; so where does that leave me and Sammi? I can't expose Mama Ella's lie. Would she go to jail? Lose her nursing license? Would CPS take Samaya away from us?*

Karina threw a pen across the room. "Damn you, Candace! You're not even here and you're still fucking up my life!" Resigned, she picked it up and went to join her grandmother in the living room where she sat playing cards with Eugenia.

"So, Miss Samaya is going to school, I hear." Ella chuckled.

Eugenia laughed, "The child already thinks she's a mini you, Rina. She's probably in there now trying to get her little backpack together." They all laughed.

"She needs to go but I still don't quite know how we're supposed to explain the relationship." Karina said.

"What's to explain? And to who? You're her mother. Period." Eugenia said. "There's no reason for anyone to question the situation and, despite what I know Ella prays for, there's no reason to believe that anything will ever change."

Although Ella's eyes were sad, she nodded, "Karina, Genie is right. As much as it pains me to admit it, Candace may never come back. It's our job to do what's best for Samaya and that, my sweet girl, is for you to continue being the wonderful mother to her that you've been since day one. It's not what any of us anticipated, but I believe that God intended for you to do this for your sister, for our family. When and if Candace comes home we'll undo whatever needs to be undone."

"Sammi has been my angel baby since the morning I found her. I couldn't love her more if she actually came out of my body. That's not the issue," Karina assured them.

She sat down between the older women. "I'll be honest, though, I do worry about how it will affect my relationship with Zander." She reached for Ella's hand. "I love him, Mama Ella. I really do. I know we're young but I'm sure that I want to spend the rest of my life with Zander. But what if he won't raise her with me, as our daughter? What if he rejects her when he finds out the real story?"

Eugenia scooted closer and reached for Karina's other hand. "Honey, Zander is a good young man, as far as I can tell. But I'mma give it to you straight – you can't expect him to take in all of this. He doesn't need to know about your sister's business. Telling him will make him or his people overthink and ask questions that don't nobody have answers to. All he needs to know is that you are standing in as the mother of this child and you'll be doing it for the rest of your life. Y'all are a package deal."

Ella broke in, "As usual Genie doesn't mince words, but I agree. You know I like Zander and your relationship seems strong. I will say, though, that Ernest and Bettina Bishop travel in different circles from our folks. Whether that's because of her family pedigree or the success of his legal career, I don't know. But people like them tend to try to get up in folks' business. Could be to help or to cast judgment – we don't need either. All they need to know is you're the smart and caring young woman who's been taking care of 'her cousin's' baby since she was born and now, you're the only mother she knows. Samaya will always hold her head high, regardless of how she came into this world."

"The Bishops don't act like that, Mama Ella." Karina replied. "Mrs. Bishop has been really kind to me, and she's included me in her social and community activities. Neither of them has ever questioned me about Sammi, but we're talking about a future with Zander as if it's definitely gonna happen. It's not like he's proposed. He's Mr. Popularity out there at Howard and everybody keeps hyping him up about his NBA prospects. No need to put all my eggs in that basket." Karina's attempt at nonchalance fell flat as Ella and Eugenia shared a look.

Registering Samaya for preschool turned out to be a good decision. She thrived in the new environment and Karina needed whatever respite she could get. Karina's days were full with classes, a part-time teacher's assistant job, homework and helping take care of the precocious child. Ella's schedule was unpredictable and Eugenia's arthritis was making it more and more difficult for her to keep up with Samaya.

One February afternoon, Karina was drawn to U. C. Berkeley's Sproul Plaza by the sound of hip hop music. She found an enthusiastic crowd cheering as members of several Black sororities and fraternities performed step routines. Karina cheered and clapped with the crowd but soon broke away. She felt a deep melancholy settling in her spirit. *College is nothing like I imagined. I wanted to pledge! Mommy talked about how much fun she had with her sorors and how much of an impact they had on the community. But there's no time. . . there's always Sammi to think about. Damn you, Candi! Where are you? Why didn't you ever call back? Mama Ella will never give up hope, but at this point Sammi is more mine than she'll ever be yours.*

Karina was disappointed that Zander couldn't come home to celebrate her twenty-first birthday, but Sonya wouldn't let her dwell on his absence. "You know he'd be here if he wasn't rehabbing. And anyway, you're in your last year of college and it's 1990! You don't need a man by your side to have fun!"

Sonya had become the "it girl" of their social circle. An extrovert by nature, spurred by ambition to build a salon empire, she made it her business to keep up with the latest hip-hop, rap and R&B artists from the Bay Area: En Vogue, Digital Underground, Tupac, MC Hammer, Toni, Tony, Tone' and E-40. As a result, Sonya always knew somebody who knew or was related to someone influential and they knew and respected her. She planned a birthday weekend for Karina that was spectacular, from spa treatments, mani/pedis, to a wild party at a local rapper's mansion. As much as she missed Zander, Karina reveled in all the attention she got that night. She couldn't deny that Sonya's world was exciting but it took her three days to recover from her first hangover.

She was even happier two weeks later when Zander came home for an entire month. But he wasn't as enthusiastic. Learning that his NBA dreams would never become a reality had been a bitter pill to swallow, especially since he had only himself to blame. Zander had been rehabbing from a broken ankle and Achilles tendon rupture when he made the life-altering decision to join a pick-up game near campus. Buoyed by his local celebrity status as Howard's all-star point guard, he ignored Elliott's urging to walk away when the guys at the park cajoled him into a game and he tripped on the uneven, rough asphalt court. The resulting ACL tear – the second in the same knee – was career ending. Karina hated to see him in pain, but privately thanked God that she wouldn't spend the next several years competing with NBA groupies.

"I can't believe how much she's grown!" Zander carefully laid a sleeping Samaya on her bed. After a full afternoon of the petting zoo, climbing on the play structure at the park, and nonstop chatter on the way home before she zonked out, Zander was exhausted and his knee ached.

"Is it just me or is her vocabulary pretty advanced for a three year old? She held a full conversation with me about the animals, what she had for lunch and dinner yesterday *and* asked me about my dorm room." Zander laughed.

"I think she's around grown-ups too much." Karina admitted. She grew quiet. "I do love her. She might as well be mine."

"I think of her as yours. I mean, for almost as long as I've known you, she's been right there. She's your mini-me. I can't imagine you without her."

Karina looked into Zander's eyes. "I wonder how that might impact us. I mean," she swallowed. "If there is more to us than undergrad, you know?"

"What do you mean, if? You trying to dump me?" he teased.

"Come here, girl." He pulled her close and started backing into her bedroom, pushing the door closed behind him. They laid on Karina's bed, facing one another.

"First of all, I know that y'all are a package deal. I've always known that. And I want the entire package."

Karina started to respond but Zander placed one finger over her lips. "Shhh. I need to 'talk' to you." He started kissing her neck, her eyelids, her cheekbones. "I have some questions."

Karina moaned. "Oh, you do? What questions?"

"Well, first of all, jokes aside, are you sure you still wanna be with me now that I won't be an NBA superstar?" He looked searchingly at Karina. "You can be honest with me. I know it's an adjustment to make."

"Are you serious? I hated the idea of all those NBA groupies hanging all over you. I can barely hold my own against the college girls always trying to take my spot."

Zander shook his head. "You really think there's ever been a competition? That's funny! Baby, you took the top spot from that very first game when I came running up to you stuttering my name." They laughed quietly.

Zander kissed the corners of her lips, her eyelids and the tip of her nose. "Let me ask you another question, how long do you think you need to get comfortable in your teaching career before you start having babies?"

"What?" Karina squealed. "What are you talking about, having babies?"

"We already have one girl and there's gonna be a pretty big age difference between her and her brothers and sisters if we don't get started soon. And I want a house full of kids! You don't have to worry about money. I'm gonna be a big-time lawyer. I mean, it won't be NBA money but we'll be good." Zander's tone was serious.

Karina pulled back. "Excuse me! I have career plans too; you're not the only one who'll be bringing in money!"

"Rina, nobody goes into teaching to be rich," Zander teased.

"Point taken, but still, I intend to be an independent woman with my own career. But back to your questions. Babies? I want at least three more babies too, but don't you think you're putting the cart before the horse, mister? I already have one baby out of wedlock. This isn't gonna be a pattern with me!" Karina laughed, hitting him with a pillow.

"Details, details! We get through these holidays, we graduate, we get married. Bada bing, bada boom."

"Sounds intriguing, but I'm gonna need an official proposal, a ring, the whole shebang," Karina insisted.

Zander raised an eyebrow. "Don't try and play me. I will come correct when the time is perfect." He blew her a kiss. "And as for the rest. Have you met Bettina Bishop? Black society has been waiting for this since I was Samaya's age!"

They laughed until the laughter turned into kisses.

SHATTERED DREAMS

Karina's head was spinning from the activity of the last few months. Each graduation – Karina from UC Berkeley and Zander from Howard University – was cause for celebration and the wedding of the two young people was the biggest event that both extended families had celebrated in a decade or more. Bay Area Black society was abuzz.

"Are you happy, Baby?" Zander asked as he sidled up behind his bride, enjoying the breathtaking view of Lake Tahoe.

"Happy doesn't begin to capture all these feelings." Karina leaned back against his broad chest. "Wasn't it sweet of Nana and Papa Lanier to send us here for our honeymoon? I can't believe they still have a timeshare. They haven't traveled in years."

"We're just being blessed left and right. I definitely wasn't expecting Mom and Dad to give us the down payment for the condo. You know Dad is still fuming because Eli and I decided not to intern at his firm this summer. He thinks we're nuts to get on the struggle bus instead of working under him." Zander laughed.

Karina smiled. "Well, I'm proud of you guys. It takes guts to do it the hard way. And I'm so grateful to your parents! I didn't think we would be homeowners this soon!"

"We are surrounded by love, that's for sure." He snapped his fingers. "Oh, I meant to tell you. One of the attorneys at that firm I'm gonna intern at spring semester agreed to draw up the adoption papers pro bono!" He did a two-step dance move. "Pretty soon little Miss Sammi will be a Bishop too." He grabbed Karina's hand, spun her around and dipped her. "He can do it for you and me at the same time."

Karina looked away. "That's not necessary. Me and Mama Ella took care of all that last year when we found out Cousin Jolene died."

"What? That was Samaya's birth mom, right? She died? You never mentioned that."

"I didn't?" Karina frowned. "It was all around the same time as Mama breaking her hip. And then I needed to get Samaya into preschool. There was so much going on. Anyhow, that paperwork is all taken care of, she's already legally my daughter. And now, with the attorney helping you, the Bishop family will be official soon!"

"You think she'll ever stop calling me Zandy and move to Daddy?" Zander asked.

"Probably around the same time I graduate from Ri-Ma to Mommy!" Karina giggled.

"Well, let's go inside and talk about her little brother for a minute." Zander looked into Karina's eyes as he lifted her up to straddle his waist and backed into the bedroom.

Three years later, Elliott sat on the park bench, wiping sweat from his brow with the bottom of his t-shirt. "Dude, it's hot as hell out here. Are you ready to actually talk or you gonna keep punishing me and that backboard for whatever's bothering you?"

Zander tossed him a bottle of water. "Always making excuses. You're just out of shape." He wiped his brow. "But you ain't the only one, bro! Let's go watch people get paid to do this."

"Oh, now we can go watch the game? You gon' need to feed me and pay for the beer," Elliott grumbled.

Showered, dressed to impress – Zander in a FUBU leather bomber jacket, black jeans and Timberland boots and Elliott in a Coogi sweater, jeans and Jordans – and ensconced at their favorite table at a bar and grill overlooking the water while Game 6 of the 1997 NBA Finals played on every screen, Zander could no longer avoid Elliott's questions.

"So, what's up with you, man? Luckily nobody at work knows you the way I do. They're all fooled by this front you're putting on but I can tell you're stressed as fuck." Elliott pressed.

Zander nursed his beer, "I feel like I'm under a microscope, man." Zander sighed, "Paul just told me they're considering shortening my partnership track."

"Way to bury the lead, man! The last person to make partner had to wait nine years and you're gonna do it in four or five? The only ones who ever get that kinda break are the white boy legacies." Elliott got up to give Zander a hug and a pat on the back. "I'm so proud of you. And you know," his eyes twinkled, "all you're doing is setting yet another challenge for me. I'm nipping at your heels."

"You're already on their radar, Eli. You keep getting assigned to the major white collar crime cases. That trial work makes you essential to the firm."

Elliott chuckled, "You don't have to try to build me up, man. As always, I know my worth. Just like in college while you were the flashy player, who was setting you up with the assists and coming back for your rebounds? You weren't the only one with scholarship money, may I remind you?"

"Dynamic duo," they said simultaneously, exchanging fist bumps.

"So, is it just work?" Elliott asked.

Zander shook his head. "I feel like Karina is slowly just fading away, man. I don't know how to reach her. Two miscarriages and an ectopic pregnancy in three years-she loses a piece of her soul every time."

"It hurts you too. Even a blind man can see that."

"I'm not gonna lie, yeah, I want a son since I already have a daughter. To be honest, sometimes I forget Sammi isn't mine. Hell, she even looks like a combination of me and Rina!"

"Dude! I thought I was imagining it! I swear she's a little mini you!" Elliott laughed.

Zander continued, "But more than wanting a son, I want my wife back. She's been so intent on having a baby that everything else got put on the back burner, including forming the non-profit she and her mother dreamed about. So now she feels like she's failing in *two* areas. She's listless and irritable and don't let her be ovulating! Then she's ready for a brother to perform. It's just too much pressure." Zander downed his beer and signaled the waitress to bring another.

"If you're complaining about doing your husbandly duty then things must be pretty bad. Maybe y'all should try counseling?"

"The one time I said something about counseling she twisted my words around and somehow decided that was my way of saying I was unhappy with our marriage – that she was failing me as a wife and then took it to mean I must be out there looking for somebody to replace her." Zander shook his head. "Two weeks of making up and what happened? She got pregnant and fourteen weeks later, another miscarriage. Dude, that was right in the middle of the SunBright trial. I was this close to telling Paul I was gonna have to take a leave of absence, but luckily Mom swooped in and started spending more time with Rina."

The bar erupted in applause and trash talk as the unlikely Steve Kerr scored the winning basket to give the Chicago Bulls their second three-peat. When the noise quieted down, Elliott leaned forward. "Yeah, I can see how this great news and Rina wanting to give you all the good stuff she got, is making you so goddamn tense!" He shook his head in despair.

Zander had to laugh. "I can see how it sounds, an abundance of riches, right? I'm just worried about Rina. She is approaching this baby making like it is a J.O.B.! But I feel like the timing is off. I'm gonna be grinding these next two years trying to make partner. She's starting to get into a groove with her students; Sammi is doing fine in school. Why rock the boat right now, you know? But if I say the wrong thing, she'll run with it and decide I'm fucking somebody at work or planning to get a divorce."

"Damn! I didn't know it was that bad. I'll tell you what I think you should do." Elliott's voice dropped and Zander had to lean in to hear him. "This is my tried and true, break-the-glass, go-to remedy when all else fails, okay?"

Bemused, Zander said, "Give it to me."

"Talk to your dad. I swear, that man can fix any problem."

"You know what? You might just be right."

<hr>

Zander was surprised to find Karina waiting up for him when he dragged himself in after another fourteen-hour day of trial. Kissing her forehead, he kicked his shoes off without untying them and stripped, anxious to get in the shower and wash away another grueling day.

"Surprised to see you up, Babe. Everything okay?" he said as he strode naked into the master bathroom.

As usual Karina was distracted by her husband's physique and felt her body reacting. Shaking it off, she focused on why she had waited up for him.

"Everything is more than okay! Guess what?"

Zander closed his eyes and let the water run over his head. He was too tired to play guessing games, but he was also too tired to squabble with his wife. Before he could come up with a safe response, she blurted out, "I got a job offer today!"

"A job offer? Since when were you looking? I thought you liked working for Berkeley Unified."

"I did, I mean I do, but I'm being recruited to work for Bay Area Prep. Not only do they have fantastic resources and training for teachers but get this . . ."

Zander started toweling off. Seeing the smile on Karina's face seemed to lift some of his fatigue. He wrapped the towel around his waist. "What baby?"

"They don't just want to hire me to teach third grade, they want to give me a fellowship to focus on bringing more socioeconomic and racial diversity into the lower school. I'll be in charge of outreach and selection of full ride scholarship recipients for each grade level." Karina was beaming.

"Wow! That sounds amazing. You're perfect for it!"

"Zander, this is the first really exciting thing to happen to me in years! It's the kind of thing me and my mother used to fantasize about but I won't have to find funding."

"I hope you accepted!"

"Me and your mom went over the pros and cons and she convinced me to do something I never would have done on my own."

"Oh Lord, what has the Queen Bee done?

"She told me to know my worth and make a counterproposal. If I'm going to be creating an entire program and still teaching, I need administrative and financial resources."

"She's not wrong about that. Still, I know it had to be hard for you to push back on your dream offer."

"It was but I did it. And guess what?" Karina started jumping up and down on the bed. "They gave me everything I asked for!"

Zander tackled her and started raining kisses all over her. "Of course they did. They would've been fools to do anything else. I'm so proud of you, Baby. And so happy that you realize how worthy you are."

The following weekend Zander dropped Samaya off at his parents' house for a visit.

"Will you look what the cat drug in!" Ernest joked, grabbing his son in a long hug. "I never get to see you anymore Mr. Trial Lawyer."

Zander laughed, "Well then I must be doing something right. How many times did you make it to family get togethers in your early days of practice Dad?"

"Touché, son, touché. Are you ready to come put in some of that sweat equity at The Bishop Firm? I told Elliott I'm ready to change the name to Bishop, Bishop & Jeffers when the time is right."

"Dad, do we have to do this every time we see each other?" Zander said in mock annoyance. "By the time me and Eli will be ready to make a move, you'll be retiring, anyway. Don't be afraid of a little friendly competition." He lightly punched his father in the shoulder.

"Before you two get any farther down this well-traveled road, let me scoot in here and get a kiss from my first born." Bettina entered the kitchen in tennis whites and reached up to hug Zander.

"Again, with the first-born stuff! Let me remind you that I'm your only child. And I swear you get younger every time I see you, Mom."

With her close-cropped jet-black hair, radiant skin, and well-toned body, Bettina could indeed pass for someone twenty years younger. She smiled broadly, revealing straight pearly white teeth. "So you say. Eli may not be my biological son, but I've held him right next to my heart since he was born. You do remember he was my godson before he moved in with us ten years later, don't you? And then there's my daughter, Karina. Are you going to try and question that relationship too?"

Holding his hands up in surrender, Zander backed away. "No ma'am, once again I stand corrected. I'm happy to hold the title of firstborn." He grinned. "Actually, I wanted to talk to you about your daughter . . ." He looked around the room.

Reading his mind, Bettina said, "Sammi is downstairs sorting through paint and carpet samples for her room."

"Her room?" Zander frowned. "Mom, didn't we talk about this?"

Ernest interrupted. "Why would you be talking about how we manage our house? Our granddaughter has her own room here, end of story. Now, what were you saying?"

"Y'all spoil that girl something awful."

"Like she doesn't get the same treatment at home!" They all laughed.

"Well, that's for a different day." Zander continued, "I came over to thank both of you."

"For what?" Bettina asked.

"Well I had no idea what Dad meant when he said, 'I'll take care of it, son' when I spoke with him last month about Rina. I've been really worried about her. The miscarriages had her spiraling, but this new job that mysteriously fell in her lap is bringing back the Rina I remember. She's excited! Staying up til all hours of the night, researching and planning."

Ernest beamed. "Good!"

"We all knew Karina would be fine, it just took her a little time to get her footing." Bettina responded. "I don't know why you're thanking us."

"Mom, I know the signs of a Queen Betty Bishop maneuver when I see them."

Ernest started chuckling but stopped abruptly when Betty cut her eyes at him.

"And what do you mean by that?" She said with a raised eyebrow.

"This is a sweetheart deal that very few baby teachers could ever hope for. And I happen to remember you mentioning that one of your sorors is affiliated with Bay Area Prep."

"Hmm, you do have a good memory. That will serve you well in your legal career." The dimple in Bettina's left cheek made a quick appearance. "It's true that Janesa Ward serves on the Board of Bay Area Prep, however you're making a leap without supporting evidence, counselor.

Zander glanced at his father. "Janesa Ward is your contact?"

Ernest raised his eyebrows but remained silent.

Bettina frowned, "Yes, she is. I know you're not worried about that old dalliance with Sofia coming out, are you?"

"Dalliance," Zander grinned. "Who uses that word anymore? But in answer to your question, Mother, I'd rather Karina not know that Sofia and I dated. You know she trips about the silliest stuff. And I haven't seen Sofia in years. I was surprised when she transferred in the middle of her Freshman year. I don't even know where she went."

"She lives in Atlanta. She transferred to one of the schools down there. I'm not sure which one. I know she doesn't come home too often because Janesa always complains about not seeing her enough. In any event, I can't imagine Janesa bringing up your dalliance to your wife. I doubt she even remembers!"

"Back to the matter at hand. I will neither confirm nor deny your assumption that I had any involvement in the job offer to Karina, but my daughter-in-law is highly qualified for this position. Not only does she have the academic credentials, she also has the drive to fulfill her mother's legacy. I've done my homework son, and I understand that Jewel Maxwell was well on her way to establishing something quite similar to the program that Karina will create for Bay Area Prep. This job will help her get back on her feet."

Bettina stared out of the kitchen window. "There's nothing like the hole in your heart from losing babies. Other people can't quite understand, maybe because they haven't felt them in their bodies, I don't know. But it's a loss that you never quite recover from. Karina has lost so much. Her parents, her sister, those babies. Every woman has to figure out how to deal with loss, grief, depression, what-have-you, in their own way. Some people go to therapy, some exercise, some lose themselves in work, some just lose themselves. Our Karina will not be lost. Not on my watch."

Zander wrapped his arms around his mother. "And that's why you will forever be the Queen Bee of this family. Thank you, Mother. I love you."

Bettina shook off the melancholy moment. "Of course, you do! I raised you right!"

Ernest grumbled, "And I just paid the tab. I didn't have nothing to do with the outcome, I guess."

Bettina tousled his hair. "Oh, hush up, you big baby. You need some attention, go find our granddaughter so she can love on you."

"Good idea! She's the only one who really appreciates me around here!" Ernest headed downstairs. "Scoot! What ya doing down there? You didn't even come give your Granddad a hug!"

Bettina turned to Zander, "I'm so glad that you and Karina married, Alexander. I'll admit that you had me a little worried about your college shenanigans, but when you committed to Karina and Samaya you made me very proud. Karina is the daughter I never had, she wears her heart on her sleeve and she loves so hard, it's really my pleasure to help her in any way I can."

"Remember when you wanted me to marry one of your high society friends' daughters?" Zander teased.

Bettina hit him with a dish towel. "Boy hush. It wasn't a 'high society' thing. It was more about the familiarity of the people you had grown up with and the group in which we socialized but I promised myself I'd never be like my mother. She fought me tooth and nail when I told her I was in love with Ernest, all because he didn't come from 'the right family.' She cared about her social standing more than she did about my happiness."

"I always wondered why we rarely saw Grandmother and Grandfather Sinclair growing up, but once they passed I didn't think much about it," Zander reflected.

"I chose Ernest, and he gave me unconditional love. I've never regretted that decision. And that's all I've ever wanted for you, son. Now get on outta here and make partner so you can gloat!"

Although there was a party going on downstairs, Ella and Bettina shared a quiet moment on the balcony of Zander and Karina's new home.

"I know they think this is their celebration," Bettina said, "but I feel like it belongs to us! Look at our babies, Ella!"

Ella smiled wide. "Girl, look at God! I prayed every day that Karina would come through the dark years whole. And that she and Samaya would build a life of love and safety with your son. I'll be honest with you, for a while I worried that she leaned too heavily on Alexander for her strength. But she's come into her own. As a wife, mother, teacher, and leader. My prayers have been answered."

Bettina reached over to squeeze Ella's hand. "Quiet as it's kept, Alexander has been the one leaning. Karina and Sammi made him grow up, and none too soon! That boy would be lost without his ladies."

The house was filled to capacity with an eclectic mixture of Zander and Karina's friends and colleagues. The décor was upscale with top-of-the-line kitchen appliances, overstuffed leather couches, and gleaming hardwood floors. The focal point of the room was the oil painting, which hung above the fireplace, that Zander commissioned of Mama Ella, Karina, and Samaya-three generations of strong Black women.

Ernest called everyone into the great room in his booming voice. "Alright y'all, let's come together to give some acknowledgment to these young people. I was a bit disappointed when the boys decided to get on the struggle bus instead of coming to the firm that was their birthright —"

Calvin Rhodes, his friend of 30 years, yelled out, "It takes a strong man to admit defeat Ern. Be strong!" Laughter erupted.

"As I was saying," Ernest rolled his eyes and continued. "I was disappointed but I couldn't be prouder now. I wouldn't have cut them any slack, but they would've always wondered if they could make it on their own. My boys answered that question for themselves and anybody else who might wonder. May I present to you the only men to have made partner at Smythe Chastain in only five years and drumroll please: the only Black partners in the history of the firm."

The attendees burst out in joy with high-fives and clapping. Elliott gave an exaggerated bow and Zander performed a pretty good impression of Michael Jackson moonwalking.

"Let's raise our glasses to the future of the legal profession," Ernest continued.

"Hold on a minute," Zander interrupted. "Even better than the promotion and our purchase of this house – that my father failed to mention." Twitters of laughter broke out. Zander reached out to pull Karina closer to his side. "Karina and I have been blessed by God's grace. We are expecting the arrival of our son in about three and a half months, y'all!"

Karina basked in the attention. Her loose-fitting dress concealed the small baby bump, so only a few people had even suspected that she was pregnant. Bettina pulled Karina aside. "I can't believe you've been keeping the baby a secret all this time."

"We've had so many disappointments that we decided to hold off until we knew it was real."

"I understand, I just wish I could've been there for you. It must've been scary for you these last few months. But that's over with now. And you're going to get your boy!" Bettina radiated with joy.

"Brace yourself, Rina. Raising boys is very different from raising girls. Samaya has been a walk in the park compared to what you – *what we* – are about to experience!" She laughed heartily, clearly looking forward to the future.

"Alexander was so headstrong; you couldn't tell that boy anything! Alexander was worse than Elliott if you can imagine that! Right after his Junior year of high school he refused to participate in Jack & Jill activities. 'Smelling hisself' is what the old folks call it. He ran around with his hair all crazy trying to look like one of those rappers. All he'd listen to was rap or maybe it was hip hop, and he changed his name to something he thought was 'cool,' I can't remember what it was right now but we weren't having it. He was just a mess."

She took a breath, "It was touch and go there for a bit between him and Ernest. They're both so stubborn. Honey, I had to pray through it. Senior year he pulled himself together. Started calling himself Zander, and brought his grades back up. He met you around that time, Karina. You were good for him. You always have been." Bettina pulled Karina in for a hug.

"And we're going to have so much fun preparing Miss Samaya to flourish. With you teaching at Bay Area Prep and her making lifelong friends with the right set, she's well on her way. I've already been laying the foundation with my sorors to be prepared to welcome my granddaughter, because you know it's never too soon! And now with this little boy coming! Baby, Ernest is beside himself!"

"Mom Betty, I am ready for all of it! I can't wait to meet our son. I want to thank you for embracing Sammi like you have. She's so lucky to have you as a grandmother."

"Hush up now! We're the lucky ones. Being her grandmother has brought me more joy than you know." She squeezed Karina's hand. Bettina had never tried to replace Jewel, but over the years she had nurtured a relationship with Karina that nearly filled that void.

As excited as everyone was about the arrival of the long-awaited baby boy, there was also cause for concern. Over the next few months, Karina started having debilitating headaches. Her blood pressure was so dangerously high that she was put on bed rest for the remainder of the pregnancy. She was adamantly against a C-section; she wanted to deliver naturally so that she and Zander could share the entire experience.

She was relieved when the contractions finally began. Zander drove Karina to the hospital and a few hours later it was time to push. "We're going to meet our boy soon, babe!" Karina beamed at Zander. The monitors in the Labor & Delivery room reassured them that their son's heartbeat was strong but it was taking longer than they expected. Zander blotted Karina's forehead with a cool cloth. They readied themselves for the next contraction.

"Okay, here we go, Karina, you want to push steadily through the entire contraction." Dr. Lenoir said.

Karina mustered all of her strength and began to push, using Zander's arm for leverage. "Stop pushing, Karina," Dr. Lenoir said, unexpectedly, while she reviewed the printout spewing from the monitor.

Karina panted, "No, I can do it."

"What's wrong? Why do you want her to stop?" Zander asked.

"The strong contractions and pushing are causing his heartbeat to dip." Taking Karina's hand she said, "Karina, I know how much you wanted a vaginal delivery, but we're going to have to get this little guy out quickly."

Karina started to panic. "No, we can do it, just one more push!"

"That's exactly what I don't want you to do. We don't have a choice, Karina. We need to get you to the OR right away." Dr. Lenoir said.

"Zander!" Karina panicked. "Do something! Don't let them cut our baby out!" She began to cry, sucking in huge gulps of air and choking as another contraction hit.

Zander gently extricated himself from his wife's grip and pulled the doctor aside. "Is this absolutely necessary, Dr. Lenoir?"

The nurses attempted to calm Karina down and prep her for surgery.

"I don't have time to sugarcoat this, Zander. We don't have a choice. If we don't get your wife into that operating room in the next few minutes, we'll lose your son. I can't promise you what the outcome will be once we get into surgery but I'm going to do my damnedest to try to save him. There's a chance we could lose one or both of them. We need to move now, understand?"

Zander's eyes filled with tears; he grabbed her arm. "Don't let my wife die."

He rushed back to Karina's side. "I'm here baby." The nurse helped him put on a paper gown, booties and bonnet as he consoled her. "I'll be right by your side the entire time, like always. Rina, I love you more than life itself, you know that don't you?"

The sincerity in Zander's eyes calmed Karina. "Yes, I know, my love. Let's go meet our son. I'm ready," she said. The medical team rushed the gurney down the hall, with Zander running alongside it, holding Karina's hand until the last possible minute.

Even though the playlist that Karina and Zander had painstakingly compiled to ease their son's entry into the world was playing through the speakers, not even Stevie Wonder's classic *Ribbon in the Sky* could ease the tension in the OR. Karina's anxiety was so intense that the doctors had given her something to calm her down. She wasn't feeling the pain anymore, but she was still alert enough to barrage Zander with questions.

"What are they doing now? Why is it taking so long?" she demanded to know.

Zander let go of her hand long enough to peek over the barricade of sterile blue paper sheets. They were soiled with blood and there was a steady drip of blood pooling on the floor under the gurney. "Is there supposed to be so much blood?" he whispered to the nurse closest to him.

She looked at him through her glasses that perched above the sterile mask covering her mouth. He couldn't understand what her eyes conveyed. She nudged him back behind the line and murmured, "They're doing everything they can, sir."

Just then the doctor lifted their son out of the bloody mess that was his wife's belly. Zander was enthralled by the sight of his son; his eyes took in his tiny feet and toes, dangling legs, the proof of his gender, and his brown arms and hands with delicate fingers splayed wide, but when he reached his face, Zander's brain registered that all was not well. Thick pale yellow tubing surrounded his son's neck obscuring Zander's view of his face. "What's wrong?" he screamed.

Karina struggled to sit up. "Something's wrong? What's happening? Where's my baby?" She cried out. "Zander!" She tugged on his arm. "Tell me! What's going on?"

The doctor was working furiously to untangle the umbilical cord wrapped tightly around the baby's neck. "As you can see, the umbilical cord is strangling your son. I'm trying to release it."

"Go faster!" Zander urged.

"It's knotted. I have to make small cuts to ensure I don't cut through to the baby's neck." Dr. Lenoir explained without looking up. Soon the baby was free of the umbilical cord but his neck and face were a mottled dark red. "The blood is not circulating. He's not breathing. We need to start CPR." Dr. Lenoir handed the baby to the neonatal nurse. They walked a few feet away to an area made ready for the baby and began working on him.

Karina watched it all in misery. "Go with our son, Zander. Watch over him."

Tears streamed down Zander's face. He looked over the barrier as Dr. Lenoir and the nurses continued to work furiously on Karina; blood continued to flow faster than their fingers could move. "I don't want to leave you, my love. I can see from here that they are working on our son."

"Don't you let our son be alone, Zander! Go to him! I'll be fine. Tell him I love him. Tell him that his Mommy loves him!" She then broke into tears.

Zander let go of her hand. As he walked past Dr. Lenoir he asked, "Is she okay? There's so much blood."

Dr. Lenoir responded, "I've stopped the bleeding for now. We'll keep her in ICU and watch her closely." She looked up at him. "I'm so sorry about the baby, Zander."

Zander ran to check on his son.

Six weeks later Karina woke to the sound of the vacuum cleaner and gospel music coming from the great room downstairs. "Please don't come up here," she whispered. Twenty minutes later Mama Ella strode into the bedroom.

"Karina, it's time for you to get up!" Mama Ella threw open the curtains, letting in the sunshine. Karina rolled over in bed, covering her head with the pillow.

"Oh no. That's not gonna work." Ella said, hands on her hips. "You've pushed Zander, Betty, Sonya, even Samaya away for weeks but that ends today. Your body has healed enough for you to get out of this bed." Ella snatched the comforter and pillows away.

"Just leave me alone," Karina groaned and curled up in a ball, her back turned toward Ella.

"Look at me." Ella turned Karina's face toward her, steeling herself to not visibly react to the deep dark circles under her eyes or her gaunt pale face. This had gone beyond a slow recovery from back-to-back surgeries. Karina's depression was taking a toll on her body and soul.

"Sugar, I know that you are devastated. No one knows more than me how much you longed for that baby. We're all mourning, and our little L.J. will live on in our hearts forever. But Rina, in losing him we almost lost you and that just about broke this family.

How would I go on without you? And Zander? If you ever doubted his love for you, Babygirl you should've been a fly on the wall when they rushed you back into surgery." She shook her head.

"It just about broke him. He tries to put on a good front for you when he comes in here, but he's barely functioning, Karina. And Samaya is suffering too. She's been peeing in the bed, forgetting her homework, I even caught her sucking her thumb the other day! As much as she loves me and Betty, going back and forth between our houses isn't working. She wants to come home. She misses you. *She needs you.*"

Karina had cried so many tears over the past six weeks. She cried for the babies she'd lost in the earliest years of her marriage. She cried at the memory of her and Zander's shared anguish when he gently extricated their son from her arms for the first and last time. She cried for the loss of the son she'd come to know through his kicks and twists and turns in her belly. The son who had grown bigger and stronger until she'd finally allowed herself to imagine him at one-, three-, and even fifteen-years old. She cried when she learned the birth had almost killed her, and that the cost of survival had been removal of her uterus. She cried when it hit her that Langston Jarell was to be the last baby she would ever carry. Finally, there were no more tears. She had nothing left to demonstrate the depth of her despair.

"Karina, you come from strong stock. From women who've known sorrow, and hard times, and have pushed on in spite of it all. That's what Black women have had to do and will always have to do. We put our faith in God. It's time to pull yourself together. Do you hear me?"

Karina looked at her in astonishment. "Mama Ella, how can I lean on a God who would let Candi have a healthy baby on a bathroom floor but snatch away all of my babies?"

Ella pulled Karina close. "Oh my sweet girl. Don't do that. Don't compare yourself to your sister or anyone else. I know it can be hard to have faith at times like this because the answer to why we must suffer is beyond our comprehension. We must trust in the Lord and lean not on our own understanding. We walk by faith, not by sight. Pray for peace, Karina."

"I'll try, Mama Ella." Karina promised, but she knew that she deserved God's punishment for keeping Candi away from her baby all those years ago. *If only it were as simple as just having faith. I'll never be able to give Zander a child. The one thing he's wanted for so many years. Will he leave me one day since I can't give him a biological child?*

PART III

THE PRESENT -2005

ALL TOGETHER NOW

"Baby, are you ready yet?" Candace struggled to mask the impatience in her tone. She folded down the corner of a page in the book she was reading, slipped off the bar stool, and walked upstairs. Entering the bedroom she was happy to find Nick fully dressed. He turned as she entered and flashed a brilliant smile.

"Hey Sweetness, don't you look sexy?" he teased as he walked over to her.

Glancing at herself in the mirror she bit her lip. "You're joking, right? The last thing I want to do is have Rina think I haven't grown up."

Nick wrapped his arms around her, inhaling her signature scent of jasmine and vanilla.

Kissing her neck, he whispered in her ear. "Hell yeah you look sexy, Sweetness. You *are* sexy! And there is no doubt that you're a grown-ass woman."

Candace smiled as Nick continued whispering, "But don't worry, everyone else will see a prim and proper community non-profit executive."

Candace extricated herself from Nick's embrace and smoothed her dress. "Good, that's exactly the look I was going for."

Nick's expression grew serious. "Candi don't go into this feeling like you owe Karina something. You were a teenager and made some poor choices but you paid your dues, in spades. She can't take that away from you. Your sister isn't any better than you; you have to promise me that you'll remember that."

"Thank you love, I appreciate that. It took many years of therapy for me to understand that self-blame is what led me to self-harm. And whatever I didn't blame myself for, I blamed on Karina. Now it's important to me to try to rebuild my relationship with my sister. Other than you, she's all the family I have left. And I've let too many years pass. My goal is for us to agree to put the past behind us."

"And if that doesn't work?"

She took a deep breath. "I'll walk away. Not run this time but make the choice to walk. Life's too short and I can't undo anything I've done in the past. I left here a child, but as you said, I'm a grown-ass woman now and I can cope if Rina can't handle me being around."

"That's my girl! Let's go see what's up with these bougie folks. And then maybe tonight we can work on our little project." He shot her a lascivious look.

Candace laughed. "You and this baby project! Have you forgotten that we've already done our part? The rest is up to God and the Stanford experts."

"Let's call it extra credit then." He laughed.

She grew serious and stroked the side of his face. "Nicky don't forget that we're fighting some pretty big odds. A baby might not be in the cards for us."

Nick swept her into his arms. "We moved back to the Bay Area so we could work with a top notch fertility team right?"

She nodded.

"And that's what we're doing. If we're meant to have a baby, cool. If not, we'll either adopt or leave it alone. We'll cross that bridge when we get to it." Nick said.

"I know how bad you want to have a baby of your own. If I

can't give one to you, I don't think it's fair to you to have to miss out on that." Candace pulled away, tears gathering in her eyes.

Nick turned her to face him. "It doesn't matter, okay? As long as I can have you by my side for the rest of my life, I'll be a happy man. Would I like to have a baby? Sure, I would. But Sweetness, you not having my baby isn't what keeps me up at night. Do you know what keeps me up at night?" She shook her head.

"Worrying that what we have is too good to be true. Do you know how crazy it is that we're still together after everything we've been through? Any other woman would've walked away from me and my bullshit years ago. What I put you through. What I drove you to—" Nick's voice broke. "Candace, I thank God every day that you stayed by my side. Who knows why you haven't been able to conceive? It's not like it's your fault. It just is what it is. I just want you - us - to be happy, alright?"

Candace nodded, burying her face in his neck and inhaling the fresh woodsy scent of his cologne. Her eyes drifted to the clock.

"Oh shit! We're gonna be late!" Candace ran to the mirror to repair the damage they had done to her hair and makeup. *'It's not like it's your fault' . . . but what if it is?*

Across town, the Bishops were also preparing for the evening. Karina adjusted the tie of her wraparound blouse and examined her face in the mirror. Her makeup and hair were perfect, but she wasn't satisfied.

Zander stepped behind her, resting his hands lightly on her hips. "Gorgeous," he murmured as he kissed her.

"Get a room!" Samaya laughed as she passed them in the hallway, her ever-present cell phone at her ear.

"Wouldn't it be nice if she was a happy, likable, child more often?" Karina mused.

Zander smiled. "Yeah, I know what you mean. I had intended to get on her case about the laundry and talking on the cell when she still has to work on her history project, but damn if I feel like dealing with the funky attitude that's sure to follow."

"That's the problem, Zander, we keep giving her passes!" She took a deep breath. "I don't have time for this right now. I have enough to worry about. But don't forget to remind me, we need to talk about this dance troupe thing."

Karina turned back to the mirror, but Zander pulled her away. "You look fine - no, perfect. Stop stressing."

"It's been so long since me and Candi spent any time together. For so many years I thought I never wanted to see her again or if I did, it would be just long enough to curse her out, and banish her from my life on my own terms. But now it feels different." Karina walked downstairs to the great room and perched on the leather recliner, careful not to wrinkle her linen slacks.

"What's different now, babe?" Zander sat beside her.

"I don't know exactly. Maybe it's because Mama Ella is gone. Maybe because the Candi in my mind was frozen in time – selfish and self-absorbed – but the Candi that showed up at Mama Ella's house was a woman. A woman who reminded me of the child she used to be. A woman who has pain in her eyes and voice, and a story to tell."

"I'm sure she does. It can't have been easy to be on her own in the streets since she was a kid."

"I know. And the little she shared the other day made it clear that she had a really rough time out there. But then I get angry all over again. She made a choice to run away! And what happened with our parents, she put it all into play." She shook her head. *And when I think about what she did to Samaya …* "I can't forgive her. I just can't."

Zander pulled her up on his lap. "Maybe it's not for you to forgive at all. Your sister will atone for her choices, and like everyone else she'll be judged by God. Maybe all you can do is let the past lie."

"After all these years of thinking I didn't want to ever see her again, now I feel like a missing limb suddenly grew back and I don't know how I managed without it." Karina said. "But as much as I missed her and don't want to argue with her, I also don't want her to think that what she did was okay."

"I doubt that she thinks it was okay, Rina. She's been carrying so much guilt around with her about your parents' deaths that it probably would've broken most people. And remember, she didn't have a support network out there – no Mama Ella, no you. But it seems like she's gotten herself together. And she's married right?"

Karina pulled away. "That's the other thing. She's married to Nick! We all thought he was gonna be her undoing." Her voice grew louder. "He was a little thug and now he's coming to my house to break bread! He was the catalyst for everything that happened." She threw her hands up in frustration.

"Wait a minute, Rina. You're jumping to conclusions. You told me that he was a wanna-be drug dealer almost eighteen years ago, your sister was crazy in love with him, and after your parents died she ran away to be with him, right?"

"More or less, yeah." Karina mumbled.

Zander laughed, "More or less. What you don't know was how much Nick pushed Candi to behave a certain way, and what she was already destined to do. It's like I keep telling you about Sammi - we can only blame so much on Darnell or Brandy. We have to accept that she's making decisions and has to learn how to anticipate, and later accept, the consequences of her actions. We don't know if Nick convinced Candace to run away. For all we know, Candace might have been the one to make the plan. They might've thought they were saving each other – the teenage mind is a mystery."

"You're right. I never really got to know Nick. I just went with the gossip. And it seemed like Candi changed into someone else because she was dating him, but it was also around the same time she started hanging out with Tiffany. I don't really know how much was due to Nick and how much was due to Tiffany. Brandy reminds me so much of Tiffany it's scary." She shook her head, trying to focus on the topic at hand. "But still, I'm so shocked that Candi and Nick are still together! I don't know how to act with him. I mean is he gonna step in here with gold teeth and a jacked-up attitude?" She sucked her teeth. "I don't need Samaya to be around all that. Candi is already someone I don't want her to be exposed to."

"Rina, I saw the brother at the funeral. He looked respectable and was obviously very concerned about your sister. I think our best bet is just to sit tight and observe. Dinner will give us a chance to get to know them. I doubt they're going to be angling to be our best friends, they're probably just as anxious as we are. Eli and Sonya are always a good time, so they'll be sure to keep the conversation light and flowing. Now, about Samaya being around Candace, maybe that's just what she needs: a fresh adult to bounce things off."

Karina stood up. "Let's not go too far, too fast. Candace may have matured, but that doesn't mean she can step into an Auntie role with Samaya. I don't know that I trust her to do that."

"Well, no, you don't trust her just yet, but you could try to be open to the possibility. Let's see what happens, okay? If you and your sister can find a way to rebuild your relationship, that's great. If not, you'll both move on and you won't have the past hanging over your head any longer."

The doorbell rang. Zander looked at his watch. "Somebody is super early. It must be Eli."

Karina's smile vanished as she followed Zander out of the room. *The past won't hang over my head. Not likely! I'm living with the past every damn day.*

Zander opened the front door ready to reprimand Elliott, but his best friend elbowed his way past him saying, "My hands were too full to use my key, quit tripping." Eli placed a grocery bag on the counter and presented a large bouquet to Karina with a flourish.

"Rina, I wanted to get here early and give you these autumn flowers for your table. I know how much you love them. And Zan, I brought us some special nonalcoholic beer that actually tastes good, since I understand we are dining with folks who do not partake of the fruit of the vine."

Karina laughed and kissed Eli's cheek. "You can be counted on to be thoughtful *and* to make an entrance, can't you Eli?" She looked him up and down, taking in the expensive shoes, silk shirt, and perfectly creased indigo slacks. "Why you looking so fly? It's just dinner at our house."

Zander said, "You know he wasn't gonna miss an opportunity to show out for Sonya." He walked up to Eli and sniffed the air around him. "Nigga even got on some new cologne." Zander laughed loudly.

Karina smiled, "Aww Eli, you still working on that project?"

"Zan, you putting too much on it. Sonya is a beautiful woman, ain't no denying that, but it ain't like a brotha is pining for her or some shit like that." Elliott shrugged, "We grown. If we're compatible, it'll happen. If not, no big thang. And don't be smelling on me like that!"

Zander and Karina shared an amused glance and dropped the subject.

Thirty minutes later, everyone had arrived and made themselves comfortable around the fire-pit on the patio overlooking the bay.

Nick stood at the banister and pointed down at the tiny houses below. "Damn, when I was a youngster living down there in the flatlands, I thought the only people who lived up here were rich white people."

Zander said, "Well we ain't rich, and we damn sure ain't white."

"But we're here!" Eli finished.

They all laughed and held their glasses for a toast.

"Is that your way of letting us know you closed on your house, Eli?" Sonya asked.

Elliott smiled. "Well, Sonya, I'm never one to steal anyone else's thunder." Zander and Karina snickered. Elliott threw them a fake frown and continued in an affected British accent, "But since you brought it up, it is true that I have acquired a home of my own a half mile from here with, if I do say so myself, an even more stunning view of the Golden Gate Bridge." He broke character and said, "Next dinner party is at my house y'all."

The room erupted with high fives, congratulations, and demands to see the pictures that Elliott had stored on his cell phone.

After a few minutes Elliott said, "As much as I appreciate the well wishes, you know what's even more exciting?" Without giving anyone time to respond, he said, "Karina's lasagna! How much longer do we have to munch on these healthy appetizers Rina? A brotha skipped lunch in anticipation of your lasagna!"

"Eli, you probably have containers of my lasagna in your freezer already."

"Objection, irrelevant!" Elliott responded.

Karina laughed and turned to the other guests. "Are y'all ready to eat? Eli is always hungry and obviously left his etiquette book back at his English manor!"

Nick was the first to respond, "Well now that I understand what's waiting for us, real estate and etiquette be damned! Let's eat!"

Everyone laughed and nodded in agreement as they headed inside.

Elliott fell into step next to Sonya. "I was thinking that maybe you could help me out, give me some decorating tips."

"What makes you think I know how to decorate?" Sonya laughed. "For all you know I'd have your place jacked up!"

Elliott's laugh faded as his gaze took in Sonya from head to toe. "You've always been perfectly laid out for every occasion. You set the standard for every woman in the room. There's no way that a woman as skilled as you are with her wardrobe wouldn't be just as good dressing up a house." He reached for her hand as he spoke.

Sonya let her hand rest lightly in his as she assessed his words. "You are one smooth-ass talker, Mr. Jeffers." She smiled. "I don't know if what you just said makes any sense, but it sounded good. I'm gonna have to continue to watch myself with you, I see."

Elliott laughed. "No need, baby. I got you."

Sonya shook her head. "Says every player, every day!" She laughed and pulled her hand away. "I'm gonna have to pass on the interior decorating, Eli, but I'm sure you have a backup or two in the wings."

"You been talking to Rina and Zander. Don't listen to them. They're just haters!" Elliott said, as he trailed after Sonya.

Light and easy conversation flowed over the dinner table as they ate. Karina was mesmerized by Nick's devotion to her sister – his eyes lit up when she spoke, he always had a slight smile on his face when he looked at her even when her attention was elsewhere, he was constantly touching her hand, twirling one of her braids, or pulling her close. Despite all of that, he didn't come across as possessive. Instead, he seemed a bit in awe of her. As for Candace, she leaned into Nick whenever he was close as if she just knew he would be there. Karina had to admit to herself that she might have been wrong about the depth of their relationship.

Forcing herself to focus on the moment, Karina asked, "Should we have dessert right away or take a minute to let our food digest?"

Sonya said, "If by digest, you mean give my stomach a chance to make some room, I vote for take a minute."

"I'm with Sonya," Candace said. "I'm about to bust!"

Elliott scoffed. "Lightweights! I thought it was time for thirds!" They all shook their heads.

Zander walked over to Karina and, stooping down, began to nuzzle her neck. "Baby, do you mind if we play a little pool before dessert?" He murmured in her ear.

She closed her eyes, reveling in the fire that was beginning to build. She took her time to respond and then whispered. "Well, since they're not leaving yet, I guess so, but you know you're playing with fire."

He gave a low growl and bit her ear, "Oh I plan to build a bonfire, and take my time putting it out." Karina bit her lip in anticipation.

To the group Zander said, "Well, if we're going to take a little break, does anyone wanna play a little pool?"

"Now you're talking," said Nick. "What about a friendly wager?"

"Oh Lord! Nicky, we're guests! Don't show out!" Candace joked, but she wore a slight frown.

"Girl, don't worry. These fools can handle themselves." Karina assured her.

The guys headed downstairs to the game room and the ladies made themselves comfortable on the plush leather couches in the great room.

"Candi, Rina hasn't told me anything! Are you here to stay? What kind of work do you do?" Sonya blurted.

Candace grinned, "I'm a Regional Director of The Sun Will Rise, an awesome non-profit that's committed to helping teens in trouble. We deal with drug use, self-harm, runaways, prostitution and pimping, sex trafficking, aging out of the foster care system, and more. There's an invisible society out there suffering. Waiting for 'the system' to step in is usually too little and too late."

Karina interrupted, "That sounds fantastic. How did you become Regional Director? Sounds pretty prestigious." She slapped her hand to her mouth. "Damn, that came out all wrong, Candi! I didn't mean . . . what I was trying to say —"

"I'm not offended, Rina. All those years ago I was one of those teens in trouble. I'm sure it's hard to imagine my trajectory."

"I am sorry, though, I really wasn't trying to judge you —"

Candace winked at Karina and continued. "The founder, Roxie Stapleton, literally saved my life – more than once – when I was going through my own personal hell in Reno. She saw something in me. I didn't understand it then, but I do now. I've had a few 'Candis' get under my skin since I've been working there. Anyway, after a couple of years with Roxie's bullying and mothering, I finally got my shit together. I started community college classes and worked part time at The Sun. Time passed and I got some letters after my name. I became the COO and now the Regional Director. We're exploring expanding to the Bay Area." She turned to Sonya. "That takes us to your first question, I'm hoping to stay in the Bay Area."

"When will you know more about your expansion efforts?" Sonya asked. "I'm a member of a Bay Area Black women entrepreneur group and we've been talking about identifying a community organization to throw our collective weight behind. The Sun Will Rise sounds like something that would interest the group. I'd love to support what you're doing."

"Thanks Sonya. We should have plans solidified before the holidays get into full swing."

They spent the next several minutes reminiscing about girl scout adventures and third and fourth grade sleepovers.

"We used to have so much fun playing dress up in your basement, Sonya!" Candace recalled. "I remember how your mom fixed up a spare room like a diva's dressing room with Goodwill clothes and costume jewelry —"

"And vanities and floor mirrors and oh my gosh all the shoes!" Karina interjected.

"We kept ourselves busy for hours while our moms studied for their Masters degrees!" Sonya said. "And if we happened to get hungry . . ."

"SNACK CABINET!" They shouted in unison and laughed.

"This was such a good idea. I wonder how the guys are getting along?" Karina said.

"Nick brought his portfolio. If he's showing his work, you're probably gonna have to go rescue Zander and Eli. My man is passionate about what he does and why he does it." Candace laughed.

"What exactly does he do?" Karina asked.

"He's an artist. His bread and butter is graphic design – stuff for small companies and corporations' brochures, logos, marketing materials. But his passion is working in acrylic, watercolor and oils. He's sold out a few gallery shows. And there are some private collectors beginning to show interest as well. He also uses mural making to redirect the youth in our programs to a more positive creative outlet for their trauma. We have contracts with municipalities and individual business owners to display the kids' art."

"That's amazing! I had no idea. I remember when we were teenagers you told me once that he was a really good artist." Karina said.

"Yep. And he's grown so much since then." Candace's pride was obvious.

"It's amazing that you all have been together all this time." Sonya said. "Did you do the breakup and make up thing that most of us did back in the day?"

"Well, our journey wasn't your typical teenage love affair, that's for sure." Candace said. "When we left the Bay Area it was us against the world. You couldn't have split us up for anything. But there were some months, hell some *years,* when Nicky was locked up and I was on my own. We were apart but it never felt like we were broken up."

"I don't mean to sound as naïve as I know this sounds, Candi, but once Nick was in jail why didn't you just come home?" Sonya asked. "Your grandmother would have taken you back, no questions asked."

"I know that now," Candace responded. "But back then? I was too ashamed." She looked at Sonya. "We go back to third grade, so I know you were raised just like me and Rina. Believe me when I say that the Reno Nicky and I ended up in was not the Circus-Circus Reno our parents took us to on weekend getaways." She sighed. "Folks were ruthless and nobody gave a damn how old you were. I did a lot of things I'm not proud of."

They sat in uncomfortable silence for a few minutes before Candace shook off her melancholy. "I saw you pull up in a Porsche, Sonya. Did you follow your dream and become an entrepreneur?"

"You know it! I own three hair salons and a beauty supply store." They all exchanged high fives. "You remember my Uncle Zeke?"

"I think my first crush was on your Uncle Zeke!" Candace giggled.

"Uncle Zeke was everybody's first crush!" Karina chimed in.

"Y'all was nasty!" Sonya laughed. "Uncle Zeke came into some money around the time we graduated from high school, and he invested in my first salon. His only criteria was that I had to take some business classes. He knew I wasn't interested in college."

"And like everyone knew, she had a head for business. Sonya parlayed that first investment into another salon. She kept telling herself she wasn't into school but somehow managed to get her B.A. and her M.B.A." Karina praised her friend.

"Impressive! What about on the personal side? Did you get married, have kids?" Candace asked.

"I'm married to my financial portfolio, and my businesses are my kids!" Sonya laughed.

"What about Eli? It's obvious he's interested in you." Candace asked.

Sonya smiled. "Eli is . . . complicated. The chemistry is undeniable, but I can't let him get the upper hand."

"Hmm, sounds like there's some juicy stuff you're not sharing." Candace said.

Sonya smiled. "My gramma said never tell all your business!" she laughed. "But anyway, I just don't think Eli's ready to settle down."

Karina raised her eyebrows. "And if he was ready?"

"Girl, let's talk about something real, like that pineapple-upside-down cake that's ready to be cut!" Sonya deflected.

Candace winked, "And let's get ours before the guys come upstairs!"

Downstairs, the guys were enjoying their time together. "I think it is fair to say we could make some money off some suckas if we went to play some pool together!" Nick tipped an imaginary glass to Zander and Eli, and they returned the toast.

"We are pretty evenly matched, my brotha!" Zander agreed.

"Hey Nick, I'd really like to take a look at your work sometime." Elliott said.

Nick grinned. "You ain't said nothing but a word - I've got my portfolio in the car. I'll be right back."

A few minutes later he spread the large portfolio out on the pool table. Elliot and Zander began to slowly turn the pages.

"Dude! You said you 'draw and do some graphic design.' I had no idea you were an artiste! These are amazing!" Zander exclaimed.

"Amazing doesn't capture it! I'd love to see these in person." Elliott said.

The canvases depicted the beauty of urban America that is often overlooked. There were children jumping double Dutch, playing hopscotch and cooling off under the spray of broken fire hydrants, an unexpected patch of sunflowers growing in the parking lot of an abandoned warehouse, a woman tucked into a sleeping bag yards away from young Black and brown boys shooting basketballs through hoops with no nets – images that evoked familiarity, despair and hope at the same time.

Nick smiled. "Gentlemen, it's that type of reaction that makes this worthwhile. These are pieces I've worked on most recently. The graphic design stuff I do for corporations. But what I'm most proud of is the work that I do with kids – turning some of that excess energy into art."

The men began to brainstorm about how they might introduce Nick to philanthropists interested in funding extra-curricular activities for marginalized youth.

"Keep in mind when you're identifying corporate types for me to meet that I do have a record. I haven't been behind bars in ten years, but some companies aren't interested in a comeback story." Nick said.

Elliott responded, "That's true. I have some well-placed fraternity brothers that aren't likely to let that derail them, but I appreciate your candor. What were you were in for?"

"Possession with intent to distribute was the longest bid. It carried a mandatory five-year sentence, and I served a little over two years. It was such a small amount that if it had been powder cocaine instead of crack, I would've got probation, or might not have even been charged at all. Other than that, let's see petty theft, public drunkenness, resisting arrest." Nick shrugged. "I was young and dumb and going through tough times."

"I can work with those. No murders or attempted murders?" Elliott confirmed.

"Hell naw, I wasn't violent. Just stupid." Nick laughed.

Zander mused, "I wonder if there's anything we can do to get any of that expunged from your record? How long have you been working with the nonprofit?"

"Eight years."

"Lemme talk to one of my buddies at the DA's office." Zander said.

"I appreciate it man, but don't put yourself out. I'm at peace with my past." Nick replied.

"That's all well and good, but you'd be amazed how many

people use their influence to clean up records far worse than yours. Why should your record become an impediment to helping our youth improve their lives, or limit the reach of your visionary artwork? Black folks have influence and networks at our disposal just like the white boys who have no problem flexing their power." Elliott said.

"I never thought about it that way. I've been focused on making amends and doing whatever good I can with what God gave me." Nick said.

"Keep that focus, Nick. Let me and Eli use the talents and resources that we've been given to do our part. But if you don't mind me asking, how did you get out of that life?" Zander asked.

"They say people come into your life for a reason, a season or a lifetime, right? Well, I met this old head, Brother Xavier, when I got that five-year sentence. He'd been big in the dope game, selling heroin, when I was just a baby. By the time I got picked up, Brother X had turned his life around and had started a prison ministry of sorts."

"Of sorts?" Zander asked.

"It wasn't about religion, the way most people think of ministry. He was more of a resource and a parental figure to young dudes, if you could imagine having a parent that knew the ins-and-outs of the game and could sniff out bullshit a mile away." Nick chuckled. "Anyway, Brother X tried to talk some sense into me the first time I got locked up, but a hard head makes a soft ass, you know? It took a while to really sink in. Brother never gave up though. He might swoop me up off the corner so we could play a game of chess or visit me when I was locked up and force me to imagine that I had a future. Then he found a way to get some of my pieces in an art gallery and they sold out! Gave me a sense of pride that I hadn't ever experienced. The rest, as they say, is some messy ass history. Brother X? He was a reason and a lifetime. Not a week goes by that I'm not in touch with him."

"Sounds like a helluva man," Elliot said.

"How long have you been sober?" asked Zander.

"Since February fourteenth, eight years ago. I played around at sobriety a few times before that but that was the last day I did drugs or took a drink."

Elliott raised his eyebrows. "That's oddly specific. Valentine's Day?"

Nick smiled. "It was the day before Candi's twenty-seventh birthday. It was one of those come-to-Jesus moments. She'd finally come out the other side and I was still straddling the fence. I wasn't all gangsta anymore, but I was still volatile. When she said she was finally ready to start living her life as a whole person again, I knew that if I didn't get my shit together, I would not be part of that journey . . ." He looked directly at them with glassy eyes. "There's no drug or liquor that can take the place of that woman. I started AA and NA meetings the next day."

"The love of a Maxwell woman is something else, ain't it man?" Zander raised his fist for a bump.

Elliott asked plaintively, "Are y'all absolutely sure there's not another sister somewhere? Maybe a first cousin?" They all laughed.

"Sonya is pretty damn close," Zander said.

"Man, you ain't gotta convince me. I'm constantly striking out, but it ain't for lack of trying! Every time I think we're almost there, she shuts me down. No matter what I say she refuses to believe I'll give up my entire roster for her." Eli whined.

"Wonder why?" Zander asked wryly.

Turning to Nick he said, "I won't lie, I was worried about Karina and Candace's reunion."

Nick nodded. "Candi was so wound up about seeing Karina for the first time in all those years, I honestly questioned if a reunion was worth it. But now I see that she really needed to be with her sister. Her spirit is lighter. I don't know the details but it's looking like they're getting closer to forgiving one another."

"Knowing my wife, it's more likely that she's tiptoeing around whatever the landmine is, instead of confronting it. But I agree that having her sister back has been good for her, especially with Mama Ella gone and Sammi doing the whole teenage angst thing." Zander said.

"Something tells me they'll work through the bumps − their

foundation of love is obviously strong. I wish we'd come back sooner. It would have done my lady some good." Nick exclaimed. "Now didn't I hear something about dessert?"

Eli rolled his eyes in ecstasy, "Dude, you think that lasagna was something? Wait until you get some of Rina's pineapple-upside-down cake!"

"Aww shit!" Nick laughed.

Zander snapped his fingers. "Oh, I forgot to tell y'all, I can get us box seats at the Raiders game this Sunday. They play the Saints. Who's in?"

When Nick picked up his phone and started scrolling without saying anything; Zander and Elliot exchanged confused looks. Then Nick held up a picture of himself wearing a Bo Jackson Raiders jersey.

Zander grinned and said, "I'll take that as a yes." They all laughed and headed upstairs to rejoin the ladies.

"Oh, y'all started dessert without us! Sneaky asses!" Nick teased as he embraced Candace from behind. She fed him a forkful of cake and Nick closed his eyes and moaned.

"Karina, this is the best pineapple-upside-down cake I have ever tasted!"

Karina grinned, "This is our grandmother's recipe. I'm surprised Candi hasn't made it for you."

Candace chimed in, "Hold on, don't judge me! The backpack I left home with did not include Mama Ella's recipe book. I remembered how to make some basic stuff, but this is the next level. You know she only pulled this out for special occasions. And I swear Rina, you must've added a secret ingredient, because this tastes more decadent than I remember!" Candace closed her eyes as she savored a forkful.

Karina felt that deep inner knot of anxiety unraveling. *She can talk about leaving with a backpack without sounding angry, that's got to be a good sign.* "Hey, I'm married to a lawyer. I will neither affirm nor deny that allegation."

They laughed and Nick said, "I guess that means when I need a cake fix I'll be knocking on your door, sister-in-law!"

"Get in line, get in line." Sonya piped in. "But not next week. Our master baker will be super busy getting ready for Halloween. She always does it up big for the kiddies at her school."

Karina smiled. "I only do the baking; the other teachers provide the ingredients."

"What do you bake, Rina?" Candace asked.

"Mostly cookies for the school Halloween festival. The kids sell the cookies to the family members who attend and use the money to fund parties for each classroom throughout the year."

"That's so sweet! Can I help?" Candace asked.

"Sure, that would be awesome. Samaya used to be my helper but she's much too busy with Senior Year activities this year, or so she says."

"Did I hear my name?" Samaya came running into the kitchen.

Karina fussed. "Sammi, why are you always running in the house?"

"Sorrryy!" Samaya groaned. Looking around the room, she flashed a bright smile. "Is grown folks' time over yet? Hey Auntie Sonya, Uncle Eli, Auntie Candi – looking fly. And you must be my new uncle? Y'all looking like Black Barbie and Ken!"

Nick took Samaya's hand and gave a slight bow. "Pleased to make your acquaintance, niece. I am indeed your Uncle Nick. But let's get something straight from jump: your Auntie Candi here might look like a honey-colored Barbie, but I ain't got nothing in common with no square-ass Ken!"

The laughter bounced off the walls. "My bad, Uncle. Now that I get a better look at you, I see what you mean. You're way too smooth for that." Samaya smiled, "Anyway, sorry to interrupt y'all, I'm just here for a piece of cake." She slipped her headphones over her ears, sliced herself a big piece of cake, and went back upstairs.

Candace grinned, "Well, back to the Halloween cookies. I'd love to help. Just tell me when."

Sonya exhaled in relief. "Thank God! I've been praying for a miracle so I wouldn't have to jump in. Baking is one thing I do not like to do!"

"Duly noted," Elliott whispered to Zander. Zander shook his head with a half-smile.

"Speaking of Halloween," Candace said, "Rina, do you remember how Mama Ella would let us turn her front yard into whatever we could dream up for Halloween?"

"Girl yes! My favorite was the creepy witches' lair, complete with the brewing cauldron we made with hot ice to create the fake smoke." Karina said. "We were so cool that the entire fourth grade must have come through to see it. I think I was a witch for at least three years in a row. But you always challenged Mommy with something different. A robot, a princess, oh, remember the dragon?" She laughed.

"I haven't even allowed myself to think about all of this in so long. Such good memories." Candace's smile carried a trace of melancholy.

Karina sighed, "We stopped doing those over-the-top decorations once Mommy, Daddy and you were gone. Later, I'd just decorate my classroom and make whatever costume Sammi wanted. She was a witch every year from four to about ten, then she was a ballerina."

Zander piped in, "Not just any ballerina, mind you. She had to have intricate tutus and matching toe shoes and special ribbons for her hair. The girl would research famous Black ballerinas and have her mama up all night trying to replicate their look."

"She must've gotten her dancing gene from me! I overheard you two talking about Ms. Bennett and her dance troupe. I love that my niece and I have something in common."

"Me too," Karina said quietly.

"Hey! We should decorate Mama Ella's yard this year!" Candace said.

Karina brightened up. "That would be fun."

"Let's see what's in Mama Ella's attic and then supplement what we need from the dollar store or the craft store," Candace said.

Sonya groaned, "Oh no! Not a craft store trip!"

"You don't cook, bake, or do crafts?" Elliott asked.

Sonya laughed, "You've never been to the craft store with Rina, have you?"

Zander moaned, "Man, it's brutal. She gets all excited searching for the best deals! And don't let her find the clearance aisle!"

"I am standing right here, you know!" Karina cleared her throat and put on a fake frown. "And stop making my sister think there's something wrong with me. I'm just a frugal shopper. Teachers have to be."

Candace reached out to pat her hand. "Don't worry Sis, I got your back! How about planning and shopping on Saturday and decorating on Sunday?"

"Count me in for Sunday!" Sonya said.

"Sounds good," Karina said. "And Candi, we can bake for the Halloween Festival the following weekend."

The conversation flowed freely and laughter bubbled like champagne. Karina's mind drifted as she thought about how smoothly the evening was going. It felt good to spend time with this version of Candace. She reminded her of the sister she had grown up with, but this woman's eyes told a story that Karina wanted to hear, and she exuded warmth and comfort that Karina needed to absorb. Karina prayed that Mama Ella's last words to her were just the incoherent ramblings of a dying woman and not a premonition.

13

KUMBAYA, MY LORD

The next morning the phone rang, rousing Karina from a deep sleep. She reached for it. "Hello?"

"Hey, did I wake you?" It was Candace.

Karina smiled, remembering the good time they'd had the night before. "No, it's okay. What's up?"

"I wanted to thank you for opening your home to us. We had a great time. I don't know when you turned into such a good cook, but that lasagna was fantastic! I'm gonna have to run an extra mile this morning to pay for it."

"Girl, who you telling? I was just trying to show off cause these hips cannot withstand that kinda meal on a regular basis."

"I'm glad you said that cause I was thinking that you must have got the better set of genes!"

"Mommy always said that Maxwell women's hips spread once they hit thirty! I guess she was right!" Karina spoke without thinking but immediately worried that bringing up their mother might trigger dissension. She exhaled in relief when Candace replied without hesitation.

"I find myself remembering all sorts of things Mommy and Daddy said or did, just out of the blue!"

"Me too. I guess that's the point. Parents hope their words will stick with you forever." After a slight pause Karina said, "So what are you up to today?"

"Actually, that's why I'm calling. I have to go to Stanford Medical Center for some lab work and imaging and I wondered if you wanted to ride out there with me. As I recall, there's a nice mall out there and I've never known a day that wasn't made for shoe shopping!"

"I know that's right!" Karina laughed, lowering her voice so as not to disturb Zander, but finding his naked torso very distracting. "Why do you need to go all the way to Stanford for testing? Is something wrong?"

Silence.

Karina blurted, "I'm sorry. That was a really personal question."

Candace laughed softly, "Well damn, you are my sister. If you can't ask, who can? I'm just not used to talking about it with anybody but Nick, but I'm the one who brought it up, right?"

It was Karina's turn to be silent.

"I'm working with the fertility clinic. Nick and I have been trying to conceive but haven't had any luck. We came out here to work with an expert team to give it one last try. I'm going to check on the implantation."

Why in the hell would you want a baby now after you threw the last one away? Karina thought, but clamped her lips shut. That was one conversation she did not want to have with Candace. Instead she said, "It's hard to believe how complicated women's bodies are. Stanford has some of the best doctors. I'm sure they'll be able to help you."

"They say it's going well. I'm just always so pessimistic about it. I have to work on that." Candace said.

"I wish I could ride with you and shopping sounds like fun. But I know myself, the whole day would be shot and I have to help Samaya with her history project. Plus Zander and I need to talk about this dance troupe thing she's throwing at us. But—"

"Oh, no problem. It was just an impulse; I didn't really expect you to go. I—"

"Not so fast! I was gonna ask you if you want to hit the gym together?" Karina interjected. "I don't know what time your appointment is, but we could go before or after. I have a 24 Hour Fitness membership and I can bring guests."

Candace's smile lit up her face. *She isn't blowing me off!* "That's much smarter than shoe shopping, especially after that dinner you cooked for us! My appointment is at 11 o'clock, so maybe we can go mid-afternoon, around 2 o'clock?"

"Sounds like a plan. Call me when you're on your way back. And good luck."

"Thanks Sis. That means a lot to me. I'll talk to you later."

Karina was lost in thought. On the one hand, all the pain, anger and near hatred that she had felt about her for so many years was right beneath the surface, waiting to be unleashed. On the other hand, she recognized in the adult Candace the person she had imitated, adored, and unconsciously missed for so many years. Being around Candace made Karina feel like she had finally come home after a long trip.

She turned to study her husband's features. She ran her hand over Zander's chest, resting it momentarily over his heart and taking comfort in its strong beat. *I don't know what I would do without him. What if everything were to come out? Would he ever forgive me?* She frowned. *I can't ever take that chance. I want to be close to Candi again but if it comes down to a choice, I won't ever give up Zander.*

Resolved in her decision, Karina lifted the sheets so she could start her husband's day off the way he ended hers.

Across town in the Myers' bedroom Nick pulled Candace back into bed. "I can't believe you're gonna leave me like this," he said, gesturing to the erection that had created a tent in the sheet. Candace laughed as she danced playfully just out of his reach.

"Baby, I'm sorry, but I don't know what traffic is gonna be like."

Nick grumbled, "Yeah, yeah, kick me to the curb! I guess this is what it's gonna be like when we're finally parents, having to sneak in a little nookie whenever we can." A cloud passed quickly over Candace's eyes.

"You squeeze that parenthood thing into every conversation, don't you?" Her laugh was slightly off.

Nick caught the change in her tone and sat up.

"Candi, I didn't mean anything by that. I told you, no matter what happens we'll be just fine." He pulled her into his arms. After a few seconds she relaxed and released the tension in her shoulders.

"It's just that I know how bad you want a baby and I'm afraid I won't be able to give you one." She valiantly held back tears.

"Hey, look at me −," he held her chin in his hand and turned her face toward him so he could look deeply into her green eyes, "Candace, I love you more than life itself. I told you I would like to be a father one day. But as long as we're raising our child together, I don't care where the baby comes from. You gotta stop pressuring yourself, Sweetness. Matter-of-fact, let's stop this fertility stuff and get started on the adoption."

Candace shook her head vehemently. "No, Nicky, I'm not ready to give up yet. The doctors said we have a decent chance of this time working out and I want more than anything to give birth to our baby."

"Well, who's to say the old-fashioned way might not still work? Let's not leave any stone unturned!" Nick said, a mischievous glint in his eye. She laughed and swatted at his wandering hand.

A few days later, Candace pulled up to Mama Ella's house and ran inside to get out of the rain. She had come to look for the Halloween decorations Mama Ella kept in the attic. She wanted some time alone to drink in the memories; sometimes being back after all these years felt overwhelming. Unlocking the door, she hung her wet jacket on the coat rack, put her purse on the table and dropped her keys in the basket.

She walked down the short hallway, pulled down the attic ladder and climbed up. She yelled, "I'm coming up," hoping to scare away any mice that may have taken up residence.

"No wonder it's so neat downstairs! Everything Mama Ella and Daddy Horace ever owned is up here! Good Lord, there must be twice as many boxes as I remember from when we were kids!" Rummaging around, she spotted a familiar box. She grabbed it and took it down to the kitchen.

As she looked through a box of pictures that she and Karina had saved over the years, her laughter bounced off the walls. "So many good times," she murmured. After fifteen minutes of reminiscing, Candace forced herself to get back to work. She left the pictures scattered on the table and climbed back up the ladder into the attic to look for the decorations.

"Jackpot!" she said when she spied a box labeled 'Skeleton.' "This must be Mr. Bones." She chuckled at the memory of the skeleton that had been a mainstay during her childhood. She and Karina took turns "dressing" Mr. Bones with jaunty hats, ties, and sport coats. "I don't know what our theme will be, but Mr. Bones, you Sir, will have a starring role." As she made her way back to the ladder with Mr. Bones, a rectangular black box that was partially obscured by a crate of trophies caught her eye.

"What the hell?" she muttered. Brow furrowed, Candace gingerly stepped closer. Abruptly she dropped Mr. Bones, pushed the crate of trophies aside and reached out to grab the box. When she saw it was her dad's old Air Jordan shoebox, she snatched her hand back and slapped it over her mouth to muffle her scream.

Candace reached a shaking hand out again, grabbed the shoebox and held it close to her chest as she clambered down the ladder. She hurried down the hallway and into the kitchen. The whooshing in her ears drowned out the staccato beat of raindrops on the roof.

"How is this possible?" she whispered placing it carefully on the table. "How did Mama Ella get this?"

Candace began pacing the room. "Think Candace, think! This doesn't make sense!" Her hand trembled as she reached to open the shoebox but then she pulled it back as if she had been burned. "I saw the garbage truck! They took it away!" She ran her hand over the top of the shoebox in a gentle, almost reverent manner.

She picked it up and sank to the floor with her back against the wall, holding it in her lap as tears ran down her cheeks. "Zora," she whispered. She cleared her throat and said it louder, "Zora. Her name was Zora." Her voice shook.

"Oh, Mama Ella, I'm so sorry that you found out that way. You found Baby Zora outside with the trash and had to bury her, all while worrying about me." Candace moaned, "I hate that I put that burden on you. All this time I've been staying away because of my shame and my fear that you would find out and you knew all along!"

Karina opened the front door, sending a gust of blustery wind and rain down the hallway into the kitchen, but Candace didn't notice. She was swept away to that afternoon nearly eighteen years ago when her life changed forever.

When Karina reached the kitchen doorway she froze at the sight of Candace clutching the shoebox.

"Zora baby," Candace whispered, "I hated myself for not making sure that you were buried properly. You were my sweet baby. I never imagined you would only take one tiny breath. I should have saved you somehow but I failed you like I failed everybody." She swiped at the tears falling from her eyes. "I wish I had known that Mama Ella was your guardian angel just like she had always been mine. I thank God that you've been resting in peace all these years."

Karina's purse slipped from her hand and skittered across the floor, and she grabbed for the kitchen countertop to steady herself. Startled, Candace looked up to see her standing there. They both began to speak, neither fully paying attention to the other.

"Rina, I need to tell you something." Her voice raspy from crying, Candace spoke quickly, relieved to finally tell the tale. "I found out I was pregnant in Texarkana. I was already five months along. At first I couldn't wrap my head around it. I was gonna find the baby a good family but then Auntie died. I came home to tell you guys and all of a sudden, the baby was coming! She was eight weeks early but she was so beautiful. She only took one breath. Nothing I did worked. I panicked."

"Candi, I didn't know what to do! And I was so angry with you . . ." Karina's voice was almost unrecognizable as emotion over took her and tears streamed down her face.

"I can't believe after all this time, to find out that Mama Ella knew – did she tell you? – No, of course she didn't, she would never do that, *but I should've told you*." Candace's voice shook with emotion. "It's been eating a hole in my soul for so long. To not be able to talk to you, of all people about the worst thing that's ever happened to me, that I've done."

"I've just never understood how you could do such a thing!" Karina screamed. "If you didn't want her there were so many other things you could've done!" She swiped the tears from her face. "You could've told Mama Ella, you could've told me! We could've helped you! Mama Ella was a nurse for Gods' sake! How could you just throw her away?"

Candace stood and walked to the window, watching the storm. She shook her head slowly and murmured to herself. "I could've come home, I could've made it up to my precious baby. I wouldn't have lost everyone. *I wouldn't have lost myself!* I was so stupid." Tears streamed down her cheeks.

Karina sank into a kitchen chair. Her tears dried up, and she spoke softly. "You took everything, Candi. In that last year, all Mommy and Daddy could focus on was you. You were constantly getting into trouble. All they did was worry about you. I was invisible. Nobody cared about my grades or how I was doing. You had always been my best friend and then you dropped me. And then Mommy and Daddy were gone because of you. When I thought it couldn't get any worse, you left me and Mama Ella for good. It almost broke her. She got old right before my eyes. Mama Ella kept saying you were going to come back and everything would be okay." She snorted. "But 'one day' never came. You knew the address just like you knew the phone number. Never even a postcard." She paused and shook her head slowly. "The only good that came out of it was our babygirl, she was all we had left. But the cost, Lord, the cost! I gave up so much. I had to grow up fast because now there was a baby to raise. Mama Ella did what she could but she still had to work so a lot fell on my shoulders—"

Candace had turned to look at Karina. She slammed her hand on the kitchen counter. "Why are you talking about Samaya right now? I'm talking about *my baby,* Zora."

Karina snapped out of her reverie and looked at Candace with disdain. "When did you name her? Before or after you stuffed her in a sneaker box and put her out with the garbage?" She sneered.

Candace closed the space between them in a millisecond. She slapped Karina so hard her head hit the back of the chair. "Don't you dare judge me! You don't know what it was like. My baby was dead. I wished it had been me! If I could have changed places with her I would have!"

As though all the energy had been drained from her body, Candace sank down into a chair at the table. She spoke quietly, looking at the shoebox."I know my baby deserved a proper burial. I've lived with the shame of not giving her one for all these years. If I had only known that Mama Ella had done that for her, so much would've been different."

Karina held a hand to her cheek. A myriad of emotions played over her face as she stared at her sister. The rain drummed steadily on the roof.

"Why didn't you tell me that Mama Ella found her and buried her, Rina?" Candace whispered. "Why didn't you beg me to come home?" She glanced at the old-fashioned yellow rotary phone bolted to the wall. "Remember the first time I called? I had only been gone a few weeks. You called me selfish and hung up on me. *I needed y'all, Rina.* I was so sick from having the baby I almost died." Candace's eyes bored into Karina's.

"When I called that second time and I begged you to send me money to come home I told you I was in bad trouble. Did you think I was high and wouldn't remember? Oh, I remember, Sis. I wasn't high. I was scared shitless."

"Candi, I . . . I've felt guilty about that for so long." Karina broke eye contact.

Candace ignored her, "Did you hear the fear in my voice when I told you I needed help? Did you even wonder what I was so scared of? I'll tell you now what you didn't give me a chance to tell you then. This white man that a pimp set me up with had drugged and raped me, and tried to strangle me to death. I barely managed to escape, but he was just a few yards away trying to find me so he could finish me off."

Karina's eyes widened in shock. "Candi, I'm so sorry. I wasn't paying attention; I didn't know!" She began to cry. "I can't tell you how many times I've gone over those conversations in my head."

"Spare me, Karina," Candace snapped. "You hung up. You didn't care if I died right then and there, and I nearly did. And I was stupid enough to make my way to Western Union, looking for the money. The money that never came." Candace's voice cracked. "What did I do that was so horrible, Rina? I snuck out to go to a sideshow and because you snitched, Mommy and Daddy died looking for me in East Oakland. Meanwhile I was laying down by the bridge at the U.C. Campus thinking I was in love." She stared at Karina. "Tell me this, if you felt so bad about hanging up on me, did you tell Mama Ella that I called and asked for help?"

Karina reached out to her sister. "Candi, please let me try to explain. I didn't know where you were or how to find you. I thought telling Mama Ella would cause her more pain. I assumed you'd call back," her voice trembled. "It was a fight, Candi. It wasn't supposed to be the last time I'd hear your voice for seventeen years."

"No, Karina, it wasn't a fight. You were the last link to my old life and you cut me off." The fire had faded from Candace's voice. "I promised myself I'd never call back, no matter how bad it got. And damn, it got so bad sometimes it took everything in me to keep my promise. But you had hurt me too much to go through that again. It took me years to stop blaming you and start taking accountability for my own actions. Mommy, Daddy, baby Zora – all dead. My only sister basically wanted me dead. So I went on a mission to convince God to just let me die too. But it seemed like it was my punishment to live and suffer."

Karina swallowed, "How did you get through those years?"

"High on something most of the time. Sometimes Nick was out of jail and we'd hustle to make it together but there was a long stretch of time that he was locked up and I was on my own." She looked Karina in the eye, "You don't wanna know the things that a young girl has to do to survive in the streets. Mommy and Daddy didn't prepare us for that life. But I was a quick learner. I had to be. And it turns out I was a survivor."

"But how, how did you manage if Nick wasn't there with you?"

Candace snorted, "Are you still that naïve? I was an addict, a thief, a hooker. I fucked or sucked whoever I had to – for money, for coke, for crack, for meth, for food, for a roof over my head. I stole, robbed, fought - whatever I needed to do, whenever I needed to do it. Roxie, the woman I told you about, would rescue me as often as I'd let her. Nick would get out and things would be cool for a while. 'Round and 'round we'd go."

Karina bit her bottom lip and shook her head. "Candi, I had no idea it was that bad."

"Seriously Rina? What did you think eighteen-year-old girls do to survive when they disappear? Why did you think I was calling home?'" Candace's voice was raw.

Karina forced herself to meet Candace's eyes and whispered, "I was so angry for so long. I wouldn't allow myself to think about what you were going through. I let Mama Ella do all the worrying and praying about you so I could hold tight to my anger and not admit how lonely I was."

"You were lonely." Candace barked sarcastically. "I was literally fighting for my survival. Some days just getting enough to eat was a miracle. I had to carry whatever I owned with me in a backpack because I had no place to call home, but you were lonely. Wow. Rina, you think you can make me feel any worse about leaving my dead baby in a shoebox? That was just the beginning of my descent into hell."

"Candi, I need to tell you something—"

"Oh no! It's not your turn to talk. You wanted to hear my story, right? You've been so angry with me for so long so here it is!" Candace took a deep breath before continuing. "It started before I ran away. Y'all didn't even notice that I tried to kill myself before I went to Texarkana."

Karina gasped. "What are you talking about?"

"I tried to drown myself in that tub right down the hall. But I forgot to put the plug in and the tub didn't fill with water. I couldn't do anything right! You found my suicide note and basically flipped me off. I was such a disappointment. Mommy and Daddy were gone. You hated me. Even Mama Ella could barely look at me. I heard her talking about me to Mrs. Jenkins. She said I was whorish! And you took every opportunity to let me know I was a slut. Which was hilarious given that I had only had sex once in my life."

She paused, allowing a tiny smile to escape. "Texarkana turned out to be a bright spot during that miserable time. Aunt Izora helped me believe my life could maybe, just maybe, get better."

Karina interrupted, "So you left knowing you were pregnant?"

Candace shook her head. "I had no idea. It took months for me to figure it out." Her lips curled into a sardonic smile. "By the time I found out it was too late to get an abortion. Thank God for Aunt Izora! Of all people, she was the one to come up with a plan to get the baby adopted so no one would ever know."

"You were gonna do that without telling Mama Ella?"

Candace nodded. "I didn't want to bring any more misery to Mama Ella's doorstep."

"So, what changed?" Karina was caught up in the story.

Candace hung her head, "Aunt Izora died."

"We found out about her passing when Mama Ella called to see if you'd gone back to Texarkana. She thought maybe that's why you'd come home unexpectedly but it never occurred to her that Aunt Izora knew you were pregnant."

"She died two weeks before I came home. I didn't want Mama Ella to come to the homegoing and see me pregnant, so I came home to tell her face-to-face. I was going to come clean about everything and ask for her help. I'd started to hope it might be possible to keep the baby. I was a mess! Scared of y'all's reaction and worried about whether Nick would ever forgive me; if he would still want to be with me." She shook her head. "Turns out, none of that mattered."

"So that's why you wouldn't hug me the day you came home from Texarkana," Karina said.

Candace nodded, "I didn't want you to feel the baby without me having a chance to tell you and Mama Ella my story first. I was completely thrown off when she said she was going to Reno with Frieda! And then you had a date with a boyfriend I'd never even heard of and you were pissed at me for being home. You clearly still hated me. Everything was just awful. I didn't want to ruin her trip or your night so I decided I'd tell you both the next day."

"But the next day the baby was born." Karina said, putting the pieces together.

"She started coming that night. I wasn't ready! She was so early, I knew something was wrong. I kept calling out for you but the music was too loud for you to hear me. I was struggling, but I made it to the living room. Even though I was pregnant, I was still pretty naïve; I hadn't ever seen . . . wasn't prepared for what I saw."

Karina's face flushed. "That was my first time," she murmured. "Candi, why didn't you say something? My God, you needed help!"

"I've asked myself that question over and over again. I was embarrassed? First babies take a long time, Mama Ella used to tell us. I had ruined so much in your life; I didn't want to ruin your special night. I thought you'd come to bed at some point. But it got really bad and then I was kind of out of it. At some point I heard the front door close and I called out for you but it was too late. I tried to make it to the phone but all of a sudden baby Zora was coming fast! I didn't know what to do. I got as far as the bathroom. Rina, she just slid out! She moved her little arms and legs once, but then she was still. I tried to get her to move again, but she wouldn't. I tried so hard. I cleared her mouth. I pushed on her chest. She was so still; like a babydoll. I had lost her too." Candace's eyes were trained on the floor.

"But why did you leave? Why put her outside?" Karina couldn't contain her curiosity.

Candace shrugged. "I panicked. I'd kept my pregnancy a secret and now my baby was dead. I couldn't burden Mama Ella with all of that. That shoebox was sacred in my mind. It came from Daddy. I walked out the door with baby Zora but then didn't know where to take her. So I put her next to the garbage can. I was probably in shock; I know that now. But at the time I thought I was behaving rationally. When I got to the bus stop it hit me that I should bury her somewhere, but like everything else I fucked that up. The garbage truck had already come and taken her away, or so I thought. I felt like I was the worst human being in the world." She began to cry again.

"Now all these years later, I know that Mama Ella came through for me like always. She picked up my baby and made sure she was buried. I don't know how it happened, but this shoebox proves it." She shook her head. "God is amazing."

Karina took Candace's hands in hers and took a deep breath. "Candi, look at me. I need to tell you something." Her voice was shaky but resolute. "There's no easy way to say this. Candi, I'm the one who found her. When I went to move the garbage can back from the curb I saw the shoebox. Then I heard something."

"What do you mean you heard something?"

"Candi, the baby wasn't dead."

"Rina, what are you saying? She was dead. At first she wasn't and then she was. She never moved again! *She was dead. Zora was dead!*" Candace's voice grew shrill.

Karina's voice was steady. "Mama Ella was convinced that's what you believed. There's a name for it − asphyxia. It could've been fatal but since the baby got gen right after she was born, the disruption in her breathing for a few minutes didn't cause long-term damage."

"What are you saying? She was alive? For how long? A few more minutes? Hours?" Candace grabbed her by the shoulders. *"Karina, tell me!"*

"We didn't know her name was Zora. Mama Ella thought the name Samaya would be perfect."

Candace's hands dropped to her sides and confusion clouded her eyes. *"Samaya?"*

A high-pitched keening came from the living room. They rushed to investigate and found Samaya on the floor, rocking back and forth, tears streaming down her face.

"Zandy said he . . . was meeting you here." She told Karina. "I, I came to surprise you. I thought we, we . . . could all have dinner. And then I heard you guys talking and I was being nosey and . . ." She spoke in a monotone voice. Her face was pale and her body was shaking.

Karina tried to pull Samaya into her arms, but the teenager pushed her away. "Don't touch me!" She screamed. "You're a liar! You've lied to me my whole life."

Candace sank onto the couch, watching them, unable to sort through her thoughts quickly enough to speak.

Karina put one hand on each side of Samaya's face. "Sammi sweetheart, listen to me, I know this is a lot to take in and it sounds crazy but hear me when I tell you that it doesn't change anything. *You are Samaya Bishop.* I am your mother in every way that matters. Zander is your father. You've been loved and cherished since the moment you came into this world. I know this is confusing but we'll work through it as a family."

Samaya jerked away. "No, *Karina*, this changes everything! *You're not my mother.* You've been *pretending* to be my mother." She pointed to Candace. "*She's my mother!* She thought I was dead and you let her think it. What kind of person does that? I can't believe Mama Ella kept this secret. And what about Zandy? Was he in on this too? What kind of family is this?"

She turned to Candace. "How can you stand to be in the same room with her? She ruined your life!"

Candace struggled for the right words. "I've made lots of poor decisions and choices that I have to own; that I can't blame on anyone else. I'm taking this all in, just like you." She moved to sit on the floor next to Samaya and reached for her hand. "What I can tell you is that *today*, learning that my baby girl did not die seventeen years ago, *is now the best day of my life.* You are a blessing, a treasure, a gift from God." Tears streamed down Candace's face.

"I'm a blessing . . . a treasure . . ." Samaya repeated. "But you left me for dead in a shoebox next to a garbage can." Pulling her hand away, she stood up. She walked to the door. *"I hate you both!"* She screamed and slammed the door behind her.

Karina and Candace stayed on the floor where Samaya had left them. Neither of them knew what to say or do next. The ticking of the grandfather clock seemed to echo through the house. Several minutes passed and they heard footsteps coming up the front steps.

Hope was dashed when Zander, instead of Samaya, entered the house. "Hey, what's up with Sammi? As I was turning the corner I saw her pull out of the driveway like a bat out of hell!" He leaned down to kiss Karina's forehead as he spoke.

Karina scrambled to come up with a story. She looked to Candace and then out of the window. "Oh, you know how she is whenever she doesn't get her way. She was trying to go to some last-minute thing with Darnell that she tried to use Brandy as a cover for. She'll get over it." Her eyes darted around the room. Candace didn't acknowledge Zander's presence.

Zander looked back and forth at them. "Well, it seems like you two are in the middle of something kinda intense. Wanna reschedule dinner, Rina?"

"Yeah, would that be okay?" she asked.

"No problem, I'll just grab an apple or something." Zander walked to the kitchen. Stopping at the table he sifted through the pictures that Candace had found in the attic. He looked at one for several seconds. Brow furrowed, he picked it up to get a better look and turned it over to read what was written on the back. He stiffened and dropped the picture back on the table. Forgetting about the apple, he strode quickly to the front door, looking straight ahead, and closed it softly behind him.

Karina gathered her things and walked towards the door.

"Just where do you think you're going?" Candace blocked her path.

"I need to go see about Samaya."

"Not so fast, little sister. You can't just drop this shit on me and take off." Candace grabbed Karina's wrist and pulled her into the living room. "Sit yo' ass down." She ordered and began to pace around the room.

"So, you're telling me that you and Mama Ella found my baby, alive, and decided to name her Samaya? You became her mother? Just like that?" She snapped her fingers. She stood in front of Karina, her body trembling with a mixture of emotions and willed her to look at her.

"Karina, all that shit you spewed at me on the phone – how the fuck is it that you didn't say a single word about finding my baby and her being alive?"

Karina hung her head. "I thought you tried to kill her and I hated you for that . . ." Karina's voice trailed off. She looked up to meet Candace's eyes. "That's what was going on in my head that day when you called. After a while, I finally heard what Mama Ella was saying and thought, well maybe she's right, maybe it was an accident. I kept thinking you'd call back but you never did. And then after so many years had passed, I was afraid that you'd take her from me."

"I called twice and both times you hung up on me. You were the closest person to me and you made it clear that you didn't care whether I lived or died, so why would I call back?" Candace laughed bitterly. "Damn, this is the first time I've wanted a drink in years. But after all you've done to me, I'll be damned if I let you take my sobriety away from me."

Candace whispered to herself. "Seven years of hell. Ten years of sobriety. God grant me the serenity, God grant me the serenity, my God, please grant me the serenity."

Karina sat silently, watching her sister grapple with her emotions. Unable to process her own.

"Tell me all of it. What was it like to raise my daughter? And when did your husband become a part of this cover-up? He must be shaking in his designer loafers now that I'm back."

Karina jumped up, wild-eyed. "No Candi, Zander has no idea!" Her words tumbled out. "I mean he knows that I'm not Samaya's birth mom but that's it. Only me, Mama Ella and Mrs. Jenkins knew the whole story. Zander adopted Samaya when we got married."

"What about her birth certificate?"

"Mama Ella had somebody at the hospital put my name on it."

Candace's eyes filled with tears. "Damn, that soon? She just blotted me out of Zora's life that quickly? I guess I really didn't matter to either one of you."

Karina frowned. "It wasn't like that. She was trying to protect you – to protect all of us. She didn't want CPS or anybody poking around so she put me there as a placeholder. She kept saying she'd get it corrected when you came home."

Karina stared out of the window, her voice grew bitter. "Mama Ella was always talking about 'when Candi comes home' this, and 'when Candi comes home' that. She didn't seem to notice or value all the sacrifices I was making. My so called 'college years'? They were a joke. I only lived on campus for a hot minute. I missed out on the parties, didn't get to pledge a sorority, always had to get right back here so I could take care of the baby and then take care of Mama Ella. All while you were out there doing whatever you wanted to do. I was just the stand-in for you. I had to be the big little sister."

"You are unbelievable, Karina! You have the audacity to say this to me? I told you the kinda shit I had to do to survive. I was out there turning tricks, smoking crack, boosting from stores, pickpocketing, and running credit card scams, Little Miss College Student, while you had whatever you needed, whenever you needed it. What do you think I would have given for a roof over my head and food in my belly? To have the privilege of changing diapers, teaching my daughter her ABCs or rubbing my grandmother's feet?" Candace sat on the couch, massaging her temples.

"You could've come home Candi!" Karina snapped. "You had the address. Shit, you had the key all these years. *You chose not to come back.*"

"I guess from your perspective it looks like a choice, Karina. Tell me something, did you ever try to find me?" Candace studied her sister's face.

Karina sat back down. "Of course we did, Candi. We called the police. We put up missing signs and called your friends."

"What about later? What about when you married this big shot lawyer who had connections?"

"He wasn't a big shot lawyer. He was young, like me, and had to work his way up through the ranks," Karina explained.

"I didn't ask for his fucking resume!" Candace yelled. "I'm asking you if you ever, as my daughter got older, tried to find me? His family had money. The people he worked for had connections. Did you at least try to find out if I was alive?"

Karina blushed. "Remember, Zander didn't know anything about you being connected to Samaya. He just knew that I had a sister who ran away with her drug dealer boyfriend. That's all."

Candace nodded her head. "Right, he was in the dark about everything. So the answer is no, you didn't try to find me. It wouldn't have been too hard; I kept using my government name." After a brief pause she looked at Karina with a sneer and said, "And you never had kids of your own."

"Samaya is ours!" Karina shouted. "We are the only parents she knows." Karina shook her head. "We always planned to have a house full of kids. I told you about the ectopic pregnancy and the miscarriages and the stillbirth. But Samaya is all we have." Karina's pain was etched into her face making her look years older.

Candace was in no mood to feel sorry for her. "So once again, you were jealous of me. You wanted what I had. I get it now."

Karina opened her mouth to respond but Candace put up her hand to stop her. "I need some time to process all of this."

Without another word they gathered their belongings and locked up the house.

14

REVELATIONS

Candace made a cup of tea and wrapped herself in a blanket, lost in thought. Nick sat at the table reviewing sketches for a client submission. Typically she loved to share this early morning time, right after sunrise, with her husband. But today she prayed he would be so absorbed in his work that he wouldn't notice her mood. She was still digesting all that had happened. She knew she'd have to tell Nick all about it but when she tried to think of how to start the conversation, her mind went blank. *My marriage is over. After everything we've been through, this is it.*

Her phone vibrated. It was Karina.

"Is Samaya with you?"

Candace frowned and sat up. "No. Why would she be?"

"She didn't come home last night. I'm scared. I think she ran away. This is déjà vu all over again." Karina's voice started to shake. "Can you please come over? I'm at home."

"We're on our way." She threw off the blanket and hurriedly got dressed, yelling instructions at Nick.

Twenty-five minutes later Candace and Nick arrived at Karina and Zander's house. Karina let them in without a word and led them into the Great Room where Zander was finishing up yet another call with one of Samaya's friends. He raised his chin at Nick and Candace in greeting and brought them up to speed.

"This isn't like her at all; she didn't come home last night, and none of her friends know where she is." Zander was an anxious ball of energy.

"I talked to some folks I know at the police department but they think I'm overreacting. They said 'teenagers do things like this.' Since she has money and a car and hasn't been gone that long they're treating me like an overprotective dad but I know my daughter . . . " He looked at Karina. "She was upset when she left Mama Ella's yesterday. I need you to walk me through it one more time cause I don't understand what happened."

Karina didn't respond. She walked aimlessly around the room picking up things and putting them back down, her lips moving as she mouthed a silent prayer.

"Karina—!" Zander's voice boomed.

"Give her some space, Zander." Nick said trying to calm him down. "Let's sit down and talk this through. I'm sure Samaya's okay, I feel it in my bones." They sat down and spoke quietly.

Candace walked over to the window and stood next to Karina. The harsh words of the night before enveloped them like a heavy cloud. Karina turned to Candace, her eyes telegraphing her despair. "Do you think she'd try to hurt herself? What if she really is like you and I won't see her for seventeen years, or ever?" With each question, Karina's voice became shriller and weaker with the last ending in sobs.

Tears sprang to Candace's eyes. She grabbed Karina by the arms. "Samaya is not me! You sound crazy. She's like you. She's smarter than me. She's not going to be gone for seventeen hours, much less seventeen years. And there's no reason to think she'd hurt herself. She's just taking some time and space to absorb everything —" she paused to wipe away her tears with the back of her hand "— I think she's punishing us!"

"What the fuck are y'all talking about?" Zander shouted.

Karina and Candace both jumped at Zander's voice. Nick walked over to them. "What's going on, Sweetness?"

Karina avoided Zander's glare, but tried to answer, "You already know that yesterday, me and Candi were, um, over at Mama Ella's house. We were talking about some stuff and um, well Sammi had come into the living room, but we didn't know it. You know how nosey she has always been. Always eavesdropping even though we've tried to get her to stop. And um . . ."

Candace broke in, no more eloquent than her sister, "Right, so we didn't know that, that she was in the house while we were talking. We said a lot of stuff that she didn't have a context for because we really didn't have the context for it ourselves. I mean, we were kind of talking through it and we were arguing. What she heard was like a shock to her, I mean really to me too, but we were trying to focus on her, on her um feelings and her uh, reaction. Then she said some things. Understandable things, you know. And then she ran out before we could talk it through with her, right Karina?"

"Right, right!" Karina nodded.

Zander couldn't take any more. Before anyone in the room could register what was happening, he quickly covered the distance between him and Karina, leaving only inches between them, towering over her. His voice was low and gravely, "Don't make me have to ask you again, Karina. What the fuck are you talking about? What was so confusing? What did my daughter overhear?"

Candace pushed Zander away from Karina. Fury emanating from her, she screamed, "You trying to put hands on my sister? You come for her, you come for me!"

Zander turned to face Candace with a frown and Nick stepped between them.

"Nah brotha, you don't want none of that. I understand you're really upset right now and it's causing you to act in ways that you'd surely regret so why don't you back up, alright?" Nick spoke calmly but there was no doubt he could escalate as quickly as Zander had.

The men locked eyes for several seconds then Zander nodded and seemed to deflate. He sank into a chair and put his head in his hands. Nick stood over him.

"I'm so sorry. Karina baby, you know I'd never hurt you. I'm just worried about Sammi, and I'm so fucking confused. And no,

Candace that's not who I am. I promise you that. Can y'all please just tell us what's going on?"

Giving Zander the benefit of the doubt, Nick sat down. The wariness in his eyes remained.

Karina and Candace sat on the loveseat across the room from their husbands. Karina cleared her throat. "Let me try again. Last night Candi and I were at Mama Ella's house talking. It's been all these years but we never had the full side of each other's stories. Samaya heard us piecing our past together."

Zander started to interrupt but Karina put up her hand to silence him. "Zander this is hard enough, could you please just let me get it out as best I can?"

He nodded and she continued, "When Zander and I met during my senior year of high school, it was just me and Mama Ella. Candi was down South. It was a really hard time for our family. I was still grieving our parents. Then Candi came home unexpectedly but she ran away the next day. Mama Ella and I had this newborn baby we were taking care of while Mama Ella was still working and I was getting ready to go to Cal." Karina swallowed hard, finding it difficult to choose her words.

"Zander, when you came along . . . it didn't feel like a good time to be super open with a lot of details and information. I mean, you were gonna be leaving for Howard and Mama Ella kept reminding me that high school flings are usually just that, even though I didn't think that's all it was. And Mama Ella said we needed to keep family business close and plus we didn't know exactly when Candi would be back."

Karina looked at the men, trying to gauge their reaction. Candace was looking at her feet. Taking a deep breath, Karina continued. "Mama Ella said we would raise her ourselves. That's when we told everybody that Cousin Jolene asked us to take care of Samaya."

Zander interrupted, "Look, Babe, I'm trying to be patient but what does your Cousin Jolene have to do with any of this? I know she was Sammi's birth mom, but that was dealt with years ago. She's been dead ever since Sammi was three. Why is this coming up now?

Sammi is missing and you want to talk about a woman who never had an impact on her life?"

Realization dawned on him. "Are you telling me that you picked yesterday to tell Candi about that and Sammi overheard you? What the fuck, Karina? We decided when Sammi was six years old that we'd never tell her you weren't her birth mom! You're the only mother she's ever known. And her birth mother was dead. It was enough that she'd know I adopted her. Even Mama Ella and my parents agreed!" Zander stood up. "And she had to hear it like it was some kinda gossip?" He started pacing around the room.

Karina glanced at Candace, took a deep breath and said, "No Zander, that's not what happened. That was all a lie. There never was a Cousin Jolene. I found Samaya in a shoebox next to the garbage can outside Mama Ella's house the day Candi ran away. We figured out that Candi had put her there. Mama Ella made up the Cousin Jolene story to cover for Candi. Mama Ella made me swear I'd never tell anybody about what really happened. She always believed Candi would come back for the baby. But Candi didn't come home and I became Samaya's mother. *I am Samaya's mother.*"

Nick went completely still and the room was silent.

Zander's face turned ashen. "Wait a minute! Are you telling me that Candi is Samaya's mother?"

He turned to look at Candace with a wild look in his eyes. *"You were pregnant and didn't tell anybody? You put your baby outside in a shoebox? What the fuck is wrong with you? My baby girl started out her life in a garbage can?"* Zander shouted.

He turned to Karina. "For seventeen years, through all the madness of our life together – school, marriage, miscarriages, your crazy insecurities, *the death of our son* – and you kept this from me? And Mama Ella, the most upstanding, churchified woman I've ever known, was part of this lie?"

The veins in Zander's neck bulged. "My daughter heard this bullshit last night? No wonder she didn't come home. This is un-fucking-believable!" He stormed out of the house. The sound of a car engine revving up reverberated through the house. Karina seemed to fold into herself. She sank back into the loveseat, face expressionless.

Nick stared at Candace, willing her to look up at him. When he finally spoke, his voice was barely a whisper. "Candace, make this make sense to me. Please."

Candace raised her eyes to meet Nick's. "I can't make it make sense, but I can finally tell you what happened. Or I can tell you what didn't happen. I didn't throw her away, Nick . . . when I left baby Zora that day she wasn't moving or breathing."

Nick's eyes narrowed in confusion. Candace explained, "Zora was the name I gave her. *She was dead.* I didn't have any doubt that she was dead. Hell, at that moment I wanted to be dead myself. I couldn't bear the thought of looking into Mama Ella and Karina's eyes and presenting them with my beautiful dead baby girl. I just couldn't do it. One more failure, one more death, one last bit of evidence that I was worthless. So I wrapped her up and put her in my special shoebox, put her outside by the curb – *not inside the garbage can.* I did go back to get her, but it was too late. And I ended up with you." Candace's heart was beating so loudly she could barely hear her own words.

"I almost died; remember when I ended up in the hospital in Reno after we got married? I couldn't tell you why I was so sick cause you were the only person who actually thought I deserved to live. I didn't even think I deserved to live. I slowly kept trying to kill myself when you were locked up – the cocaine, the , the drinking, putting myself in dangerous situations . . . My parents were dead, my baby was dead, I was dead to my sister and my grandmother. But God kept me alive. And somehow you and I came through it all and made a life together. Finally, God started whispering to me. He made me think there was some seed in me worth nurturing, worth living for, so I've been trying to help other girls find their way. And I learned to give myself a little tiny bit of grace."

She inhaled sharply. "And last night, after all these years, I found out that Zora had somehow survived; that Zora is now Samaya. I'm still trying to take it all in." Candace's voice had grown softer but she was determined to tell her truth and not hide behind it.

Nick sat with his arms crossed, his face expressionless, staring at her. Several moments passed. "That's a touching story. But I have one question, Candace." He leaned forward and his voice grew deeper and louder. "Where the fuck did baby Zora come from in the first place?"

The layers of polish sloughed off and the boy who grew up without parents, hustling in the streets to survive, emerged. "You telling me you was the Virgin Mary of Berkeley? We was *together* Candi, and *we had never had sex!* What, you thought I forgot that part? We was *waiting until the right time*; until you was *ready*. Shit, we even waited more than a month after we got married!" He could barely hold back his disgust. "I was willing to jump through any hoop, do anything for you." He stood and strode over to Candace, towering over her.

"I would've died for you, Candi! I damn near did more times than I can count!" He started pacing around the room as though his body couldn't hold the energy any longer. "All the shit we've been through? We've been down holes as deep as any two people could go together and you kept this from me? I've never held anything you've done against you! Nothing could ever have spoiled you in my mind. You know you've always been my world. After the miscarriages, and tears and the damn fertility treatments, *you still couldn't tell me you had a baby?*"

He stopped suddenly and turned to look at Candace who had sunk down into the cushions of the chair, tears streaming down her face. A mix of emotions clouded Nick's face, the anger seemed to suddenly dissipate, replaced with raw pain. He rushed to her and dropped to his knees, taking her hands in his. He whispered, "Wait a minute did somebody force himself on you? *Baby is that what happened? You didn't tell me because somebody raped you?*"

Candace looked at him, knowing that her response would impact the rest of her life. She took a deep breath and cradled Nick's face in her hands. "Oh Nicky, no, it wasn't rape — it was an impulsive, one-time dumb decision of an immature girl. It happened the night my parents died and it became inconsequential, until it wasn't. Then it was a secret, from everybody, a secret that I didn't think our relationship would survive. I don't know if there was a time along the way that we could have handled it if I'd told you the truth. What I do know is that the love between me and you grew stronger over the years. But I never wanted to be less than who you believed me to be." Candace paused, searching his eyes for forgiveness.

Nick slowly and carefully removed Candace's hands from his face, his expression inscrutable, his eyes never leaving hers. "I never thought anything could break us. But as my grandmother would say, keep living, Boy, keep living." With that, he walked out, closing the front door quietly behind him.

Karina and Candace were speechless. Unable to comprehend that both of their husbands were gone, they threw themselves at the most pressing problem.

Karina spoke first. "Samaya! We have to find her."

Pulling herself together, Candace said, "Let me make some calls."

"I'll create a flyer. We need to post them all over." Karina opened her laptop as Candace scrolled through her phone.

"Rashad? Hey, it's Candi Maxwell-Myers. Listen, I need your help. We have a seventeen-year-old runaway. She's been gone since last night – first timer, not street smart, emotionally driven, mobile with access to cash. This one's personal. Can you please activate your teen street team for me? I'll text a pic. Yeah, I suspect she'll stay in the Bay Area for now. Thanks so much, I'll check in with you later." She ended the call.

Karina looked at Candace quizzically, "Activate the teen street team? Who was that?"

"Rashad Ali is the Director of the non-profit we're considering merging with. He'll make sure that all the spots that are kept 'secret' from adults and social workers are checked and he'll report to me if there's a sighting, without spooking Samaya."

Karina frowned, "Samaya isn't a 'runaway' like that. She doesn't know anything about secret spots."

"We don't have time for this shit, Rina. We need to be on the same page, for once." She snapped, then took a deep breath. "Sorry, I'm just . . ." Candace closed her eyes. "Let's call it triggered by all of this. You know, finding out about Zora, or Samaya, I mean, and then her running away. Thinking about everything that happened to me when I ran away." Her voice trailed off. "I can't fail her again."

Karina's expression was unreadable. "Yeah, we wouldn't want that to happen." She said, in a flat tone.

Stung, Candace blinked back tears.

"I'd better call Mom Betty!" Karina said.

"Who is that? Do you think Samaya's with her?" Candace asked.

"She's Zander's mother. All these phone calls to Sammi's friends will have gotten back to their mothers and grandmothers and then to Mom Betty. They're all connected through Jack & Jill, the Links, the AKAs and Deltas. She'll be frantic."

"Oh, Zander comes from that kind of money," Candace murmured.

"What's that supposed to mean?"

"What do you think it's supposed to mean?" Candace snapped. "You know we didn't come from that kind of generational wealth. Exclusionary, bougie folks, summering at Oak Bluffs, memberships at exclusive country clubs, cotillions . . ."

"For your information, it's not what we thought it was. They're all very nice. We all just want our kids to be supported and to have the best experiences they can have in this world where the cards are stacked against them. Why shouldn't they be able to have carefree summers, play tennis, ride horses and yes, even be debutantes?"

Candace snorted. "Well clearly you've been indoctrinated to the 'our kind of people' way of thinking."

"You're so dramatic! I'm setting my daughter up for success, period."

"I don't have time for this. You go on and call the ladies of lineage or whatever so they can check the country club Rec room to see if Samaya is there. I'm gonna stay on track and have my folks look for her where I know she's likely to be!"

"Wait a minute, Candi. Don't get beside yourself. Samaya is *my* daughter. Don't think that a few weeks of being around is gonna make you an expert on her."

"Now is not the time, Rina. *Yours, mine, ours.* Samaya is missing, period. You've been telling me the whole time I've been back that she's been hanging out with Brandy for months, right? From what I've seen, Brandy is not summering in Oak Bluffs or practicing for the cotillion, is she?"

Karina rolled her eyes.

"Like I said, I'm gonna have my folks look for Samaya where regular teenagers go when they don't want to be found and where predators know to seek them out." Candace pushed past Karina.

Rashad clasped Nick's hand. "It's been a long time, brother. I'm glad to see you but so sorry it has to be under these circumstances."

"Same here, man. I'm kinda stressed about my niece. Has Candi already reached out to you?"

"Yeah, I was just about to call her with an update."

"Is it good news or bad news?"

"More like a progress report. We know some of where she's been, but not where she is right now. She was at a sideshow near 98th and Foothill late last night or really early this morning. Her car was seen parked not too far from there and she was spotted walking around and watching while some dudes were battling it out in the intersection."

"Was she by herself?"

"As far as we know. She wasn't seen talking to anybody in particular but we're not sure if she left alone."

"Candi is gon' lose her mind when she hears this!" Nick stood up to leave.

"Don't you want to make the call to Candi with me?" Rashad asked.

"Nah man, you handle that please. I'mma ride around that part of town and ask a few questions." He turned back. "Hey man, no need to tell Candi I was here. I'll reach out if and when I get some more news."

Elliott was shocked when he opened his front door and saw the anguish in Zander's eyes.

"Get dressed Eli, I need you." Zander went to the kitchen sink and splashed water on his face. "Hurry. It's Sammi."

"What's wrong with Sammi?" Elliott ran upstairs, returning a few minutes later, yanking a t-shirt over his head, pulling on sweatpants and jamming his feet into sneakers. "Zander, say something! What's going on? Do I need my gun?"

"I don't know; yeah, maybe. Bring it just in case."

Elliott reached atop the kitchen cabinet to retrieve a 9mm handgun and clip. "I'll drive. You talk." They raced to Elliott's car.

Zander hesitated, "Man, I don't know where to go." He banged his fist over and over on the dashboard. "Sammi ran away. She took her car but left her phone. None of her friends claim to have heard from her."

"Ran away? Why?"

"It's a long ass, fucked up story, but bottom line, she found out about her real mother."

"Her real mother? What are you talking about?"

Zander ran his hand over his head. "Not too long after me and Rina started dating, her and Mama Ella had a newborn at the house that they said belonged to a cousin from down south. Long story short, Karina is the only mother Sammi has ever known. We all agreed to keep it a secret."

Elliott stared at Zander for a long beat. "You're my brother and you never told me this? I thought you met Karina soon after she had a baby and the daddy just wasn't in the picture."

"What difference would it have made, man? It was her family's business. And when we got serious, it didn't matter to me."

"So Sammi learned Karina isn't her biological mother and she freaked out? But why would she run away?" He answered his own question. "I guess learning about it so soon after Mama Ella's death might have put her on emotional overload." He started the car.

"Where are we going?" Zander asked.

"I'm thinking we go check out that skateboard park in Alameda. I saw Sammi picking up Brandy and a couple other kids over there not too long ago. One dude had a board."

"And you didn't think to mention that to me?"

"Dude, you gave your 17-year-old a car and a midnight curfew and I'm supposed to report back her Saturday afternoon movements? Plus, the kids looked harmless enough. Sweat jackets, jeans, Vans, kinda artsy/dance types."

After a few minutes Zander said, "There's more to the story."

Elliot glanced at him. "Isn't there always? What else happened?"

"I'm still wrapping my mind around all this and I'm telling you up front, I do not have answers to all the questions you're about to throw at me."

"Would you stop with the preambles and just spill it?" Elliott demanded.

"Turns out, Candace is Sammi's birth mom."

"What!" Elliott shouted.

Zander nodded. He could barely believe it himself. "No one knew she was pregnant. She had the baby by herself at Mama Ella's house and thought it was dead so she ran away. Mama Ella revived her, I think, I'm not sure about all the details. Then she and Karina pretended like the baby belonged to a cousin from down South."

"And Karina never thought it was important to tell you this?"

"It never would've come out, if Candi hadn't come home. How much longer 'til we get there man?" Zander felt like he was losing his mind. "My daughter has been dealing with this since last night. I need to find her."

"Almost there. Damn, my goddaughter's head has to be spinning. No wonder she wanted to be far away from both Rina and Candi."

"Man, if I'd realized, if I'd just put two and two together . . ."

"I know you're stressing, Zan, but there is no way you could've known any of this. You came into the picture after all this was set in motion. Hell, you didn't even meet Candi til a few weeks ago."

"This shit is so fucking complicated . . ." Zander started to speak again, then he closed his eyes and rested his head in his hands. "Damn Eli. You don't understand, man. *We're talking about my daughter.*"

"Give me a little credit. I know in your heart there's no difference between Sammi and that little boy y'all lost." He parked the car and they got out. "Let's see if she's here or if anyone has seen her." Ten minutes later Elliott murmured, "I'm sorry Zan. I was really hoping she'd be here."

Zander nodded. "Can I drive? I think better when I'm driving."

As they rode, Zander replayed the events of the past few hours, hoping that answers would crystallize. "So, we know Sammi was in the living room listening to Rina and Candi hash out their old shit. Is there anything that she heard that might connect to where she is now? That's the question."

They rode in silence until Zander murmured, "I wonder?" Buoyed by a thought he didn't dare speak out loud, he maneuvered to the freeway and sped up.

Candace found Karina sitting on the back patio smoking a cigarette. "You smoke? I didn't see that one coming."

Karina tipped the ash into a makeshift ashtray made of aluminum foil. "Not really. But I needed something to calm my nerves. Zander quit a few years ago, but he keeps a stash in his desk drawer. He thinks I don't know." She laughed dryly. "I'm not the only one with secrets."

"I'm not gonna touch that one. Anyway, I just talked to Rashad."

Karina smashed the butt in the ashtray. "Why didn't you tell me he was on the phone? What did he say? Did they find her?"

Candace sat down next to her. "Slow down. Try to keep it together, okay?"

Karina's eyes glistened. "Oh no, what is it, Candi? Tell me." There was both fear and urgency in her voice.

"We don't know where she is, yet, but we know where she was."

"When? Where? Tell me!"

"Around 3 o'clock she was at a sideshow on 98th and Foothill. Her car was parked nearby. She wasn't seen with anyone in particular. All we know is that by 5 o'clock when the crowd had dispersed, she wasn't seen anymore and her car had been moved."

"I don't understand. A sideshow! That doesn't make sense." Karina got up and ran into the kitchen, Candace right behind her. She began to frantically search through a pile of Oakland Tribunes stacked by the backdoor.

"What are you doing?" Candace asked.

Karina muttered to herself, "Where is it?" She found what she was looking for and slammed the newspaper on the table. "We read that article together a few days ago! A fifteen-year-old girl died at a sideshow last weekend, Candi! One of the cars spun out of control. Sammi swore to me that she's never been and would never go to a sideshow! Your information just can't be right."

Candace pushed the newspaper aside. "I hear you, Sis, but my folks know what they're doing. I don't know why she was at that sideshow last night but she was definitely there."

Karina murmured, "Why is this happening again? I begged you not to go to the sideshow that night. I told you that there had been a shooting and you went anyway. Sammi is you all over again. Somebody is going to die . . . it's already been written."

Tamping down her own fears, Candace tried to calm her sister down.

"Let's not catastrophize. Nobody is going to die. Let's focus on what we know: we know she was moving about on her own for hours after she left us. We know she isn't at any of the local hospitals and nothing has been on the police scanner about an accident involving anyone fitting her description. And it's only been a few hours since she was last seen alive and well."

The doorbell interrupted them. Karina's eyes grew big. "I'm too scared to answer it."

Candace willed her heart to stop racing and hurried to the front door. "It's Sonya!

Sonya rushed inside. "I was in L.A. I jumped on the first plane home when I got Rina's message and took a cab here. Sammi ran away? I can't even get my mind around that. What happened?"

Karina leaned into Sonya's embrace, tears streaming down her cheeks. "She's gone, Sonya. She's gone. Somebody is gonna die tonight – either my baby or my man or even both and it's all my fault. Mama Ella warned me."

Astonished, Sonya opened her mouth to respond but Candace spoke first. "Stop saying somebody is gonna die, Karina! And what do you mean Mama Ella warned you?"

"Right before she died, she told me. She grabbed my wrist and said, 'every shut eye ain't sleep, all goodbyes ain't gone and what's done in the dark always comes to light.'" Karina shook her head, depleted. Looking at Candace, she said. "I had a bad feeling when you came back. I knew it couldn't stay buried. Why didn't I tell her?" Karina collapsed on the couch.

Sonya looked from one sister to the other. "Tell her what? You're both talking in riddles. What happened to my goddaughter and what does it have to do with Candi coming back?"

"You tell her," Karina said. "I can't. I'm going to the bathroom. I need to wash my face."

Sonya turned to Candace with her hands on her hips. "Candi?"

"Pull up a chair, girl. You ain't ready for this."

Ten minutes later, the story was told. Sonya sat back in her chair, processing all that she had heard. "I can't believe Rina kept this from me all these years," she said. Gazing intently at Candace she said, "Has anyone asked how *you're* doing? This is so much for you to take in." She wrapped her arms around her old friend and rocked her as Candace finally released the torrent of tears she had been holding back.

Karina returned, her expression unreadable as she watched Candace cry and Sonya comfort her. After a few moments Candace pulled away and gathered herself. Sonya turned to Karina, "Come here girl, I know you're hurting too." She wrapped her arms around Karina. Ignoring Karina's stiffness, Sonya whispered in her ear, "I will always be here for you. I love you so much." Karina nodded and pulled away. She sat at the table gazing at the newspaper article.

Candace asked Sonya. "Will you be here for a bit?"

"Girl, where am I gonna go?" Sonya asked.

"I don't want to leave Rina alone, but I need to get some air. I'll have my phone with me. I'll call if I hear anything. Call me if anything changes."

As she headed down the hill, Candace wondered out loud, "What are the chances that she went back to Mama Ella's house?" Doubtful, but glad to have a specific destination in mind, she drove onto the freeway.

The house was quiet – and empty. Candace thought back to that night when she lost track of Tiffany at the sideshow. The crowd was a living being, sucking her in deeper and dragging her farther and farther from where she had last seen her friend. She remembered the fear and panic when those guys surrounded her and couldn't help but imagine Samaya experiencing the same things. *Why would she go to a sideshow now? What was she thinking?*

Candace replayed the conversation she'd had with Karina that Samaya had overheard. *What did we say before we knew she was here?* Candace wracked her brain. Then she remembered. She heard her own voice. "What did I do that was so horrible? I snuck out to go to a sideshow and because you snitched, Mommy and Daddy died looking for me in East Oakland. Meanwhile I was laying down by the bridge at the U.C. Campus thinking I was in love."

Suddenly she knew. Candace ran to her car, praying she was right. Ten minutes later she parked her car on the street near the Sproul Plaza campus entrance. She took off running across the courtyard and veered off the paved path. The overcast day combined with dense foliage made it difficult to make out the bridge at first, but she found it. Stopping in a small clearing Candace leaned over to catch her breath. *I think this is where Rell and I were that night.* She scanned the area when a movement to her right caught her attention. It was Samaya trying to hide behind a tree.

"Samaya Bishop! Do not take another step!" Candace called out.

Samaya peeked around the tree. "Are the others with you?"

Candace ran to her. "No, I'm by myself. Let me look at you. Are you okay?" Candace ran her hands over Samaya, reassuring herself that she had not been hurt. She cupped her face in her hands and checked her pupils. "Are you on something? Did anyone hurt you?"

"I'm fine. No, I'm not on anything. I don't use drugs."

"You're not fine. Your world was turned upside down. You ran away. You've been out all night seeing and maybe doing all kinds of crazy stuff. Just tell me if anyone touched you, hurt you in any way."

"No. I stayed to myself."

Satisfied that Samaya was physically intact, Candace asked, "Is it okay if I hug you?"

Samaya's eyes overflowed and she leaned into her mother's embrace. They stood together in silent acknowledgement of their bond.

"We need to call Rina and Zander. They're worried sick."

Samaya pulled away. "I really don't want to talk to Ri-Ma yet. That's why I couldn't stay at home. I knew she was going to try to make me *process and communicate.* And Zandy is gonna be so mad he'll probably never forgive me. I just want to be left alone."

"I understand. Let's get you home and not worry about what happens next right now, okay?"

Candace checked her phone but didn't have service. "We'll call when we get closer to the street."

They walked slowly, holding hands.

"I don't know what to call you," Samaya said suddenly. "I had just gotten used to Auntie and now . . ."

Candace stopped and turned to face her. "Sugar, we have all the time in the world to untangle our feelings and develop our own relationship, okay? Names, titles . . . none of that matters when it comes right down to it." Candace held her daughter's hands in hers. "Rina has raised you since you weren't even an hour old. And look at what an awesome job she's done. I wish with all my heart that it had been me, but that doesn't matter. You'll never have to choose between us, do you hear me? Never. Got it?"

Samaya smiled, "Got it."

A few minutes later they reached the courtyard. Candace had pulled out her phone to call Karina when Samaya said, "So much for a hiding place."

Candace looked up to see Zander and Elliott running towards them. When Zander reached Samaya he wrapped her into a bear hug and held her tightly for a few minutes before kissing her forehead. "Sammi! You scared the hell out of me!"

"I'm sorry Zandy. I just . . ." Samaya looked down at her feet.

"We don't have to talk about it right now. Just tell me you're okay." He lifted her chin.

"I am." Seeing the doubtful expression on his face, Samaya repeated, "I am, Zandy, really. I'm just tired."

Elliott came forward and hugged Samaya. "I need some of that too. Got me out here strapped, goddaughter."

"Oh, Lord!" Samaya's eyes grew big. "Uncle Eli, who were you going to shoot?"

"Whoever was shootable." He shrugged.

In spite of the circumstances, they all laughed. As they neared the sidewalk Samaya said, "Hey, I know, um, Auntie," she stumbled over the word, "found me because she figured out what I'd heard her and Ri-Ma talking about, but how did you know where to find me, Zandy?"

Zander stiffened and then chuckled. "Haven't I always told you that you can count on me? I have magic Daddy powers." He tugged at her ponytail. "And folks are on alert all over the Bay Area. It was just a matter of time for me and Uncle Eli to hit all the likely places."

Elliott pulled Zander aside while Sammi talked with Candace. "So when you suddenly decided to head up to the campus to look for her you were using your so-called magic Daddy powers?"

Zander frowned. "We found her and she's safe. That's all that matters, Eli. Thanks for having my back."

"Having each other's back is what we do." Elliott held Zander's gaze for an extra beat. "That's such a coincidence that Candi was already here."

Zander turned toward the sound of Karina's scream of joy emanating from Candace's cell phone.

"Yes, Sis, I promise she's okay. Talk to her?" She looked at Samaya, who was backing away shaking her head no.

"Um, she's tired and not too chatty, but she's all in one piece. We'll see you soon, okay?" Candace put her phone away and gave Samaya's hand a squeeze.

Zander said, "I'll drive Sammi's car with her and we'll meet you guys at the house." Zander and Samaya headed towards her car, leaving Elliott and Candace alone.

"It was really lucky that you knew where to find her." Elliott said.

"I've been her, out in the streets by myself. I just had to put myself in her shoes, so to speak." Candace looked at Elliott, "I'm sure you've heard what kicked this all off."

"Yeah, to be honest I'm still reeling. It never occurred to me that Karina wasn't Sammi's biological mother. And I didn't know much of anything about you." He took in the circles under her eyes. "So how are you doing with this huge revelation?"

"It's a lot. I can't really talk about it right now." Candace didn't make eye contact.

Elliott patted her arm. "You don't owe me any explanations."

She gave him an appreciative smile. "I'm gonna take a minute to pull myself together."

"Take my phone number." He put his phone number into her cell phone. "Candi, you can call me anytime about anything." He gave her a hug and walked to his car.

Candace sat in her car. Her hands were shaking. *I need Nicky.* She pulled out her phone. He answered immediately with a gruff. "Yeah?"

"It's me." Candace said.

"I know that, what's up?" he barked.

"I wanted to let you know we found Samaya. She's safe." Candace's voice was soft and tentative.

"That's a real relief." Nick exhaled loudly. "I been out in the streets looking too. Thanks for letting me know."

Candace hesitated. "Are you at home? I was hoping we could talk."

"Nah, not a good time for all that."

"I don't have to come home right now. Maybe we can meet up for dinner someplace first?"

"Dinner? This ain't some kind of minor disagreement, Candace. This is betrayal. You think a steak dinner will smooth over betrayal?"

Before she could come up with a response, he said. "I'm gonna take a ride up the coast. I'll be outta here in ten minutes. Don't come here until I leave."

"Up the coast?" Candace's voice grew shrill. "How long will you be gone? Don't you think we should be together to work through all of this? Plus, we have appointments coming up soon."

"I can't deal with any of that right now. I don't know how long I'll be gone but I know that seeing you right now ain't a good idea."

"Nicky, I love you. I always have. We've proven we can get through anything together." She began to cry.

Nick's voice was somber. "I don't know about that. I don't know who you are, who *we* are anymore. You've been lying to me for a long time." He disconnected the call.

Candace was on emotional overload. *If I have to deal with one more thing, I'm gonna need to find a meeting.* She contemplated calling Roxie. *What am I gonna say? I need you to be my sponsor right now because I found out that my niece is really my dead baby that I never told anybody about and my husband is leaving me? Nah, too much. Hard enough to think it — there's no way I can say it out loud.*

Instead, she drove to her grandmother's house. Once inside, she laid on Mama Ella's bed, absorbing comfort from the vanilla and lavender scent that permeated the room. *I refuse to believe this is the end. This is supposed to be our beginning.* She gently traced circles over her abdomen as tears pooled in her ears.

15

TAKE IT TO THE GRAVE

Karina and Sonya waited in the driveway for Zander and Samaya. Sonya had urged her to feel Samaya out before pushing her to engage. Karina had agreed, but as soon as they arrived she pulled Samaya out of the car, examining her for injuries and smoothing her hair.

"Are you okay? We were so worried," she murmured.

Samaya pulled away. "I'm fine. I just want to lay down."

Karina's heart sank when she saw the rejection in her daughter's eyes. "Alright sweetie, I'll make you something to eat."

"I'm not hungry. I just want to be left alone." Sonya stepped aside to let Samaya pass, giving her hand a squeeze. Samaya stayed silent but squeezed back and walked upstairs to her bedroom, closing the door behind her.

"Just leave her be," Zander said.

Karina turned to him, "Maybe we can talk —"

Zander cut her off, "Me and my daughter need space. The last thing I want to do right now is talk to you, Karina."

He turned to Elliott, who was leaning against his car fender. "Yo brother, I'm gonna stick close to Sammi. My car can stay at your place. I'll holla at ya a little later, okay?"

Elliott walked over to give him a hug. He turned to Karina. "Rina, I'm always here whenever you need me."

Sonya motioned to Elliott. "Don't make more of this than it is, but can you give me a ride home?"

He grinned. "How long have I been trying to take you for a ride?"

Sonya rolled her eyes and said, "That's not what I mean, Eli. I just need to get home."

He whispered as he opened the car door for Sonya, "You know you wanna talk about all this madness as much as I do!" Sonya winked and got in.

As they drove away, Zander and Karina walked into the house. "I'll be upstairs in the guest room; I wanna be close to Sammi."

He left Karina standing in the foyer.

A few minutes after Zander closed the door to the guest room, Karina knocked and entered. "I know you asked for space Baby, but we need to talk, please."

Zander was incredulous. "Suddenly it's urgent for you to talk to me about something you kept secret for seventeen years?"

"I know it was wrong of me not to tell you. But Zander, it really didn't have anything to do with you. The secret was to protect my sister at first and then Samaya."

"Nothing to do with me? It has everything to do with me, Karina. Everything! I made decisions based on what I believed to be true!"

Karina nodded. "Okay, I agree that it wasn't fair for you not to know the whole story. But what would've changed? At the end of the day, why does it matter that she was my sister's baby instead of my cousin's? We were in love. You've loved Samaya from the beginning. We would've still had this life together."

"Nothing would've changed? You don't know that! That's so classic Karina; you make decisions based on facts *you* decide are relevant." He shook his head in frustration. "Just leave me alone, please. I need time to think."

Karina sighed, "I'll be downstairs. We can talk later after you get some rest." She closed the door behind herself.

Zander picked up his cell phone and called his parents' house.

"Hey Mom. Yes, she's okay. She's resting. It's a long story. I know you and Dad need to be brought up to speed, but to be honest I can't handle another conversation about this right now. I need your help. Karina keeps badgering me to talk it out with her but I can't deal with her right now. Can you get her out of the house? Maybe she'll confide in you, I don't know, but nothing good will come of us talking right now."

Thirty minutes later Karina knocked on the bedroom door and opened it slowly. "I just wanted to tell you that your mother's here." Karina sat on the bed. "She asked me to ride with her to Sacramento to pick up the centerpieces for the banquet. I guess the world doesn't stop turning, huh?" The corner of her mouth turned down. "I don't want her to drive all that way by herself but I'd rather stay here and talk with you."

"You should go with Mom."

She hesitated at the door. "Okay. Maybe we can talk when I get back."

He didn't answer.

Nick hugged the curves of Highway 1, pushing the limits of his car. An oncoming car flashed its lights and blew its horn, warning him that the passing lane had ended and a big rig was on its tail.

"Yeah, I see it. Who gives a fuck, man? If it's my time, it's my time!" Nick yelled.

At the last second he jerked his car to the right, scraping the fender against the sheared shale of the mountainside. Rubber burned, the brakes squealed, and the rear end of the car spun out before coming to a shuddering stop. The truck missed him by mere inches. The driver laid on the horn and let out a long string of expletives. Nick got out of the car, saluted him with a pint of cognac, and took a long swig. A motorcycle cop pulled up behind him.

"On a suicide mission, my man?" The middle-aged Latino

officer shook his head, noting the additional bottles on the passenger seat. Nick, standing near the trunk of the car, offered no resistance.

"Officer, may I reach into my pocket, please? I'd like to give you something," he slurred.

The cop looked in his eyes. "How about I reach in? Is there anything in there that will hurt me? Any needles?"

"No, Sir." Nick shook his head.

The officer pulled out a small velvet bag from Nick's inner pocket. "Is this it?"

Nick said, "Yep. Inside that bag, sir, are eight chips representing my eight years of sobriety." He tried to snap his fingers but failed. "Done. All because they were built on a lie. On the lie that there was nothing, nothing that could come between me and my lady. Man, I would've laid down my life for her because she was the one true thing in this world. But she betrayed me, man. She betrayed me." He broke down into tears.

"Alright man, we've all been there, or somewhere along that path, but no one is worth losing your life or endangering the lives of others. I'm gonna take you in on a DUI. A squad car will be here in a minute. You have the right to remain silent . . ."

***

"Mom Betty, I'm pretty sure our marriage is over." Karina anxiously twisted the straps of her purse.

"Darling, you and Alexander have weathered many storms together. There's no reason to believe you won't get through this one. What you should focus on right now is Samaya. Thank the Lord she's back home safely!"

"Yes, amen to that." Karina whispered.

"Now Karina, you know I'm not one to pry. Ella and I both believed in waiting on the sidelines until you all decided to share. But this business with your sister and Samaya doesn't feel like something we can wait on to be unveiled. That seems to be at the root of the problem, the waiting. What are you willing to tell me, dear? We have a long drive to Sacramento and back and I'm a pretty good listener."

"Mom Betty, you've been the only mother figure I've had over these nearly fifteen years. You gave me the room to treat Mama Ella like a grandmother in her later years. I appreciate you so much. I don't know if I've ever told you that." Karina's eyes were glossy with tears and she reached over to rub her mother-in-law's hand.

"It's hard to even know where to start. I mean, you already know about the night my parents died. You may not know that the rift between me and Candi had started before then. We had drifted apart. That night she snuck out I tattled to my parents. I told them everything Candi had been doing wrong and looking back I can finally admit that I embellished it all to make it sound worse; they went out in a panic looking for her." Karina paused. "They never came back."

"Oh darling, that doesn't make it your fault." Bettina got off at the next exit, parked and turned to Karina.

"Candi and I blamed each other. A couple months later, she left me too. She went to stay with our great aunt in Texas. Mama Ella and I limped along without her. We didn't know that Candi had gotten pregnant that night of our parents' death. While Candi was away I met Zander. It was like he saved my life, Mom Betty. When Candi came back that day in April, it wasn't obvious that she was pregnant. She was home for one night. The next morning there was a baby on the curb and Candi was gone."

Karina's voice trembled, "But I was home the night Candi had the baby. I was home with Zander, Mom. Candi needed my help and I ignored her. I was too busy being grown. Having sex for the first time. I didn't help my sister when she needed me most. The baby almost died. My sister could've died." Karina couldn't stop crying. "I never told anyone that. Not even Mama Ella. When Zander finds out, it will be one more reason for him to hate me! It's been my responsibility to take care of Samaya since then. She's been my baby ever since I picked her up off that curb because God gave me a second chance after I'd almost killed her."

Bettina got out of the car and went to open Karina's door. She pulled her out and held her closely. "This is so much to have held onto for so many years, Karina. You're still looking at this and feeling it from the perspective of a sixteen-year-old girl. You're taking on a mountain of responsibility from circumstances that were beyond your control."

"You haven't heard the worst of it, Mom Betty." Karina's eyes darted around the parking lot as though she were afraid someone would overhear her. "Candi called home for help. Twice. The first time was just a few weeks after she ran away. She wanted to come home and I hung up on her. I didn't tell Mama Ella. I was so angry with her. But I knew I was wrong. The day before Zander left for Howard, she called again. I thought she was high and being dramatic. She said she was in trouble and needed money and I hung up because Zander rang the doorbell and I didn't want anything to interfere with our last night together. I figured she'd call back eventually. But she didn't." Karina looked at Bettina.

"After a while I didn't want her to. Zander and I were getting married and we were going to raise Sammi as our daughter. And then I lost all of our babies. Samaya is the only child we'll ever have. I worry so much that Zander will find somebody who can give him a biological child, it makes me act crazy jealous. If he does step out on me, it'll be my own fault. And after this, he's probably packing, him and Samaya," she rambled.

"And now I know that Candi really was in trouble that day she called. Her life was literally in danger. She begged me for help, Mom Betty and I hung up on her. I never sent her the money. I never told her that her baby was alive and then I spent the next seventeen years raising her as my own. How much lower can a person go?" Karina quickly wiped away her tears.

Bettina was quiet for a while. She tipped Karina's chin up. "What you've shared, my darling, is your truth. That's all anyone can ever demand of you. Whether it's my son, your sister or anyone else. That's all you have to offer. You and your sister have a lot to work through, but she came back; she survived and she's here. And I believe, given some time, Zander will come around. But you have to give him a chance to absorb it all.

"Karina, you've never been 'less than.' Zander has chosen you and has never, to my knowledge, given you reason to believe he wants anyone else. But when it comes down to it, you are more than Zander's wife. You always have been. You don't exist in his shadow. You are a capable, loving mother and a creative, intelligent, and empathetic educator. Regardless of how your marriage shakes out, you are Karina Joelle Maxwell Bishop and all that represents, do you hear me?"

Karina squared her shoulders and a faint smile appeared. "Yes, Ma'am."

Bettina winked. "Now let's finish our trip and get back to Samaya and provide her with the support and love she needs; not necessarily what she wants right now, but what we know she needs. We'll get her the best therapist in the Bay Area and ultimately, she'll be fine. Biological motherhood is only one way to create a family; Elliott couldn't be more my son if I'd birthed him. Samaya is your daughter, through and through. As for you and Candace, I do hope the two of you will be open to therapy as well. It seems to me that you've spent long enough apart. And, maybe more importantly, Samaya deserves the option of having her biological mother in her life."

Karina frowned. "I don't know about all that."

"You were fine about having her around as her Auntie, even though you knew the truth. Your reticence is all about your ego, Karina. You need to work through that and keep Samaya at the center."

Karina bit her lip as she absorbed Bettina's candid advice.

Zander knocked softly on Samaya's door and peeked in. She was sleeping. He softly closed the door and went downstairs to make a call.

"Candi, hey it's Zander. We need to talk. Can you come over to the house right now?"

"Is Sammi okay? What's going on?"

"Yeah, she's okay, she's sleeping."

"Zander, I'm exhausted. I can't handle another Karina showdown right now."

"Karina's not here. I need to talk to you – alone. Can you come now, please? It's important."

Something in his voice made Candace sit up. "Alright, I'm on my way."

Zander opened the front door as soon as he saw Candace's car pull into the driveway. He motioned her inside, holding a finger to his lips.

"Sammi's sleeping upstairs. Let's go out back."

Candace followed him through the kitchen outside to the patio. "What's going on?" she asked. "Where's Karina?"

"This has been such a crazy couple of days," Zander said as he sat down and pulled a pack of cigarettes out of his pocket. "Do you mind?"

Candace shook her head as she reached for one and took the seat next to him.

"Rina's in Sacramento with my mother, thank God. I can't deal with her right now. My head is spinning. I can't believe she and Mama Ella lied to me all these years. I feel like a fool. And you," he turned to look at her, "how can you possibly forgive Karina and move on? She robbed you of so much."

Candace contemplated her answer. "I think it's more about acceptance than forgiveness. Despite my ignorance and my mistakes, my baby didn't die. God had a plan for her. And I guess what I went through, as bad as it was, was part of God's plan for me."

Candace took a long drag on the cigarette and exhaled before continuing. "My feelings about Karina and Mama Ella are all jumbled up. I'm so thankful to them for saving my baby. And knowing my grandmother, I'm not surprised that she tried to protect my reputation. But I'll be honest, it's harder for me to wrap my mind about Rina's role in this. In those early years I called home, twice. She could've told me about the baby or at least told Mama Ella that I was trying to come home."

Candace stubbed out the cigarette in the ashtray. "Did she leave me out there in the cold because she hated me, like I thought? Or was it because she didn't want to give Samaya up? Either way, she stole a part of my life. I've missed so much — first steps, skinned knees, bedtime stories, all the birthdays and Christmases and dance performances . . ." Her voice trailed off.

"I wish I could answer your questions," Zander replied. "But what I *can* tell you is that her world has revolved around Sammi as long as I've known her. She's always put Sammi's needs above her own, even if that would've meant the end of our relationship. I always knew they were a package deal."

"I can't even wrap my mind around Samaya, Zander. She's everything I've ever dreamed of in a daughter. I have to thank you both for that." Her eyes filled with tears. "The only constant, the only unconditional love I've had in my life since I left home was Nick. And I may have lost him. It's too painful to think of us not being together after all we've been through. But I'm a survivor. I've learned that about myself. I'm not going to let any of this break me. I have my sobriety, a career, and a chance at getting to know the awesome young woman that I helped create."

Zander considered her response. "You're incredibly resilient. You should be proud of yourself. As for Nick, I'm just getting to know the brother, but the way he talks about you and your history together — that man loves you with his entire being. A baby is a huge secret, but it was a lie of omission under pretty unique circumstances; maybe with some time he'll find a way to deal with it. You have a lot of years invested in each other, just like me and Rina."

He looked away. "But Karina took it way farther. It wasn't a lie of omission. She lied to me from the very beginning and kept layering lies on top of lies. She made me complicit in her web of lies!"

He stood up and paced around the small patio area. "But now that I realize . . . now that I have all the pieces of the puzzle, I guess I bear some responsibility too. I'm pissed at Rina for keeping secrets, but I did too. Just not for as long as her. I didn't say anything when I saw the picture of you."

"Picture?" Candace frowned. "What are you talking about?"

"Remember yesterday when I got to Mama Ella's after Samaya drove off and Rina didn't want to go to dinner? I went to the kitchen to get an apple and I saw a pile of pictures on the kitchen table. Looked like somebody had been going through them. There was a photo strip of you and another girl and somebody had written 'Tiffany and CC–1986' on the back."

"Oh yeah. Those were my wild days. I was wearing too much makeup and acting grown." Candace paused before continuing, "When I found it, I realized it was taken the night that Zora, um Samaya, was conceived."

"Yeah. I remember." Zander looked in Candace's eyes.

"What do you mean, you remember?" She frowned.

"I remember everything about that night. I don't know if it was the makeup or the outfit, but I thought I was with an older girl. I hadn't made the connection, but when I saw the picture I recognized you right away. I don't know why it took me so long." He shook his head.

Candace studied Zander's face. Suddenly it all clicked. Horrified, she slapped her hand over her mouth. "Oh my God! This isn't possible. You cannot be Rell! No!"

"I'm not surprised you didn't recognize me. I had dreadlocks – well twists really – and I was hella skinny. Rell was short for Jarell, my middle name. Not too long after that night, I cut my hair, bulked up for basketball, and started using Zander. I even grew a couple inches." He laughed.

Candace stared at Zander as though seeing him for the first time. She thought back to the time she spent with Rell but it was all a bit fuzzy compared to the vivid memories of her parents' death hours later. Still, she recognized Rell in Zander's more mature features, now that she knew to look. When she could finally speak, her voice shook, "So it wasn't a lucky coincidence that you showed up on campus to look for Sammi this morning, after all."

"No, it wasn't." Zander smiled.

Candace leaned forward in her seat, elbows on her knees, head in her hands. "I don't know how much more I can take today, Lord," she said quietly.

"You should have told me you were pregnant, Candi. Me and my parents would've helped you. Everything would've been different," Zander said.

"Now you're gonna judge me? How could I have told you? I didn't know your last name, or apparently your real name, much less your phone number!" Candi snarled.

She couldn't sustain her anger. "So much happened that night. My parents died because they were looking for me while I was laying up with you. You can't imagine how guilty I felt. It didn't even occur to me I could be pregnant until I was five months along. To be honest, even if I had known how to get in touch with you, I probably wouldn't have. We didn't know each other. I was going to put her up for adoption."

She paused. "But when she came and I held her in my arms, I knew I could never give her up. And then she stopped breathing and I thought she'd died." She sighed heavily.

Zander shook his head. "It never crossed my mind that the baby belonged to Rina's sister. Or that the girl I'd spent that time with was her sister. The few pictures I saw of Candace over the years didn't look like C.C. and I never questioned her story about Cousin Jolene."

"There was no reason for you to doubt the story. And like you said, you didn't have all the pieces of the puzzle."

"You're right. But Candi, we need to brace ourselves for the fallout. That's why I called you over here. Maybe we should arrange for a therapist to be with us when we talk to Rina. And I think Nick should be there. I'm thinking we don't tell Sammi until Rina and Nick have a chance to take it all in though."

Candace's eyes grew wide and her heart started to race. "The fallout? No!" She stood up and gripped Zander's forearm. "Nothing else is coming out. Do you hear me? Nothing else! There's no point. It's too much for anyone to handle. Sammi's too young and in too much pain right now to deal with this. You've been her father for as long as she can remember, that hasn't changed. And Karina is all I have left. If she found out, it would break her. There's been too much competition between us for too long. You're hers and hers alone. And Nick never needs to put a face to Rell, especially not after making friends with you. My marriage definitely will not survive that revelation."

Zander pried her fingers off his arm and was silent for a long time. "I don't know," he sighed. "What if it all comes out later? Do we want to be held accountable for keeping this from them? The other secret is already out."

"We can't blow up our lives over a one-night stand when we were teenagers, Zander!" Candace was on the verge of tears.

Zander ground out the cigarette. "I don't know what to do. Karina loses her shit over women she imagines I've slept with." He plopped back down in a chair and sighed, "You're right. There's no way I can tell her I've been with her sister and think our marriage won't fall apart."

He sat forward and looked earnestly at Candace. "But this is about more than your marriage or mine. This is about Sammi, and we have to put her first."

"Don't you see? This is the one secret that we can control. The two of us are the only people in the world who know this, right?" Candace said.

"I never told Eli about C.C. or that night." Zander said.

"I told Rina about Rell, but it's clear that she never put it together." Candace said.

"That summer I tried to get my family to call me Rell, but they wouldn't. When school started, I went back to A.J. or Alexander. I introduced myself to Karina as Zander, hoping it sounded cool and it stuck."

"So there's no reason to believe anyone will ever figure out this last detail." Candace said.

"You're right. We *could* keep this a secret. But should we? Would it matter to Sammi to know?"

"I know I haven't been a mother very long, but my gut tells me it would just add more confusion to her life. I know Samaya couldn't possibly love you anymore than she already does. And as for Rina, Zander if this comes out she'll always wonder if there's something going on between us."

He nodded. "That's a fact. I can't tell you how many times she has accused me of sleeping with other women!"

"Did you step out on her?" Candace asked.

"No! Not once in our marriage! I meant those vows. I've never understood why she's so insecure about our relationship."

"That didn't start with you," Candace said. "She was insecure in high school. Her insecurity and jealousy had a lot to do with our falling out. Along with my selfishness and lack of empathy."

Candace locked eyes with Zander. "Our priorities have to be our daughter's well-being and saving our marriages. C.C. Maxwell was a mixed up, immature girl who *never* met Rell Bishop and doesn't even know who Samaya's biological father is. We take this to the grave."

Zander took Candace's hands into his. "C.C. Maxwell was a beautiful person, inside and out. Rell Bishop would have been lucky to have spent five minutes in her presence." He raised her hands to his lips and kissed them. "Agreed. To the grave."

Candace took the path from the backyard to her car. Zander walked into the kitchen and noticed water trickling out of the faucet. *Did Samaya come downstairs? Oh God, please don't let her have overheard!* He took the stairs two at a time and eased her bedroom door open. Samaya was curled up in bed, eyes shut tight. Zander closed the door quietly and exhaled.

THE END

A NOTE FROM THE AUTHOR

Hello Reader!

Done in the Dark is my debut novel - I'm looking forward to hearing your reactions. Let me know what worked and what didn't. Were there characters you loved (or loved to hate)? Were you left wanting more? Was there anything that surprised you?

Join the TamFam to be the first to hear about my writing journey and gain insight into the backgrounds of the DITD characters. You might even get access to lost chapters and side stories! Go to my website to join: www.TamaraMorganAuthor.com. You can find me on IG and FB @TamaraWritesBooks, on TikTok @Tamara_Writes_Stories, and on Amazon.com/author/tamarawritesbooks. Ask your local bookstore to stock DITD! Thanks for reading and spreading the word!

Tamara

ACKNOWLEDGMENTS

There are a few people who have always believed that I was an author. Not a lawyer who likes to write on the side, but an actual author who was stuck practicing law. My daughters Brianni, Jessi, and Shonetta, sister Danielle, and sisters from other mothers, Karen Lewis and Karen Williams – all believed in me before I believed in myself. Without the six of you, I doubt I would have had the courage to take on this new challenge. I love you beyond measure.

My village of friends and family who nurture and encourage me is too extensive to list, but a few must be singled out for always keeping it real and showing up every single time I need them: Ronetta Morgan, Taneshia Lewis, Tonya Ward, Jay Larry, Rhonda Andrew, Darnella Davis, Tiffany Thomas and Ti'Ara Williams - thank you from the bottom of my heart.

A special thank you to Mrs. Karen Lewis for being my Auntie and guiding light and for introducing me to Black literature. Toni Morrison opened a new world to me. You planted the seed that has grown into the luscious garden that empowers, motivates, and sustains me.

Thank you to my beta readers – Karla Marie Banks, Jamikia Davis, Nekisha Goodwin, Mrs. Karen Lewis, Natriece Spicer, Mrs. Donna Thomas – for your time, enthusiasm, input and honesty. Because of you, Done in the Dark is a better book.

To my phenomenal editor, Carol Taylor, I appreciate your partnership and patience. You made me dig deeper, reach higher, and hardest of all, delete, delete, delete! Thank you for nudging me to let my characters tell their own story.

Jermaine Haggerty of GraphixMain, LLC you are nothing short of amazing! Your artistic ability to piece together my ramblings, reactions and incessant need for 'just a little tweak' to come up with such powerful images that evoke the essence of the book was more than I had imagined possible. Thank you so very much.

Whenever I feel doubt or question my abilities it seems I'm touched in some way by one of my angels: my mother, Beverly Mason - my hummingbird; Deborah Broyles, my mentor and muse; Karen Williams, my bestie and cheerleader; and Emmanuel Morgan, my forever love.

My cup continually overflows.

www.ingramcontent.com/pod-product-compliance
Lightning Source LLC
Chambersburg PA
CBHW022107310726
48972CB00007B/1915